THE
PHOENIX
AND THE
CROWN

Also by Rachel Terry

<u>The Guardians Duology</u>

Lightbringer

Flameseeker

<u>Atlas Sea</u>

The Phoenix and the Crown

THE PHOENIX AND THE CROWN

RACHEL TERRY

PHARUS PRESS

For my brother, Josh

(Even though you probably won't read this book.)

INDRIS
Palace
Brisban
Palace
ALARA

Palace
DAERA
ATLAS SEA
The Pirate Haven
AMBERLEIGH
Witch Wood

PROLOGUE

The woman crept cautiously out onto the balcony, casting a furtive glance behind her. There was no one there, she knew, but that didn't stop her from looking. There were guards everywhere in this castle and she couldn't afford to be seen, knowing the danger she was putting herself in. Putting them both in.

But it would be worth it, if she succeeded.

Breathing hard, she placed the basket she had been carrying down in the middle of the semi-circular balcony, turning it slightly so that the searing sunlight wasn't in the baby's face. She looked down at the small figure swaddled in the white blankets, who had been in her care for only a short time.

"Goodbye, little one," she whispered and then fled.

Moments later, a shadow fell over the basket and the balcony, moving in slow circles as a hawk swooped down to perch atop the basket's handle. The baby peered up at the bird, not knowing what to make of it, reaching up with one tiny hand. The hawk surveyed the hand that rose up toward it with yellow-orange eyes, making a soft sound.

There was no time to waste. The hawk wrapped its talons securely around the basket handle and heaved its load up into the air, taking care not to upset its passenger. It weighed more than the hawk had expected, but it was to be a brief trip.

A short time later, the hawk returned, depositing the basket back onto the balcony. The woman, who had been keeping a careful eye out from a safe distance, hurried to collect it, shutting the windowed doors to the balcony after her, feeling relief descend over her.

It was done.

CHAPTER 1

Varrian waited for the sound of the attendant's footsteps to recede down the passage, the door closing quietly behind him, before turning his attention back to the sealed envelope in his hand. The red wax seal, bearing the image of a griffon—the symbol of the kingdom of Alara—seemed to glare up at him, daring him to open it.

Any correspondence from the southern kingdom these days was a welcome sight and yet Varrian found he was hesitant to open it, fearful of what it might say. *To hell with this,* he thought shortly, snatching the letter opener up from the table and slicing through the envelope.

The paper within was thick, of good quality. Stepping closer to the open window, where the gray daylight streamed in, his eyes quickly scanned the message. It was addressed to him, naturally, from queen Thalia herself. He had received enough missives by now to recognize her flowing script.

Varrian let out a sigh, inhaling deeply of the heavy, humid air streaming through the window, heralding the coming storm.

He read the message a second time, more slowly, as if afraid he had missed something. No, it was exactly as it had been at first glance.

When the messenger had first arrived, informing him of the letter that had just come from Alara, he had feared the worst. He'd come to fear the worst over the past decade.

Folding the letter, but keeping it in his hand, Varrian surveyed the village below through the tall, thin pane of glass, and the woods leading to the harbor and sea beyond.

The harbor was not as full as it had once been, nor as full as he would have liked. The sky was overcast, as it always seemed to be these last ten years, giving his kingdom a gray tinge. This was a rare moment when it was not raining, but that would come soon enough. Already he could see the clouds gathered threateningly on the horizon.

Varrian could have done with some sun himself, but he supposed, resting his hands on the window ledge, that he should be grateful for whatever good fortune they got.

The people in the villages would be thankful for a respite from the incessant rain, however brief. *It will come again. It always does.*

He fingered the parchment in his hand and pondered, not for the first time, the differences between his kingdom and Alara, their neighbor to the south. Tropical. Warm. Sunny. Bright, beautiful, cheerful—that was Alara, or at least the image they portrayed on one of his diplomatic visits there.

He had swallowed his pride and gone himself to appeal for aid. His younger sister, Annabelle, had wanted to go, to champion the cause of the people herself, but he had refused her.

This was a serious matter, one the king himself should handle. How would it look, after all, for him to send the princess in his stead while he remained here?

But now it seemed that Annie would get her wish, he thought, glancing down at queen Thalia's letter once more.

Annabelle had recently come of age, not two months ago, and Thalia was once more extending them an olive branch.

A way out of their predicament, by suggesting an official alliance between the two kingdoms.

All they had to do was reach out and take it. And in exchange, Annabelle would find herself betrothed to the crown prince of Alara, Kain.

Varrian was unsure how Annabelle would take the news—she had wanted to travel to Alara, yes, but living there permanently with one's husband was a different sort of arrangement altogether and he dreaded to think what her reaction would be.

She loved this kingdom, and so did he. It was unfair to ask her to leave it and everything she had ever known behind. But it was of little consequence, he reminded himself. She didn't have a choice in the matter. None of them did, if they wanted to ensure Alara's good graces.

And Daera's future.

Like it or not, and Varrian most assuredly did not, Daera was at Alara's mercy. The northern kingdom had suffered greatly from famine for the past decade and it showed no sign of letting up any time soon.

Ten years ago, the weather had suddenly taken a turn for the worse. Some had believed it to be only a short spell, a phase that would return to normal given enough time. Those people were still waiting, ten years later, if they were even still alive.

The sun refused to shine and it rained nearly every day. Crops rotted in their fields. The great forests, the main source of export for the northern kingdom, were dying more and more with each passing day.

The neighboring islands, unaffected by the inclement weather, could still grow food, but the prices had risen exorbitantly. And with their main source of income gone, Daera could ill afford it.

Increasingly, they found themselves relying on aid shipments from Alara, but even that was not enough. More often than not, the much-needed supplies never reached Daeran shores, pilfered and plundered along the way by the many pirates who roamed the Atlas Sea.

Varrian clenched his hand into a fist, unintentionally crumpling the letter. When it had first arrived, he had half-feared that it was the same news he had heard so many times, he could recite the messages in his sleep. Another letter informing him that yet another Alaran shipment had been lost to the sea-faring brigands.

Or worse, that Alara would cease sending aid altogether, no longer willing to take the risk.

Pirates presented a menace to both kingdoms and it seemed there was nothing to be done. Any that were caught and tried were promptly hanged for their crimes, their corpses strung up and displayed in chains at the docks to discourage others from doing the same.

Little good it did. For every pirate that was captured, there were still more out there. Varrian would have considered issuing letters of marque and commissioning privateers to hunt down the pirates, as Alara had done, but with the food shortage, his kingdom simply couldn't afford it.

They couldn't afford anything these days. At this rate, it wouldn't be long before his family starved along with everyone else.

Accepting the offer was the only way, but even so, Varrian balked at the idea of sending Annie to stay—permanently—in the southern kingdom.

Alara had problems of its own. For the past twenty years, witch-hunts had been a common occurrence in Alara. Anyone who was found guilty of being a witch was sentenced to death, typically by burning. Varrian had heard rumors that such hunts had increased in intensity to the point where anyone merely suspected of being a witch was executed—and the reasons for suspicion were myriad.

A birthmark or an unfortunately shaped scar might be enough to mark one as a witch as easily as having the wrong kind of pet, believed to be a familiar, or even a neighbor's personal dislike.

Understandably, witches had fled, seeking sanctuary in Daera, where witchcraft was not outlawed and witches were theoretically safe, though Varrian was unsure for how much longer.

Rumors had reached him that some believed Daera to be cursed, that its poor weather was somehow the fault of a malevolent witch. That he or she—or all of them together—were causing the crops to rot in their fields and the sun refuse to shine.

For his part, Varrian didn't put much stock in such rumors. Mostly, those deemed witches seemed to be a relatively benevolent lot. And it didn't make much sense that a witch would so publicly announce their presence in this day and age by doing something so drastic.

It was not something one flaunted. The witches had gone into hiding, if there truly were any left after twenty years of persecution and ten of famine.

Still, the weather *was* a bit odd, even he had to admit that. If he were a superstitious man, he might even have been tempted to believe that Daera had been cursed. A kingdom where the sun did not shine.

His stomach twisted into a knot. What had they done to deserve such a thing?

What had children done to watch as their parents starved, withering away before their very eyes, giving all their food to their children and sparing none for themselves, until, with their parents gone and unable to provide, the children eventually succumbed as well?

What had parents done to be faced with the choice of watching their children slowly starve or kill them themselves, in whatever manner they deemed quicker and more humane?

To have entire villages empty, deserted, the inhabitants having all fled or died, the roofs caving in beneath the weight of the incessant rain?

Varrian sighed again. He didn't want to think on such things or about witches or any curse.

He needed to find a way to solve the problem or he very soon would not have a kingdom left. *One can hardly rule over a mound of corpses,* he thought grimly.

With the acceptance of the offer of marriage and the alliance formalized, Alara might be more motivated to do something about the pirate scourge and thus ensure the shipments arrived unmolested.

He would have to wait for Annabelle to return to discuss it with her. She had taken the opportunity, since it wasn't pouring down rain for once, to go out riding. It was one of her few pleasures and he hadn't had the heart to refuse her, despite the ever-growing danger.

Naturally, he'd sent guards to accompany her, despite her wishes.

Varrian hoped she would agree to this proposal without a fuss. He loathed confrontation, but he would pull rank and force her if necessary. *Pray it won't come to that.*

Heaving one more sigh, he turned away from the window, resolving himself to wait.

CHAPTER 2

The squish of mud accompanied Annie as her horse's hooves sank into the mire of what had once been dirt streets through a village. She could hear the guards' mounts having similar luck behind her. The towns closest to the palace were fortunate enough to have cobblestone streets, though admittedly now in need of some repair, but the further away one got, the roads became merely dirt, having long since permanently turned to mud from the torrential rains.

Annie would have preferred to venture into the villages in the forest. She would have preferred not to have guards accompany her. But Varrian had asked her not to go there and insisted they go with her, sticking to her side like nursemaids.

Feeling the comfortable gait of the horse rocking beneath her, she looked around, surveying the townspeople she saw.

Those nearest the harbor and castle had fared better than most. Their clothes looked faded and patched in places, since no one could afford new ones, but their faces lacked the dirty desperation of those further in. Though thin, their bones were not yet visible. But unless something could be done about the famine, that would not last.

A woman taking in clothing from a hanging line paused in her work to survey the royal procession. Everywhere they went, they attracted attention, not all of it friendly, and Annie was uncomfortably aware of the eyes watching her every move.

She had never before been afraid to go out riding alone, never felt as though she had anything to fear from her subjects. But Varrian's fears of an attempted kidnapping, in the hope of enough ransom money to be able to afford the ever-rising cost of food, were not wholly misplaced, she had to admit.

Desperation made people do a lot of things, no matter how foolish or dangerous.

She tried her best to push her fear aside and enjoy what now constituted pleasant weather in Daera. Today was one of the precious days where it was dry and the people were making the most of it.

Annie gently slowed her chestnut mare to a stop. An old man blocked half the road. His wagon of vegetables—cabbages by the look of them—had become mired in the mud and his mule, a pathetic creature with patches of fur missing and nearly as thin as her owner, seemed unable to pull the cart free.

Logan, the captain of her guard, was about to steer his horse around the obstruction and continue on their way, but Annie reached out a hand to stop him.

"Aren't you going to help the man?" she demanded, gesturing at the old man tugging futilely at his mule's reins, trying to encourage her to move.

Logan was a large man, broad in the shoulders, but with a youthful appearance that belied his age. He sighed but brooked no argument, signaling to his other men and swinging down from the saddle, his feet squelching in the muck.

Annie watched as they braced the cart and attempted to heave it forward. A few of the men cursed as the treacherous mud slipped beneath them and they nearly lost their footing.

She surveyed the poor state of the farmer's cabbages and thought to herself that they were hardly worth salvaging, their leaves a sickly color and riddled with mold. Still, they were some of the better specimens she'd seen.

Casting a quick look around as the wheels began to roll forward, and determining that no one was paying her any mind, Annie wheeled her mare around and urged her down a side street at a canter. She braced herself for a shout behind, calling her to stop, but it never came.

Part of her felt bad for using the pretense of offering the old man aid as a means of escape, but she truly had wanted to help. *We helped each other,* she told herself as the wind caught the hood of her cloak and pulled it off, freeing her long black hair, which would undoubtedly become hopelessly tangled by the time she returned to the palace. *When isn't it tangled, though?*

She slowed her horse as she reached the docks, noticing that there were fewer and fewer ships docked there all the time. The waves of the Atlas Sea lapped at the pier and a few gulls cried forlornly overhead. *It would be so much more beautiful with the sun out,* she thought with a stab of pity.

Laborers toiled, unloading what precious supplies there were from the ships currently moored there, depositing the crates, sacks and barrels to be carried to the warehouses or stores lining the docks.

Annie turned to make her way down toward the beach, drawing up short as she spotted two urchins beneath a gnarled apple tree. The boy was completely barefoot, while the girl had a pair of dingy stockings on, but no shoes. Her pinafore was smudged with dirt, as though she'd fallen down. They both hopped up and down, their tiny hands reaching for the red fruit that was hopelessly high. All of the lower fruit that may have once been in reach had, unsurprisingly, been taken already.

Clicking her tongue, Annie urged the mare over toward them. As the horse approached, the two children stopped what they were doing and drew back, as though intimidated by such a large animal. Or, more likely, by what the horse represented.

Only the wealthy could afford to keep such creatures now.

"It's all right," Annie called. "You're not in any trouble."

She swung down from the saddle, securing the reins around one of the tree's lower branches. Unclipping her cloak and laying it across the saddle, she craned her neck up to survey the apples that dangled tantalizingly out of reach.

She pointed to them. "They look good, don't they?"

The children nodded shyly, the girl hiding slightly behind the boy.

Well, there was nothing for it. Even on horseback, she wouldn't have been able to reach. Heaving a deep breath, Annie placed her boot in the hollow where the trunk of the tree split, grabbed ahold of the trunk and hauled herself up. The children might have been able to climb up themselves, if they'd been tall enough to reach the foothold.

Annie had learned long ago not to look down and so she didn't, though she was still tempted. Not for the first time, she was thankful she'd chosen to wear riding trousers. Scaling this tree in a dress would have been a nightmare.

Her hair, which never did well in humidity, was soon sticking to her cheeks and forehead and she could feel perspiration gathering under her arms, dampening the material of her blouse.

Clenching her teeth, she tried to ignore the unpleasantness and kept climbing. She let out an involuntary gasp as her footing gave way and for a breathless moment, her body had begun to swing out over the drop before she managed to steady herself.

Heart thudding, she remained there for a moment. The sought-after fruit was only a few feet away. Trying not to think about how much harder getting down would be than getting up, Annie heaved herself upward, closing the remaining distance. Her palm was sweaty and bleeding from where the bark had cut her and she wiped it off on the leg of her trousers before plucking one of the apples. She stuffed her pockets full of them until there were no more to be had.

Only then did she allow herself to look down.

Her stomach hollowed out at the sight of the dizzying drop beneath her. Telling herself there was no hurry, yet also aware that by now Logan and the guards must have finished helping the old man and were searching for her, she began the wary descent toward the ground.

She let out a breath of relief when her feet were once more safely on the ground and then turned to the children, who were eyeing her with wide-eyed admiration.

Smiling, she withdrew the apples from her pockets and held them out. "Here you go."

Tiny hands shot forward to snatch the apples, though they remembered their manners and thanked her. Annie just hoped that there were no worms in the fruit. One couldn't always tell by looking.

It appeared not, or else the children ate them anyway. The girl paused and then offered one of the apples to Annie.

She felt her face heat. "Oh, no, thank you. You keep it."

Even if she'd been ravenous, she didn't think she could have taken it, knowing how much more it meant to them.

The little girl pointed to the horse, which had turned to pick dismally at the grass. "For the horse, then."

The mare turned as the girl offered her the apple. Unlike Annie, the horse had no compunction about taking it. The girl laughed as the horse's lips brushed against her palm. And then the apple was gone.

"What are your names?" Annie asked. The children had finished eating and turned their attention to the horse, stroking its coat.

"Ophelia," the girl replied, while the boy answered, "Albert."

"Do you live nearby?"

Ophelia nodded, her shyness having worn off. "Our Da owns the inn, over there."

Annie followed where the girl pointed and thought she could make out the correct building.

"Your Highness!"

Annie let out a sigh.

Albert and Ophelia ducked behind Annie as thundering hoofbeats announced Logan's arrival. He jerked hard on the reins, bringing his horse to a halt before them, his handsome face marred by anger.

"We've been searching all over the village for you! What were you thinking, running off like that? Your brother will have my head if something happens to you!"

"I don't think Albert and Ophelia meant me any harm," Annie retorted, glaring at him, daring him to disagree with her.

He was not mollified. "I think it prudent that we return to the palace. I doubt this weather will hold."

He nodded toward the sky and she followed his gaze, seeing he was right. Dark clouds gathered to the west, even darker gray than those that always lurked over the kingdom.

But she refused to allow him the satisfaction of being right. "It always looks like it's going to rain, Logan," she said, untying her mare from the tree and swinging up into the saddle before he could dismount and offer her assistance.

She looked down at the two children, her expression softening. "It was nice to meet you. I hope to see you again." Though she knew she wouldn't, if Logan had his way.

The captain was silent as they made their way back, his shoulders taut with anger. Fortunately, he didn't comment on her wind-blown appearance.

"Did you succeed in freeing that man's cart?" Annie inquired.

"If you had stayed where you were supposed to, perhaps you'd know," he replied, and then, as if his anger were evaporating now that they were headed back, added, "Yes, we did."

She could understand his frustration. This was not the first time she'd done something like this. Suddenly, she felt remorseful, despite all her bravado. It was never her intention to get Logan or any of the other guards into trouble. She hadn't stopped to think of them, now or any time before. Perhaps she should, before she chose to do something so impetuous.

She hunkered down in the saddle, trying to make herself appear smaller, but she didn't offer an apology. She still had her pride.

The rest of the ride back was spent in silence. As the castle came into view, visible between the trees, Annie glanced up, surveying the weathered stone, the tiles that were cracked or missing from some of the spires. It, too, had seen better days. Her gaze settled on the glass windows on the roof. The greenhouse. Her workshop. A sudden sense of urgency filled her.

She handed her horse off to one of the attendants at the stables and ducked inside the castle, hurrying up the stairs.

Time was running out. The apples would help Ophelia and Albert, but it wouldn't last. They were the reason she was doing this. And she'd come so close!

She had chosen the greenhouse as her base of operations, a laboratory of sorts, the walls and roof entirely composed of as many windows as possible, to allow the meager light to filter through.

Annie marched up to her latest experiment, boots ringing on the floor, and stopped short. The blackberry vine was shriveled. She let out a breath of dismay. It had all happened so fast.

She turned and glanced at the other wilted plants lining the tables. All the other failed hybrids she'd experimented with. She'd had the highest hopes for this latest one, watering it incessantly, trying to emulate the weather conditions outside.

For once, the plant had displayed no outward effect to the overwatering. But there was another problem. One Annie had yet to find a solution for.

The lack of sunlight.

Without it, the plants all eventually withered away, either choked by too much water or starved for sunlight. And Annie, despite all her knowledge of plants, could not create that.

Annie leaned against the table, staring down at her latest failure, letting the disappointment wash over her. Then she straightened and picked up her notes, going over the newest entries, determined to find where she'd gone wrong.

She couldn't give up. People like Albert and Ophelia were counting on her. She could engineer a plant that would bear fruit, survive the torrential rains, require little to no sunlight, and be able to thrive in Daera's cooler climate. She could and she would. She had to!

But time, that ever scarce commodity, was not on her side. And every day, another failure, another setback, more people out there dying.

So engrossed was she in her notes that she didn't hear Varrian come in behind her until he cleared his throat.

Annie spun around, nearly dropping the papers.

"Hard at work, I see," he remarked. "Any luck?"

Annie's shoulders slumped. "I've finally got a variant that will survive the rains, but it needs sunlight."

Varrian nodded, his expression pensive. He was a good twelve years older than her, though the lines in his face made him look older than thirty.

His thick brown hair desperately needed to make the acquaintance of a comb. He wore a coat of violet velvet brocade, trimmed in silver, with buttons to match—Daera's colors. It should have looked quite elegant on him, and perhaps in a better time it would have, but now the fabric was rumpled.

Her eyes strayed to the envelope he held in one hand. "What's that?"

"Oh." He held it up as if only now noticing it. "A missive from Alara."

"Are they finally cutting off aid? Too risky with all the pirates? Not that we get much aid from them as it is…"

"No. Something better. They've sent an offer of marriage."

Annie stared at him. The southern kingdom had sent such offers in the past, but their father, who had been king at the time, had always disregarded them, saying that they should wait until Annie was at least eighteen. Now that such a day had come, it didn't surprise her that they would try again.

"Aquillus and I have discussed it and I have accepted the offer."

Annie swallowed. "Is that really necessary? Surely, there's some other way—"

"There is no other way, Annabelle."

"But—" She protested, gesturing to the room around them. "My work. It's not finished, but…I can make it work. I can, Varrian. I know it. I just need more time."

"I wish there was more time," Varrian said, resignation heavy in his voice. "But there isn't. The kingdom is nearly bankrupt from having to constantly buy supplies from Alara and Indris. So many people have died already or simply moved away. If we wait any longer, I fear there won't be a kingdom left."

"Is it really aid if we have to pay for it?" Annie asked, unable to hide the bitterness she felt.

Varrian rubbed at his eyes. "At least this way, by agreeing to the proposal, Alara feels they're getting something out of it. We both are. It wouldn't be so difficult if not for those damned brigands."

Pirates, Annie thought with a sharp twist of fury coiling in her chest.

The pirates who preyed upon Alaran aid shipments, preventing them from ever reaching Daeran shores. Or if the Alaran ships did get through, it was only after they'd been plundered of anything of value.

Varrian had even sent Daeran ships to Alara, in the hope that they might fare better, since Alara seemed increasingly reluctant to risk their own ships. The same fate befell them. Most simply never returned.

"You know I wouldn't ask you to do this if there were any other way," Varrian went on. "I appreciate your talents and I think it's impressive, what you've managed to accomplish. But we've simply run out of time."

"I understand," Annie said stiffly. "What do we get in return?"

"With the alliance sealed by the marriage, Alara will be sending more aid and offering the support of their navy to hunt down the pirates."

A surge of anger speared through Annie at the thought. Little better than common thieves, they were, preying upon the weak and vulnerable. She'd even heard pirates sometimes stooped to raiding coastal towns and villages, raping and plundering where they wished. She wasn't supposed to hear such things, but servants gossiped. Especially her maids.

She raised her chin. "You've already given Alara your answer?"

He nodded.

"When do I leave?"

"As soon as the ship is ready. It's still being outfitted with supplies. And I've arranged for two escorts, just in case any of those brigands get any ideas."

"I should go prepare, then."

Varrian stepped aside, allowing her to squeeze past. She headed for the stairs that led up to her quarters at the top of one of the spiraling towers, but footsteps in the hall made her stop and turn.

Aquillus, one of Varrian's advisors, stood there. He was an older man with silvery gray hair and sharp green eyes. Annie had always liked him and had come to view him as more of a father figure than an advisor. The sight of him twisted her heart. Another reminder of what she would be leaving behind.

"I hear you are leaving us," he said softly.

"Yes," Annie confessed, a sudden thought occurring to her. Accepting this proposal meant she would be engaged to the crown prince of Alara and yet she realized she knew next to nothing about him. He'd hardly been her first concern. "Have you ever met the Alaran prince? I'm afraid I don't know much about him."

"Prince Kain? Not recently. It's been many years so I regret I can't accurately comment on his character."

"Pity. I hope I will like him, but I suppose like doesn't really have anything to do with it, does it?"

Aquillus smiled wryly. "You will be helping your people tremendously, Your Highness. Far more than a few apples."

Annie started, opening her mouth to ask how he knew about that when she'd only returned a short time ago, but with a wink, he'd turned and walked back down the stairs.

Annie sighed and continued on her way, thinking how odd it would be to marry a man she'd never met. Of course, she'd get to know him before the wedding ever took place. They wouldn't be expected to wed immediately upon her arrival.

She tried to view the upcoming trip with a sense of optimism and excitement. It represented a new life for her. A chance to escape the deplorable conditions of her own kingdom while at the same time doing something to remedy those conditions.

Privately though, she felt saddened by the fact that this arrangement meant she would have to leave her home behind, likely never to see it again.

Don't wallow in self-pity, she told herself fiercely, brushing away unshed tears. This wasn't about her, it was about the people who were out there suffering. She wanted to help them another way, but if she could help them in this way, then so be it.

Who was she kidding anyway? It was a naïve fantasy, a nice dream, to think she could singlehandedly save the kingdom by crossbreeding a plant variety that would thrive under their current conditions and provide food so they didn't have to seek aid elsewhere.

Her mother might have been able to work it out, but she wasn't here. Annie was and she wasn't going to let her pride lead to any more suffering.

She had tried and she had failed. But in the end, she could still save her people, even if it wasn't in the way she had hoped.

CHAPTER 3

Ben drew on the clay pipe between his lips, glancing up at the man seated across from him as he exhaled the smoke through his nose. He had never personally met the man on the other side of the table—Leroux—but he knew one thing about him. The man was about to lose his pigs.

Or he would, if Ben could pull this off.

On the way back to Daera, the *Phoenix* had anchored off the coast of Indris, one of the neighboring islands, mostly to pick up gossip. The real shore leave would come once they reached Amberleigh, the infamous pirate haven.

For now, it was merely a brief hour's stop at one of the local taverns. For Ben, it was a rare moment of indulgence. Neither smoking nor gambling were allowed on ship and he rarely took advantage of shore leave the way his men did. Ordinarily, he would not have engaged in a game of chance. He wasn't opposed to taking risks, but he preferred them to be calculated rather than left up to fate or chance, whichever one was partial to.

But Charles Leroux, who had already been well into his cups when Ben and part of his crew arrived, had boasted of the prizes he had recently taken. Most of it didn't particularly interest Ben at the moment, except for the mention of several large hogs, fattened and primed for slaughter.

There was no better place to find such creatures than Indris. Ben unconsciously clenched his fingers as he considered what was at stake. How much those animals would mean to the starving people of Daera.

The *Phoenix* was already laden with cargo of her own, but it wouldn't hurt to add a few plump pigs into the mix, especially given that Daera was their next destination.

Of course, all of that depended upon him winning.

If he didn't, he stood to lose five hundred ducats, no small amount. He supposed he could have used the money to offer to buy the pigs outright, but why bother paying when you could essentially steal them from under someone's nose?

"*Careful,*" hissed a voice in his ear.

Ben felt the hawk on his shoulder shift his weight, adjusting his footing.

It's not really up to me, is it? he thought silently, knowing better than to reply to Horus out loud in unfamiliar territory.

The Hen and Horsewhip Inn wasn't his usual haunt. The lighting was dim, the air heavy with the scent of beer and likely other, less pleasant aromas, but his pungent tobacco smoke blessedly masked the rest.

Charles Leroux held a pair of dice in his hand, his eyes not on Ben but nervously glancing at the hawk perched on his shoulder. Horus seemed to make the man uneasy and Ben was not surprised. The bird's sharp orange eyes seemed to glitter with forbidden knowledge an ordinary hawk should not know.

His crew had grown accustomed to the bird and some of the men believed Horus spoke to their captain. Others were more reluctant. Perhaps Leroux had heard the tales and was unsettled by them.

Passage, as the game they were playing was called, was relatively simple compared to other games of chance. The first player rolled the dice and if he rolled a double, the sum was added to the third die. If the total was less than ten, he lost, but if it was equal to or greater than ten, he won. If a double was not rolled, the dice were passed to the second player.

So far, they'd been at it for a few minutes, with both parties failing to roll doubles. But it was only a matter of time. The question was, which one would it be and would it be enough?

Leroux blew on the dice in his hand and rolled them onto the tabletop. A low chuckle came from Horus. A three and a five.

The dice changed hands once again.

"This is it," Horus muttered and Ben felt the bird's talons tighten their hold on his shoulder. *"I can feel it."*

You'd better be right about this, Ben thought, beginning to tire of the game and not wanting to be late to the rendezvous.

He tossed the dice upon the table without ceremony, feeling a sense of grim satisfaction as they each turned up a four. The third dice had rolled a six, more than enough.

Despite his drunken state, dismay spread across Leroux's pockmarked face. He was sober enough to know he'd lost. Cheers went up behind Ben from members of his crew. Leroux's men didn't look the least bit pleased, likely having hoped to sell the hogs for an exorbitant amount in Daera. Ben eyed them, wondering if they intended to cause trouble over the loss.

He pushed his chair back and stood quickly. "Well, lads, we'd love to stay and chat, but it's time we were off."

He gave Leroux an ironic sort of salute and then made his way toward the docks. All that was left now was to collect the pigs and weigh anchor.

Once the cargo had been collected and transferred to the *Phoenix*, Ben gave the order to depart. A storm was in the air and he wanted to be done and gone before it arrived—not that it truly mattered.

He could feel it approaching, though still unseen, by the smell of lightning in the air and the way the hair on his arms stood on end, beneath the sleeves of his coat. He could hear a faint ringing in his ears, so quiet that if he tried to concentrate on it, it seemed to fade away, only to flare again the moment he let his mind wander.

The deck became a flurry of activity as orders were given to cast off. Crew members hurried about to trim the square sails to catch the wind. Horus's keen eyes watched as the sheet and tack lines were hauled in and the sheet ropes released.

Canvas snapped taut above their heads in the wind and Ben's blond hair stirred slightly where it protruded from beneath his hat. The *Phoenix* surged forward eagerly as the wind caught in her sails, pulling away from the Indris harbor.

She was a three-masted, square-rigged frigate, making her one of the largest pirate vessels sailing the Atlas Sea. Ben had made special modifications to her, including adding several more guns so that she was heavily armed.

Despite her bulk and weight, she was the fastest frigate in these waters. Rumors flew about how the ship moved with a speed that was almost unnatural, as if propelled by the sea gods themselves, and could turn and corner with far more ease and maneuverability than she had any right to.

Ben smiled to himself from the helm, resting his arms on the wheel. Ordinarily, his quartermaster, Terrance, would occupy this post, but Ben enjoyed the feeling of guiding his ship personally. Besides, old habits died hard.

He felt a rush of pride, feeling the power of the ship beneath him, the *Phoenix*'s dark hull slicing through the waves, making good time.

With full canvas set and a favorable wind, she arrived at her destination before the storm broke. It was always difficult to tell what time of day it was in Daera, for the gray clouds obscured the sun. It looked the same in midmorning as it did midafternoon and so Ben was forced to rely on the ship's bells, proclaiming it was four o'clock.

The *Phoenix* anchored off the coast of Daera rather than make port at the harbor where she would be too conspicuous. Though they meant the people of Daera no harm—quite the opposite in fact—they were still a pirate vessel and the *Phoenix* had something of a reputation. She would not fail to be recognized.

The plundered supplies they had gathered throughout the past two weeks were hauled up to the main deck and loaded aboard the *Phoenix*'s two longboats. Not everything went. The pirates kept behind the common necessities: casks of ale and water and enough food to hold them over until they next made port. And of course any personal loot the crew had received as part of their share.

While overseeing the preparation of the longboats, Ben turned to the hawk perched on his shoulder. "All right, Horus. You know what to do."

The hawk let out a short cry and launched into the air, the wind from his wings buffeting Ben's face. He watched as the bird vanished into the distance, listening to the sounds of his men shuffling on the deck, the sails flapping gently, and the ocean lapping against the sides of the ship. He could just barely make out the shore in the distance and the figures standing there.

A few minutes later, a shriek split the air and Ben raised one arm. With a flap of wings, Horus alighted on his hand, talons wrapping around his leather glove.

"*All clear, Captain,*" the bird murmured.

Ben nodded to the hawk, hurrying to join the men who would be accompanying him to shore. The two longboats, laden with their treasures, were quickly lowered down into the water. The trip to shore took longer than Horus had covered it in the air, but they soon reached land.

The hawk had been true to his word. Standing a few feet away, separate from the small crowd that had gathered, was a woman, clad in a blue-gray dress, the hood of a cloak covering her head. Horus, who had been perched on the longboat's prow, called a greeting. The figure reached up with one hand to pull the cloak's hood down, revealing a mane of wild red hair.

The woman's gray eyes glinted and she strode forward toward them. "Benjamin."

Ben finished helping his men haul the boats up onto the sand and then turned to nod a greeting. "Aunt Calida."

"Encounter any trouble?"

"No more than usual."

The villagers she had brought with her moved forward to help unload the supplies from the longboats and into the waiting wagons. Calida had brought her own, pulled by her ancient black and white mare.

Ben moved over to the horse, stroking her neck with one gloved hand. "Hello, Edith."

He glanced up, spying Lorelei, a midwife and friend of his aunt's, among the crowd. She waved but did not approach him, busy as she was helping the others.

Leaving the horse, Ben turned to help his quartermaster, Terrance, with the cages of pigs. They had nearly taken up an entire boat by themselves. He was glad to be rid of them. Unlike other animals, pigs were notorious for not faring well at sea and a seasick pig was the last thing anyone wanted on board. By the time they had finished, Terrance's dark skin glistened with sweat and Ben was wishing he'd thought to leave his scarlet coat behind.

"How is your shoulder, Terrance?" Calida called.

The quartermaster grinned. "Bearing up."

"I could mix up some more poultice, if you'd like."

"No need, ma'am. But thanks all the same."

"Suit yourself," Calida replied, turning her gray gaze on her nephew. She studied him silently for a moment, as though reassuring herself that he was as well as he claimed.

Finally, she remarked, "Your hair is longer than the last time I saw you."

"Haven't got around to cutting it yet, I s'pose," he replied, though in truth, he intended to take a knife to it as soon as they made port in Amberleigh. It was getting too long for his liking.

He'd never been fond of tying his hair in a queue at the back of his neck. However unlikely, it was still something to grab ahold of in battle, like a rope attached to the back of one's head. He preferred to hack it off until it just touched his collar in the back and the tips of his ears, nearly but not quite reaching his eyebrows. He needed to be able to see in a fight.

"Growing out your beard, too, I see," Calida said, her tone light and teasing. "Or have you just not gotten around to shaving that either?"

"Keep tellin' 'im it looks like a spot o' dirt," Terrance remarked, clapping Ben good-naturedly on the shoulder.

He gave the man a half-hearted glower, running gloved fingers along his jaw. "It'll grow out, just give it time."

All three of them knew it was a lie. He'd never been able to grow much more than stubble, something the men constantly teased him about.

"Any of these supplies come from Berchmoore?" Calida asked, thankfully changing the subject.

Ben shook his head. "No. I don't know what the old boy's up to. Haven't seen him for some time."

"Well, he doesn't strike me as the type to go into hiding somewhere with his tail tucked between his legs. He's too crafty for that. Suppose it's too much to hope he's gone into retirement."

Ben grinned. "Aye, but if I see him, I'll give him my regards."

"By all means," his aunt cautioned, "but don't go looking for trouble."

"Me?" Ben said with mock astonishment. "Look for trouble? Whatever gave you that idea?"

Calida pursed her lips. "Trouble seems to have a way of finding you, whether you go looking for it or not. So maybe don't bite off more than you can chew, hm?"

Ben waved a hand, acknowledging that he'd heard her and dismissing it all at once.

Before Calida could admonish him anymore, lightning flashed overhead, briefly casting a silver glow over the beach around them, the rumble of thunder following close behind.

"Time we were off, sir!" Terrance called.

Ben nodded to him, turning back to his aunt. "I'll return in a fortnight."

"I'll be here."

He removed his hat, bowing to her briefly, and then was on his way. He would have preferred to stay and chat a while longer, but there was nothing to be done about it, with a storm bearing down on them.

Besides, Calida and the villagers needed to get the supplies safely stored away in one of the warehouses before the worst of it broke loose.

It had begun to sprinkle as they headed back out to where the *Phoenix* was anchored. Ben glanced over his shoulder as the men rowed. Calida stood on the shore, watching them. Her hood had been pulled over her face again, hiding her features.

She watched them for a time and then turned to her horse, leading it and the cart after the others.

CHAPTER 4

By the time she reached town, the skies had opened and rain was pouring freely down, soaking Calida's cloak as she guided her aging mare, Edith, through the muddy side streets, following after Lorelei and the others.

Weather permitting, they would have begun distributing the supplies to the needy straight away, and though she privately doubted those desperate enough would have been deterred by the nasty weather, no one wanted to catch their death out in the deluge.

Lorelei was catching her breath as the last of the supplies were unloaded, taking advantage of a brief respite, shielded by the warehouse. Rain drummed on the roof overhead and she raised her voice to be heard over the din.

"I'd invite you back to my place for a cup of tea," Lorelei said to Calida. "But it's a bit of a way to walk in this weather. What say you to a pint at Daniel's instead?"

Calida liked the idea just fine. It would be good to see Daniel again and catch up on the latest news. He usually attended the supply drop-offs when he could, but running a public house, even in these times, was busy work, and Calida wasn't surprised he hadn't been present.

Still, she hesitated.

The pub would offer far less privacy than a cozy discussion at Lorelei's house. But she had known the two of them long enough to rely on them to be discreet.

"Sounds lovely," she replied, "so long as you're buying."

Lorelei grinned, water dripping down her face, and led the way outside back into the torrent of water. Fortunately, a small stable had been built behind the pub a few years ago to protect patrons' animals from any bad weather. More often than not, it would have been needed—if people still had their animals.

Unhooking Edith from the cart and securing her in one of the stalls to be seen to by one of the attendants, Calida followed Lorelei inside. She shucked off her cloak and left it hanging by the door to dry.

The lanterns hanging from the ceiling had been lit, casting a dim golden glow. The fireplace in the corner crackled heartily, suffusing the room with warmth. Unsurprisingly, the pub wasn't crowded, with only a few patrons present.

Where once it had bustled with business, now Daniel struggled to make ends meet. The famine ensured that people spent all their money on food, clothing and shelter. Even so, Calida was surprised by the amount of people who still managed to purchase a drink or two, a way to numb the pain and allow them to forget about their current troubles for a short time.

She would have liked to sit close to the fire, but naturally so did everyone else. Lorelei chose a table in the far corner, as far away from the others as possible.

Calida sat down warily, her eyes never settling in one place, glancing up at the rafters, to the stairs nestled across from the hearth that led to the inn above, to the massive stag head mounted over the fire, flicking to the door, calculating what exits she had available should the need for them arise.

Daniel had been standing behind the bar and came over to join them upon noticing their arrival. He was a tall man, though not broad, with hair that had once been brown, but was now mostly gray, prematurely aged.

"What can I get for you ladies?" he asked.

"Ale, if you've got it," Lorelei replied, the typical poison of choice.

Calida had always been partial to a nice red wine herself, but Daniel wasn't likely to have that, and those days were far behind her. She finally settled on tea.

"Sure you don't want something stronger?" Daniel inquired. "You might, after you hear what I have to tell you."

Calida's stomach clenched, but she fought to keep her composure. "No, tea will be fine."

Daniel nodded and went to fetch the drinks himself rather than call one of the barmaids to do it, leaving Calida's mind racing as to what news he may have uncovered. It seemed to take him ages to return and when he did, she wrapped her hands around the teacup to keep from fidgeting.

He joined them at the table, his back to the other customers. "Now then, first things first. The supplies arrive all right?"

"Yes," Calida answered, sipping her tea. It was weak and tepid, but it would suffice. "Though I fear it won't be enough."

Daniel frowned. "Not if the rumors I've heard are to be believed."

"Why? What have you heard?"

As the proprietor of a pub, Daniel was uniquely placed to hear rumors and gossip before anyone else and he was usually more knowledgeable than either of them as to the latest comings and goings. Although Lorelei's position as a midwife and Calida's own as a healer provided some news, neither of their clients were likely to be drunk and as inclined to talk as Daniel's were.

"I had a customer stop in here the other day, a farmer on his way to one of the markets, he said, and he had to pass through the village of Wymore. You'll never guess what he found there."

"We're not going to like this, are we?" Lorelei muttered.

"Don't keep us in suspense, Daniel," Calida said, a bit more testily than she'd intended. She could tell that Lorelei was right. They weren't going to like it one bit and that knowledge made her irritable.

"The whole village was gone."

"Gone? As in destroyed?" Lorelei sought to clarify. "Or abandoned?"

Several villages had been abandoned and left behind by the former tenants who had lived there. Such properties usually belonged to a wealthy landowner, who hired the people on to work at the farms. Now, with so many unable to afford their rent, the landowners had decided to force them out and gave them no choice but to comply by tearing down their roofs. Empty, roof-less homes were not an uncommon sight.

"Gone as in everyone there was dead," Daniel answered grimly. "Apparently for a few days, at least. Bodies just lying in the streets and muck. People don't have the strength to give them proper burials, so the dead simply lie where they fall."

Lorelei reached up to cover her mouth with one hand, too horrified to speak. Calida swore with feeling, one of the more colorful expressions she'd picked up from Ben.

It was one of the worst reports they'd received, though hardly surprising. The area around Wymore had been one of the hardest hit. All of the farming communities were, relying as they did on their crops succeeding every year, only to watch them languish and rot in the fields for a decade now.

"He said he looked around for survivors and called out to see if there was any response, but there was no answer," Daniel said, his shoulders slumping.

Calida was beginning to wish she'd listened to his earlier suggestion and added something stronger to her tea.

Lorelei toyed with her tankard of ale, spinning it slowly on the tabletop. "I've been called out to attend births where the mother is so thin, she can't survive giving birth, if she even makes it to that point. Some are so malnourished that they lose the baby entirely because they can't provide enough sustenance for themselves, much less for a second life."

Calida glanced up. Though her friend's voice remained steady, the anguish was plain in her face. Lorelei's features, which had once seemed plump and somehow still youthful despite the passage of years, had since thinned and grown lined. Her brown hair was streaked with gray at her left temple.

The midwife looked up suddenly, her hazel eyes meeting Calida's gaze. "You were right."

"About what?" she asked, startled.

"The boy."

Calida looked down at her hands. "Yes, I suppose I was." *Although he's not a boy anymore, is he?*

She felt a sudden rush of affection for her nephew, so intense it was almost painful. Closing her eyes, she pictured how he had looked earlier on the beach, wondering if he truly was as all right as he claimed, if there was something she'd overlooked.

Calida could see him now, as clearly as if he stood before her once more. The angle of his jaw, the slight bump in the bridge of his nose that he had hated as a child, but grown to accept. The golden color of his hair, in contrast to his eyebrows, which were dark brown. But most of all, the blue of his eyes. Those eyes…that reminded her of the sea and the life she'd left behind.

She always hated watching him leave, returning to his ship. Though she knew it was necessary, she feared he might not return, that this would be the last time she would lay eyes on him, and so she memorized each of their visits. Anything could happen out on the sea, after all.

Calida pushed the thoughts away. Ben was well out of her reach now and she would have to trust that he would keep his wits about him.

With an effort, she once more returned her attention to her companions.

Daniel frowned, as though wrestling with some internal decision. "I've been trying to do what I can to reverse some of the crop damage—subtly of course—but it's too extensive."

"You shouldn't have taken that risk!" Calida admonished, and then quickly eyed the other customers to make sure they hadn't heard her outburst. Lowering her voice, she went on, "You know what they're saying. You know what people think. A witch is behind this."

"Do you truly believe that?" Lorelei asked softly.

"Yes. I do. What other explanation is there?"

Daniel nodded. "Not only do I believe it, but I think I know who it is. Mordred. I've heard rumors of a man matching his description, though thankfully, he hasn't passed through here. Not that I'm aware of, at least."

Calida felt a chill snake down her spine and it had nothing to do with the cold rain still pouring down outside, streaking the windows. It was a name they were all familiar with. *The witch who hunts witches.*

She shook her head, not bothering to hide her skepticism. "He can't control the weather, Daniel."

One wouldn't even need an earth witch if they were intent on ruining a kingdom's harvest year after year. Not if they could simply cause it to rain nearly every day and the sun refuse to shine. That would be enough. Crops rotting in their fields or too waterlogged to sprout to begin with.

"She's right," Lorelei whispered. "If Mordred is here, it's for another reason."

Daniel looked from one woman to the other. "You don't think—?"

"Of course," Calida replied. "She won't have given up."

He stared at her. "So all of this…?"

"No," Calida said, feeling a stab of guilt all the same. "There must be something more to it. Her ambition runs deep. It always has."

"If Mordred is here, you need to leave," Lorelei insisted.

"I'm not going anywhere," Calida said, with more resolve than she felt. *Where would I go? There's nowhere left…*

For twenty years, she'd made this place her home, the little cabin in the forest. In all that time, no one had come for her, no one had disturbed her peace or threatened her life.

But nothing lasted forever and now it seemed all of that was about to change. She'd dared to hope for a time that perhaps she'd been forgotten. It had all been so long ago…

Now she saw how naïve that belief was. She would never be forgotten, just as she herself could never forget, and this would never end.

Calida supposed she could try one of the neighboring islands, but that would mean packing up and starting anew, leaving behind everything familiar and comfortable. The people she had come to know and the life she had built for herself, in spite of everything. She'd done it once and did not fancy ever doing it again. When she'd arrived in Daera, she'd silently vowed to herself that she *would* never do it again.

She was done running.

The home that had come to feel safe no longer did. The illusion had been shattered, all in the span of one evening. Calida resented Daniel for it, even though she knew it wasn't his fault. He was only trying to protect her.

If Mordred was in Daera, they were in danger, too.

Daniel sighed. "I feared you would say that."

"I can't run forever," Calida replied firmly. "None of us can."

"Then what should we do?" Lorelei asked. "Go after him ourselves?"

"I wouldn't. Mordred is dangerous. He's turned his own kind in before; I can't imagine he's changed his ways."

"So we just lay low and wait for him to find us?" Daniel demanded. "I don't like the sound of that. I'd rather take the fight to him."

"Don't do anything stupid," Calida snapped. "You have a family to think of. Besides, it's me he wants. We all know that."

He pursed his lips but said nothing. She was right.

Calida stood abruptly. "I should go. I've spent too much time here as it is."

"Will you be all right heading home in this storm?" Lorelei asked. It had yet to let up outside.

"I should be."

"I'll let you know if I hear anything more," Daniel said tersely.

"Very well. You know where to find me."

"And you I."

And then she was gone, fetching her still-damp cloak by the door and leaving the shelter of the pub behind to enter the tempest once more, wondering how Ben was faring in the awful weather.

CHAPTER 5

The queen of Alara peeled up the wax seal on the folded letter that had been delivered to her moments before. She had sent the servant away and reclined comfortably back in her chair by the fire. Thalia regarded the sealed message for a moment and then unfolded the parchment slowly, hardly daring to hope. She had received several responses in the past, each marked with Daera's seal, and each one only brought setbacks and disappointments.

Her eyes quickly roamed over the handwritten response. Varrian's answer was concise and brief, cutting straight to the heart of the matter. She had her answer. An eager thrill went through her as she finished the letter. Her eyes raised to look at her husband, seated across from her in front of the fire, slumped in a chair of his own.

He was staring into the flames, not at her. One withered hand rested on the side of the chair, the other clasping a wine glass of dark red liquid. His silk clothes were rumpled, appearing slightly too large for him. Time had not been a friend to the man.

A hound rested on the carpet at his feet. The only sound in the room was the crackling and occasional pop of the fire as the logs settled. Two crossed swords hung above the mantel and the wall behind the king was decorated with a rich red tapestry, depicting a regal gold griffin, the kingdom's symbol.

Some of the castle rooms had a tendency to become chilly, though it really was much too warm outside for a fire. Her husband always insisted on having one anyway and Thalia allowed him his little eccentricities.

"Niklaus, they've accepted."

The king started, as though snapping out of a trance. His head turned to face her. There were lines at the corners of his sharp blue eyes. "What did you say, dear?"

Queen Thalia smiled, holding up the letter. "The king of Daera has accepted the offer of marriage. You see, it says here: 'The kingdom of Daera graciously accepts the kingdom of Alara's proposal regarding the betrothal of Princess Annabelle Grace to Crown Prince Kain.'"

How good it felt to read those words after so many years of trying and failing. Thalia felt a surge of triumph.

But Niklaus waved a hand dismissively. "Nonsense. He's too young to get married."

Thalia's smile wavered. "That's for us to determine, dear. We're his parents, after all. It's our duty to do what is best for him and the kingdom. As it is his duty as prince to marry."

"He's only a child. And I don't see the need to ally ourselves with that kingdom."

"Age is not always a measure of maturity," Thalia replied. *Unfortunately.* "Kain is of the proper age to be married and as for Daera, they're starving." She spread her hands, speaking slowly and calmly, as though to a child. "They need our help." *Far more than we need theirs.*

The king frowned. He looked like he wanted to argue, but the thought died before it could fully form. "Whatever you say, my dear. You always know better than I when it comes to these matters."

The queen folded the letter and stood abruptly as a knock came from the door. "Enter."

A second messenger strode in, bowing, and handed her another letter, this one not nearly as ostentatious as the first. Thalia dismissed the servant and glanced down at it. The parchment was plain and there was no ornate wax seal.

She glanced over at her husband, who seemed to have dozed off again. She tucked the letter, unopened, into a pocket in her skirt and crossed to where the king sat, patting one of his hands. "Finish your medicine, dear." She nodded to the glass gripped in one hand and walked to the door to call for an attendant.

The king eyed the glass as though seeing it for the first time, downing what liquid remained. A red liveried servant hurried to the door to answer Thalia's call.

She gestured to her husband with one hand, her fingers glittering with rings. "Take him to his bed."

The attendant bowed smartly and moved to help the king to his feet, beginning to lead him away.

Niklaus glanced over his shoulder at his wife. "Are you coming to bed, darling?"

Thalia gave him a small smile, waving him on. "You go ahead. I'll be along shortly."

The king nodded, his head slumping forward languorously. From the look in his eyes, the queen knew he would be asleep long before she arrived.

* * *

Rodek slowly traced the mark on the queen's back with one finger. It was slightly raised, like a scar, and darker than the rest of her tanned skin. The mark lay at the base of her spine, at the small of her back, and he knew its shape and edges intimately. It had always reminded him a bit of an anchor without a stock, though he'd never voiced such thoughts.

The queen's private chambers were dimly lit, a few lighted candelabras casting flickering shadows over the room. A great window stood to the right of the bed; Rodek was facing it but the curtains had been drawn to block the view of the night sky. The bed itself was large, with a canopy stretching high above their heads. Its gauzy curtains were also mostly drawn.

Somewhere to the side of the room was an empty and cold hearth. There were no guards or servants present, as in the rest of the castle. The two of them were alone.

Thalia shifted suddenly, raising herself up off the pillows into a sitting position. The silk covers slid off of her like water as she got up from the bed. She threw the curtains back, her long fiery hair falling over her shoulders and down her back to conceal the mark.

Rodek propped himself up with one arm. Thalia's bare feet pattered softly on the hard floor as she walked over to a nearby chair. She picked up the robe that had been draped over it, shrugging it on. From the way she left her hair trapped beneath the garment, not bothering to free it, he could tell she was agitated.

He watched her, refusing to look away, as she crossed to the window and parted the thick curtains that blocked it, staring out at the night as silvery moonlight illuminated the room. The robe she had donned was slightly sheer and did little to disguise her figure. His eyes roamed over her, the tense way she held herself only confirming his suspicions.

But Rodek remained silent. He had dealt with many of her moods over the years and was accustomed to her volatile personality, her fiery temper that matched her hair. If there was something she wished to confide in him, he would wait rather than ask.

Thalia fished in the pocket of her robe, withdrawing a folded letter and reading it again for the third time. She had yet to tell him what it was about, but he had no doubt that it was to blame for her unease.

"I've received word from Mordred," she said at last, still facing the window. "He's found nothing." She folded the letter once more and tucked it away, muttering to herself, "Though if he's found Daniel, it's only a matter of time…"

"Who's Daniel?" Rodek asked, interest piqued. The name was new to him.

She turned, a grin slowly spreading across her lips. "An old friend."

"What sort of friend?" He was liking this conversation less and less by the moment.

She let out a short, husky laugh. "Jealous, are we?" She didn't give him time to answer. "Isn't that sweet. But you've nothing to worry about." She turned back to face the window, effectively dismissing that line of questioning.

Rodek wasn't convinced. If anything, he felt even more irritated than before. But it came as no surprise. Such was the way with Thalia, always dodging questions. She took no small amount of pleasure in toying with him and watching him squirm.

"Fine," he replied, as nonchalantly as possible. "Keep your secrets."

She was silent for a few moments more and then, as if the previous exchange had never happened, said, "Daera has accepted the marriage proposal. I expect the princess should arrive in a week's time." Thalia looked over her shoulder at him. "I don't want any of your pirates anywhere in sight, you understand? In fact, it's best if they avoid the Brisban Strait altogether for the time being."

"You've nothing to worry about," Rodek replied, throwing her earlier words back at her. "What did Kain say when he heard the news? I imagine he was simply thrilled." *The brat.*

"What's there for him to say about it?" Thalia answered. "He knows what's expected of him."

Rodek grunted noncommittally, but didn't let the matter go. *Two can play at this game.* He knew what the queen's son was, just as she did, no matter how she may try to defend him privately.

"I heard just the other day that he rode one of the horses so hard, it died."

Thalia adjusted her robe. "Yes, well, I'm sure he was just over-eager."

Rodek frowned. He hadn't come to the queen's bedchamber to bicker and it appeared that was all they would be doing tonight. He threw the covers off and stood, fetching his clothes from where they'd fallen, beginning to dress.

He would leave, but not before getting in one last parting shot.

"Well, I hope he treats his wife better than he treats those horses."

CHAPTER 6

Two days after meeting with Varrian, Annie found herself boarding a ship bound for Alara. It was a massive galleon, loaded with supplies for the journey and any personal belongings she was to bring with her. The main deck crawled with men and Annie found the rolling, pitching motion of the ship upset her stomach, so she mostly remained in her cabin, situated beneath the helm.

Ordinarily, the captain of a vessel would have resided there, but since she was royalty on board, she had been granted its sole use for the duration of the journey, for which she was grateful.

She had a bed all to herself, albeit smaller than she was used to, and best of all, the cabin contained a private bathroom.

The galleon was escorted by two of Daera's ships of the line, to discourage any pirates that might see the large ship as a potential prize. Traditionally, galleons were known for transporting treasure and though there was none aboard, Annie was aware that she could be considered that treasure and held for ransom if captured.

To her delight, Aquillus had accompanied her, as an ambassador, and would stay until things had been settled before returning to Daera. He remained on deck for much of the trip, leaving Annie with only one of her maids, Maddie, for company and her chaperone, Florence. The woman appeared ancient to Annie, her hair gray and pulled back in a no-nonsense manner. She would follow Annie around wherever she went to ensure she didn't get into any trouble before the wedding could take place. Annie had rolled her eyes at that.

The first few days passed without incident. The galleon sailed with a man o' war on either side and though several ships had been spotted in the distance, none approached.

Annie groaned and turned over in her bunk, trying to fight down a rising wave of seasickness. The wind had picked up earlier that morning and she worried that a storm was coming. The waves buffeted the ship more intensely than before and sent her stomach churning.

Maddie sat at the table in the cabin, which had been laid with fresh fruit. She'd been trying to encourage Annie to eat something for the past half hour. Though the slices of oranges and pineapple looked enticing, and would be considered rare delicacies these days, Annie could hardly bring herself to glance at them.

"You need to eat something, Your Highness," the maid said, popping an apple slice into her mouth. "It might help you feel better."

Maddie was young, perhaps slightly younger than Annie herself. She wore a plain gray dress with a white pinafore fitted over it. Her dark brown hair was pinned up and kept in place beneath a lace cap.

Annie's own hair was loose and tangled on the pillow. Maddie would have to comb the snarls out of it later and pin it up in some elaborate, uncomfortable fashion that would take forever to get just right, before she was introduced to the prince. Annie was no good with hair, hers being thick and slightly curling; she'd always found it impossible to manage and had long since given up.

She wasn't wearing her best gown either, as she would be required to later on. There was no point at the moment, since she'd likely only be sick all over it.

"No, thank you," she replied to the maid. "I'm not hungry." The truth was just the opposite, but she doubted she'd be able to keep anything down for long.

"You might consider going up on deck, miss," Maddie suggested. "The fresh air might help. I'll come with you, if you like."

It was the last thing Annie wanted, because it required her to move and she doubted her footing on the rolling deck, but she supposed it was better than simply laying there. At least if she was going to be sick, the railing would be within easy reach.

"Very well," she conceded. "You go on ahead. I'll be just a moment."

When Maddie had left, closing the cabin door behind her, Annie hauled herself to her feet, stumbling over to the glass windows at the back of the stern. Several of her plants had been secured there, where the sunlight could reach them.

She'd selected her most hopeful hybrids to bring along and she sighed as she looked at them, thinking of all that rested on them. She had to find a way to make this work.

Her laboratory had to remain behind in Daera, but that didn't mean her work had to stop. Hopefully, crossbreeding some of these varieties with Alaran plants would finally give her the result she'd toiled so long for.

Alara received more rainfall than Daera—at least until the weather had turned—so it followed that their plants would have to be hardier to such things.

Or so Annie hoped. Really, it didn't matter much now. With the alliance secured, the pressure to find a way to save her kingdom didn't weigh on Annie as much as it had only a short time ago.

She turned, following after Maddie, onto the quarter deck. She inhaled deeply as a gust of wind hit her in the face, breathing in the scent of the sea and the damp wood of the ship.

Annie gripped the rail and gazed around, past the ship escorting her. They were surrounded by the unending blue of the sea, not a stretch of land anywhere in sight.

She swallowed. It made her feel very much alone, in spite of the crew going about their tasks. Standing there, she could almost believe that they were the only beings in the entire world, that the rest of it had somehow ceased to be.

She shook her head, thinking herself fanciful. Large white sails flapped gently above her as they were stirred by the wind. Even higher, suspended from the gilded truck on the mainmast was the purple flag of Daera, whipping in the breeze, its white horse rampant.

Listening to the waves slap against the hull of the ship and the quiet billowing of the canvas, Annie had momentarily forgotten about her seasickness.

A voice called out from above. "Sail, ho!"

"Where away?" a second voice replied, though Annie wasn't sure who had spoken—the captain maybe?

"Larboard beam, three points abaft, sir!"

Annie had no idea what the exchange meant and she spun about wildly, searching for the aforementioned sail, but her untrained eyes could see nothing.

The captain stood on the left side of the deck, a spyglass raised to his eye. Apparently, the other vessel was still too far away to make out many details, because no orders were given to either ignore, flee, or roll out the guns.

Slowly, the sighted ship came into view for Annie and she squinted, trying to make out if it were friend or foe. The blood-red sails it boasted did not instill her with confidence, for Daeran naval vessels did not have such sails and, as far as she knew, neither did Alaran ships, even though red was the color of the southern kingdom.

She turned to the captain, still eyeing the ship every now and then with his spyglass. "What colors is she flying?"

The captain pursed his lips into a thin, hard line. "She's not flying any."

Annie felt her stomach bottom out, the same way it had when she'd climbed the tree for Ophelia and Albert and nearly fallen, the sensation of solid ground suddenly disappearing from beneath her.

"Mind," the captain added, "you usually can't tell by colors alone. Most vessels carry every type there is and haul them up based on the situation to deceive."

That did little to relieve Annie's anxiety. "But at least there's no pirate flag." She'd heard of the infamous black flag. Though the individual designs may vary, they usually involved some reference to death.

"That's no guarantee either. Some of those dogs don't run up their colors until they're just about to attack."

Nausea having returned in full force, there was nothing Annie could do but stand there helpless at the rail and watch as the other ship continued to approach. It was large enough to be imposing, nearly the same size as the warship escorting her.

"Pirates!" Maddie breathed, at her elbow. "Real life pirates, chasing us. Imagine that! If only Gertrude were here to see this. She'd never believe me if I told her."

Gertrude was Maddie's sister, back in Daera. Right now, Annie didn't much care that Maddie wanted to brag to her sibling about the harrowing situation. She wouldn't get the chance if these were real pirates and they found themselves boarded and slaughtered.

She'd heard plenty of grisly tales from the maids about what pirates did to their victims. Being female, she and

Maddie likely wouldn't be killed—at least not initially—but she dreaded to think what other horrors might await them.

The approaching vessel was now close enough that if she squinted, she could make out distant figures in the rigging or on the deck, but could not discern any details. Annie was unsure whether she was grateful for that fact or if it only made her more apprehensive.

But it was the figurehead that caught and held her attention. A large bird had been carved out of the wood, resembling a bird of prey, its sharp beak open, wings spread out behind it on the bow.

A shriek sounded above and Annie looked up to see a hawk soaring lazily overhead. Her brow crinkled in confusion. What was a bird like that doing so far out, in the middle of the ocean?

The larboard man o' war fired a warning shot, the report echoing across the waves and Annie jumped, hawk forgotten. The shot fell well clear of the scarlet-sailed ship, splashing harmlessly into the water, but it had the intended effect. The unknown vessel made no attempt to come closer, though it continued to stalk them.

Annie was thankful that her brother had had the foresight to assign her escorts and she breathed out a sigh of relief as the other ship retreated slightly. It hung back, staying out of the escorts' firing range, but it never again attempted to creep closer or engage them.

She continued to watch the ship throughout the day, as did the captain and several of the officers. She heard snatches of conversation from the crew, muttering nervously amongst themselves. The tension was palpable in the air, the unease remaining. Surely if the other vessel had been a friend, it would have bothered to identify itself by now?

Her fingers twitched, itching to have a rapier at her belt. Little good it would have done against the other ship's guns, but she would have felt a little safer, with a weapon at her side.

The unknown ship was still trailing them by the time the sun set and the order was given to extinguish all lanterns to hide them from view in case the vessel had purposefully waited until nightfall before launching an assault.

The scarlet ship, though, kept its lanterns lit, and with a full moon and clear skies, the Daeran ships were still clearly visible despite their efforts to the contrary.

When Annie awoke the next morning, she immediately hurried to peer out the stern windows and saw that the mysterious ship was still there, lurking at their backs as before.

Only when they reached Alaran waters, the blue sea intermingling with green hues, did the other vessel veer off and begin to tack away from them.

Annie felt her tension ease away as she watched it fade ever farther from view. She wasn't certain that it had been a pirate vessel, but perhaps Maddie would have an interesting story to tell after all.

CHAPTER 7

The island of Amberleigh rested off Alara's coast, but it belonged to and was ruled by neither kingdom. It was the largest of a small cluster of islands and happened to be the most popular pirate haven in the Atlas Sea.

As they drew near, the deeper hues of the Atlas Sea began to give way to lighter, clearer blues. Glancing over the side, Ben caught flashes of silver, light winking off the scales of fish in the pools of aquamarine water.

The harbor was crowded as usual when the *Phoenix* made port, the ships on display ranging from sloops and schooners to brigantines and one or two frigates such as the *Phoenix* herself. Here, there was no reason to fear anchoring at the docks as there would be in one of the kingdoms.

Amberleigh had deep water in its harbor, eliminating the need for longboats. Ben glanced around at the other ships docked there and sent Horus to have a look around, the hawk's eyesight far better than his own. He recognized several of the ships, but not the one he was looking for. Horus reported similarly. Berchmoore's ship was nowhere to be found, but that didn't necessarily mean the man wasn't on the island.

It was dusk by the time they arrived, the setting sun casting an orange glow across the quiet waves, staining the sky pink. It was Ben's favorite time of day and the best time to be in Amberleigh. Leaving the boatswain, Macaulay, in charge of the anchor watch, the rest of the crew departed to enjoy some much-needed and well-earned shore leave.

It was an opportunity not to be missed, a chance for the crew to go ashore, sell their share of the plunder, and spend their coin as they saw fit.

Terrance and Sharpe were both waiting for Ben as he walked across the gangplank and set foot on the dock. Sharpe was one of the many musketeers on board and the best shot of them all, which was precisely why the crew not only tolerated but respected her, despite the fact that she was the only female crewmember.

She was tall for a woman. With her chest bound, she could pass for a man at first glance. Her black hair was secured in a braid, not unlike some of the men. Her skin was very dark, making the light patches stand out all the more starkly.

"What are you two still doing here?" Ben asked as he reached them. "Would have thought you'd been off by now."

"Just waiting for you, Cap'n," Terrance replied, flashing him a grin.

"Well I'm here now."

The two fell in step beside him, Horus flying on ahead. Ben's long red coat swished against the fabric of his trousers as they walked through the streets. The air was warm and humid and he was already beginning to sweat, wishing he'd left the coat behind.

Though Amberleigh was neutral territory, welcoming to all pirates, occasional fighting still took place, despite it technically being outlawed. Ben walked with his cutlass sheathed at his side and one pistol tucked into his belt, in plain sight for all to see. Sharpe had the most weapons of any of them, with as many pistols stuffed into her baldric as possible.

With nightfall approaching, Amberleigh was a flurry of activity, the island not truly coming to life until after dark. The buildings and houses that lined the streets and alleys were mainly constructed of wood or brick. The windows were alight with golden glows, the air heavy with the smell of smoking wood, cooked meat, gunpowder, alcohol, and the ever-present scent of unwashed human.

A few people danced in the streets—most likely drunkenly from the look of them—to a fast, jolly tune being played on a fiddle. Somewhere, a gunshot went off and they passed several individuals sprawled in alleys or in the street itself, out cold.

"Would be so easy to pick their pockets right now," Sharpe muttered.

"Doubt there'd be much point," Terrance replied. "They probably don't have anything on them, having spent it all on rum."

"There are worse things to spend one's money on," Ben remarked. He'd always been partial to rum more than any other drink and he knew that's where they were headed.

A destination had never been spoken aloud, but the Black Horse tavern was a destination one couldn't afford to pass up on a trip to Amberleigh.

"Aye," Sharpe agreed as she pressed closer to him to avoid a pair of men who were in the middle of a brawl over skies only knew what. "That's what I intend to squander my ill-gotten gains on. And I can already guess Terrance's plans for the evening."

Terrance grinned over at her. "Maybe I'll pay Rosa a visit later, eh, Cap'n?" He nudged Ben with his elbow.

Ben ignored him, so used to the ribbing by now that it no longer phased him. He wouldn't have stood for such behavior from some of the other crew, but he and Terrance had been giving each other a hard time ever since they'd met as cabin boys under the command of Captain Lussard.

Terrance's jests were cut short as they reached their destination. The Black Horse tavern was a large, squatting sort of building, with two floors and walls made of timber the color of stone. Its cross-hatched windows were lit faintly in welcome.

The interior was dimly lit, the only source of lighting coming from the lanterns hanging from the ceiling and the individual candles on the tables, the flames flickering gently. A few sets of eyes raised in their direction as they entered, but most paid no mind, already well into their cups, deep in conversation or giving one of the serving girls their undivided attention.

Their boots echoed softly on the wood floor as they made their way through the room, around occupied tables, until they came to one in the corner. Ben always tried to find a table in the corner, if at all possible, so one didn't have to watch one's back. Horus hopped off his shoulder to perch on the back of the chair opposite from the one Ben took, Terrance and Sharpe sitting down beside him.

He reached up, removing his hat and running gloved fingers through his damp hair as he surveyed the room.

A few musicians in an opposite corner were singing some bawdy song, strumming along on a lute. A large boar could be seen roasting on a spit over a roaring fire. Barmaids, dressed in their plain white and brown dresses, hurried about, delivering ale and food to patrons, bosoms threatening to overflow.

"Busy place tonight," Sharpe remarked, reclining back in her chair.

It didn't take long for one of the barmaids to notice them and hurry over. Terrance ordered an ale while Sharpe and Ben both ordered rum. Ben pulled out his pipe and went about lighting it, listening to the conversation going on around them as they waited.

There were several sailors seated at the bar, but what caught his attention was the pretty blonde barmaid refilling their drinks.

"They say the prince is to be married soon," she said, likely by way of idle conversation.

"Wha' 'appened, luv?" one of the sailors asked loudly. "'E turn ya down again?"

His companion tugged at the barmaid's skirt. "Can't see why."

She shot him a glare, slapping his hand away. "Keep talkin' like that and I'll 'ave the proprietor call up your tab right now!"

"Well mebbe I *can* see 'ow 'e turned ya down…"

She shook her head. "He's to be married to the Daeran princess, they say. She's to be escorted to the kingdom."

Horus perked up at that. "*You don't think—?*"

Ben nodded wordlessly.

The hawk didn't need to say what he was thinking. Ben was certain he knew. There were times when they each seemed to instinctively know what the other was thinking. He'd known the hawk the entirety of his life, but he also knew better than to believe that's all it was.

One of the sailors raised a hand. "Eh, don't see why we should care, seeing as 'ow we wasn't invited to the nuptials."

"Yeah," his companion said with feeling, adjusting the collar of his dingy shirt, which may once have been white. "What would I wear anyway?"

"Thought you was wearing yer best clothes right now!"

Ben smirked at that, tuning out the conversation as the two men started bickering, exchanging insults back and forth, each trying to outdo the other.

The barmaid that had taken their orders had returned, setting the drinks on the table. "Anything else I can do for you?"

He glanced up at her smiling, expectant face. She intentionally leaned over the edge of the table, but Ben met her eyes, flicking her a coin. "No, thanks, love. That'll do for now, but I'll keep you posted."

She flashed him a grin and went on her way to attend to other customers.

Sharpe smirked. "You'll 'keep her posted', eh?"

Ben shrugged, extinguishing his pipe and taking a long swig of rum. "Course. I might order a few more of these before the night's out."

In the end, he didn't, finishing the one tankard of rum and then standing. "I think I'll go call on Rosa."

"Go ahead," Sharpe replied. "We'll be here. Or rather, I will be."

"Enjoy yourself, Cap'n," Terrance said, waving him on.

Ben smiled grimly to himself and fetched his hat, stepping outside. Horus followed, perching on his shoulder. The air had blessedly cooled off with the setting of the sun, but it remained muggy.

"They swallowed it hook, line, and sinker, didn't they?" the hawk mused.

Rosa ran a large bawdy house on the other end of town, near the docks. Over the years, she had made a name for herself, first as a common prostitute—if one could call her that—and now as a madam herself, chosen as the previous madam's successor.

But more than that, she had developed a knack for knowing precisely how to find what it was a man wanted, be it company for the night or a cheap bottle of rum. If you wanted something, you went to Rosa.

And that included information.

Her girls were paid to be spies as much as entertainers.

The house was quite large, painted white, with gaudy red shutters on the windows.

Immediately upon entering, there was a small bar area to the right, where patrons could purchase spirts not served at any of the local taverns. Occasionally, Rosa would greet guests personally.

There were chairs and tables where patrons could sit and drink or merely talk before retreating upstairs. Some of the entrances to other rooms were blocked by long, flowing curtains and Ben could guess what they shielded from view.

Faintly, from behind one such curtain, he could hear music being played. The air smelled heavily of perfume. Ben ignored all of it, going straight to Rosa's office and knocking, adjusting the cravat at his neck.

The door opened almost instantly to reveal Rosa herself standing there. A curvaceous woman, she was quite beautiful, her blonde hair falling to her chin in delicate waves. Her true age was unknown, but her face had a youthful appearance to it, one that was both enchanting and disarming. It was a face you instinctively trusted—and were drawn to. Little wonder she had collected so many secrets over the years.

She wore a loose, frilly white shirt, the collar open, the neckline plunging. She had on a deep green vest over the shirt, matching her long skirt, beneath which protruded a pair of dainty silk slippers.

She eyed him. "I wondered when you'd next darken my door." She stepped aside. "Come in."

"Thank you," he replied, handing her his hat and coat as had become habit. "How're things here?" he asked as she waved him into a chair.

The office looked more like a boudoir, complete with a fake fireplace. A large desk stood against one wall. Two comfortable chairs rested before the false hearth, a table between them, and there were settees and lounges elsewhere in the room. The furniture was decorated in colors of cream and rose.

Beside the desk, a bookshelf stood, filled to the brim. Through a half-closed door, Ben spied a glimpse of her bedroom, if she chose to stay at the house. A bathtub peeked out from behind a room divider.

"Much the same as always," she replied. "You want a drink?"

Ben accepted, even though he'd just come from the tavern. Rosa only traded in the best of everything. She moved over to the desk, uncapping a crystal decanter and pouring two drinks.

"Seen anyone new around?" Ben asked as he took the glass she offered him.

"No, but I recently saw a mutual acquaintance of ours." She sat down across from him, green eyes fixed on him, her gaze unusually serious. "He's been asking about you."

"Berchmoore?"

She nodded, taking a drink.

"Me?" Ben said, surprised. The pleasant warmth of the rum he'd imbibed earlier was beginning to fade. "Why would he be asking about me?"

It had been two years and if the man was plotting something, he'd had yet to make a move.

Because he knows that little tub of his is no match for the Phoenix, he thought with no small amount of pride.

"It appears he's legal now," Rosa answered. "Got a commission from the Alaran navy to hunt down pirates. And there have been rumors of others who have done the same."

Ben curled his lip. "Turncoats. If that's true, I'm surprised he had the balls to show his face here."

"Well, be that as it may, you know there's one pirate above all he'd love to get his hands on." She raised her arched eyebrows at him.

Ben smiled at her. "I'm not worried."

"I think perhaps you ought to be. He's got a new ship, bigger this time."

If Berchmoore at last had a bigger ship, one he believed could possibly challenge the *Phoenix*, it made sense that he would finally make his move. *But I have an advantage he never will.*

Ben reached out one gloved hand to stroke Horus's feathers. "Is he here now? I didn't see his ship earlier when we dropped anchor, but if he has a new one, I obviously didn't know what to look for."

"No. He left a few days ago."

"What's this new ship of his look like?"

"I don't know," Rosa confessed. "Never seen it myself, but I heard she's called the *Black Dagger*."

"Well, I'll keep an eye out for him," he said, to mollify her.

"Keep your wits about you. He'd love nothing more than to truss you up like a goose and march you into Brisban. And I'd hate to see that happen." She reached out, stroking his cheek with one hand.

But despite her flirting, he could see the fear reflected in her eyes, a tightness about her lips.

He gave her a full grin, hoping to ease her fear. "Don't worry yourself over it, Rosa. He'd have to catch me first and there's not a ship that sails the Atlas Sea that can catch my *Phoenix*."

"You may be right," she said, settling back into her chair.

He chatted with her for a little while longer and then took his leave, paying her for the information as always, and heading back to his cabin aboard the *Phoenix*, a pleasant warmth in his chest from the alcohol, his mind preoccupied with Berchmoore.

He had meant what he said when he'd promised Rosa that he would be keeping an eye out for his former shipmate. In fact, he intended to actively seek him out.

As a rule, most pirates refrained from preying on each other. Instead, they hunted vessels belonging to the kingdoms, since they were viewed as a common enemy to all pirates. But Ben was one of the few that not only targeted other pirates, but refused to attack Daeran ships, and that had made him more than a few enemies.

None more hellbent on revenge than Berchmoore.

But he'd had people challenge him before and they soon came to regret it. Berchmoore would be no different.

Ben set his jaw, feeling eager rather than anxious. He was rather looking forward to it.

It was time he paid Berchmoore back for that night two years ago.

CHAPTER 8

The streets of the village were dark and deserted as Daniel closed the pub for the night and made his way back home. Only a few torches placed here and there offered any sort of light. With the sky in Daera almost always overcast, one couldn't rely on the moon, but Daniel had walked this path every night for nearly twenty years and he could have found his way without the meager torchlight.

He'd begun to hear rumors of a stranger spotted in the next village over, though the description was lacking. The newcomer appeared to be a man and never spoke much to anyone or stayed in one place for long.

That was no proof that the stranger was Mordred, as Daniel believed. Men matching Mordred's description had been seen in Daera, but he would need something more definitive if he were to convince Calida to leave.

Daniel glanced over his shoulder. There was nothing unusual about tonight, nothing that should have made him feel apprehensive, but he couldn't shake the feeling that someone was following him—or at the very least, watching his movements closely.

But the street was empty, save for a few who had passed out drunk and lay where they'd collapsed, or those who were too weak from hunger to move out of the streets. *They would make poor witnesses if anything were to happen,* he thought, then chastised himself for letting his imagination get the better of him.

He kept going, the hair on the back of his neck prickling in warning. Unconsciously, he had quickened his pace and tried to avoid looking over his shoulder. He doubted he would see anything, even if there was something there.

Daniel started at a scurrying noise to his left, but it was only a couple of rats scuttling through the mud on the lookout for any scraps they could get their hands on.

He exhaled heavily, trying to reassure himself that it was all in his head and to put it out of his mind. He had never been so relieved to arrive at his front door as he was on this night, but arrived he had—safely and without incident.

It was his own paranoia, his own surety that someone had been sneaking around looking for him, Lorelei or Calida, that was beginning to get to him. Fact or fiction, he had convinced himself of its reality and now he was seeing threats and potential stalkers everywhere.

Ridiculous.

Taking his key from his pocket, Daniel unlocked the door to his small cottage near the edge of the village and let himself in. His two children, Albert and Ophelia, came to greet him almost immediately. He'd made a habit over the years of occasionally closing the pub early, after dinner had been served, to be able to come home and enjoy a late dinner of his own with his family.

His wife, Miriam, was in the kitchen, preparing dinner. She had managed to find a chicken at the market—a rarity nowadays—and some carrots that hadn't looked too poorly. She smiled at him as he came in.

As the usual routine of the evening meal, reading to the children and then putting them to bed, played out, Daniel had nearly forgotten his earlier misgivings. It wasn't until

Ophelia and Albert had retired for the night and the house grew quiet that the unwelcome thoughts resurfaced.

"What is it?" Miriam asked, making him look up.

She was seated across from him in their spartan living room, mending a hole in one of Albert's socks, since patching clothing was more economical than buying new ones, even when the old clothes looked more like ugly patchwork quilts than clothing.

Daniel hadn't realized his poor mood had been so obvious but he should have known better than to think he could hide it from his wife. Her keen brown eyes studied his face, waiting patiently without pressing him.

Her face was still beautiful, though lined. It gave her an air of wisdom, he thought, though the years had not been kind to her. *Nor to any of us.* He was able to afford food for his family, at least, where most struggled or failed altogether.

"It's nothing," he replied, realizing he'd been staring at her without saying a word.

"It's not the children, is it?"

"No. It's not the children," Daniel answered, though skies knew Albert was too thin for his age and Ophelia's clothes were too big for her, hanging loose where a healthy, well-fed child would have filled them out.

"The famine, then," Miriam concluded. It was always the famine.

"Yes," he sighed, thankful he didn't have to tell her the truth. He hated lying to her, but a lie was simpler than the truth. *The truth would be impossible.* "Have you had any visitors lately?" he asked suddenly, unable to resist.

"What sort of visitors?" she asked, brow furrowing. "Mrs. Lynn stopped by earlier. She'd needed some help with the washing and I'd promised to assist her."

"No one unusual, though?"

"No," she said slowly. "No one who hasn't stopped by before. Why?"

He shrugged. "Just wondering." But from the look on her face, he knew he had failed to convince her.

As much as he would have liked to pour the truth out to her, to have someone to share the burden with, he could not. Not without explaining the entirety of it and that would keep them there all night.

He had often wondered in the past if he had made a mistake in not confiding to his wife that he was a witch, a persecuted minority. It was what had driven him to seek refuge in Daera twenty years ago, when the witch-hunts began. Miriam knew nothing of his former life and there was no way to make her understand.

He'd been one of the lucky ones to escape, but if his fears were right and Mordred was in Daera, then his past now threatened to catch up with him.

Daniel rubbed a hand over his face. How could he explain such a thing? He hadn't told Miriam all those years ago, when they'd first met, out of fear. Fear that she would leave him, fear that he would inadvertently put her in danger simply by her knowing.

Thank goodness neither Albert nor Ophelia were born with a witch-mark. That would have meant that he had passed his power on to them and put them in danger. He would have been forced to confess the truth then and there, had such been the case, but it blessedly hadn't been.

Perhaps I should have listened to Lorelei… The midwife was of the opinion that marrying someone who was not a witch would only lead to disaster. She wasn't willing to put them in harm's way or drag them into her predicament and so she had never married. If she held herself to the standard of only wedding a fellow witch, skies knew there were precious few left to go around. Or if there were more, they'd hidden themselves well and didn't show their true natures.

It was a little late to be having second thoughts now.

Daniel glanced over at Miriam, intent once more on her work, and wondered how he had ever managed to marry such a woman. *Through lies and keeping secrets,* a voice taunted in the back of his mind.

He stood abruptly. "I'm off to bed." He couldn't stand to sit there and ponder such things any longer.

She followed him half an hour later and he was still awake when she joined him in the bedroom.

* * *

The woods bordering the village were thick and shadowed, offering many hiding places. It was understandable why the villagers seemed to avoid the woods at night, almost as though there was something inherently wicked about the forest, though it had nothing on the Witch Wood.

What it did have was a clear view of Daniel's house at the end of the lane, all the while concealing the figure standing there in silent vigil.

They watched as the last lamp went out within the home, plunging the windows into darkness. The figure continued to observe for the better part of an hour, but nothing within the house stirred. Any inhabitants had retired for the night.

Silently, the shadowed figure turned and walked away.

CHAPTER 9

As agreed upon, an Alaran vessel did come forth to meet Annie and her escorts, guiding them safely through the strait and into the kingdom's harbor. Annie was simply relieved that the mysterious ship that had been trailing them was gone; there had been no other sign of a threat and no more ships had appeared on the horizon, save for the one that would meet her.

The harbor was large, even bigger than Daera's, with many fine and impressive ships already docked there. Even her escort warships paled in comparison to the might of Alara's navy.

Annie could just make out the castle from where she stood on the docks, though it was impossible to discern any details from this distance. It seemed to sit on a hill, not far from the sea, with towns and villages laying sprawled out before it.

Maddie, Florence, and Aquillus remained close by her side as the trunks and crates were brought up and unloaded from the ship. They didn't have long to wait before their welcoming party arrived.

Annie blinked in the bright sunlight, shielding her eyes with her hand as she looked around. Oh, how long it had been since she'd last seen the sun! Even when it had dared show its face in Daera, it hadn't seemed so bright and warm. It felt wonderful on her skin after so many years spent living in darkness and she tipped her head back, letting her hand fall away, to soak up its warmth. In minutes, she was sweating from the tropical heat, but she didn't care.

She opened her eyes as two lines of Alaran soldiers rode up, side by side, each mounted on fabulous white steeds. Both soldier and mount alike were decked out in Alara's colors of red and gold, aside from the man who rode at the head of the gathering. He wore deep forest green and was seated on a magnificent chestnut stallion.

Behind his horse were four rider-less white horses that pulled a gilded carriage, surrounded on all sides by the mounted soldiers. Maddie was gawking at the blatant finery of it all. Even Annie, who was used to luxury, found herself slightly taken aback.

Daera would be hard-pressed to match such a display. There were probably more horses parading before her now than remained in her entire country. The famine had taken the vast majority of them.

She hadn't even reached the castle yet and it was already apparent how much wealthier Alara was than its northern counterpart.

The man in green swung down from his horse, his polished boots hitting the wood of the dock lightly. He approached with a calm, confident air, and Annie suddenly wondered, with a stab of alarm, if *this* was the prince.

Surely not! But then…she'd never met him before and so had no way of knowing.

He was well-dressed, of course, but surely, he wouldn't meet her here, on the docks. *Unless he was over-eager.* What alarmed her most, though, was his age. He had a handsome face, in a rugged sort of way, with a strong jaw and regal cheekbones, but he might have been twice her age! He was at least as old as Varrian, if not more.

He bowed at the waist as he reached her and, as was customary, Annie extended one hand in his direction. He took it gently, the material of his glove brushing against her.

"Your Royal Highness," he said, pressing a kiss to her hand and releasing her. "Welcome to Alara." He straightened. "My name is Rodek, the royal advisor, and at the queen's behest, I am here to escort you to the palace."

Annie sighed inwardly with relief, hoping it wasn't outwardly obvious. This man wasn't the prince, then. Just an advisor.

She inclined her head to him. "Thank you. I look forward to it."

In truth, she was feeling rather nauseous again, even though she was no longer on the pitching deck of a ship. So this man wasn't the prince, but she would still meet him eventually, along with the king and queen. She would finally lay eyes on the man she was expected to spend the rest of her life with.

The thought filled her with apprehension, hoping that he was pleasant enough—and if she were completely honest—easy on the eyes as well, but at the same time fearing he wouldn't be.

If Rodek noticed her discomfort, he was too well-bred to show it. "Very well, if you'll come with me…"

He guided her over to where the carriage sat, Maddie and Florence following. Aquillus would have a horse of his own, so he and Rodek could discuss on the way to the palace, one advisor to another. Rodek opened the carriage door himself and stepped aside, offering a hand in case Annie needed help climbing inside.

Ordinarily, she would have politely declined and gone up the stairs by herself. But seeing as how the sickening feeling in her stomach had yet to dissipate, she gratefully accepted the offer.

The ceiling of the carriage was shaped like a dome, with windows on either side, currently covered with velvet curtains. The carriage, for the most part, was white, with the wheels, curtains and velvet seat cushions all gold. There were two rows of seats and Annie took the one that would allow her to face the front of the carriage, scooting over to the window.

Maddie and Florence followed, taking the seat opposite, their eyes fixed on the golden carpet. Rodek shut the door securely behind them and disappeared, likely going to fetch his horse. A moment later, there was a flick of a whip and the carriage lurched forward, surrounded by the clacking of hooves.

Annie drew back the curtains, peering through the window at the passing scenery beyond. Some of the village streets they passed reminded her of home.

Nearest the harbor, waterways and smaller piers branched off, the sea channeled through the village itself. The buildings here were tall, multi-storied, crammed closely together, the tiles of their roofs earthy browns or reds.

People wandered about, from one storefront to the next, haggling, dressed in a variety of styles. Some were clearly sailors, others wealthy merchants. More than once, Annie saw a bag of coins exchange hands.

Palm trees sprouted between buildings, wherever there was free space to be had, providing shade. Annie's gaze was immediately drawn to the stalls of fresh fruit, their colors vibrant, their size large, round and inviting. There was also more than enough fresh seafood, its pungent but not unpleasant aroma filling the air.

It made sense that this would be the first sight potential travelers and customers would see upon entering the city, a reflection of the positive image Alara wished to embody. But as the carriage drifted further from the harbor, a different side of the southern kingdom was quickly revealed.

Not all of the villages shared in the wealth of the sea trade. Here, the houses were short, squat, one dimensional. These were also crowded together, nearly on top of one another, and all seemed to be constructed of the same drab timber. The streets were dingy and an unpleasant smell hung in the air, detectable even within the confines of the carriage.

Peasant women went about their chores, washing and hanging up clothes, haggling with merchants at their stalls. Children, their pale faces streaked with dirt or soot, played in the streets or begged. There were few men to be seen and Annie assumed they must be busy working elsewhere. But everyone they passed paused to glance up at the regal procession that strolled by.

Yes, Alara had poor of its own. Not everyone, it seemed, shared in the wealth. But even these peasants had it better than those back in Daera. Worn and faded their clothes may be, but their faces were not hollowed out by hunger. Their bones did not press against their skin, giving them the appearance of the living dead more than real human beings.

Perhaps the vendors did charge too much for their produce—as one woman they passed loudly proclaimed—but at least they *had* food to sell and argue over. The people of Daera had nothing.

And that, Annie reminded herself, *is why you are here.*

The village was soon left behind, the castle coming into view in all its glory. It was a massive, sprawling monster of a building, with spires and towers stretching higher than the castle she called home in Daera. It was a thing of gleaming gold trim and adornment set against ivory stone. Everywhere one looked, there seemed to be glass filling the walls. There was even a glass roof for much of the structure. Its every surface shone, the sun winking off the glass, the statues carved with lifelike resemblance. There were no cracks to be seen, no faded tiles, or dull exteriors.

Annie felt a dull ache in her chest as she thought of all the people back home in Daera. It was probably raining there, cloudy at the very least. *To live in a place like this every day…*

The villages and towns closer to the castle were more affluent, the houses narrow but tall, with balconies and terraces. She watched women walk along the streets, or riding in open carriages, dressed in lovely silk gowns. The houses were all painted garish colors, some with flowers in the window boxes. The colors seemed incredibly bright when all one knew was drab.

Trapped in Daera, Annie had had no idea that a place like this could exist. It gave her a vision of what Daera could become in the future.

And then the carriage had halted, the door had opened, and Annie was escorted up the grand stairs and into the palace in a daze, staring around at all its polished splendor as if she were a peasant girl instead of a princess.

The white marble floors, the high vaulted ceilings with their glass domes offering a perfect view of the sky with its white clouds, the gilded chandeliers, the many floor-to-ceiling windows, the sheer number of servants and guards bustling around, all dressed in red and gold livery. Rodek led them through the winding halls, past pillars and columns, their footsteps echoing on a floor so polished it was almost like looking in a mirror.

Past gleaming marble and glass—oh, the glass! It was everywhere Annie looked, making her feel as though one wrong step would shatter it and bring the whole place down around her.

Finally, Rodek halted before a door in the west wing. "These chambers are all yours, Your Royal Highness. I will leave you now, to settle in and rest after your journey. Tonight, we will host a ball in your honor, to celebrate your arrival and to announce your betrothal to His Royal Highness. There, you will be introduced to everyone officially. You will be provided with all the servants you require, who know their way around the castle, to assist you and help you prepare for tonight."

Annie felt her lips twist at the mention of the ball. Really, they needn't have gone to all that fuss. But then, looking around, this was hardly a place where they refrained from indulging in the ostentatious.

"I am most grateful for your assistance," she said. "Before you go, I have one request to ask of you. Is there a spare room that I might utilize as a greenhouse? I've brought some plants from Daera along with me, you see."

If he thought her request odd, he didn't show it. Annie was beginning to realize just how little this man gave away. Looking at his handsome face, she had no idea what he might be thinking.

"Yes, of course," he replied. "If you'll follow me, I will escort you there."

"Thank you."

She followed dutifully behind him, glancing over her shoulder at her attendants. Some of them were depositing her luggage in her quarters and the others carefully carried her plants.

Rodek led her to a conservatory, filled with a riot of color. The roof was a glass dome and the walls were composed entirely of tall, thin windows, completely surrounding the circular room on all sides.

Annie sucked in a breath of the warm, slightly humid air as she took in all the plants arranged before her, many of which were unfamiliar to her. It was precisely what she had hoped for.

"I trust this will suffice?" Rodek asked.

Annie assured him that it would.

He bowed. "Until tonight, then, Highness, I shall bid you goodbye." He kissed her hand a final time and then was off, striding briskly back the way he'd come, boots echoing on the marble floor, until he was out of sight.

As soon as her attendants had set the plants down, Annie shooed them away, wanting to see to this task herself. With the utmost care, she placed each of the plants where she wanted them, trimmed away any brown or dead leaves, and watered those that needed it.

She turned to the Alaran plants, wanting nothing more than to observe them and take notes, already dreaming about the ways she could crossbreed them with her Daeran varieties.

But she didn't get very far. She was tired after her journey and her mind refused to focus, distracted by her unfamiliar surroundings and reeling with questions yet to be answered.

Annie sighed and reluctantly shut the notebook her servants had brought, filled with her notes and sketches. Her work would have to wait.

She returned to the quarters she'd been escorted to, her earlier misgivings returning. A ball! She hadn't been told anything about a ball. The anxious fluttering in her stomach redoubled.

Maddie had been waiting for her. "Come on, miss," she said eagerly. "Let's see what room they've given you!"

They stepped inside, gazing around and the maid gave a gasp, "It's so lovely!"

It was, of course, like everything else in that castle. There was so much gold trimming, it made Annie's eyes hurt to look at it. She wondered if it was real or fake, and if it was real, how much it had cost.

How many hungry people would that much gold feed?

Her bedroom consisted of a large, canopied bed, the red sheets smooth as running water. A chandelier dangled in front of the bed. There was a wardrobe, a dresser, lush, thick carpets, and a single tall window, which opened out onto a balcony.

The adjacent, main room, was larger, with sofas, divans, and chairs for sitting and several grand chandeliers. Candelabras were made to look like elegant figures. There was a portrait on the wall, but no one Annie recognized. There were tables with potted plants and a hearth against one wall, though Annie doubted it would be needed in this tropical heat.

Room dividers for dressing behind stood at the far end of the room, near a dressing table with a large circular mirror and a chair seated in front. A door led to the next room, which contained bedchambers for the maids and servants, always at her beck and call within a moment's notice.

At least there was a solid ceiling above her head, not a glass dome. She would have felt too exposed sleeping in a room made of glass, like she was little more than an exhibit. Something foreign to be stared at, observed and put on display.

"I could get used to a place like this," Maddie muttered, admiring the wallpaper. The maid turned to her. "Are you all right, miss? You look a bit pale."

"I'm fine, Maddie, thank you. It's all just a bit much to take in at once, I expect."

"Well, I'll leave you to rest for a bit, miss. Big night tonight. Got to make a good first impression!"

The maid curtsied and then headed through that far door into the servants' quarters. Annie turned and walked back to her bedroom as one in a trance.

After a week at sea, she needed to rest if she was expected to attend a ball tonight and meet the Alaran royals. But with all that had happened, the odds that sleep would come did not seem favorable.

Annie ignored the bed and stood at the window, gazing down at the sprawling towns below. Her chambers really *were* high up and she suddenly had the morbid thought of wondering what it would be like to fall from such a place.

She shook her head, stepping back. Her mind always did come up with strange thoughts when she was tired. Reluctantly, she turned to the bed and collapsed onto it, certain her prediction of sleep evading her would prove true.

She was wrong.

It seemed like only a second's time had passed between the instant Annie sank onto the bed and closed her eyes and Maddie rousing her. The maid set to work immediately on taming the princess's wild black curls, which had become tangled in the wind from her time spent at the rail of the ship. The snarls proved to be quite painful to yank out and Annie sat there, at the dressing table mirror, gritting her teeth with tears in her eyes.

Just as Rodek had promised, other maids from the castle were sent to attend to her. There was a brief debate over which of the gowns she should choose.

In the end, Annie selected her deep purple dress, since it was the color of her kingdom. It was a bulky, cumbersome thing, with thick petticoats beneath to fluff out the taffeta skirt. The bodice had been cinched tight and it showed off more cleavage than Annie would have liked. She would have liked to be in trousers, but that would not do.

Her shoes were silver, the heels high to increase her height. White gloves that covered her arms to the elbow completed the look.

At last, the maids stepped back to admire their work, allowing Annie to observe her reflection in the mirror. Her thick black hair was piled atop her head, leaving a few curls loose to frame her face. Two silver earrings dangled in plain view. Her sleeves were off the shoulder, the gown alternating between dark and light shades of purple as it caught the light.

It wasn't perfect or the most comfortable thing she'd ever worn, but Annie refrained from voicing any such misgivings. The maids seemed delighted with the result.

"You look beautiful, my lady," Maddie murmured.

Annie flashed her maid what she hoped was a grateful smile, and hoped that the king, queen, and prince would agree.

Attendants came to fetch her and she left her maids behind, following as they led her through the unfamiliar corridors of the castle to the ball room. Florence trailed behind as her chaperone, hanging back at a discreet distance.

The sun had set and moonlight filtered through the glass ceiling of the ballroom, bathing everything with a silvery glow.

Someone announced her as she entered. "Her Royal Highness, Princess Annabelle of Daera!"

It seemed to Annie that every head in the room swiveled in her direction. Her breath caught in her chest. She could feel her resolve begin to slip away, frozen, pinned by the force of so many gazes upon her at once. But a familiar figure appeared by her side.

"You look lovely, Highness." *Rodek.*

She nodded to him, not trusting herself to speak, but grateful for the rescue.

He offered her his arm. "Come. I'll take you to the king and queen."

She accepted it, thankful to have something to lean on at that moment. She gazed around at the room as they walked, trying her best to ignore the whispers and low murmurs of those around them as they watched her pass.

An orchestra played softly on a dais on the other side of the room. There were tables, draped with white cloths, that held row upon row of exquisite dishes and servants bustled about carrying drinks and other refreshments on trays. The ballroom was lit by hanging chandeliers and sconces on the walls, in addition to the moonlight pouring through the ceiling. The sheer amount of people in the room made the air feel uncomfortably warm to Annie, or perhaps she was just flushed from all the attention.

Everywhere she looked, she was met with a riot of color from the women's gowns, in stark contrast to the panther black of the men's suits. Jewels winked in the light, at throats, dangling from ears, and even threaded through hair.

Rodek guided her deftly through the throng of people, over to where three figures stood at the head of the room. "Your Majesties, may I present Princess Annabelle of Daera."

Annie released her hold on Rodek's arm to give a shy curtsy, trying to control a sudden rush of nerves. These were the people upon whom Daera's future depended.

Rodek gestured to the woman who stepped forward. "Her Majesty, Queen Thalia of Alara."

The queen was a tall woman, though she may have been wearing heels as Annie was, and quite striking. She wore a lavish scarlet gown, inlaid with golden beads that winked as she moved. Her bright red hair was left flowing freely down her back. She had full lips and peered at Annie with deep blue eyes.

"What a pleasure it is to finally meet you," the queen murmured. "I hope you're enjoying your stay thus far."

"Very much, Your Majesty," Annie replied. It was the only suitable answer. "You have such a beautiful kingdom."

"Indeed." Thalia nodded. "I see you've already met Rodek, my advisor."

She lifted a hand to gesture to the man and as she did so, Annie caught a whiff of a fragrant floral perfume. It made her feel slightly lightheaded and immediately she was struck with the certainty that she ought to know which flower the scent came from. It was intimately familiar, to the point where she had to have smelled it before, but no name or image came to mind.

Annie shook her head to clear it. "Yes, ma'am."

The queen said nothing more and Rodek moved on to introduce the man standing beside her.

"His Majesty, King Niklaus of Alara."

The queen's husband was dressed similarly in the kingdom's colors of red and gold, medals pinned to the breast of his jacket. He had blond hair, with a resplendent mustache and beard and kind blue eyes. Annie exchanged brief pleasantries with him, but he seemed distracted and she glanced at the wine glass he held, wondering if that was to blame.

Her heart leapt as Rodek turned to the last figure. "His Royal Highness, Prince Kain of Alara."

Kain was nearly the spitting image of his mother. He had both her fiery hair and her deep blue eyes, but didn't seem to resemble his father at all. He, too, was dressed in a red military-style uniform.

To her relief, he was quite handsome, more so than she had expected, with a sculpted jaw and good cheekbones.

She curtsied to him and extended one gloved hand. "Pleasure to meet you, Your Highness."

He reached out to kiss her hand, the picture of grace and politeness itself, all suave and sophisticated. In contrast, it made her feel all the more clumsy and out of place.

"The pleasure's all mine, Highness." He smiled at her, revealing a dimple on one cheek. "You're even more beautiful than they say."

"Your Highness is too kind," Annie replied, desperately wishing she had a fan or something to cool herself with— and also consequently hide behind.

It felt odd having to address him by his title, but it would be that way even if they were married. No, not if. *When.* This man was her future husband. She could hardly believe her luck. She had been so worried that he would be a boor or else dreadfully dull. She nearly laughed at herself for having worried over nothing.

"Would you care to dance?" he inquired.

"Certainly," she said, nodding, hoping she didn't seem too eager.

Kain offered his arm much the way Rodek had and Annie obligingly took it as he guided her out into the center of the ballroom. She stood, facing him, and he placed a hand on her back.

It was a bit difficult to move in her stiff dress as he began to lead her into a waltz of sorts, but she hardly noticed. The room seemed to swirl by, a mass of floating lights and colorful tapestries. The air seemed warmer and more stifling than before.

They were surrounded on all sides by crowds of gathered guests, each one's gaze seemingly locked on her and the prince. None of them were dancing, likely waiting until the prince had completed the first dance.

The monarchs were waiting, too. The king looked proud and Annie saw the queen murmur something to Rodek, who nodded in agreement.

And then the dance was over, with Annie twirling one more time, her skirts swirling around her legs, leaving her and the prince standing still, facing each other. He bowed to her and she curtsied to him as the audience applauded around them.

"Thank you for granting me the honor of this dance, my lady," the prince said.

Annie hoped her smile didn't look as wobbly as it felt. "The pleasure's all mine."

"Come," the prince suggested. "I'll introduce you to some of the lords and ladies."

Most of the lords seemed dreadfully old to Annie, their hair either graying or making a hasty retreat altogether, but a few were closer to her own age. None of them had anything much of importance to say, making small talk and exchanging pleasantries, but mostly commenting on what a handsome couple the two of them made, embarrassing Annie further.

She found chatting to their wives to be slightly less uncomfortable and more engaging, just. Mostly it was more congratulations on their engagement and upcoming marriage, asking if she could confide in them any juicy tidbits about the wedding ceremony. Annie did her best to smile, laugh along, and wave their questions off.

She doubted she would—or could—remember all their faces, much less their names, or whom she should make sure to steer clear of. It was all a blur; so many people she didn't recognize or know, but getting introduced to all at once.

The only people she knew here were Aquillus, Maddie, Florence, and the other servants she'd brought with her. It was a stark reminder of just how alone she really was.

At long last, the prince steered her back over to where the king and queen waited. Rodek still stood nearby, a little bit behind the queen but still very close in his proximity. Aquillus stood off to the side, engaged in a conversation with one of the lords. Annie met his gaze for a moment, but didn't want to interrupt.

Rodek and the queen were engrossed in a private conversation as well and so Annie turned to the king.

"It's a lovely ball, Your Majesty," she remarked.

"I'm glad you think so. I hope you're enjoying yourself."

"Oh, yes. Very much, sir."

He peered closely at her, squinting slightly. "Is everything all right, Highness? You seem preoccupied."

Annie hadn't realized she'd reached up to fidget with one of her silver earrings and she promptly lowered her hand. "Oh, no, sir. I'm just a bit worried, I suppose."

The king nodded. "I see. About your kingdom, no doubt. I've heard the news. It's quite distressing. I remember when Daera was a grand kingdom, to rival this one, in fact."

"My brother does what he can," Annie murmured. *But it isn't enough.*

"A good man," the king agreed. "Always was opposed to the idea of witch-hunts, as I recall. Thought they were cruel, messy affairs that people took advantage of to get their way. If you didn't like someone, you could simply accuse them of being a witch and whether or not it was true, like as not they would be found guilty anyway. You could get rid of someone just like that." He snapped his fingers for emphasis.

Annie thought this commentary odd coming from the monarch of the kingdom known far and wide for its own witch-hunts. "People did that? Accusing someone of being a witch just to be rid of them?"

"Oh, yes. Usually because the accuser stood to gain something, like the accused's land or property or belongings of some sort. Or perhaps the accused had knowledge that, if revealed, would ruin the accuser, so the easiest solution would be to accuse them of witchcraft." He shrugged his bony shoulders. "No one would believe the word of an accused witch."

"That's awful," Annie exclaimed.

The king looked down at the contents of his wine glass. "Yes, well… It wasn't always like that."

Queen Thalia materialized at the king's shoulder. She patted his arm in a soothing manner. "Now, now, dear. I'm sure our guest doesn't want to hear such maudlin tales of the past. It's getting late. I'll send someone to fetch your medicine."

She turned to Rodek, snapping her fingers. He hurried away silently, melting into the crowd.

Thalia turned to Annie. "You'll have to forgive him, Your Highness. I'm afraid my husband is not well."

"I'm sorry to hear that."

Thalia nodded slowly. "I understand you must be concerned for your kingdom, but let me set your mind at ease. I've been discussing such matters with your brother's advisor, Aquillus. We have another shipment of supplies for your people, scheduled to make sail as soon as possible."

Annie bowed her head. "Thank you, Your Majesty. We would be eternally grateful."

Neither the queen or king said anything more. Rodek returned a short time later, carrying a small vial of red liquid. He took the king's wine glass and poured the vial's contents in, swirled it slightly, and presented it to the queen with a bow.

She took it from him, offering it to the king. "Here you are, dear."

He accepted it wordlessly and downed the glass of wine.

Thalia smiled apologetically to Anine. "I think it best if he retires for the night." She signaled to a servant, murmuring something to them, and they began to lead the king away.

Annie turned her attention back to the prince, standing at her shoulder. "I'm sorry to hear that your father is not well."

"Don't worry yourself over it. He's been ill for years, I'm afraid."

"What's wrong with him, if I may ask?"

"His mind is going. Sometimes he can't remember who he is, who we are, or even where he is." He pressed his lips together. "It's a shame." He brightened suddenly, as though shaking off the low mood that had come over him. "Say, I was thinking that tomorrow you and I might do a bit of riding, tour the kingdom. I'd love the opportunity to show the people my future bride and their future queen—and to show you your future kingdom. Would you like that?"

Annie blinked rapidly, caught off-guard by the sudden shift in subject. "Y—yes, I think that might be a good idea, Your Highness."

"Excellent," the prince replied, flaunting that smile again. "It's a date, then."

Annie summoned her own smile in response to his. "Indeed."

The night stretched on, the ball interrupted briefly for a dinner, until Annie finally excused herself, having grown tired. She bid a goodnight to the queen and prince and then followed the summoned servant as they escorted her back to her quarters.

She was grateful to leave behind the stifling ballroom and just be alone with her own thoughts, but her maids rushed forward to question her as they helped her out of her gown.

"Did you meet the prince?" Maddie asked.

"I did."

"Was he handsome?"

"Very much so."

The maid plucked a few silver pins out of her hair. "Did you dance with him?"

Annie laughed. "It was a ball, Maddie. Of course I did."

The maid sighed dramatically. "You're a lucky girl."

Yes, Annie thought, imagining the starving peasants back in Daera. *I am lucky.*

She glanced at the new maids she'd been assigned. "I heard the king is ill. Is that true?"

"Oh, yes," one of them, Aliya, said, nodding. "He's been that way since around the time his father died. Can't seem to remember things very well anymore. Sad, really, what grief does to some people."

The other maids verified the claim.

"Poor man," Annie murmured. "I'm sorry to hear it."

But the man seemed to recall the witch-hunts well enough. Or was he merely making it all up? Annie had no way of knowing. She knew what a famine was like, but not a witch-hunt, and she was grateful that they didn't occur in Daera. But the idea of someone accusing their neighbor of being a witch, simply because they desired that person's property for themselves, struck her as a bit extreme.

It took the maids some time to help her out of the unwieldy gown and into a simple nightgown. By the time they were finished, Annie was exhausted and in no mood for further conversation or questions. Her servants bid her goodnight and retreated into their own quarters, leaving her alone in her bedroom.

Annie sank down onto the bed, but this time, sleep did not come so quickly. Her mind kept drifting back to the king and his condition and what he had said to her of the witch-hunts. But mostly she lay there thinking about the prince and his proposition for tomorrow's activity.

She wasn't foolish enough to entertain the notion that one could fall in love overnight, but she was surprised by how charming the prince had been. Of all the possible outcomes, she felt she had won the best.

Of course, she barely knew him, but that would come in time, as they got to know each other better.

Annie sighed, finally releasing her fears about him. She was rather looking forward to what was to come and to seeing him again.

She froze, sitting up. Had she heard something outside? She crept to the door, her suspicions proven correct—she could hear voices raised in anger.

She pulled her door open and stuck her head out, glancing both ways down the hall, but could see no one. One voice was female while the other was clearly male, but she couldn't make out any of the words or identify who the voices belonged to. She ducked back inside, shutting the door.

The argument went on for several more minutes and then abruptly ended, leaving her none the wiser as to who it had been or what they had been arguing about.

CHAPTER 10

Mordred glanced over his shoulder at the sound of approaching hooves and wheels squelching in the muck. He'd been wading through Daera's pathetic excuses for roads for over an hour now and his boots and the fringes of his cloak were caked in dried mud, adding to his appearance as an ordinary beggar. He stopped limping, giving the appearance of allowing his bad leg to rest, and raised a hand to hail the cart coming his way.

The old nag pulling the cart halted beside him and Mordred called up to the man perched on the seat, "Where are you headed?"

"Steelrest," came the reply.

"Mind if I hitch a ride?"

The driver jerked his head toward the cart behind him. "Wagon's empty. Climb in."

Mordred hobbled around the wagon and heaved himself up, truly grateful to be off his feet. The man flicked the reins and the cart shuddered as it rolled into motion once more.

"Come from the market, did you?" Mordred asked, gesturing at the emptiness of the wagon.

The driver grunted. "Sold what I had. Wasn't worth much, of course, but better than nothing."

"You're a farmer, then?"

"Not the one I used to be, but I make do. Used to have such a bountiful crop that you couldn't fit it all in one wagon. Even if they don't rot in the fields, you're lucky if the cabbages are as big as your fist."

Mordred made a noise of sympathy. "It's the same everywhere."

"Even the roads are terrible," the farmer muttered, swearing under his breath as the wagon jolted.

"It's worse up north." Mordred couldn't see the man's face with his back to him and he dearly wished he could, to judge his reaction to his next remark. "They're saying a witch is to blame."

The man scoffed. "Just a bad bit of weather, that's all."

"Season after season? For ten years?"

That gave the man pause. He remained silent for several moments, as though giving the matter serious thought. At last, he turned to glance back at his passenger. "I had heard something to that effect. I dunno about all that; what's a witch to gain from this? Still, you'd think bad luck would have turned by now."

Mordred nodded. "I couldn't say, but I always did think it was a bad idea when Daera let the witches in, after they fled from Alara. We were fine until they came; we didn't have such problems until they arrived." He adjusted his cloak against the chill in the air. "If you ask me, Alara was on to something. They chased all the witches out and look at them—prosperous and with a hell of a lot better weather than us."

The farmer said nothing more, but Mordred heard him mutter under his breath, "Maybe they was on to something, after all."

The remainder of the trip was uneventful, but Mordred didn't care. He had accomplished his task. The seeds of doubt had been sown, as they had in each village he passed through.

The farmer, whose name he hadn't bothered to ask, nor had any interest in learning, dropped him off on the outskirts of town, telling him that if he was hungry, he might be able to get something from the Crow's Nest Inn.

Mordred thanked him civilly enough and went on his way, returning to the task that occupied his every waking moment. Subtly searching until he found what he was looking for. And he had a feeling that he might find her very soon.

* * *

Daniel wanted nothing more than to lock up the pub for the night and go home to Miriam and the children. It had been a long day. Each one was, but they seemed to get longer as time went on. He'd have already gone home but he was waiting for his last customer to leave.

Crawley, more often than not, was one of the last to leave. He was a thin, grizzled old man, who had lost more teeth than he now possessed. But he had ears like a fox and if there was any news, you could be sure Crawley had heard of it.

Not only that, but he was always eager for company and that made him loose-lipped.

Daniel made his way over toward Crawley's table. The old man looked up. "I was just about to go on my way." As if he were afraid that Daniel would throw him out for staying so late.

Daniel sat down across from him. "No need to hurry, Crawley," he lied, though that's what he would have preferred the old man do. "Hear anything new lately?"

Crawley shook his head. "Nothing I'd imagine you'd want to hear, sir."

"Nevertheless," Daniel encouraged him.

"The Baides lost their baby," Crawley said, looking down into his tankard as if that made the words easier. "The younger one. Too small to survive, I suppose. I heard some sailors down by the docks earlier saying that fewer and fewer ships are docking all the time and that the king might do well to consider instituting higher wharfage fees to make up for it. But then who would come, I ask you?"

Daniel nodded, not particularly interested in any of this—though the loss of the child was sad. "What about travelers? Have you seen any strangers lately?"

"Just the usual bunch. Can't imagine there'd be many travelers passing through these parts anymore."

Daniel was disappointed, but hardly surprised. If Mordred had been in Daera longer than he'd supposed, he might have already found a way to fit in and hide in plain sight. If he didn't appear unusual—and he would take pains to ensure that he did not—then no one would pay him any heed.

"Why?" Crawley added, more perceptive than he should have been for putting away so much liquor. "You lookin' for someone?"

Daniel briefly debated admitting that he was and giving Crawley a description of what he remembered of Mordred's appearance, but then thought better of it. It had been many years ago and the man likely looked nothing like he once had.

Besides, Crawley had already told him that he hadn't seen anyone unusual. There was no need to drag the old man into this mess and put him in unnecessary danger.

"No," Daniel answered, not giving any further explanation for having asked.

Crawley shrugged. "Sorry I couldn't be of more help to you." He downed the last swallow of his ale, settled his account, and shambled off into the night, at last leaving Daniel to close up for the evening.

He sighed and stood, making his way to the back of the bar to fetch a rag to wipe off the last table, telling himself he could do this and then go home. He had just reached the bar, his fingers closing around the damp cloth, when the door creaked open behind him, a cool draft of air flowing into the room.

"We're closed for the night," he said without turning. "You'll have to come back tomorrow."

Only then did he turn and felt his muscles lock, clenching the rag in his fist, as he laid eyes on his late-night visitor. He couldn't bring himself to speak the name, but he didn't have to.

"You'd turn away an old friend?" Mordred rumbled.

Daniel had been right in his earlier assumption that the witch-hunter looked nothing at all like he used to. His skin still had the same sallow complexion, the same over-long face with its over-long nose. But his lank black hair was gone, replaced by the smooth dome of his bald head. He was clean-shaven, the only hair on his head being his two thick black eyebrows, sprouting over eyes so dark they looked black themselves.

Daniel exhaled softly, the initial shock beginning to wear off. "Mordred." He tossed the rag back onto the counter. "What do you want? I doubt you came here because you simply wanted a pint."

"How right you are. I'm looking for someone and I think you can help me find them."

"I think not," Daniel retorted, eyes scanning the room. Mordred stood between him and the exit, but he thought he might be able to dart out the back door, if he was quick enough. *And then what?*

Mordred grinned, a gruesome thing that made it look like his face was about to split in two. He spread his hands and Daniel thought he saw something move on Mordred's shoulder, beneath his clothes. "Come now, Daniel, don't be a fool. You have two choices: help me, or hinder me. Just tell me where I can find Calida and I'll be on my way. There's no need for you to die."

Daniel hissed through his teeth, both out of nerves and anger. "As if I can trust anything that comes out of your mouth. You're a witch-killer. A murderer of your own kind. And for what? Just so you could save your own neck?"

"I've managed to survive where others haven't. You'd do well to reconsider, Daniel."

"I don't know how you live with yourself. I'd rather die than condemn innocent people to be slaughtered!"

"That can be arranged," Mordred sneered. "But first, we'll see how talkative you become."

He raised a hand and Daniel felt the floor tremble as the earth heaved beneath it. The wooden floorboards split beneath his feet as a massive hole opened up. He cried out, frantically trying to catch himself. Splinters and exposed nails stabbed at his hands as he fought for purchase, but continued to slide.

One of the boards had warped violently, bending back on itself and he latched onto it, clinging for dear life, most of his body hanging over the yawning abyss that had opened up underneath him. He knew the cellars lay below, but if he fell down there, escape would be all but impossible. Mordred could simply collapse the earthen walls down upon him.

* * *

Mordred wished he could simply stand back and watch Daniel struggle, but it was a luxury he could not afford. He knew a large tree stood outside the pub; he'd seen it on his way inside.

Unlike some of the trees in Alara, this one did not have nails driven into its trunk, which warded off witches like him and hindered them from using their power. With witches allowed freely here in Daera, there was nothing to stop him.

He backed away toward the door. Daniel stopped his struggling for a moment and Mordred could see the confusion in his eyes, wondering why the witch-hunter was retreating in his moment of triumph.

Mordred reached out toward the tree, forcing it to bend, its roots upending in the moist earth, the wood creaking as it began to topple over. Daniel, perhaps realizing what he was doing, let go of his fragile hold and plummeted down into the cellar as the tree came crashing through the far wall, smashing the roof in with it.

No doubt the noise would attract the neighbors—lights were already blooming in the nearest windows. Mordred waited while they filed out into the night air, murmuring confused questions. Some had hastily thrown jackets or trousers over their nightclothes, but most hadn't bothered.

There were gasps as people pointed at the downed tree.

"Is anyone hurt?" one woman asked.

"The only person who would have been in there this time of night would be Daniel," a man replied.

"If he was in there, he'd have been crushed!"

"Hurry!" Mordred called. "Help me look for him. If he's still here, we need to get him out."

Searching for Daniel's corpse among the wreckage was a task that would be accomplished much faster with the help of the unwitting village folk. They rushed forward to help one of their own, shifting fallen timbers and debris, but their efforts proved fruitless.

Daniel was not to be found among the wreckage.

With the search over, the townspeople returned to wondering what had happened and how the tree had come to collapse onto the inn.

"It wasn't storming," one pointed out. Nor was there the slightest hint of wind.

"No," Mordred spoke up, raising his voice to be heard. "A storm did not do this. This is the work of a witch. Don't you see?" He stepped up to the fallen trunk, gesturing to it. "This tree was not dead or rotting, but solid and strong. It had probably stood for a hundred years and should have for a hundred more! Look for yourselves and tell me how it could have come crashing down."

A few stepped forward to examine the tree and he heard murmurs of agreement, concluding that such a tree should not have toppled in perfectly calm weather.

"We must find this witch!" he called. "Justice must be done."

Mordred stepped away, glancing at the ruins of the inn. If Daniel wasn't here, then where was he? Leaving the crowd to mutter amongst themselves, he crept away, slipping into the darkness. They were too preoccupied with the fallen tree to notice.

"*He got away,*" a soft, high-pitched voice hissed. Mordred felt little claws make their way across his tunic briefly and then a rat climbed out from beneath his cloak to perch on his shoulder.

"Yes," he agreed. *But there's no point in chasing after him. Who knows where he's gone?* But Mordred had a pretty good idea.

Either Daniel had gone home or he'd run straight to warn Calida. Regardless, he hadn't told Mordred what he wanted to know and since Daniel was Mordred's best way of obtaining that information, he intended to try again.

"*Yes,*" the rat murmured, understanding his intentions perfectly. "*Why chase after him when you can make him come to you?*"

There was a light still on when Mordred reached Daniel's house. He sent the rat scurrying up to the window sill to peer inside. Anyone within who happened to be looking out would be able to see little or nothing, their night vision destroyed by the bright lights.

"*Just the woman,*" the rat reported when he'd returned.

"The children must be in bed, then," Mordred said. Daniel hadn't gone home. *But he will come to me.*

Mordred turned away, withdrawing a dagger from his belt, and scoring a deep X into the wood of the tree nearest the house. He made his way into the forest, up the hill near the outskirts of the village, marking the trees as he went.

Only when he was satisfied that he'd gone far enough did he stop and peer back at the little house whose lighted windows were still visible through the darkness.

The water table was very high from all the rain, the ground saturated with moisture. It had made uprooting the massive tree outside the pub easier than it should have been.

The witch-hunter raised both hands, exerting his will over the damp hillside. It put up some resistance, but soon gave way. A wave of earth slid free, rushing down the hill, uprooting trees, picking up speed as it neared the village.

And in the path of the landslide was a tiny house in which a wife was still awake, her two small children asleep within, waiting for a husband and father who would not return.

The villagers would soon come knocking, thinking they might find Daniel there and inform him of what had happened to the pub.

But what they would find when they arrived was another matter.

CHAPTER 11

Calida's eyes flew open, staring at the white ceiling of her bedroom, though it was beginning to look more yellow these days. She couldn't say what had awoken her; it was blessedly not storming tonight as it so often did. It was still dark outside; a sliver of moonlight fell through the gap in her drapes, falling across her sheet.

She lay there for some time, trying to return to sleep, but failing. She sighed, not wishing to get up. The air was chilly and the bed was the warmest place in the cottage. There was a fireplace in the kitchen, but she refrained from lighting it if at all possible, fearful that the wrong person might see the smoke coming through the chimney deep in the forest.

Admitting that she was to get no more rest that night, Calida threw off the covers and made her way to the door, the floorboards cold and creaking beneath her bare feet. She snatched her shawl and wrapped it around her shoulders.

Opening the door, she peered out, letting her eyes scan the darkened house. But it was empty. Dark, cold, and empty. She stepped out into the hallway, jumping as something scraped against the window in the front of the house.

But it was only a tree branch, moving in the wind. She could see it from where she stood. She sighed again, scolding herself for letting Daniel's warning go to her head.

Calida leaned against the wall, glancing up at the round mirror hanging across from her. The backing was beginning to come off. She'd always had good night vision and she didn't need to light a candle to make out her reflection.

Though witches aged at the same rate as ordinary humans, they often retained a more youthful appearance for longer. But standing there in the darkened hallway, Calida just thought she looked old. It wasn't from any wrinkles—though there were crow's feet at the corners of her eyes—but from her eyes themselves.

They looked dull and sad, as if she had seen more than she should have at her age of forty-two. And there were times she *felt* it, too. In the long, lonely hours when she missed companionship.

Unlike so many others, she hadn't lost her familiar during the witch-hunts in Alara, and yet she had lost him all the same. The house had once held laughter. Now there was nearly no sign at all of the boy who had once lived here. *Oh, how different things might have been…*

Calida reached up, absently touching the thick curling hair that fell past her shoulders, thinking of the man who had liked nothing more than to run his fingers through it. A dull ache blossomed in her chest, quickly growing into a white-hot ball of rage that time had done nothing to diminish. *Funny how even after so much time, old wounds can still ache.*

A knock came from the door, startling her out of her reminiscing. She shook herself, grateful for the interruption, and headed for the door. It didn't do to dwell.

"Who's there?" she called, thinking one of her patients must have hurt themselves somehow and needed to be seen to. Perhaps a wife had burned a hand while fixing dinner for her family.

"It's Daniel," came the reply.

Calida's eyes widened and she hurriedly unbolted the door and threw it open to reveal the figure of Daniel standing there. His posture had a defeated, exhausted look about it, but his eyes were alert and darting around anxiously.

"What's wrong?" Calida demanded. "Is it Miriam? One of the children?"

"They're fine," he replied, pushing past her and into the kitchen. "It's Mordred."

"What about him?" she asked, securing the door and bustling about the kitchen to light some candles.

Figuring this was one of her exceptions, she stacked some logs in the fireplace and lit it, stepping back as warmth slowly began to suffuse the room.

It illuminated the small wooden table with its two chairs, the pitcher she had left on its surface, not bothering to put it away. Shelves stood against the wall, crammed with the crystals she had collected, along with any interesting stones she had taken a liking to. There were jars of herbs and preserved fruits and vegetables. Bundles of dried herbs and onions hung down from the ceiling. A chair stood against the wall, a basket of flowers resting on it.

Below the circular, cross-hatched windows stood a low bookshelf, so full some of the books had been turned sideways and laid on top of each other. And everywhere one looked, there seemed to be explosions of green. Plants hung, draped from above the window, cluttering up every spare inch of shelf space, and ivy vines tumbled down the side of the hearth. Her pride and joy, Calida liked to think these were some of the healthiest plants in Daera, sheltered from the incessant rain and given unceasingly tender care.

There had been a time she'd hated plants, and though her views had changed, she'd never been able to deny that she had a way with them.

Turning from the fire, Calida faced Daniel and in the wan light saw the extent of his injuries for the first time. "Your hands!" she cried, taking in the mangled flesh.

He was bleeding from his temple and stood at an awkward angle, putting most of his weight on his left leg.

"Sit down!" she snapped, which he gratefully did. "There's no need to stand on ceremony. Now tell me what happened."

She turned to her shelves, where among the other bric-a-brac she kept numerous pots of salve, jars and containers, and colorful vials of liquid.

As she sorted through them, Daniel explained what had happened. He had let go of his hold as the tree fell, dropping down into the cellar below, and thus avoided being crushed. He had managed to claw his way out and flee, but he had landed awkwardly and Calida thought it a miracle that he hadn't broken an ankle.

"I came here as fast as I could," he finished. "I had to warn you."

"Were you followed here?" She glanced at the windows, but could see nothing of the world outside.

"I don't think so. I was very careful, doubling back and taking a circuitous route, or I'd have been here sooner."

Calida fell silent, intent now on her work. She applied one of the salves to Daniel's ravaged hands and bandaged them, cleaned the blood off his temple and out of his hair and applied a makeshift brace to his injured ankle. It was the best she could do on such short notice.

"I'll make you some tea," she offered. Not only would it help calm him down, but it would accelerate the healing process.

"No," Daniel protested, rising unsteadily to his feet. "Thank you, but I should go. I've put you in danger merely by coming here. Besides," he added, before she could argue, "he's out there looking for me. I need to get Miriam and the children out of here. If you know what's good for you, you'll do the same."

"And go where? I'm perfectly safe where I am." Her cottage was deep in the forest, nestled amongst the trees, and though it was quite difficult to find, she wasn't as certain of her safety as she sounded. "Mordred hasn't found me yet. For all he knows, I could be living in a cave somewhere."

"I'm serious, Calida," Daniel said, in a tone she'd rarely ever heard him use.

She exhaled heavily, not wanting to press the issue. "Fine. If you must go, be careful, at least."

He nodded tersely and then was gone, leaving her alone in the house once more.

* * *

It seemed to Daniel that the trip back through the forest took ages, constantly on edge as he was. He kept imagining that he heard noises behind him and glancing fearfully over his shoulder, only to see nothing.

He was fortunate enough not to encounter anyone. He paused near the edge of the woods, blinking in the moonlight. One side of the hill had sheared away, the landslide leaving raw, gaping, exposed earth behind.

Still, there had been reports of mudslides before, in other parts of the kingdom. That sort of thing was to be expected with all the rain they'd had. He didn't think anything of it until he'd reached the outskirts of the village and laid eyes on what the landslide had struck.

Daniel felt his blood run cold, as though someone had laid a freezing hand on the back of his neck.

Where his house should have stood was now a mound of earth, some pieces of debris sticking out, just visible. The wave of earth had crushed his home and swallowed it entirely.

For a moment, he could only stare. And then he was rushing forward, calling out his wife's name, shouting for Ophelia and Albert, daring to hope that they had somehow found a way to escape.

No one answered his calls. He tossed a board aside, sinking his hands into the thick mud, ignoring the pain it caused, throwing fistfuls of it out of the way as he desperately tried to dig through to where his family must be trapped.

It was a hopeless venture. For every handful he removed, there seemed no change. It was simply too big a task for one man and there was no point anyway.

And then he realized what a complete fool he was. He was an earth witch! What was he doing trying to sift through the muck with his bare hands? He cursed himself, his panic having made him careless, not thinking straight. The earth heaved and parted for him, quickly revealing its secrets.

He did not like what he found.

Letting out a sob, Daniel sank to his knees. He looked down at his bandaged hands—now covered with mud, the motionless bodies of his family, buried alive, mud still clinging to their pale faces—and began to cry.

What a fool he'd been! His first thought should have been for his family—not for Calida. He should have run to them and seen them to safety first before running off to warn her. She could take care of herself, but they were helpless.

After all, Mordred obviously didn't know where she lived, or he never would have bothered with Daniel himself. But if he'd learned the location of the pub and that Daniel worked there, what was to stop him from finding out where his family lived?

"You should have told me when I asked you."

Daniel whirled around, already knowing who he would see. "*You!*" he snarled. "You did this!"

"I gave you a chance," Mordred said, without the slightest hint of pity. "No one can say I didn't. Perhaps you'll tell me now."

Daniel rose to his feet, furiously blinking back tears. "I'll tell you *nothing!*"

"Don't be so sure." Mordred held one hand out, a silent threat hanging in the air.

Daniel clenched his fists, his entire body trembling with barely suppressed rage. "I'll kill you for this." His voice was so low, it was nearly a hiss. "I won't tell you where she is!" Not after the price he had paid to keep it a secret.

Mordred must have judged something in his expression and decided that Daniel really wasn't going to give up the sought-after information, because he said, "Then you can join your family."

Daniel lunged at him.

CHAPTER 12

Whatever else the kingdom of Alara may have been, it certainly was as beautiful as the rumors claimed. Annie and Kain set out in the middle of the afternoon. She had been waiting impatiently since waking that morning, eager to see him again and tour the kingdom that was to be her new home.

The day had dawned bright and clear, once more sunny and warm. Kain led the way on his black steed and Annie followed, trying to ignore the entourage behind them. It felt good to get out of the castle and let the sun bathe her skin.

Kain didn't take her to the forest riding paths, saying he'd leave that for another day. Instead, they toured through the villages, the prince more than happy to show off his future bride to the people.

At first, Annie was flattered by all the attention, but before long, she began to feel more like a trophy that was being flaunted. Still, she did her best to smile and wave. The last thing she wanted was to appear sulky.

And really, there was nothing to sulk about. The weather was lovely, Annie was able to wear trousers again—for riding only—and whether she would admit it to herself or not, she enjoyed sneaking glances at Kain, who looked quite dashing in riding clothes.

From there, they headed along the shore, with its white sand, following the slope as they approached a watchtower in the distance. Several of the palace guards had accompanied them and, of course, Annie's chaperone, Florence.

The tower they approached sat at the edge of the coast, on a strip of land that stretched out into the water. It reminded Annie of a lighthouse, but the prince informed her that it was an observation point. It was a tall, imposing figure of a building, made of weathered gray brick with glass windows at the very top. Annie might have been able to believe it truly was a lighthouse, if not for the cannons jutting from its tops, to be used in defense of the shoreline.

The horses were left at the tower's base, in the care of most of the guards. The remaining soldiers and Florence followed the prince and Annie as they began ascending the stairs that spiraled up within.

Annie made the mistake of glancing down halfway up the stairs. The sheer sight of how high they were—and the idea of how dreadful the plummeting drop from here would be— made her head spin and her vision swim. She clutched the rail with one hand for support, her breathing suddenly quick and shallow. Why did heights have to bother her so?

Kain was a few steps ahead of her and turned to glance back. "You all right, Highness?" He made no attempt to come back for her.

"Yes," Annie replied, taking a deep breath. "I'm fine."

She forced herself to keep going and managed to reach the top without further incident. Florence was wheezing for breath by that point, a grating sound that Annie did her best to ignore.

The moment she set foot at the top made it instantly worth the climb. The sight made her pause and she drifted over to the windows as though in a trance.

The windows were more than twice her height, completely surrounding the top of the observatory. Peering out, she could see that they were indeed very high up; the rocky ground on which the base of the tower stood seemed miles away. But if one looked up and out, there was little but blue-green water as far as the eye could see, the ocean stretching out infinitely, the water's surface glittering in the sun. White seabirds soared toward the outlines of islands just visible in the distance.

The prince joined her at the window. "Beautiful, isn't it?"

"It is, Your Highness."

"Please, call me Kain."

She glanced across the room at her chaperone, but Florence appeared to still be catching her breath. "Is that really proper?"

"I insist," he replied, smiling at her.

"Well, if you insist."

He turned back to face the view. "I remember when my father first brought me here. It offers a perfect view for the autumnal meteor shower."

Of course, there were no meteors falling now, but Annie looked anyway, imagining what they must have looked like.

"I imagine the star gazing is quite good," she said appreciatively. Perhaps she'd have to come back one night and see for herself.

"We used to do a lot of that," Kain added. "My father and I. We used to do a lot of things together." His brow suddenly furrowed, jaw clenching, his voice turning bitter. "But that was a long time ago. Before he decided he'd rather stay in front of the fire. Before the drink."

Drink? Annie had been told that the king's memory was going, not that he was a drunkard, but she knew better than to ask.

Annie was uncertain if he hoped for a reaction from her, but she didn't know what to say and so remained silent. Was it possible that the king wasn't ill at all, but simply a drunkard and his family disguised his drinking by saying he was merely taking medicine? She supposed it wasn't that farfetched. After all, the truth would be far more disgraceful. No doubt the family viewed perceived illness as being preferable.

She turned to one of the spyglasses set up along the room and peered through it. There wasn't much to see. The closest islands were too far away to make out any details at this distance. Mostly it was just sparkling blue water.

Annie turned the glass to the north, not expecting to see anything of interest. But what she did see made her freeze.

It was a lone ship, flying no colors. She still couldn't make out what type it may have been, but she spied three masts. But the most important feature was its blood-red sails, resplendent in the sun.

She drew back, remembering how the ship had followed her on the way to Alara, flying the color of neither navy. The crew had been tense, unnerved by its presence, fearing the vessel to be pirates. It had never been confirmed either way.

Annie turned to Kain. "Your naval ships don't have red sails, do they?" She'd seen several warships docked in the main harbor upon first arriving and all of them had white sails.

"No, why?"

She moved over so he could peer through the spyglass, pointing out the window in the general direction she'd seen the ship. "Is that a pirate ship? So close to the mainland? Isn't this the northern shipping lane?"

He bent to peer through as she had done. When he pulled back, he didn't look the least bit alarmed, which sat at odds with his response. "Well, yes. But you have nothing to fear. That must be one of ours."

"One of yours?"

"A privateer," Kain explained. "Licensed by the crown to hunt down pirates." He smiled at her. "Desperate times and all that. But now that our kingdoms have an alliance, we can work together and get rid of the brigands for good."

Annie felt relief rush over her. If the red-sailed ship was a legal privateer working for Alara, it made sense as to why it had followed her to the southern kingdom.

It hadn't been pirates after all.

CHAPTER 13

The mist was still thick when Lorelei stepped out of the house she'd been called out to. The morning air was chilly and damp, fog having rolled in from the sea, cloaking everything in white. She shivered, wanting nothing more than to return home for a bracing cup of tea and crawl into bed. But she needed to stop by the market first, such as it was.

Her work as a midwife ensured a steady flow of income—there were always women needing her services, though less and less of them survived. This one had been a breech birth, one of the more difficult cases, but it had had a happy ending. A rare success story.

Lorelei felt pleased with a job well done and the coins jingled in her pocket softly as she walked. Not that there was much to spend them on at the markets these days. Prices had only increased and if there did happen to be anything edible, it was too expensive for the average shopper.

She arrived on the market street to find the stalls empty and deserted. It was early in the morning, to be sure, but the stalls should have been opened by now. Lorelei felt a moment's panic, fearing that the kingdom had finally run out of produce to sell, before she heard several voices murmuring from up ahead.

Hurrying forward, the mist seemed to part before her, revealing a crowd that had gathered in front of the tree that stood in the middle of the village square, beside the well. Their heads were craned upward, staring at something, and Lorelei looked up, eyes drawn to the sight that had so captivated them.

She let out a gasp, nearly dropping her bag of medical supplies. She covered her mouth with one hand, staring in horror at what hung from the tree.

Daniel dangled from his ankles, suspended upside down, his arms bound behind him, the end of the rope hidden among the thick branches. His white hair hung limply toward the ground.

Even from a distance, Lorelei could tell that he was dead, his face discolored by the pooling blood.

Snapping out of her shock, she began to listen to what the villagers around her were saying.

"First the inn, now this," one said.

Lorelei wanted to ask what they meant, but could not find her voice and was afraid of drawing attention to herself. The villagers may have been questioning who could have done this and why, but she had no such doubts herself and it frightened her.

She hadn't seen this sort of sight since fleeing Alara. The onlookers might not understand the significance of displaying a dead body upside down, but she did. Traditionally, in Alara, witches were burned to death or weighted down with heavy millstones and thrown into the river.

But those had been public executions. Spectacles meant to make an example.

Those who were discovered or suspected of being a witch within villages had a different sort of justice meted out upon them. There was no ceremony, no trial. They'd simply been killed and strung up in such a manner, proclaiming to the remaining villagers that not only was this individual a witch, but you could expect the same fate if you, too, were found out.

"The old man was right," one of the men muttered. "A witch has done this."

You're not wrong, Lorelei thought wryly.

"But why?" one of the women cried, clutching a small child closer to her. "What did Daniel do to warrant such a thing? Are we, any of us, safe in our beds?"

The crowd devolved into an argument about whether or not a witch was to blame for the kingdom's ills and Lorelei crept away, not wanting to remain or stare at the awful sight a moment longer.

She could imagine who had put such ideas into the villagers' heads and she didn't like it. She could easily see this spiraling out of control, to become like Alara all over again. People were already afraid, desperate, hungry. They felt helpless and that made them dangerous.

If they felt that flushing out the witch that hid among them would put an end to their troubles, it would take little to entice them to such action.

I have to find Calida and tell her.

Morning shopping forgotten, Lorelei headed away from the villages and deep into the woods, fighting the sick feeling in her stomach. She couldn't keep from casting nervous glances over her shoulder, half-expecting to see Mordred behind her.

What if he had been among the crowd, waiting to see who showed up? But there was no one there whenever she looked. The other half of her was worried what she might find upon arriving at Calida's cottage. What if Daniel had told Mordred the truth?

She scolded herself for even thinking such a thing. Daniel would never have done that! But that did not lessen her fear.

Lorelei arrived at Calida's cottage, thankful that there was no outward sign of trouble. The same faded brown walls, badly needing a new coat of paint, scarcely visible beneath the choking, clinging ivy, the same green roof, the windows with their gray shutters and flowers.

She pounded on the door more forcefully than she'd meant to and breathed a sigh of relief when Calida answered.

"Lorelei? What's happened? You look awful." She moved aside to allow the midwife inside. "It's Daniel, isn't it?"

Lorelei looked at her sharply in surprise. Knowing the future was not something a witch could do, and yet sometimes Calida made her wonder. "How did you know?"

Calida shut the door behind her. "He came here last night. Mordred confronted him in the pub as he was closing up for the night and collapsed a tree on top of it. Daniel managed to get away and came here to warn me. He left soon after to get Miriam and the children to safety." She shrugged. "It was the only thing I could think of."

Lorelei's eyes landed on the traveling case laid out on the kitchen table, stuffed with hastily organized clothes. "Going somewhere?"

"Daniel warned me I should leave. I just thought it best to have something packed at a moment's notice. Just in case."

"He's dead," Lorelei sighed, sinking down into one of the chairs by the window where she could keep an eye out. One of its legs was shorter than the others. "That's what I came to tell you. I found his body hanging from the tree by the well."

Calida's eyes darkened. She closed and latched the case and snatched her cloak from a peg on the back of the door. "Show me."

Taking Calida's horse would be too conspicuous with Mordred likely still lurking around somewhere. Calida pulled up the hood on her cloak to hide her flaming hair and Lorelei did the same, hiding her face. They would have to walk.

* * *

Calida had expected to feel anger upon hearing the news, but all she'd felt was shock. *The anger will come later,* she told herself as they walked through the woods toward their destination.

The crowd Lorelei had mentioned was gone by the time they arrived. The midwife had explained about the superstition and fear that had spread through the crowd and Calida could understand why they had left, not wanting any part of the strange and frightening forces that had done this.

It left them with a clear view of Daniel's body hanging from the tree. No one had bothered to cut him down. It was just as Lorelei had described.

Rage burst to life inside Calida, consuming and destroying every other emotion until all she wanted to do was murder Mordred herself. But even as she thought such a thing, she knew that it was not only Mordred that her anger was directed at.

Damn her sister and her greed.

"We should cut him down," Lorelei whispered.

Calida couldn't have agreed more, but practicality had to win out over sentimentality. "No. Mordred could be watching, waiting to see if we do exactly that. The moment we do, he'll know who we are." *Who else would do it?* Not the townspeople. They had fled in fear.

Lorelei didn't press the issue, seeing the wisdom in Calida's argument even if she didn't like it. "What about his family? You said he went to fetch them. What became of them?"

"It doesn't appear he ever arrived," Calida replied. "We should check on them. If she's heard the news, Miriam will be devastated."

But a second horrific sight greeted them when they arrived at the former location of Daniel's home. The little cottage had been swallowed and buried beneath thick, black earth.

"Skies above," Lorelei whispered. "If they were inside when it happened…"

There was no point in searching for evidence to the contrary. Calida knew they must be dead. An entire family wiped out in one night.

"The children…" Lorelei went on. "I knew Mordred could be cruel, but this… They were innocent."

They weren't innocent of being a witch's spawn. "Come. Let's get away from this dreadful place."

Lorelei turned away from the sight and followed after Calida. "What do we do now? Daniel told you to go somewhere else and I think he's right."

As much as she hated to admit it, Calida now agreed as well, though it still felt like she'd be admitting defeat by running. *What's the difference between this and fleeing Alara?*

But all she said was, "I can't go anywhere until Ben returns for the next drop-off. Otherwise, I have no way of getting word to him as to where I've gone." *Or why.* That one would be interesting to come up with. "Besides," she added, voice hardening, "we don't want Mordred finding him."

Lorelei knew better than to argue with Calida when she used *that* tone. "How long until he returns?"

"Tomorrow," Calida replied. *Barring some unforeseeable delay…*

"I think we can survive one more day," Lorelei conceded. "Though I didn't pack anything."

Calida agreed that they should both stick together. It was safer and even if Calida took Daniel's advice and left, Lorelei would still be in danger if she stayed behind.

"I should have enough for both of us," she said, adjusting her grip on the valise handle. "We can stay in the abandoned mill. It's close enough to the rendezvous site."

She might have suggested staying in one of the warehouses that the supplies were sometimes stored in. They were large enough to hide in, certainly, but there was also much more traffic in and around them and the chance of discovery would be all the higher. It wasn't worth the risk.

They made their way to the coastline, past where she typically met Ben. The abandoned mill slowly came into view, though it was hard to make it out if one didn't know where or what to look for. It was falling apart and choked with overgrown foliage, much the same as Calida's cottage. The water wheel had been dismantled entirely, though the river still flowed through on its way to the sea.

Parts of the building had collapsed over the years and the two women had to step over fallen boards of timber. It was rather a large building, with several floors, and they headed for the third. It would give them the opportunity to dart back to the ground floor to make a quick escape if necessary, or continue on to the roof.

But most importantly, it provided a vantage point to the sea, where Calida could keep an eye out for the *Phoenix*.

Lorelei settled down on the floor, leaning against the stone wall, beneath one of the large half-broken windows. "Bit spartan, isn't it? But I suppose it won't be for long and I've had worse." She paused, adjusting her skirts. "Where will you go once you've spoken to him?"

"Indris, maybe," Calida replied, watching the sea, but in truth, she had no idea.

Fleeing to Daera had been the obvious choice when she'd had to run in the past, since the northern kingdom was a safe haven for witches. But the other islands were not so certain and she was not familiar with them as she had come to be with Daera over the years.

There was a part of her that hoped Ben would not come back to the northern kingdom, though she knew he would. He wanted to help the starving people as much as she did, but now she feared it was too dangerous, even more for him than for her.

Stay away, Benjamin. It's no longer safe for you here.

CHAPTER 14

It had already begun to sprinkle lightly by the time the *Phoenix* dropped anchor at the rendezvous site. Thunder rumbled overhead and streaks of lightning flickered in the clouds. The air was heavy with the scent of rain and electricity. The sea was choppy, slapping against the frigate's hull.

"We're early, sir," Terrance murmured at Ben's shoulder. "I don't know if they'll be there yet."

Ben grunted and brushed his bangs out of his eyes, but the wind blew them right back. He was glad he'd taken a knife to his hair before leaving Amberleigh and sheared it back to the preferred length or else it would only be giving him more trouble.

Sensing the coming storm, he had decided to set sail for the rendezvous site earlier than normal, hoping to arrive before it broke. They would be cutting it rather close. The storm was holding off for the moment, but arriving so early meant that the villagers and his aunt may not be waiting for them as usual.

Ben didn't like the look of the approaching clouds. They were vast, monstrous things that seemed to swirl in the wind, although it was hard to tell in the poor lighting.

It reflected his mood perfectly. Since leaving Amberleigh, he hadn't managed to catch sight of Berchmoore's new ship. He wasn't certain what type of vessel he was even supposed to be looking for, having only a name to go off of. But the Atlas Sea was a large swath of water to cover, even with an advantage, and they'd had little time to go about looking for the privateer, what with having to restock supplies to bring back to Daera.

"*I see people on the beach,*" Horus informed him, perched on his shoulder.

Good. "We'll get a little closer," Ben informed his quartermaster. "Ready the longboats. We do this now and then get out of here, before the storm breaks."

"Sir." Terrance nodded and went off to see to the longboats.

"I don't like the look of that," Sharpe remarked, craning her head up, echoing his earlier thoughts as she surveyed the sky.

"It'll hold off," Ben said, not a trace of uncertainty in his voice. Perhaps it was a reckless thing to say. But they had time, providing they didn't mess about. They'd be long gone and out of harm's way before the storm hit.

"Aye," was all Sharpe said in reply. She would be staying on the ship as lookout. Her musket was slung over one shoulder, intricately decorated in tribal designs from her home of Indris.

The trip to shore was rougher than usual. The longboats were more susceptible to being buffeted and capsized than the larger frigate, but they managed it without incident. Ben stepped onto the sand, walking a few paces away from the others.

"All right, men, let's get this job done!" he heard Terrance bark.

The villagers moved forward to help, but Ben noticed that Calida hung back, merely watching. There was no sign of her horse or cart.

"Where's Edith?" he asked, fearing the aging mare had finally died.

"I'll explain later," Calida said quietly. Her face was taut, eyes darting around and he noted that Lorelei seemed to stick close to her.

He wasn't satisfied with the answer, but gave her a curt nod and turned back to help his men unload the supplies. The more hands helping, the sooner they could weigh anchor.

Only when all the supplies had been transferred into the villagers' possession and they began to head away did Calida speak again. "Come with me."

She turned, along with Lorelei, and began leading him away from the shore, toward an old dilapidated building nearly hidden at the wood's edge. Ben forced down his frustration, dismissing all but one of the longboats to go ahead and return to the *Phoenix* and followed, hoping whatever was so important wouldn't take long. Terrance followed after him.

Calida paused in the doorway of the old mill. "I think it best if you wait outside, Terrance."

Ben turned to his quartermaster and shared a glance that said the other man understood. He clapped Terrance on the shoulder and followed his aunt inside the crumbling building.

"What's this all about? We can't stay long."

"I know," Calida said. "I wanted to tell you that we're going to have to find another drop-off site. This one is no longer safe."

"Why?"

"Daniel was killed, two nights ago, along with his family."

Ben stared at his aunt, hardly comprehending the words. "Wh—what? Why? Who would want to do that?" He hadn't known Daniel too terribly well. The man hadn't been able to attend the supply exchanges much since he owned and operated a pub, but the news still came as a shock.

He had seen plenty during his years on the sea, enough to know that people could be cruel and vicious when it suited them—and sometimes even when it did not. But people rarely killed without a reason.

Even the children...

Lorelei glanced at Calida, who pursed her lips. Ben got the feeling she didn't relish having to answer his questions. "A man named Mordred."

The name meant nothing to Ben. "Who is he? Should I know him?"

"No reason you should. He's a witch who hunts other witches."

Ben suddenly felt cold despite his scarlet coat. The sensation warred with his earlier shock, but he refused to let either emotion show. He hadn't maintained his rank as captain by letting every emotion he felt play across his face.

"You're telling me Daniel is—was—a witch."

"Yes," Calida nodded.

Ben crossed his arms. "I'm sorry," he said and truly meant it. "But what does that have to do with it being too dangerous for you to stay here?"

Although he suspected he already knew the answer.

Calida took a deep breath, looking as though she were about to endure something painful, when the sharp report of a gunshot rang out.

Lorelei jumped and Ben whirled around to face the windows. "What the hell—"

He rushed outside, meeting Terrance at the door. "It was Sharpe," the quartermaster reported, "shooting at something here on the beach, but I don't know what."

"Horus—" But the hawk knew what Ben was asking before he'd even completed the thought. Horus sprang from his shoulder, taking to the air, searching for what it was that Sharpe had fired at.

The wind had come up, whipping now, and Ben had to reach up with one hand to keep his hat on. Calida and Lorelei's hair was whipped wildly and they had to brush it out of their eyes to see.

The dark clouds had closed in, the lighting even poorer than it had been earlier. Horus came swooping back down and Ben held up one hand so the hawk could land, wrapping his talons around his gloved fingers.

"There's a man, lying due east," the hawk reported.

Ben relayed to his companions what the hawk had said and squinted, searching the beach. A streak of lightning arced down, striking the water and illuminating the world around it for a brief second.

"There!" he called, pointing.

He could see the figure of a man lying on the sand, one hand clutching his leg as he tried to crawl forward. It was hard to make him out, dressed as he was in all black, but the bald dome of his head stood out starkly.

"Mordred!" Lorelei exclaimed.

So this is the witch-hunter. Ben supposed he should have felt fear, but it was difficult to be afraid with the man brought to his knees and forced to crawl, with the wind howling in his ears, the rain lashing at his skin as it began to fall more heavily than a mere sprinkle.

Horus let out a sudden shriek in order to be heard over the wind. *"Rats!"*

Ben failed to comprehend what the hawk was talking about until he saw the dark wave swarming over the sand toward them. It moved so fluidly, it might have been mistaken for water in the darkness.

But when lightning lit up the sky, it became clear that Horus was right. It was not water, but countless small, dark bodies racing toward them.

"Run!" Calida shouted.

Horus leapt off Ben's shoulder and Terrance drew his pistol as they all bolted for the remaining longboat. Now, for the first time, Ben felt a prickle of fear. He already despised rats. They didn't have the fear of humans that mice did, but did have more than their share of aggression. They would eat a man alive if hungry enough and given the opportunity. He didn't intend to give any of them such a chance.

A shot rang out as Terrance fired at the swarm, but even if his shot had hit home, there were far too many.

The two women clambered into the boat first and Ben and Terrance shoved against it, pushing it out into the water. If they could get out into the open sea, they would be safe. Rats could swim, but if they decided to risk it, they could also be drowned.

Ben kicked out at a rat that had gotten too close and waded out into the water, climbing up along with Terrance. The boat threatened to topple over in the choppy sea, but he forced it to stay steady.

Terrance grabbed an oar, but there was little point. The waves were already carrying them rapidly away, toward the waiting *Phoenix*.

"They're still coming!" Lorelei cried.

Ben glanced over his shoulder and saw she was right— the rats had leapt into the water and were paddling after them, refusing to give up the pursuit.

But unlike the rats, the ocean was not Mordred's to command.

Behind the longboat, the water heaved and rose as it surged into a massive wave. Ben clenched his fist and the wave collapsed, crashing down on the hapless rats below, dragging them into the depths.

He exhaled a shaky breath and turned to find Calida's gray eyes fixed on him. He looked away and did not meet her gaze again the rest of the way to the *Phoenix*.

It seemed to take ages as the longboat was hoisted up and by the time they set foot on the deck, the clouds had fully opened up, the rain pouring down in sheets.

"Are you all right?" Sharpe shouted over the noise of the downpour, musket still gripped in her hands.

Ben nodded briefly. "Weigh anchor!" he bellowed, bidding the storm edge around them to the east.

As soon as the heavy anchor was pulled up, the *Phoenix*'s massive sails stretched taut, filled with a strong tailwind. The shore of Daera began to fade into the distance. The immediate danger was past, the worst of the storm passing them by. Not wanting to stay out in the rain, but wanting answers, Ben sent Calida and Lorelei into his cabin beneath the helm.

He made to follow them and then glanced at Sharpe. "You'd better come, too," he said softly.

She followed after him, propping her musket in the corner and he closed the door behind her. The room was spacious as far as cabins went, made possible by the large size of the ship. The entire back wall of the stern was made up of windows, now obscured by lashing rain.

The bed was on the right side of the room, set into its own compartment to keep it from moving around. All of the furniture was anchored to the floor. There were two guns—stern chasers—though their gun ports were currently closed, used to fire at anyone who may be pursuing the *Phoenix*.

They were rarely used. More often than not, it was she that did the pursuing.

Horus flew across the room to land on his wooden perch. Ben shed his outer coat and his hat and went about lighting a few of the ship's lanterns, suffusing the cabin with a weak, but warm glow. The storm continued to howl outside, but in here, they were safe and dry.

He crossed over to the chest near the foot of the bed and withdrew a bottle of rum. "I can already tell that this is going to be one of those conversations that requires a drink or two. Can I tempt anyone else?"

Lorelei and Calida both declined, but Sharpe accepted and he passed her one of the bottles before shutting the trunk again. The others were already seated around the table in the center of the room and he joined them, uncorking the bottle.

The table's surface was littered with scattered maps and charts and the occasional spare dagger or pistol, but no one seemed to mind.

He sighed, debating how best to begin and turned to his sharpshooter. "You knew that man on the beach." It wasn't a question.

Before tonight, he himself had never heard of Mordred, he was certain of it. But he also knew Sharpe would never have shot the man in such poor lighting, at that distance, in a storm, without knowing his intentions, unless she had a damn good reason. Unless she knew who he was.

A spark of anger flickered in her brown eyes. "I know him," she said, taking a long swig of rum. "But I didn't realize it was him until the wind blew his hood off and I saw his face."

Ben silently marveled at Sharpe's vision, particularly in dim lighting. Sometimes he wondered if she wasn't a witch, as some claimed, but he knew that they only thought such things because of her skin.

Because she looked different.

"He's a witch-hunter," Ben muttered, downing some of his own rum and savoring the slow spreading of warmth through his chest. "Or so I'm told."

Sharpe shook her head. "I don't know him as any witch-hunter. Only as a cruel man. Most people know that sugar is grown on Indris, among other things. But what most don't know is that when families couldn't pay their taxes, Mordred took some of their children. I don't know what he did to all of them, but I know what he did to me.

"He sold me to one of the rich landowners. My master taught me how to hunt the wild boars so he could sell the meat and the pelts. When I got good enough, he would take me to shooting competitions, bragging to his friends that he had a shooter that could beat any of theirs." Sharpe smirked. "They laughed, finding the idea absurd that a girl, and a Black one at that, could beat any of their sharpshooters. But the money they had to fork over told a different story."

Ben listened in silence, absorbing this new revelation. He'd known that Sharpe had lived on Indris and that she'd learned to shoot with the buccaneers on that island, but he hadn't known the rest of the circumstances. She had never told him and he hadn't asked.

He didn't even know her full name—no one on board did. She'd only ever gone by the name of Sharpe. It was the only name she'd ever given.

"It went on like that," she continued, "until he decided he owned more than just my trigger finger." Her jaw tightened. "So, one night I put a bullet in his head and left."

Ben glanced down at the table. He knew the story of how she'd come to be a part of the crew. A former member had planned to mutiny against Captain Lussard and, having heard of her skill, hired Sharpe to kill him while they were docked at Indris.

But she had seen an opportunity to get off that island and taken it. She'd reported the mutiny to the captain and thus earned his good graces. Her skill with a musket had earned the respect of the crew and secured her place among them.

The rest of it was news to Ben. He felt a rush of pity for her, unable to imagine the sort of horrors she'd had to endure, being taken from her parents at such a young age and then treated as a piece of property.

But Sharpe didn't want his pity. She was a strong woman and a valuable member of his crew. Battle-hardened and forged by her experiences. She was ruthless in battle; he'd seen it for himself.

Little wonder she had shot Mordred.

But Mordred hadn't been there looking for her. She had been safely out of reach on board the *Phoenix*. He couldn't have known she was even there. But he hadn't been slinking around the abandoned mill for no reason.

Ben sighed. "Mordred was outside the mill for a reason, looking for someone." He looked at his aunt. "You said he's a witch who hunts other witches. He already killed Daniel because he was a witch, but you said we needed to move to a different location because it was no longer safe here. Daniel can't have been the only person Mordred was after if he was still hanging around. And the only reason he would be after you is…"

"Is if I am a witch," Calida finished. "I am. And Lorelei is too."

Lorelei was a surprise, but Ben couldn't really say he was stunned by his aunt's revelation.

"Well," he murmured, this time meeting Calida's gaze. "That explains a great deal."

Ben was relieved when he at last had his cabin all to himself again. Calida and Lorelei had been given use of one of the officer's cabins for the time being, though Calida had claimed she was fine with staying on deck once the rain stopped. Under normal circumstances, Ben would have offered them use of his own cabin, but nothing about what had happened was normal. He needed to be alone so he could think.

Well, not entirely alone. Horus remained with him, as always, on the perch Ben had made for him. But he had no secrets that the hawk didn't know about.

He wasn't surprised that Sharpe had never chosen to confide in him, although his pride was slightly stung. He was the captain, had been now for several years, and he had to be somewhat aloof, to be seen as above reproach and in command at all times.

But when he had first met her, he'd been quartermaster and that role was entirely different. He had mingled with the crew, getting to know them personally, because it was his responsibility to settle any disputes or concerns they may have. He needed to seem personable and approachable to win their trust. And yet she had never told him.

You're not the only one with secrets, he reminded himself.

He had long suspected that his aunt was a witch, though he wondered why she had never told him. Even earlier, when they were all gathered around the table, she hadn't delved too deeply into the subject. Ben was convinced she knew more than she was telling him, even now.

He sighed, running his gloved hands over his face. The world outside his windows was now the darkness of night. The sun had set behind the clouds. He pulled his boots off and sank down onto the bed, listening to the familiar creak and groan of the ship around him. The gentle swaying motion of the ship, which had once kept him awake all night when he'd first come on board and hadn't yet grown accustomed to it, would lull him to sleep now if he let it.

But he doubted he could sleep after what he'd learned today. He wished he could ask Captain Lussard the many questions spinning around in his mind, but the captain was dead. Ben was the captain now. He had loyal crew members like Terrance and Sharpe to rely on, but as leader, he couldn't ever completely rely on anyone the way they could rely on him.

And he was dreading the inevitable conversation with his aunt. She may not have brought it up today, but he had seen the look in her gray eyes and knew that she knew more than she was letting on—but so was he. They both knew that the other knew more than they were admitting to.

Secrets. One that he would go to his grave before giving up—or more likely would go to his grave because of it.

In the privacy of his own cabin, Ben allowed himself to do something he rarely ever did and peeled his black leather gloves off. It had been ingrained in him from an early age that this was something never to be done. Not in public. Not where others could see.

There was nothing unusual about his left hand, save for the fact that the skin was paler, from lack of sun exposure. It was his right hand that condemned him.

He stared at the birthmark on the back of his right hand. He couldn't decide what he thought it looked like, but then, he'd never had the imagination for that kind of thing.

Ben snorted to himself. Birthmark, indeed. It was, but that's not all it was, and it certainly wasn't what people like Mordred would think if they saw it. They had another name for it, a name that necessitated its constant concealment.

Witch-mark.

CHAPTER 15

"Y"ou're just not trying hard enough!" Thalia cried, throwing her hands in the air in frustration.

Kain was seated before her at a wooden table, in front of a bowl of water. It was a small room, with the far wall entirely composed of one large window. A suit of armor rested behind the table, the walls draped with tapestries and maps. A small podium stood at the head of the room, the smaller desk beside it littered with papers, candles, ink and quills. Ordinarily, this was the room in which the prince received lessons from his tutors, but today he had a different teacher and task.

He tugged at his red hair, his pale skin flushed. A pair of white gloves sat discarded at the very edge of the table. "I'm trying as hard as I can," he protested.

His mother shouldn't have been surprised. This wasn't the first time they'd been through this—or the last, he suspected. The result was always dissatisfactory.

Thalia took a deep breath in an effort to calm herself and continued to pace around the table. "Fine. Try again."

The prince closed his eyes, reaching out his right hand toward the bowl of water. With his gloves removed, the birthmark on the top of that hand was clearly visible, identical to Thalia's own.

He had been sitting there, trying to will the water within the bowl to move for the past forty minutes and the water hadn't so much as rippled. At this point, he'd have settled for the slightest flicker of movement.

Kain had tried different approaches: reaching out toward the bowl, clasping his hands firmly in front of him, both with his eyes open and closed, all to no avail. He was surprised his mother hadn't demanded he try doing a handstand out of desperation.

Thalia tapped her fingers impatiently on her arm as she paced, arms crossed. She'd tried all sorts of tests over the years, from giving him a potted plant and ordering him to make it grow or wither, to giving animals commands or trying to change the weather. It didn't seem to matter. Every test she presented was as unsuccessful as the last and her displeasure was mounting.

Her son had reached adulthood; the day of coming of age had come and gone. He should be able to perform such simple tasks by now. Causing water to ripple should have been one of the easiest, provided he was a sky witch. After all, he was *her* son. He bared her mark and though his father may not have a drop of magic blood in him, Kain was still a half-witch.

At last, he gave a cry of frustration and lowered his hand to the table with a thud. "I can't do this."

An orange body appeared over the edge of the table as Thalia's fox leapt up. Kain glared at the animal in disgust. She'd once ordered him to try and speak with it, but he couldn't understand anything the animal may have been trying to tell him.

Not an earth witch, then, had been her conclusion, since they were known to be able to communicate with animals aside from just their familiars. But Kain didn't feel like much of a sky witch, either. He'd never shown an ounce of magic and would have been convinced he wasn't a witch at all but for the mark on his hand proclaiming otherwise.

"Yes, you can," Thalia snapped. "You just don't want to."

He sprang to his feet, knocking his chair back and causing the fox to emit a growl. "How can you say that?"

"What other explanation is there? Either you are unable to perform the tasks or unwilling. Since you bear a witch-mark, it must be the latter! You always were lazy. Unmotivated."

Perhaps that was because things had always come easily to him. Or, more likely, perhaps his apathy was a response to the fact that, no matter how hard he tried, his efforts and achievements went unacknowledged.

"What difference does it make whether I can do these things or not?"

Thalia stopped her pacing, slamming her fist down on the table, sending the water sloshing over the edge of the bowl and the fox to jump. Her dark blue eyes were lit from within with fury.

"It makes all the difference!"

She didn't say as much, but Kain knew what she meant. What good was he if he hadn't inherited her power? She would always love him less if he turned out to be ordinary. Perhaps she wouldn't love him at all. The threat was there, hanging in the air, unspoken.

His eyes narrowed. "I am still the prince, whether I can conjure a wave or not!" He snatched up the bowl and flung it savagely across the room. It shattered against the far wall, water spraying everywhere. "Nothing will change that!" He seized his white gloves, tugged them on, spun around, and made for the door.

"Kain!" Thalia barked. "I did not dismiss you!"

He ignored her, yanking open the door to reveal the princess standing there. She let out a gasp of surprise, twin spots of color rising to her cheeks at having been discovered eavesdropping. Kain wasn't sure how much, if anything, she may have heard, but the thought of her being witness to his failure fueled his fury.

His surge of anger strengthened at the sight of her. She was beautiful, there was no denying that, but that only made him angrier still. He wished she were ugly, wished that it were easier to hate her, this girl he did not know, nor wished to.

This girl he would shortly be married to. He was tired of having to be charming to her, of feigning an interest in someone he had no interest in.

Looking at Annie now, he didn't see *her* so much as yet another reminder of the way Thalia orchestrated every aspect of his life.

Kain shoved past her and stalked down the hallway, boots echoing on the marble floor.

* * *

Annie turned to the queen, still wearing her startled expression. Thalia forced herself to smile. "Please excuse him, Your Highness. These are very trying times, as I'm sure you understand."

She nodded, dropping a curtsy. "Your Majesty." Eager to be gone, she darted after Kain.

Thalia grit her teeth, closing the door. In the aspect of his temper, at least, Kain was her son. She took a deep breath, reaching up to straighten the circlet at her brow. The boy should have been able to perform at least *some* magic by now.

It reminded her of her childhood, when she'd been sent to the Erlohn monastery with Calida. All children who were born in Alara with witch-marks were sent there to be trained by elder witches in the use of their powers and to be selected by a familiar. She had been chosen by Jade, her fox, and Calida by Horus. And while her sister had excelled in the use of her earth magic, all too happy to play in the dirt, Thalia had kept her powers a secret, pretending instead that she had none at all.

She hadn't wanted any of the elders or other initiates to know just how powerful she could become, but instead had observed the others, searching for any that could be useful to her later on.

But there was no reason for Kain to hide his powers, to pretend he had none at all, the way she had done.

It was an established fact that magic ran in families, though it could skip over someone or an entire generation without explanation. Even if Kain had no magic of his own, his child very well could.

Though she still believed in her heart that Kain was simply a late bloomer, it made Thalia all the more eager to arrange for the wedding ceremony as soon as possible.

* * *

The day had dawned sunny, pleasant and warm, if a bit humid. Kain had promised to show Annie the forest trails he had mentioned before. They were very beautiful, the paths wide and spacious, lined with white stones, the trees tall and green, bending over the paths slightly to block most of the sun's heat. The shade they cast was lovely, the sound of the breeze rustling the leaves even more so.

In fact, everything about it was lovely and Annie might have enjoyed it if not for her companion.

The prince was in an ugly mood. He didn't look at her and barely spoke, and when he did, it was in terse, clipped tones. There was a tension to his shoulders, the tightness of his lips, the furrowing of his brow. All of it radiated barely suppressed anger. He still looked handsome, only now with the added impression that he was sulking.

When she'd asked him if everything was all right, he'd nearly bitten her head off. Annie had not asked him anything more since. She hadn't heard much of his argument with the queen from her position outside the door, but she was certain that it was the two of them that she'd heard arguing previously, the night she'd arrived.

129

What had Kain meant when he said he was still the prince, whether he could conjure a wave or not, and that nothing would change that? How could anything change the fact that he was the prince?

The king and queen had no other children. It wasn't as though he could be passed over for the throne.

Kain's foul mood cast a shadow over the afternoon outing and Annie was secretly glad when they left the trails behind and made for the village streets. She presumed they'd soon head back for the castle.

Villagers were out in full force, taking advantage of the pleasant weather. Though she felt out of place, Annie tried to smile and wave at them as she had before, making an effort to at least acknowledge them, unlike their brooding prince.

More than once, children darted between the legs of their horses, causing them to nearly get trampled and the horses to toss their heads in displeasure.

"Would serve them right if they got run over," Kain muttered beneath his breath. "Stupid creatures."

"That's a terrible thing to say," Annie admonished. "They're just children. They don't know any better."

"Well they ought to," he retorted, twisting around in his saddle to glower at her.

Annie stared past him, her attention on a weathered old peddler who stood just a few paces ahead of them. The man let out a cry of dismay as the axle on his cart broke, the wheel collapsing, the sudden shift in movement causing apples to tumble out of the cart, spilling into the streets.

The children let out shrieks of delight, darting back into the streets, happily trying to chase down the fruit as it rolled back toward the horses.

One child darted between the legs of Kain's horse. It let out a scream, rearing suddenly. Kain yanked on its reins, sharply turning its head, the bit biting into the corners of its mouth. Its eyes rolled, the whites visible.

Annie reached out a hand toward the reins to try and steady the animal, but it was too late. Kain fell from the saddle, landing hard on the cobblestones below.

She snatched the reins, the horse dancing madly, its hooves crashing down on several of the red apples, crushing them. Kain barely managed to avoid the animal's thrashing feet. The child screamed and backed away, the fruit forgotten. The guards that had accompanied the two royals were shouting, trying to restore order.

The old peddler was kneeling on the ground, trying futilely to gather up the fallen apples. He glanced forlornly at the ones that had been trampled and ruined. Annie's heart bled for him, thinking of her own people back in Daera and how much the fruit probably meant to this man.

He had probably hoped to sell the apples and now he wouldn't receive as much money for them, with some being destroyed and the others likely bruised.

Handing the reins to the guard at her side, Annie swung down from her saddle and knelt to help the old man. He looked up at her, his expression one of mixed surprise and gratitude, at the sight of the princess lowering herself to the stones, dirt staining the knees of her trousers. A crowd had gathered, stopping what they were doing to watch, and the guards shouted at them to get back.

Wincing, Kain had gotten to his feet, his uniform rumpled, a trace of blood at his temple. "What are you doing?" he demanded.

Annie looked up, brushing away the hair that had fallen in her face. "Helping."

Something in the prince's expression changed. He bent down, picking up a single apple, turning it so that it caught the light as he studied it ponderously. "That fall could have killed me and yet you didn't even bother to ascertain whether I was all right before crawling around in the dirt with a commoner."

Annie swallowed, deeming it wiser to stay silent than risk saying the wrong thing and setting him off. She felt a prick of guilt; she should have made sure he was unhurt and was sorry she hadn't. But she feared Kain intended to make her sorrier still.

No slight had been intended and she was tempted to say that he appeared perfectly fine to her, but knew better than to point that out.

Her silence only seemed to irritate him further. "Think he's better than I am, do you?" he said quietly, jerking his chin at the peddler.

Annie stood, brushing herself off, and held out a hand for the apple he still held. "Give it back, Kain. Please."

"You know," he said, ignoring her, "my parents own everything in this kingdom. These streets, livestock, and these apples, of course." He tossed the apple gently in the air; it smacked down into his gloved palm. "Stands to reason, then, that I can do with them whatever I *please*."

He threw the apple then, the fruit striking the kneeling peddler. Annie flinched, blinking, gaping in shock and outrage. In a split second, the prince had bent down, snatched up several more and sent them flying toward the old man and the children who were still milling around.

Annie moved in front of the peddler, using her body to shield him and felt several of the projectiles hit home.

"Stop it!" she cried, but Kain ignored her.

Some of the crowd that had gathered to watch suddenly surged forward, grappling at the apples and hurling them back at the prince. As Annie watched, the guards immediately tried to intervene, hurrying forward to restrain the crowd, sunlight glinting off drawn swords.

Annie helped the peddler to his feet, guiding him around the corner of the nearest building where it offered at least some shelter.

Then she stalked back over to her horse, leaping into the saddle. She turned her horse around and began to ride away, having had enough and wanting nothing more than to get away from the disgusting sight.

"Where are you going?" Kain called above the din.

"I can find my own way back to the palace," she snarled.

"See that you do!"

She dug her heels into the horse's sides and the animal leapt forward, surging away from the brawl behind her. The village and its people passed by in a blur as the horse galloped past.

The wind stung her cheeks and her eyes, tangling in her hair, but not as much as the sting she imagined she could still feel of the apples striking her back.

The prince's behavior mortified and frightened her. His reaction had been entirely inappropriate for one of his standing and out of proportion. He had behaved like another person entirely, utterly out of character from the way he normally was. Or, more accurately, how *she* knew him to be. Perhaps this was who Kain really was, and the charming, suave prince she thought she knew had all been just an act.

She knew he'd been having a bad day, but that did not excuse or warrant such a response. His anger had been completely out of control. What kind of person attacks the most vulnerable, those who are helpless?

The thought was disturbing, but even more alarming still was the fact that this was the man she was supposed to marry. How would he treat her once they were wed and he didn't have to pretend to like her anymore?

He hadn't stopped throwing the apples even after he'd begun striking her instead of the old man. He simply hadn't cared.

She shuddered, feeling the smooth motion of the horse's muscles beneath her as it carried her further away. If only she could keep riding, all the way back to Daera. Decimated though her kingdom was, at least she belonged there.

The people, she reminded herself. *You're doing this for the people.* But even that reminder was not strong enough in that moment to make facing down years of being trapped in an abusive marriage in any way appealing or seemingly worth it, no matter who she was suffering for.

And yet, she could not go back. This was the only way in which she could help her starving people. *By marrying him.* The thought nearly made her sob aloud.

This was not what she wanted! This was not how she was meant to help her people! She was meant for so much more, if only someone had seen fit to inform the universe… It wasn't bloody fair!

She choked the sob back, forcing down her feelings. She didn't want to cry. It wouldn't help anyone. There was nothing to be done for her situation now but try and make the best of it.

At least she wasn't starving to death, slowly wasting away to nothing. So many had it so much worse and she couldn't lose sight of that.

Annie slowed her horse as she reached the docks and dismounted, eyeing the ships anchored there. Pity she couldn't sail away either. She would go back to the castle, paste on a smile, and pretend nothing was amiss. Eventually.

For now, she wanted to stay away for as long as possible. The thought of confronting Kain again made her stomach coil into knots.

She lingered, walking among the dockworkers and sailors, inhaling the salty brine of the sea air. But her freedom was to be short-lived. Naturally, her absence hadn't gone unnoticed and she froze as she spotted some of the palace guards, in their scarlet livery, poking around at the edge of the docks, no doubt searching for a runaway princess.

Panic seized her. She wasn't ready to go back yet. Knowing that if they spotted her horse, they would find her immediately, she gave the creature a slap on the hindquarters to send it away. Undoubtedly, it could find its own way back.

She looked around hastily for a place she could hide, but there was nowhere to go without being seen. The guards were quite close now. All they needed was to look in her direction and it would be over.

Desperate, Annie looked down at a stack of crates and barrels just to her left. Hardly knowing what she was doing, she tugged off the lid of one of the crates and ducked down inside, squeezing herself into an impossible position. She plopped the lid back on, plunging herself into darkness.

Through one of several small holes in the sides, she could see the guards' boots walking across the wooden planks of the dock, but they passed her hiding spot.

She let out a quiet breath, only then realizing how cramped she was in the tiny space. She lay atop some kind of canvas cloth and she supposed she ought to be thankful the crate hadn't been filled with something uncomfortable or flat-out disgusting.

Annie wasn't sure how long she should remain hidden, or how long she'd already been in the crate for that matter. It felt like hours. One of her legs was starting to fall asleep and she was developing a crick in her neck.

This was stupid, she thought, about to push up the lid and climb out when she suddenly felt the crate lift off the ground, shifting as it did so. She stifled a gasp, trying to keep from being rocked about, and heard a muffled grunt outside.

What the hell had she been thinking when she'd crawled in here? This was probably intended to be loaded onto some ship and transported to skies knew where. *I should say something before it's too late.* It would be embarrassing, but she could swallow her pride and salvage the situation.

But her voice wouldn't work. What would they think when she was eventually discovered? She couldn't stay in here forever. She could already feel her face heat in anticipation of how embarrassed she'd be.

At last, the crate was mercifully set down and Annie peered out of one of the holes. True enough, the crate now rested on one of the ship's decks. She could see several men milling around and didn't like the look of them.

Perhaps it was the black tattoos covering their arms or their rough appearance. None of them seemed to be wearing any shoes and their trousers were tattered about the knees. One wore a red bandana around his forehead, his ear studded with rings.

She crept back from the hole, thinking it best to stay silent. But then what? Surely one of the guards would find her before long. *But they don't know you're hiding in a crate, you fool!*

She continued to keep watch, stiffening whenever one of the men ventured too close to the crate, but none of them touched it again. A man she'd never seen before walked on board and she heard the order to weigh anchor given, silently cursing herself and her stupidity.

Annie felt the ship rock beneath her and through her little spy-hole, saw the dock slowly begin to fade from view. *Now you've done it!* The fact that she was away from Kain was no longer of any consolation.

Suddenly, the lid of the crate was whisked away and Annie gasped, momentarily blinded by the sun.

"Blimey!" a voice exclaimed.

Annie felt a strong grip clamp down on her arm and struggled against it as she was raised up out of the crate. She blinked away the bright spots in her vision to see that it was the man with the red bandana who had ahold of her.

"Bloody 'ell!" a second man cried, who seemed to be missing an ear. "Where did you find 'er?"

"Stowed away in this crate," red bandana said, gesturing to the wooden box.

At such close proximity, Annie noticed that the man was missing quite a few teeth, but what he lacked most of all was personal hygiene. The stench that rolled off of him made her eyes water.

She still had no idea who these men were, but the one thing she *did* know was that she did not want to stay anywhere near them. She struggled, squirming against the man's grip, but he held her firm. "Let go of me!"

If only she had a rapier in her hand! She'd have seen to it that they quickly regretted their impudence.

"Ooh, a feisty one," remarked red bandana. "Just how I like 'em." He made a crude gesture, eliciting laughter from his companions. His cracked lips peeled back in a grim smile. "Wot do ya say, eh, poppet?"

I'll tell you precisely what I think, she thought, spitting at him. It wasn't a very ladylike thing to do, but at that moment, she didn't care.

"Why you—" Red bandana drew back with a growl. "I'll teach you to know your place." He drew back one hand and struck her across the face. Annie yelped, her cheek stinging from the blow.

No one had ever hit her before. No one would have dared.

"What should we do with her?" missing-ear asked.

"She's a stowaway," a third spoke up. "Throw 'er o'er the side."

"Don't be daft," missing-ear snapped. "Look at her clothes. She's a posh'un, she is. Would fetch a pretty penny, I think."

"The Captain'll be the judge o' that."

"I say we 'ave some fun first and decide what to do with 'er later," red bandana growled.

He leered forward, pressing against her. Annie tried to back away, but pressed up against the rail, there was nowhere to go but the sea below. Hands began to paw at her and she let out a scream.

"What in skies' name is going on 'ere?" a voice bellowed.

The sailor stepped back and Annie gasped, suddenly free. The crowd parted and a newcomer stepped forward. Annie recognized him as the man she'd spotted earlier. Based on his clothes and the way the men responded to him, he must have been the captain they spoke of.

He wore a long blue frockcoat and one of those ridiculous powdered wigs that some of the Alaran lords had favored the night of the ball Annie had attended. A dark brown hat sat atop the wig. He had a scraggly beard, dark eyes, and a weathered, craggy face that reminded Annie of a cliffside. She guessed him to be somewhere in his fifties, but to her, he seemed quite old. She eyed the sword hanging at his side and the pistols strapped across his chest.

"Well what do we 'ave 'ere?" he muttered, studying her.

"A stowaway, Captain Berchmoore," red bandana spoke up. "Found 'er in that crate."

"Clark thought she might be worth sumthin," missing-ear added. "We could ransom 'er."

"Bad luck to have a woman aboard…" someone muttered. "We should dump her over the side and be done with it."

The man—Captain Berchmoore—held up a hand to silence the opinions. "Stray too far from 'ome, did we?"

Annie jerked the hem of her outer top, straightening it. "I demand that you let me go," she said, doing her best to glower at him and appear unafraid, even as her heart galloped at the thought of what would have happened had he not arrived when he did.

"Do you now?" Berchmoore asked, rather tauntingly. "And who are you to make such a demand?"

Annie hesitated, unsure whether to answer the question honestly or not. If she revealed her identity, they might well decide to ransom her because she would indeed be worth something. But that also meant they likely wouldn't harm her, if they thought they could get something for her. In the end, she decided it worth the risk to use her title to dissuade them from keeping her—or trying anything else.

She drew herself up. "I am Princess Annabelle Grace of Daera. Release me and no harm will come to you."

For a moment, Berchmoore stared at her in shock, as if taken off-guard by her sudden proclamation. Then he burst out laughing, so hard he doubled over, and the men around him joined in as if on cue.

When he straightened, he fixed her with a hard stare. "And I'm the king's cousin!"

They don't believe me, she realized, with a dawning horror. *None of them do.*

"It's the truth!" she protested.

"Dressed like that? Princesses don't wear trousers! And what would 'Er 'Ighness be doing 'iding in a crate, mm? You're nothing but trouble, that's what you are," Berchmoore growled, clamping a hand down on her arm. "We'll decide what to do with you later, *Your 'Ighness.*"

Annie cried out as he whisked her forward, across the deck, to where a closed door stood beneath the helm. He pushed it open and threw her inside. Annie stumbled, barely managing to keep her balance.

She whirled around. "You're pirates!" She was fairly certain now that was what these men must be. No honest sailor would treat a woman so.

Berchmoore bared his teeth at her. More than a few were capped in gold. "Privateers. I got me license. It's all perfectly legal. We work for the crown now."

Annie recalled what Kain had said about the crown having hired some of the pirates to hunt down their own.

"Now, you'd best stay 'ere while I think of what to do with you. Safer that way if the men can't get to you," he added with a wicked grin, shutting the door.

Annie remained where she stood, taking in her new surroundings.

She was in a small room, a cabin of some sort. There was a rather elaborate bed set adjacent to a cross-hatched window overlooking the sea beyond. There was a desk and a chest. The ceiling was low and for once she was grateful that she'd always been on the shorter side. Still, Annie had the feeling of being in a cramped space. Every piece of furniture in the room seemed to be attached to the floorboards to keep it in place.

Just as she had been stuck here to keep her in place.

She took in all of this in a matter of seconds, but she didn't pay it much mind. She whirled on the door, tugging on it, but finding it locked. Feeling rage surge through her, Annie pounded on the door with her fists until they ached, screaming for them to let her out, but no one came. The door did not unlock or open.

At last, she slumped to the floor in defeat, wishing she had stayed by the prince's side, wishing she was there now.

The bitter irony did not escape her.

The morning following the narrow escape from Mordred found the *Phoenix* making good time toward Amberleigh, but even with a supernatural advantage, the frigate couldn't cover the distance in one day. With Calida and Lorelei forced to flee Daera, the ship's entire routine was off. There was no point in tracking down Alaran vessels or privateers in order to take their supplies as they usually would have, if there was no rendezvous point at which to drop them off.

Still, daily life aboard ship went on. Scrubbing the decks, tallowing masts, and shifting provisions were just a few such tasks and the crew bustled about, hard at work. Calida and Lorelei roamed around but mostly stayed out of the crew's way, having no knowledge of how to help, until finally Lorelei retreated below decks, suffering from seasickness.

Ben wasn't surprised to find Calida outside his cabin door at midday, as he returned from checking their supplies below decks. The *Phoenix* was always low on provisions immediately following a drop-off in Daera and they would need to find more prey before too long.

His aunt looked as though she'd been waiting for him.

They stepped into his cabin where they could speak in relative privacy, something always lacking on a ship.

Ben closed the door behind him. "I'd expected you to talk to me last night."

"I wanted to," she replied, looking at the room around her. "But I couldn't very well do that with the rest of them present, now could I?" She sighed, her eyes straying back to him. "You know, don't you?"

It was a vague question, but Ben knew exactly what she was referring to.

"Yes," he said simply. There was no point in denying it and he was fairly certain she knew the truth anyway. "Captain Lussard told me. He thought it was safer for me to know about my abilities and what I could do."

"He never told me that he told you…"

Ben shrugged. "Likely never got the chance."

He thought briefly of his former captain. Lussard had been a large man, barrel chested, with a deep laugh that could be heard across the room. Ben had left Calida at the age of eight and gone to sea with Lussard as a cabin boy, working his way up through the ranks.

He brought himself back to the present, fixing his aunt with a direct look. "Why did you never tell me?"

"Because I believed you'd be safer not knowing." A spark of defiance flared in her gray eyes. "And I was right."

"How can you say that?" Ben exclaimed.

"Really? After your little demonstration last night?" Calida demanded. "What do you think you're doing, showing off your power so blatantly in front of a witch-hunter? Lorelei and I are both earth witches. Mordred knows neither of us could have conjured that wave. Therefore, there must be a sky witch on board."

"Those rats were following us," Ben protested. "I had to do something."

"We would have been safely on board the *Phoenix* and away before they ever reached us. But that's not the point. That wasn't the only time you've ever used your powers, is it? I've heard the stories, though I wasn't sure I believed them until now."

The stories. Of course. Ben had heard the rumors surrounding him and his ship. How the *Phoenix* moved unnaturally fast for a ship of her size, how no one could outrun her, how the wind and waves alike seemed to favor her and work against her prey.

All because he manipulated the wind and water to his advantage, just as Calida accused him of doing.

Ben frowned at his aunt. "How else do you expect a ship of this size to catch any prey?"

"It's hardly necessary now, though, is it? You have a reputation built up. The moment your quarry spots this ship, they ought to surrender without a fight or a chase. There's no need to use your powers anymore."

She had something of a point, though he refused to admit it. He crossed his arms. "I suppose I've just grown accustomed to using them."

"That's what worries me. Do you think no one else has guessed the truth? What about your crew?"

"Even if they suspect the truth, why should they care? All they care about is the fact that I keep their pockets lined."

Calida glared at him. "Well they may not care, but I'm sure Alara would, seeing as how it's their ships you attack. Are you trying to put a target on your back? Bad enough that you're a pirate, but if they find out you're a witch as well, they'll come for you."

As if they aren't already, Ben thought, thinking of Berchmoore. "I'd like to see them try. It's because I'm a witch that it wouldn't matter, if they even dared."

"Well, pride go before a fall."

"Look," Ben snapped, suddenly quite angry at her lack of faith in him, "just because you're afraid to use your powers doesn't mean I should be. I wouldn't be where I am now if I hadn't done what I did."

"At least that explains how you rose through the ranks so quickly," she muttered.

Ben scoffed. "I got through the ranks so quickly because I'm a good sailor. My gifts just happened to compliment it. If you don't like it, then you shouldn't have sent me away."

"I sent you to sea because I thought it would be safer than on land," Calida retorted. "Clearly, I was wrong."

She whirled, her dark blue dress swirling about her ankles, and left him there.

He made a small noise between his teeth and stalked out of the cabin. Only then did he realize he'd meant to ask her what she and Lorelei planned to do now that they couldn't go back to Daera. That only made him angrier still, but he wasn't going to broach the issue now.

Sharpe was standing over by the rail not too far away. She cocked an eyebrow at him. No doubt his fury was written all over his face.

His expression softened as he made his way over to her. There was something he wanted to ask her, too. "I've been meaning to ask... About what happened—"

The muscles in her jaw hardened. "If you're going to ask me about Mordred, don't. I've said all I want to say."

"I only wondered why you didn't kill him out there on the beach."

She drew her arms up across her chest. "It was dark and raining and with that wind—"

"I know you, Sharpe," Ben interrupted. "You don't miss." *Unless you want to and I can't imagine why you would.*

The corner of her mouth turned up in a smirk. "No." Her eyes were flinty. "I wanted him to crawl. To be afraid, like I was all those years ago. I just wanted him to know what it felt like." She shrugged. "Petty, I know."

"Ruthless," he corrected. "But I don't have you on this crew because you're a saint."

The smirk turned into a smile. "No," she said softly.

Ben nodded to her and walked away, the argument with Calida all but forgotten.

* * *

Calida stalked back below decks, making her way to the cabin she'd been given to share with Lorelei for the duration, wondering how her nephew could be both so stubborn and so stupid. *You know who he gets it from.*

She suddenly felt exhausted, grateful at least that, despite the turn the conversation had taken, he hadn't asked her what she intended to do now. She had no idea. There was time enough to think of a solution later.

Lorelei was still lying on the bed where Calida had left her. "Feel any better?"

"Hardly," Lorelei replied, sitting up a little. "How could I, with the way this tub rocks and creaks constantly?"

Calida smothered a smile, hoping Lorelei wouldn't notice in the dim lighting below decks. The air was stuffy down here, smelling of damp, which made sense. The wood of the ship was always wet.

"It's an acquired taste, I suppose," she answered. *Much like Ben himself.*

"I take it the talk didn't go too well? You didn't look best pleased when you came in."

Calida silently cursed her inability to conceal her emotions. "Not as well as I would have liked. But I was right. He does know."

"What else does he know? You didn't tell him the truth, did you?"

"Of course not, Lorelei! And you know very well why I can't."

"He's going to find out eventually."

Maybe not. Maybe she could keep the whole thing hidden away from him forever. That would be ideal. But she hadn't told him that he was a witch and yet he'd contrived a way to find that out. Why should this be any different? How could she assume that any secret was safe?

"I know," she sighed. "But he's not ready to know that yet."

Lorelei grimaced, though whether from a fresh bout of nausea or the topic of conversation, Calida wasn't sure. "We may not have a choice, what with Mordred. If he saw that wave…"

Calida frowned, her fingers curling into fists at her sides. Mordred couldn't have failed to see it. And if he saw it, he'd go straight to *her*. "Yes…we'll have to do something about him…"

* * *

Business was booming in Amberleigh and Berchmoore was acutely aware that he wasn't sharing in the wealth and fortune. Not yet, anyway. It was only a matter of time.

He sat in the Black Horse tavern, one of the many located throughout the island, with a plate of roasted boar and a tankard of mead sat before him, ruminating over the best course of action regarding the strange girl aboard his ship.

She had refused to change her story, still claiming she was the princess. He'd left her locked in his cabin while he and the crew went ashore. Berchmoore was certain that, whoever she really was, she was worth some money, if he played his cards right.

But the prospect wasn't without its risks. He seriously doubted the wild claim she'd made that she was the princess.

After all, didn't all girls fancy themselves princesses at some point? Not that he would know. More likely she was some rich merchant's daughter and he was willing to bet that her father would pay a pretty penny to get her back safe and sound.

The problem was, they couldn't send word to her father until she confessed to who she really was. And the crew was getting restless.

His men were divided over what to do. Some wanted to ransom her, while others wanted her gone as soon as possible, due to the belief that it was bad luck to have a woman on board. Berchmoore himself thought that in this case, it might be rather good luck, but that didn't stop some of them from wanting to pitch her over the side. A fight had nearly broken out over the differing opinions.

No, this would not do. Whatever it was Berchmoore decided, he needed to act soon.

If he couldn't figure out who she was and thus what to do with her, perhaps the smartest thing would be to sail back to Alara, take her to shore in one of the longboats and leave her there. They wouldn't get any money out of it, but they'd be rid of the temptation and the trouble.

That's what women really were, anyway: trouble.

Berchmoore chewed on a piece of boar, but his appetite was gone. It was rather tough, anyway. Certainly not the best he'd ever had. Now the buccaneers of Indris, on the other hand—they knew how to cure some boar.

"I hear they still haven't found the princess."

Berchmoore looked up suddenly, gazing around to try and find the source of the voice that had spoken, his curiosity piqued. *There!* There were two sailors seated at one table not far from his, one of the barmaids standing beside them.

"She missing?" the other sailor asked. He had a tufty white beard, sunken gums and, it appeared, no teeth.

"You haven't heard?" his companion exclaimed. He was larger, younger, but with a scruffy beard of his own. If Berchmoore didn't know any better, he might be tempted to think the two were related, father and son perhaps. "She went missing yesterday. The palace is all in an uproar about it. There are guards crawling all over the place, but they haven't had any luck finding her."

"No one knows where she's gone," the barmaid added, giving a delicate little shudder. "It's almost as if she vanished into thin air. Oh, the poor thing!"

One of the sailors grunted. "Maybe she doesn't want to be found. Maybe she ran away so she didn't have to marry that godawful prince what's-his-face. You'll never believe what I heard he did…"

But Berchmoore was no longer listening. The real princess had gone missing yesterday and yesterday that mysterious girl turned up on his ship. Berchmoore didn't care much for coincidences. Perhaps she had been telling the truth after all and he had been too stupid to see it.

You fool! He had the *princess* on board his ship, locked in his cabin, right now and he hadn't even known it. Well this certainly changed things.

He couldn't very well ransom the princess. He didn't imagine the royals would be too pleased to learn he'd taken her, however unknowingly. She had crawled into one of his crates, for skies' sake! How could he be held accountable for that?

No, the only course of action available to him now would be to take her back to Alara. If he explained what happened and told the truth, perhaps they would be grateful to him for returning their wayward princess to them safe and sound.

He wondered how exactly she had come to be in that crate in the first place.

Maybe she really did run away from the prince.

He stood, striding up to the counter to settle his account. His business was concluded in Amberleigh and it was time to leave. None of the other pirates or privateers present knew he had her and he intended to keep it that way.

* * *

Annie was relieved to be up on the main deck, the breeze stirring her hair. Fresh air was always preferable on a ship and she had grown tired of being sequestered in the great cabin. Berchmoore had let her out, saying that he believed her claim now, and that he would take her back to Alara, drop her off, and explain what had happened to the authorities.

She wasn't sure what had made him change his mind, but she was grateful. She supposed she couldn't really be too upset with him. It wasn't as though he had kidnapped her. It was her own fault that she'd ended up in this situation. But she didn't fancy seeing the queen's reaction, or Kain's, when they learned that she had hidden in a crate and been carried on board. It was too humiliating.

Annie did her best not to think about it, focusing instead on the blue-green water and the distant horizon. Out of the corner of her eye, she was also keeping a close watch on the crew. Uncouth as they were, she wouldn't put it past them to try something now that she was out in the open and accessible, but they kept their distance.

Movement overhead caught her attention and she looked up to see the silhouette of a hawk soaring lazily over the ship. Annie squinted, unsure she was seeing correctly.

As she watched, the bird alighted on the mainmast yard. She wasn't the only one to notice the hawk's presence. Some of the men had as well and a few pointed and muttered amongst themselves.

Annie turned away from the railing, studying the odd scene laid out before her. Some of the men's postures had turned rigid, their faces uneasy. Perhaps the sighting of a hawk on open waters was some sort of sailor superstition that she was unaware of. An omen, perhaps?

The bird hadn't moved from its perch; it didn't seem to be doing anything and she couldn't understand why they would be so afraid.

"The captain won't like it," one of the men muttered.

A few others had hurried to the railing, peering out across the sea, but there was nothing out there—Annie had been staring at it for a decent amount of time and seen nothing.

Suddenly, a pile of bird droppings landed unceremoniously on the deck with a splat, narrowly missing one of the men standing there.

"Why you—" he growled, pulling his pistol from his belt.

The man she had seen before, the one with the missing ear, clapped a hand down on his wrist. "Are you mad?" he hissed. "You shoot that bird and you're a dead man."

Now Annie was convinced the hawk must be some sort of superstition. Killing one must be bad luck. Reluctantly, the man lowered his gun and shoved it back into his belt, eyes glittering balefully up at the bird.

"Go on!" missing-ear shouted. "Get outta 'ere!"

The hawk let out a shriek and took off, flying back toward the stern and then the open sea.

* * *

Ben opened his eyes as the connection with Horus severed. The hawk was on his way back. One of the strange abilities he'd discovered regarding familiars was that one could link their vision with the animal's, but to do so, he had to surrender his own vision first. If he closed his eyes, he could see what Horus saw, if he wished. It made the bird all the more invaluable as a companion, able to fly ahead and scout out ships before they were even in sight. And a hawk's eyes missed nothing.

He remained standing at the helm, impatiently waiting for his bird to return to him. For the first time in weeks, excitement speared through him like lightning at the prospect of a chase.

At last, Horus's outline came into view. The hawk flew up to land on his shoulder. "*I think you'll want to take a look at that one.*"

Horus didn't have to say it—Ben had seen for himself and there was not a chance he was going to let this one get away. They had both, through their shared vision, seen the name of the ship written on the back of her stern.

The *Black Dagger*.

Berchmoore's ship.

Finally, after weeks of searching, Ben had found him.

"Did you see her?" Horus asked. *"The girl?"*

Ben nodded. The same girl they had seen traveling on board the princess's ship was now on board Berchmoore's. He didn't know what Berchmoore thought he was doing with her, but even if he hadn't already had his mind made up, this would have made the decision for him. They couldn't turn away. Aside from the fact that he had been waiting for this moment, something had to be done.

He waited until the ship had come into view in the distance and then gave the order for Terrance to take over at the helm. "All stations! Make ready the guns! It's Berchmoore, boys. Let's give him our best welcome."

Cheers went up from the assembled men. They were just as familiar with Berchmoore as he was. This would be the first time they had purposefully sought out the other captain—and the first time challenging his new ship. He and Ben had come to an agreement to avoid each other and stuck with it, though just barely.

There had been occasions when Berchmoore's former ship had been spotted, sometimes drifting too close for comfort, but the man had never tried anything. A few warning shots fired had scared him off. He knew he was no match for the *Phoenix*'s superior firepower.

But now, with a new, bigger vessel under his command…what would his response be? Fight? Or flight, as he usually chose?

Having heard the commotion, Calida hurried up from below decks, lifting her skirts slightly as she navigated the stairs. She walked up to him, leaning close, her tone confidential. "Is this wise?"

He glanced at her but couldn't summon up the irritation he'd felt toward her that morning. The bad mood that had hung about him like a dark cloud was gone, replaced by an electric energy. Eagerness flowed through him at the prospect of confronting Berchmoore again after so long. He felt that energy rippling through the crew, galvanizing them into action.

"We're pirates, Aunt Calida. This is what we do. But you and Lorelei might want to stay below. I don't foresee things turning nasty, but Berchmoore's got himself a new ship. He might want to show off."

His aunt frowned at him, but did not argue. She knew this is what he did for a living, what he lived and breathed. She may not trust his judgement when it came to the use of his power, but she ought to trust him on this.

She turned and retreated back below decks, the safest place to be during an engagement. The cabins along the stern were one of the most dangerous, the stern being the most vulnerable part of a ship. The lower one could go, the better.

Ben could see the gun crews getting into formation around the guns on the main deck and knew they were doing the same on the gun deck. Sharpe had collected her musket and was leading her fellow marksmen up the ratlines to the best vantage point.

"Sharpe!" Ben called.

"Aye, Captain?"

"When we get in range, injure a few of them, if you can, but don't kill anyone."

"Aye, sir."

He wanted to send a message to Berchmoore, not slaughter his men. Some of the crew probably hadn't even been aboard the *Phoenix* at the same time as Berchmoore. They were innocent bystanders in this vendetta. He wouldn't give the order to mercilessly open fire on them unless they chose to stand and fight, which would provoke a response.

It was rather unthinkable, but if the unthinkable did happen, the *Phoenix* was ready. All forty guns of her.

* * *

Only when the ship appeared in the distance did the crew think to inform Berchmoore. His mood was already black when he stepped out of his cabin, spyglass in hand, and his worst fears were confirmed.

The report of the hawk was bad enough—there was only one thing that could mean—but the scarlet sails eliminated any doubts that may have lingered.

Berchmoore had never understood the red sails himself. The ship had had white canvas when she'd been captured and what was wrong with that? She'd been an Alaran warship, albeit one of the smaller ones, and had been reborn as the *Phoenix*, dead to her old life. No longer a warship but a pirate vessel. A rover, a brigand, a sea wolf.

But red dye was expensive and to waste such a thing on sails, which could be so easily damaged… It was a testament to the aggression and power of the ship herself—and to the ego of the man who captained her.

Berchmoore felt a range of emotions flicker through him at the sight of the other ship. Fear, chased away by disbelief, followed quickly by outrage. *How the hell did Knight know? How had he found out about the princess being on board?*

For that must be the reason the *Phoenix* was now making an appearance. It had been two years, after all, and they had agreed to stay out of each other's way. The girl was the only explanation for this sudden change in behavior.

Berchmoore was half-tempted to give the order to roll out the guns. After all, the *Dagger* was larger than his last ship. She was a frigate herself, perhaps big enough to challenge the *Phoenix*. But at what cost? How much damage would be inflicted before victory was secured? *If* it was secured.

If the *Phoenix* caught up to them and they were boarded, the other crew would take anything of value that they found, including the princess. Berchmoore couldn't let that happen, but if he stood his ground and fought, Knight might suppose he was doing it because he had something on board he considered worth fighting for.

No, that would only pique Knight's curiosity.

"Sir? Your orders?"

He had forgotten that his quartermaster was still at his elbow, waiting for an answer. "Roll out all canvas."

"Sir?"

"We're gonna try and outrun the bastard."

It was a stupid plan, foolish to consider, even for a moment. But Knight had forced his hand and, short of surrendering, Berchmoore was out of options. The rumors didn't exist for no reason.

No one could outrun that ship, but Berchmoore was going to try it anyway.

* * *

The approaching ship had closed in fast. Annie could now make out details and she recognized it as the same scarlet-sailed ship that had followed her to Alara and that she had glimpsed from the observation tower with Kain.

She felt a surge of relief. "Oh, it's another privateer." Perhaps the palace had somehow found out what had happened to her and sent the other ship to retrieve her.

Captain Berchmoore whirled on her. "Privateer!" He snorted in disbelief. "That's a pirate, girlie."

Annie stared at him, not believing him for a moment. But as a privateer himself, Berchmoore would be best suited to know who his fellow privateers were and who they were not. She had seen his license in his cabin while she'd been locked in there. The piece of parchment had borne the queen's signature.

She looked back at the nearing ship, her stomach knotting in fear. When the scarlet-sailed ship had been following her to Alara, she'd assumed that it had been pirates and had feared that it would make a move to fire upon them, only for it to veer away as soon as they reached Alaran waters.

The second time she'd seen it, it had *been* in Alaran waters. Kain had mistook it for a privateer because, logically, what pirate would be brazen enough to be caught so deeply in hostile waters?

The pirate ship was very close now and a warning shot erupted from one of its bow chasers, smashing into the stern. Wood splintered, glass shattering, debris thrown into the air. Annie screamed, ducking down, shielding her head with her arms.

If she had been in that cabin…

Berchmoore uttered an oath. "Get 'er below!" he shouted to one of his crew, jabbing a knobby finger in her direction.

Annie felt herself gripped by the elbow and steered toward one of the hatches.

She went without a fuss.

* * *

As Ben had predicted, Berchmoore had opted to run instead of fight. But with a favorable tailwind stretching the *Phoenix*'s canvas taut and a headwind simultaneously working against Berchmoore, he didn't stand a chance.

The bow chaser's shot crashing through their stern was the final nail in the proverbial coffin.

A white flag was hoisted up on the mizzenmast truck, announcing his surrender. And Sharpe hadn't had to fire a single shot.

The *Phoenix* pulled alongside the *Dagger*, gun ports still open, guns bristling menacingly. Ben was aware that at this range, a broadside would be devastating. But a trap was unlikely. Berchmoore's own gun ports remained closed. Putting up a fight had never been his intention.

Grappling hooks were thrown over, securing the two ships together, and gangplanks lowered. Terrance went ahead, leading some of the crew to disarm the privateers, and Ben followed with the rest, Sharpe at his elbow, musket slung over her shoulder. Horus circled overhead, looking for any signs of sudden movement or a trap. Calida and Lorelei remained on board, out of sight.

Berchmoore had been relieved of his weapons and he looked far more furious than any of his crew. His face was a mottled red, the veins in his neck bulging as he fought to suppress his rage.

He looked exactly as Ben had remembered, except now he sported one of those hideous powdered wigs. Berchmoore hadn't had much hair to begin with when he'd been on the *Phoenix*, but it hadn't seemed to bother him then. Perhaps the wig was intended to conceal pockmarks he'd acquired from contracting the pox. That was Ben's suspicion, anyway.

Ben smiled at Berchmoore, putting on his best wolfish grin. With a flick of the wrist, he signaled to Terrance to take some of the crew and begin searching below for anything of value, transferring it to their own ship.

"I'd heard about your new ship, Berchmoore," Ben said. "I must admit, I'm hurt that you didn't invite me on board." He turned slowly, observing his surroundings. "It's nice. Although it would look a lot nicer without that gaping hole in the stern."

Somehow, Berchmoore managed to get a grip on his anger. He exhaled heavily through his nose. "What do you want, Knight? We 'ad an agreement, last I 'eard."

"That we did," Ben nodded. "But you see, I heard this interesting little rumor that you were looking for me. That you're a privateer now. Gone legit. Got yourself a nice little license and everything."

"Times are changing, Knight. The age of piracy is comin' to an end. I just decided I wanted to be on the winning side."

"And how's that working out for you?"

Berchmoore was saved from having to reply by the reemergence of Terrance, dragging the girl Ben and Horus had seen earlier. He had both hands around her arms, struggling to keep ahold of her as she squirmed and protested, kicking at his legs. The quartermaster was swearing under his breath.

Ben raised an eyebrow. He'd wondered briefly what Berchmoore had done with the girl when he hadn't seen her on deck when they'd crossed over. If he'd hoped to hide her somewhere to keep them from finding her, it was a doomed venture. Ben had already known she was on board.

"Let go of me!" the girl snarled, trying to twist free of Terrance's grip and this time, he let her go, having already wrestled her up on deck.

She glared around at them, eyes glittering with anger. Her gaze settled on Ben as Horus swooped down to land on his shoulder. She was afraid, he could tell, but trying to hide it beneath her anger.

She was short and slender, with a pleasing figure. Her trousers were a light tan color, black boots reaching her knees. She wore a white, silk collared shirt beneath a dark sleeveless outer top, its bodice styled like a corset.

Her hair reached the middle of her back, thick, curling and black as a moonless night. An ugly, purpling bruise marred one cheek and Ben found himself wondering if one of Berchmoore's men had done it—and what else they might have done to her.

But it was her eyes that snared his attention—bright, green, and filled with fury. She glared at him as if she could spear him with the force of her gaze alone. If looks could kill, he was certain he would already be dead.

"Well, well, well," he drawled. "What do we have here? When I heard you'd turned privateer, Berchmoore, I knew you'd lowered your standards, but I didn't think you'd stoop to kidnapping."

"She's a stowaway!" Berchmoore exploded, spittle flying from his mouth. "She was 'iding in one of our crates. Didn't know it until we already 'ad 'er aboard."

Ben eyed him, trying to gauge whether he guessed at the girl's likely identity or not. If not, he wasn't about to tell him.

He snorted. "She doesn't look like a stowaway. What were you planning to do? Ransom her? Auction her off to the highest bidder?"

"He's telling the truth," the girl snapped. "I am a stowaway. It was an accident."

"Be that as it may," Ben said. "I'm afraid this ship is no place for a lady and I can't, in good faith, leave you with a man like Berchmoore."

"Now just a minute, Knight—" Berchmoore growled, taking a step forward. Sharpe lowered her musket from her shoulder into a ready position. "You can take all our supplies. Every crate, every box. Just leave the girl."

Ben frowned. Maybe he did know. "Taken a shine to her, have you? I've got a better idea. Why don't we take all your supplies and, since you said it yourself that she stowed away in one of your crates, we'll take her off your hands, too."

Berchmoore scowled. "Bad luck to 'ave a woman on board, you know." His eyes flicked to Sharpe.

"It certainly was for you," Ben retorted.

One of the men emerged from below, carrying a crate. "That's the last of it, sir."

"Excellent. Quartermaster, are the guns spiked?"

"Aye, Captain," Terrance replied with a grin.

With the guns spiked, the *Phoenix* was free to pull away from the other ship without fear of being fired upon. Ben could have ordered the rudder disabled as well, but there was no chance of Berchmoore's ship catching up to their own.

Ben nodded to the other captain. "Berchmoore. Always a pleasure."

The older man was practically foaming at the mouth. "You'll regret this, Knight," he hissed. "Mark my words. You may be lucky, but one day, that luck'll run out. I'd like nothing more than to slit your throat myself, but I'll settle for seeing you swing from a gibbet in the Alaran 'arbor!"

"That's a nice dream, Berchmoore. Maybe one day it'll even come true, but you'll forgive me if I doubt it." Ben turned to the girl. "Well, miss, if you'd kindly get on board, we'll be on our way. I think you'll find the accommodations infinitely more to your liking."

She frowned at him, but said nothing as she proceeded him across one of the lowered gangplanks. Ben followed along with Sharpe. At some point, Lorelei had come up from below decks. She met Ben's gaze as he followed the girl, before turning and darting back down the stairs.

The gangplanks were withdrawn, the grappling hooks removed, and the *Phoenix* began pulling away from the *Black Dagger*.

The crew returned to their stations, once more going about their tasks, but the girl remained standing in the middle of the deck.

Ben walked up to her. "Well, who do I have the pleasure of rescuing?"

Her lip curled. "Rescuing? You're pirates!"

"Guilty as charged. Although I supposed *we* would be privateers if the kingdom of Daera saw fit to give us a letter of marque."

"I can't imagine why they would do such a thing."

He sighed, crossing his arms. "Who are you?"

Though he suspected she was the princess, he didn't know that for certain—nor was he likely to if she didn't tell him.

"A merchant's daughter."

"Do you have a name?"

"Why should I share mine?" she demanded, crossing her arms and mimicking his pose. "You haven't given me yours."

"Ah, yes, where are my manners?" He swept off his hat and bowed to her, somewhat mockingly. "Benjamin Knight, Captain of the *Phoenix*, at your service. And you are?"

"I already told you," she replied haughtily. "A merchant's daughter."

"All right," Ben said, putting his hat back on. "Don't tell me." *Skies, she was vexing.* "In the meantime, you can stay in the cabin and rethink your decision."

He steered her over to the cabin door and resisted the urge to push her in. She walked inside on her own, back ramrod straight, chin raised defiantly. She reminded him of a stubborn child. Ben closed the door after her, rolling his eyes.

He only wanted to be certain of her identity so he could figure out what to do with her. He certainly didn't want to keep her on board a moment longer than he had to. He had more guests than he knew what to do with at the moment.

Princess or not, she was clearly someone wealthy. The daughter of some noble, perhaps. Though he couldn't fathom why she would have stowed away on Berchmoore's ship.

And what if she was the princess? What then? With Berchmoore's ship fading into the distance, Ben turned his attention to a new dilemma—one he'd put them all in, if his suspicions turned out to be correct.

He chewed his lip, thinking it over, but coming no closer to a solution.

"How did it go? I heard a shot."

He turned as his aunt climbed up on deck.

"One of the bow chasers," he said quickly. "Berchmoore surrendered after that. Look, I need your advice on something."

Her gray eyes widened slightly. "Would this be about the girl you brought on board? Lorelei mentioned something about it."

"Yes. She refuses to tell me her name, but she's clearly someone wealthy. The point is, Horus previously saw her on a Daeran ship bound for Alara. I think she's the princess."

"You think?" Calida exclaimed. "What in skies' name were you thinking, bringing the princess on board?"

"Suspected princess," Ben protested weakly, but he strongly believed that was precisely who she was. "What was I supposed to do? Leave her in Berchmoore's hands? Out of the question!"

"Well what are you going to do with her? You can't take her back to Alara."

Ben bit his lip again and when he spoke, he tried to sound more confident than he felt. "We'll take her back to Daera."

CHAPTER 17

Night had fallen by the time he and Calida next spoke. The crew was still excited over the haul they had taken from Berchmoore. The watches had been doled out and snatches of laughter or faint singing drifted on the air.

The ship's lanterns had been lit, casting faint but warm glows in the darkness. They would be extinguished for the night soon, but not yet. The sails above shifted softly in the gentle breeze. Ben stood still for a moment, letting the wind ruffle his hair. He'd taken his hat off; it was too warm to comfortably wear it for long periods of time, so close to Alara's tropical waters.

Calida came up to him, her voice soft. "Do you still intend to take the princess back to Daera?"

"If she even is the princess." Ben cast a glance over his shoulder at his closed cabin door. He had not set foot within it since escorting the girl there.

She nodded. "It's a good plan. And at the same time, you can drop Lorelei and I off."

He turned to her. "You can't go back to Daera. It isn't safe."

"Mordred has moved on," she countered. "As soon as we escaped on board your ship, there was no reason for him to stay."

"You're more than welcome to stay here permanently," he offered. "You are my aunt, after all." Difficult as she could be at times, she was the only family he had. "You're family."

She smiled, a rare occurrence. He wished she did it more often. It made her look younger and less careworn. "I appreciate the offer. But a ship is no home for an earth witch."

"Well, the offer still stands, if you change your mind." He stared over the side at the moonlight reflecting off the waves. "You said we would have to find a new drop-off site. That Daera was no longer safe. Why the sudden change of heart?"

Calida frowned. "I can't keep running forever. Sooner or later, Mordred will have to be faced."

Ben wasn't satisfied with the answer. "Is this because of me? Because Mordred saw my power?"

Calida didn't reply, but that was an answer in and of itself.

He sighed. "Were either of my parents a witch?"

"No," she said, her voice still quiet but firm. "You know what they were."

What *they were, not* who *they were,* he thought bitterly, but supposed he should be grateful. Some people didn't know even that much.

"That's why your mother ended up the way she did," Calida added. "She had no powers or skills with which to make a living."

Ben sighed. He didn't like thinking of his parents. According to his aunt, their story was not a happy one. It certainly hadn't been a love match. His father had been a sailor and he'd met his mother one evening when he came into port.

One night of passion, paid for in gold.

It hurt him to think of his mother being treated that way. Reduced by circumstances to a common whore and he her bastard child. Aunt Calida had always taught him from a young age to treat women with respect.

That, combined with his mother's story, was why he had never patronized prostitutes, despite what his crew believed about Rosa. Paying a woman just so he could use her had never appealed to Ben. It certainly didn't seem very respectful, though he supposed it was mildly better than not paying at all, the way some did.

And Rosa…her story wasn't dissimilar to his mother's. She'd had a husband once. He'd been a merchant sailor, one of several willing to do business with Daera. Until Alara tried to strongarm them. He'd refused and shortly thereafter, he was attacked and killed by pirates.

At least that was the official line.

Rosa didn't believe it and she blamed the southern kingdom for her husband's death. With him gone, the breadwinner of the family, she was forced to turn to prostitution as a means of surviving. Just like Ben's mother.

Shortly after, Calida had told him, his own father had died at sea in a storm and his mother succumbed to illness. Ben didn't remember his mother and his father, he never would have met anyway. He had lived with Calida all his life, until she'd sent him to sea to sail with Captain Lussard.

He'd always thought of Captain Lussard as a father figure, of sorts, and even came to believe that the man might *be* his father, despite what his aunt claimed. But Lussard had refuted that.

And now he was dead, too, and it was just Aunt Calida left.

Ben suddenly felt guilty for the way he had treated her. "About that disagreement we had…" he said suddenly, feeling the urge to make restitution. "I'm sorry—"

Calida waved the apology away. "Don't worry about it. When are you going to inform Her Highness that you're taking her back to Daera?"

"Tomorrow. I don't have the energy to face her tonight."

She nodded. "Right. Goodnight, then."

"Goodnight."

Ben listened to the sound of her retreating footsteps as she walked away, leaving him alone. He rubbed his face, suddenly exhausted by the day's events. He wanted nothing more than to retire to his cabin and catch a few hours' sleep, but he couldn't.

Not with the princess, or whoever she was, in his cabin.

And even if she were someone else, if he went in there with her, the rumors would fly. The last thing he needed was to be accused of compromising the princess's virtue. If that didn't give either kingdom reason to hunt him down, he didn't know what would.

He would have to content himself with sleeping out on the open deck, uncomfortable though it was. He'd done it plenty of times as an ordinary sailor, the open air preferable to sleeping below in the cramped quarters and stuffy, damp air, surrounded by the smell of fellow unwashed men. And at least it was a clear night, not raining or storming. The sky was cloudless, no sign of impending bad weather.

Still, he missed his bed.

Ben huffed, laying down on the deck and staring up at the stars through the shrouds, sails and ratlines.

It was going to be a long night.

* * *

Annie hadn't wanted to sleep in the cabin bed. Being on this ship alone was enough to make her uncomfortable but the idea of sleeping in someone else's bed—specifically Benjamin's—was even worse.

But no one entered the cabin to tell her to go somewhere else and she certainly wasn't going to willingly stay up all night. She was already exhausted from having to deal with Berchmoore and she would need her wits about her for what was to come. She needed a place to sleep and the bed would have to do.

She reflected on her current circumstances as she settled down with a sense of disbelief. Not only was she locked inside a cabin again, this time it was on a pirate ship. She didn't know how she was ever going to get back to Alara now. Berchmoore had finally come to his senses and agreed to take her back, only to be attacked and boarded by pirates.

She honestly felt as though she could scream in frustration. Little wonder that Alara had hired some former pirates as privateers to hunt them down. They were a menace and something had to be done.

But Berchmoore hadn't even tried to fight back. Going after pirates was supposed to be his job and at the first sight of one, he turned tail and fled!

She slept fitfully, returning to consciousness several times, expecting Benjamin to enter the cabin and find her in his bed. She doubted that he would have taken too kindly to her commandeering his sleeping place and she half-expected him to try and claim it back.

But he didn't. She was still alone.

Her hair was a tangled mess by the time morning rolled around, knotted and sticking up at odd angles from all the tossing and turning she had done. She'd never grow accustomed to sleeping on board a ship, with its incessant creaking and rolling.

Annie wanted nothing more than a hot bath. It had been two days since she'd last had one and she was beginning to feel the effects. Her hair was starting to become oily and when that happened, it became lank rather than thick and curling.

She sighed, sitting on the edge of the bed. She'd even slept in her clothes since she had nothing to change into. How long would she be expected to stay here? There was no way to know. She had refused to tell Benjamin who she really was, since that had gone oh so very well when she'd told Berchmoore.

Pirates were an opportunistic lot. If she had told them who she was, they'd have taken advantage of it. No, better to stay quiet. Waiting was a far better option than being ransomed.

A knock sounded on the cabin door, causing her to jump. When she didn't reply, it swung slowly open and Benjamin poked his head in. "Oh, good. You're decent."

"Of course I am!" she snapped, feeling her face flush. "What did you expect?"

He stepped inside, shutting the door behind him. "And a good morning to you, too. Hope you slept well."

Annie didn't know what to make of the remark. He was probably trying to trick her somehow, being polite to throw her off-guard, to lower her defenses.

"Well enough," she said stiffly.

For a moment, they stood there studying each other. Thankfully, there was no sign of the hawk this morning. Ben looked exactly the same as he had the previous day, except the feathered hat was gone.

From the expensive taste of his clothes, she had assumed he must be the captain the moment she'd laid eyes on him. He wore a long scarlet coat that fell to his knees, the cuffs, collar, and lapels were black with gold trim. Beneath that was a frilly white shirt, tucked into black trousers, which were themselves tucked into polished black boots that nearly reached his knees. A sheathed sword hung at his side, partially concealed by his coat.

His skin was tanned from time spent out in the sun. His golden hair was shaggy, the fringe nearly falling into his eyes. His eyes, focused on her, were very blue. She felt as though she had seen them somewhere before, but couldn't think where.

But the most perplexing feature had to be his age. He looked scarcely older than she was. Twenty, perhaps? He struck her as a bit young to be a pirate captain, but she didn't comment on that.

He held out one hand, gesturing that she take a seat at the table in the middle of the room. Reluctantly, she did so and he sat across from her.

"I've sent word to the galley to have breakfast brought up."

"You needn't have," Annie said coolly. "I'm not hungry." That couldn't have been further from the truth. She felt rather ravenous, nearly light-headed from it, but she wasn't going to admit that to him.

"No, indeed," he replied. "But you are an esteemed guest."

His use of *esteemed* puzzled her, but she supposed a guest was better than a prisoner. Someone rapped on the door and Benjamin bid them enter. One of the crew, a man Annie didn't recognize, walked in, bearing a tray.

"Breakfast, sir," he said, laying the plates out on the table and retreating.

Annie gazed down at the plate set before her. There was a piece of fish—haddock, perhaps—a biscuit that looked rather hard, a few olives, and an orange. It was far from a royal banquet, but Annie had anticipated much worse. They'd even provided her with a knife and fork, the latter of which she hadn't known pirates were even aware of.

Giving her a knife seemed dangerous, but Benjamin didn't look the least bit concerned.

"No need to stand on ceremony," he remarked, pushing his chair back and crossing the room to one of the chests. He bent down and removed a bottle of some unknown, dark-colored liquid.

He resumed his seat at the table, pulling the cork out of the bottle and taking a swig of it. She noticed he still wore his black leather gloves and thought it odd he hadn't removed them.

"What is that?" she asked, nodding to the bottle as she stabbed her fork into one of the olives.

"Rum," he replied. "Want some? If not, I'm sure we have some claret around here somewhere, if that's more to your liking."

"No, thank you," she said primly, nibbling at the olive. "Isn't it a bit early for that?"

"It's never too early for a drink, Princess."

She froze with the olive halfway to her mouth. Slowly, she lowered the fork, resting it on the edge of her plate. "What did you call me?"

She must have heard wrong. She must have.

"I called you 'Princess'," Benjamin said, popping one of the orange slices into his mouth. "Or would 'Your Highness' be more appropriate?"

"How did you know?" she demanded.

"I've known from the moment you came aboard." His lips twisted into a mocking smile. "A little bird told me."

"Fine. Keep your secrets."

She leaned back in her chair, trying to assume an air of nonchalance, but her heart was pounding. He knew. Trying to keep the fear out of her voice, she asked the question that frightened her the most. "What do you intend to do with me now that you've kidnapped me?"

He rolled his eyes. "I didn't kidnap you. I rescued you."

"Oh, yes, just like you've rescued the other woman on board that I saw."

"What, do you think I just sail around, kidnapping women for my own amusement?"

"I don't know what to think," she retorted, slicing into her fish with the knife and fork so she wouldn't have to look at him. "But I wouldn't put anything past a pirate."

"Lorelei, the woman you saw, is a friend of my aunt, Calida, who is also on board. I've known them my entire life and you can ask them yourself if you're still not satisfied." He waited until she met his gaze before adding, "I only wanted to know who you were so I'd know where to take you. I don't intend to keep you here any longer than necessary, princess, contrary to whatever you may believe. I think that arrangement will be to your liking."

Annie stared at him, chewing her fish slowly. It surprisingly wasn't bad, but she wasn't touching the biscuit. "So you'll take me back to Alara?" she asked softly.

He grimaced. "I'd like to, understand. I would if I could. But as a pirate, I can't exactly waltz into the Alaran harbor and drop anchor, can I?"

"What about the beaches?"

"I can't do that either. I'd have to sail too far into Alaran waters in order to even reach one that was relatively secluded."

"Well that didn't stop you from sailing in Alaran waters before." She sat back in her chair, crossing her arms, feeling a trace of smugness at the surprise that flickered across his face. "You were in the northern shipping lane. I saw you from one of the observation towers."

"Did you?" Benjamin said, sounding unimpressed. "There's a world of difference between being in the northern shipping lane and doing what you suggest. Besides, I was there looking for Alaran merchantmen to waylay so there was something to make the risk worthwhile. Contrary to popular belief, there is a limit even to what *I* can do."

"Actually, I don't find that hard to believe at all," Annie retorted. "So if you're not going to take me back to Alara, what are you going to do?"

From the look on his face, she could well imagine that he was tempted to throw her over the side as a means to be rid of her.

Perhaps it wasn't wise to antagonize someone who had the power to see to it that she disappeared and was never heard from again, but Annie couldn't help it. This was the enemy, seated across from her. A pirate. One who preyed on innocent vessels and robbed them for all they were worth. One who was to blame for her people starving to death.

"I'm taking you back to Daera."

"*Back to Daera?*" Annie exclaimed, hardly daring to believe her luck.

If she were returned home, she could plead her case to Varrian. She would explain to him how vile Kain had turned out to be. Surely after he heard that, he would call the alliance off and would refuse to return her to Alara.

That was all she had wanted, after all. Was that not how she came to be in this regrettable position?

She could return to her laboratory and her plants, her experiments. She could finally achieve the breakthrough she'd been working toward. She could still save her people. They would find another way.

On the other hand, what would she tell him to explain her presence when she was supposed to be in Alara? Would he be angry with her for running away? At squandering the opportunity she—no, they all—had been given? Surely, once she explained about Kain, he would understand.

"What am I supposed to tell my brother?" she murmured, not really speaking to Benjamin, but he reacted anyway.

"Your brother?"

"The king! I'll need to explain how I came to arrive in Daera and I can hardly tell him I stowed away on Berchmoore's ship!" Her face heated at the thought of it.

Benjamin raised one eyebrow. They were brown, not golden like his hair. "How should I know? You're a clever girl. You'll think of something."

"Like *what?*" she demanded, more to annoy him further than because she expected a real answer.

Benjamin rolled his eyes, throwing his hands up. "I don't *know.* Tell him you were kidnapped by pirates and they threw you overboard, but you were picked up by a passing merchantman and delivered safely to shore."

Annie glared at him. Was he messing with her or did he really expect Varrian to believe that? "Now you're just making fun of me. Having a laugh at my expense."

"I wish I found this amusing," he muttered, getting to his feet. "As it is, I have to take Calida and Lorelei back to Daera anyway. We should arrive within another two days or so, but until then, princess, I'm afraid we're stuck with each other's company."

"Stop calling me 'princess'."

"That is what you are, is it not?"

"I have a name," she muttered, feeling very petulant.

"Do you?" he challenged, crossing his arms. "I don't know it."

"It's Annabelle, but I prefer Annie."

She half-expected him to mock her further, but instead, he nodded thoughtfully. "All right, Annie. My name you already know, but I go by Ben."

Was it just her imagination, or did he seem marginally less hostile than before? She watched him leave, wondering how she had come to be on a first name basis with a pirate.

* * *

The *Black Dagger* limped back into Alara's port like a wounded dog with its tail tucked between its legs, the hole that had been blown into the stern on full display. What wasn't so visible was the empty hold below, once stuffed with cargo, now pitifully sparse.

Berchmoore was confident the ship's carpenter could repair the damage, of course. That was what the man was paid for, after all. But it would take some time, valuable time that he could have been using to hunt Knight down and make good on the threat he'd promised.

But as it was, being a legal privateer meant being bound by certain rules. He needed to report to Rodek and inform him what had transpired. He wasn't looking forward to admitting that the princess had been on board his ship. He'd tell the truth, of course, but Berchmoore wasn't convinced it would be believed.

But the fact that Knight had taken the princess would undoubtedly be of interest to Rodek and the crown. It gave them the perfect reason for hunting him down and Berchmoore intended to be in on it.

He met Rodek in one of the small meeting rooms at the palace, near the entrance. He'd never ventured very far inside, but to be at the castle at all was a feat most people could only dream of.

The room, the only part of the interior he'd ever seen, had always struck him as gaudy. The wallpaper was a bright red and every spare inch seemed stuffed to the gills with clutter. The chairs were low, with short legs, and what little padding they had did nothing to give them a more comfortable appearance.

Red velvet fabric was draped over the hearth and elaborate rugs covered the cool stone floor. A large, heavy clock sat upon the mantel. Every bit of shelving was covered in vases, busts, or candlesticks, all of it appearing extremely fragile.

It made Berchmoore uncomfortable, feeling like he had to watch his step every time he set foot in here. There was no place for such frippery on a ship. He was a man who could appreciate practicality and he didn't see much of it here.

Rodek nodded curtly to him. "Berchmoore. You were due to report in two days ago. I trust you have a good reason for your tardiness."

Berchmoore bowed slightly. "I do. I'm sorry to report that my ship was attacked by pirates and is in need of some repair." He wasn't concerned about the cost, where he once would have been. As a legal privateer in the employ of Alara, the kingdom would foot the bill. "The pirates, unfortunately, escaped."

Rodek's lips turned down. Nothing Berchmoore said was pleasing him any. "Most unfortunate."

Berchmoore fingered the hat in his hands. "I do 'ave some information that I think will be of great interest to the crown. The princess was on board my ship—"

"Why would the princess be on *your* ship?" Rodek thundered.

Berchmoore held up one placating hand. "'Ear me out. She stowed away in one of the crates that was to be loaded onto the ship. My crew didn't realize it until it was too late and there she was. What she was doing 'iding in a crate, I don't know, but she claimed to be the princess and when I 'eard she was missing, I believed 'er."

Rodek tapped his fingers on his arm. "Go on."

"I was on my way back to Alara once I realized who she was, to return 'er safe and sound to the palace. Only as I said, I was attacked by those pirates and they took 'er."

"Who are these pirates?"

"Knight, the captain's name is. Benjamin Knight." Berchmoore practically spat the words out. He'd never get used to hearing the title 'captain' before Knight's name where it should have belonged to him and him alone. "Ship's called the *Phoenix*, sir. Can't mistake 'er. Large frigate, she is. Blood-red sails. Used to be one of the Alaran navy, if memory serves me."

"Is that so?" Rodek said, voice dangerously low. "Well, if what you say is to be believed and the princess is indeed on board, Berchmoore, I think you'd better come with me. The queen should hear of this."

* * *

"There's still no word on the princess, Your Majesty."

The messenger's words did not please queen Thalia. She paced back and forth in front of him, her footsteps echoing in the large space that was the throne room. Tall, thin windows stretched up toward the vaulted ceiling, behind two thrones. Each was seated on a raised dais, glittering red and gold. The floor was marble, shimmering blue and gold if the light struck it a certain way.

"She's been missing for nearly two days!" Thalia exclaimed. "Where could she have gone? She can't have just disappeared into thin air!"

The messenger had no answer for her, of course, and she dismissed him with an angry flick of the hand.

The news of the princess's disappearance had not been the only ill tidings to reach her ears. There had been talk of a riot in the streets, her own son the instigator. *The fool.*

With the princess having vanished, her hopes of one day having a gifted witch in the family now hung in the balance. She'd dispatched soldiers to scour the entire kingdom, far and wide, but thus far their efforts had proven fruitless.

She whirled around as the throne room door burst open to see a familiar figure clad in black, his cloak trailing behind him as he strode into the room. *Mordred.* There was a bandage around one of his thighs and he walked with a bit of a limp.

Thalia felt a surge of hope, tinged with excitement. Mordred would only return to the kingdom if he had news and she dared to let herself dream that perhaps her sister had been dealt with at last.

He walked up to her, kneeling with difficulty, head lowered. "Your Majesty."

"Mordred," Thalia greeted him with the tone one would take with an old friend. "What news have you for me? Surely you've come to tell me that my sister is no more, have you not?"

Mordred straightened. He was taller than her, but only by a few inches. How different he looked now than when she'd first met him.

He had been at the monastery as a child, with her and Calida. He'd been a poor student at best; the elders certainly never expected him to become a great witch. He'd been impatient, impetuous and determined to prove them wrong.

"I did find her," he replied. "Along with Daniel, whom I managed to kill. I trailed Calida and Lorelei to the beach, but they fled on board a pirate ship."

Thalia frowned. "A pirate ship? Then why are you here instead of hunting them down?"

"Because there is a witch on board."

"Not Calida or Lorelei, surely. Their earth witch powers are of no use when they're not on land."

"No, Your Majesty. Someone else. One of the crew, perhaps. Whoever it is, they are a sky witch. I sent my rats out into the water after them and a large wave was suddenly summoned to crush them."

Thalia felt a chill shoot through her as though a cold draft were seeping through one of the windows. *A sky witch.* The rarer of the two types and, in her opinion, the most powerful.

Powerful enough to challenge her, perhaps.

"What ship was this?" she whispered.

"I didn't get a good look at it. It was dark and they were too far out. But it looked like, during one of the lightning strikes, it had red sails."

The throne room door opened once more and Rodek strode in, followed by another man. "Your Majesty. May I present Captain Berchmoore, one of your privateers. He has some information I'm sure you'll want to hear."

"Indeed?" Thalia listened as Berchmoore explained about the princess and the pirates that had taken her.

"It was Knight and the *Phoenix*, Your Majesty. Should be easy enough to track them down, on account of the red sails. Can't miss it."

"Red sails, you say?" Thalia shared a glance with Mordred. "And this pirate has the princess?"

"'E did when I last saw 'im."

The same pirate ship that had helped Calida and Lorelei escape had also kidnapped the princess. And somewhere on that ship, there was a sky witch.

"Do you know this man, Berchmoore? This pirate captain?"

"More of a lad than a man," the privateer murmured. "But yes, I've 'ad some dealings with 'im in the past."

"Does he have any witches on his crew?"

"I wouldn't know about that, Your Majesty. But 'e does 'ave this sharpshooter. A woman. They say she can 'it a man right between the eyes from five 'undred yards out. Uncanny, if you ask me."

"What about passengers? Does he make a habit of having them on board?"

"Knight? No. 'Tis a pirate ship, not a ferry. Least I didn't see any when 'e boarded us."

Which meant that either Calida and Lorelei had been hidden somewhere or they'd already been taken and dropped off elsewhere. Either was possible.

"The witch could have been a passenger on board as easily as a member of the crew, in which case, they could already have been set down somewhere," Thalia mused. "Either way, we'll need this captain alive to tell us who they were and, if indeed there was a passenger on board, where they were taken."

"I suppose they could still be on board," Rodek remarked. "But perhaps that's asking too much of luck."

"Regardless," Thalia said briskly. "If the princess is on board, we must find her and bring her back. Her safety is paramount. I want this *Phoenix* tracked down and the captain brought in *alive*, do you understand? Berchmoore, since you have personal experience with this pirate, I will appoint the task to you. Mordred and Rodek will assist you."

Berchmoore bowed low. "With pleasure, Your Majesty. Though I doubt you'll take Knight alive. Not that one."

Thalia glanced at Mordred. "We'll see about that. You have your orders. You're dismissed."

It was a pity, she thought as they left, that Mordred's powers would be of no use if they confronted the sky witch at sea. But she hadn't tasked him with hunting down other witches for no reason. He was nothing if not resourceful. After all, he'd managed to find a way at the monastery all those years ago.

Since she herself had purposefully concealed her own power, the other students believed the lie that she had none and that had made her a target for their cruelty. But Mordred had stood up for her, along with Calida, and he had quickly been assimilated into their little group.

She remembered vividly one day when the meaner students, those who had a vicious streak in them, had been particularly nasty. One of them had pushed Thalia down and her fox, Jade, had tried to come to her defense, only to be savagely kicked aside for her trouble.

The attack on her familiar angered Thalia worse than anything they'd ever done to her personally. It was the closest she'd ever come to unleashing her power on them. The temptation to try and call down lightning was nearly too great to resist.

Fortunately, she didn't have to. Mordred's rat had gone on the offensive, making good work of its nasty little teeth. And then Horus had come swooping down to rake the child with his talons.

Mordred and Calida hadn't had to lift a finger that day.

Thalia recalled the three of them going to sit by the river afterward. "You need to be careful," she'd told Calida. "The elders could have him taken away." She nodded to where Horus sat perched by the other familiars.

It wasn't the first time her sister had ordered the hawk to attack someone.

But her sister had merely shrugged. "I'm not worried."

As it was, such a thing never came to pass and Thalia had continued to train her powers in secret, with Mordred and Calida covering for her. Their little group came to be inseparable at the monastery.

But it wasn't to be.

How different things are now, Thalia thought to herself.

CHAPTER 18

Annie remained in the cabin for the rest of the day, brooding over what Ben had said. Two more days to reach Daera? That wasn't possible. Berchmoore had been heading toward Alara when the *Phoenix* had caught up to them. It took a week's time, give or take depending on the weather, to traverse the Atlas Sea from one kingdom to the other. To make the journey in a grand total of three days was simply not possible.

And yet, if she only had to suffer her current circumstances for another two days, Annie supposed she could manage that. Even a week, if need be. Ben did not set foot in the cabin again, leaving her completely alone, much to her surprise.

By the end of the second day, however, she had nearly gone out of her mind with boredom. The lingering nausea, courtesy of the ship's rolling motion, nearly sent her racing out onto the deck, darting for the rail. But she had vowed to remain inside, wanting to stay as far away from the brigands as possible, not having forgotten the reception she'd received on Berchmoore's ship.

It was stuffy inside the cabin and dreadfully dull. Annie had nothing with which to occupy her time, other than sleeping, and one could only do so much of that.

At last, with one full day of travel to go, if Ben were to be believed, Annie opened the cabin door and peeked out, a wave of fresh air striking her in the face.

Darkness had fallen, but lanterns had been lit at various locations around the ship, giving off enough light to see by. The sky was clear, the moonlight further illuminating her surroundings.

Above her head, the canvas stretched taut with the force of a strong tailwind, urging the ship on. The speed was welcome—the sooner she was back in Daera the better—but it did nothing for her stomach.

Letting out a moan, Annie hurried to the side, slumping against the rail, shutting her eyes, waiting for the wave of nausea to pass.

"It might be a bit hard now, but you should focus on the horizon."

Her eyes snapped open. Ben had joined her at the rail. His feathered hat was gone, but he still wore the scarlet coat. Her eyes flicked to the small gold hoop in his left earlobe as it caught the light.

She turned to face forward once more. There was just enough light still staining the edge of the sky, allowing her to make out the horizon in the distance. She didn't want his help, didn't want to listen to him, to be indebted to him in any way, or even for him to be right, but as another wave of seasickness hit, Annie was willing to do anything for a bit of relief.

And so she fixed her gaze on the horizon.

Slowly, the sky darkened further and the horizon faded from view. Though she hated to admit it, the trick had worked and she felt better than before.

She expected Ben to gloat, but he didn't. He hadn't said another word and seemed to have all but forgotten her existence. He was leaning with his arms propped against the railing, eyes closed, the breeze stirring through his hair.

He didn't seem to have a care in the world and certainly didn't look as though his sins weighed the least bit on his mind.

She swallowed, not wanting to forget what he was. She doubted she was even capable of that. Had he killed people before? Surely he must have. That's what pirates did.

Still…looking around, there was nothing that distinguished this ship from the one that had brought her to Alara.

Further down, toward the bow, snatches of a fiddle drifted on the wind. She could just make out the murmur of a voice, but not the words being sung.

Ben opened his eyes and turned toward the sound. "You should join us, princess."

Annie backed away. "No, thank you. I think I'll turn in for the night."

He shrugged. "Your loss."

Leaving her at the rail, he moved toward the light and the sound. Annie remained where she was, until, compelled by curiosity, she found herself edging closer. She stopped nearby, careful to stay beyond the lamplight, and took in the scene.

A small group of the crew had gathered. Some stood, others sat on crates or barrels. One played the fiddle she had heard, in a fast, jaunty tune she didn't recognize. The others clapped in time or stomped their feet, belting out the words to a shanty that was equally unfamiliar to her.

They were more eager than skillful, slightly off-key, and Annie glanced at the bottles some of them held, the liquid sloshing within. But the joy was real enough.

As she watched, Ben approached the only other woman present, her dark skin dappled with lighter patches. He must have asked her to dance because the next thing she knew, they had moved to the middle of the deck, the crew hollering and whistling at them. The two linked arms and spun to the rhythm of the song. They moved with more enthusiasm than grace, laughing, neither taking themselves seriously.

Annie's heart fluttered in her chest, conflicting emotions warring within. Ben was quite handsome when he smiled, in a devilish sort of way. But then, Kain had been handsome, too, and she couldn't forget how that had turned out.

But their carefree joy was infectious. Annie found herself wishing she could shrug off her own cares, if only for a moment, and join them. It was incongruous with everything she knew, everything she'd been told. These fearsome pirates—looking anything but—laughing, cavorting, having fun.

Across the deck, Ben glanced up, their gazes meeting. He flashed her a grin, as though challenging her to give in to that temptation and join in.

The lightness she had felt only a moment ago vanished. Annie turned and made her way back to the cabin beneath the helm, the sound of the fiddle following her.

* * *

True to Ben's word, it took the *Phoenix* a total of three days to reach Daera, covering the distance far quicker than any other ship would have been able to—but not nearly fast enough for his liking. The sooner they could set the princess on board, the better. He knew she didn't want to remain a second longer than she had to and he wholeheartedly agreed.

For the most part, they'd avoided each other, her staying in the cabin and he busying himself with various things that needed to be seen to. So it was less her acerbic personality that made him eager for her to be gone, and more that he just wanted the use of his cabin back.

The *Phoenix* dropped anchor offshore, where she usually did to drop-off supplies. Since they had taken all of Berchmoore's, Ben didn't see why they shouldn't put them to shore along with Calida, Lorelei and the princess. The order to bring the supplies up from the hold was given and they were loaded into the longboats as so many times before.

"What are all these for?" Annie asked, gesturing at the supplies around her.

"You'll see," was all Ben said in reply.

It took several trips to bring it all ashore, with Annie, Lorelei and Calida taking up part of the room on the initial trip. This wasn't a scheduled visit, so there were no villagers already assembled, waiting. Lorelei volunteered to go inform them and she set off on foot.

Ben took the opportunity to go over to his aunt. "Are you sure about this?"

"Don't worry," she replied. "Mordred's long gone."

Ben had to admit that Mordred would have little reason to remain in Daera looking for them since he had seen them leave. The witch-hunter had no way of knowing where Ben might drop the two women off. They could be anywhere for all he knew.

Still, he wasn't convinced it was the wisest decision. But this was his aunt's home, had been his home, and he could understand why she wouldn't want to leave it.

Annie stood off to one side, arms crossed as though she were cold. A chill breeze was coming off the sea, so very unlike the warm Alaran waters and, as always, the sky threatened rain.

His instinct was to offer her the use of his coat for the time being, but he resisted the urge. She'd probably only scoff at him and say it needed a good washing before she'd ever let it anywhere near her. He could just imagine her voice in his head telling him that red was *so* not her color.

He snorted in a mixture of amusement and disgust, relieved when Lorelei returned, bringing the townspeople with her. Annie watched as they led their few horses and carts onto the beach and the supplies were slowly loaded on.

Her eyes were wide as if she couldn't believe what she was seeing. "What are you doing?"

Ben looked at her, debating what to say and settled on the truth, simple as it was. "Helping."

She was no fool. She saw how familiar the people seemed with the task, added to the fact that they had come when Lorelei asked, and said, "This isn't the first time you've done this, is it?"

He had to admit she was perceptive. He shook his head.

She continued to watch the proceedings and something about her expression softened. "You didn't tell me that you did this."

"Would you have believed me if I had?" he asked quietly.

Suddenly, Annie seemed very interested in the sand beneath her feet. She didn't grace his question with an answer, but the meaning was clear. "Why do you do it? What's in it for you?"

He put his hands in his pockets. "I grew up in this kingdom. It's sad to see what it's become. I wanted to help, if I could. Besides, some of this stuff is theirs. I'm just seeing it gets to where it belongs."

She looked at him then, eyes narrowed. "What do you mean?"

"Come here. There's something I want you to see." He walked over to where one of the larger barrels was still standing, waiting for its turn to be loaded onto a cart and carried away. He rapped on the lid with one gloved knuckle. "Look familiar?"

Annie didn't say anything. She didn't have to. They both recognized the rampant white horse of Daera painted on the lid.

"What's in it?" she finally asked.

Ben pried the lid off to reveal a container full of salted pork. It wasn't the most delicious or filling meal to ever exist, but to a starving kingdom, it was priceless.

He put the lid back on and hit it with his fist so it lay flat. "We took it off Berchmoore's ship if you'll recall. It's not the first time I've encountered Daeran goods where they don't belong."

Annie looked like she was still trying to make sense of it. "But…what does it mean? Why would Berchmoore have this?"

Ben frowned. "There are two possibilities. One is that he took it from a pirate who had robbed a Daeran ship, which I find unlikely. Or, he took it from a Daeran ship himself."

"But he's an Alaran privateer!"

He gave her a look. "A privateer is nothing but a legal pirate. I know Berchmoore, princess. Once a pirate…" *Always a pirate.*

"But you said it yourself! He could have taken it from an actual pirate."

"He could have, but as I said, it's unlikely."

"I would think it's very likely! We've been dealing with pirate attacks for years. That's why so few of our supply shipments come through. That's why Alara's hired privateers in the first place."

He stared at her, tempted to say more. What he knew, and what he only suspected. But she wouldn't believe him and why would she? The sea might be his world, but the kingdom was hers and there was no reason for her to believe the word of a man she viewed as nothing more than a criminal.

"I just thought you should know," he muttered.

Her shoulders had slumped and she remained silent as the rest of the supplies were loaded and carted off. Duty done, it was time for the *Phoenix* to be off. It didn't do to linger.

Ben took a deep breath and turned to Annie once more. "Well, princess, this is where I leave you. Calida and Lorelei will help you from here. With any amount of luck, we'll never see each other again."

But his words lacked the brutal sincerity they might have had that first day.

* * *

Annie didn't hang around to watch until the ship was out of sight. She could make her own way back to the palace.

Borrowing a horse from one of the villagers, promising to return it and to see to it that they were handsomely compensated for their efforts, she rode hard for the castle in the distance.

Her mind was a whirlwind and she felt slightly numb inside, trying to make sense of all that had happened and she had learned, and in the end comprehending none of it.

For one thing, she hadn't expected this moment to ever be truly real. There had been some part of her that doubted the pirates' intentions, that they would ever return her home at all. But they had and that was far from the most surprising thing about them.

They were helping her people. All this time she had spent locked away, experimenting with her plants and ultimately getting nowhere, forced to accept an arranged marriage in another kingdom to save her people and here they were—pirates!—actually accomplishing something.

To those people on the beach, their efforts weren't nothing. How many lives had they saved? They had made more of an impact, done more for her people, than she ever had, though not for lack of trying.

Shame heated her face at the thought of how harshly she had judged them. And yet, they were still pirates. Were they not partially to blame for the famine in the first place, or at least how bad it had become, due to the lack of aid making it to Daeran shores?

Ben's insinuations disturbed her most of all. If Alaran privateers were attacking Daeran ships that traveled to the southern kingdom for aid, what did that mean? The implications were ugly, hideous even, and Annie did not want to entertain the thought a moment longer.

But once planted, the seed of doubt was not easily uprooted.

Alaran ships often arrived with few supplies on board— if they arrived at all—claiming the rest were taken in pirate raids. When Varrian sent his own ships, they told similar tales, of being attacked along the way and divested of their provisions.

What if they weren't pirates at all, but Alaran privateers?

Why would Alara do such a thing? Why would they pay their own privateers to attack their own ships—or that of their allies—taking away much-needed aid?

It didn't make sense. Any of it.

Annie shook her head. She would tell Varrian her concerns. He would know what to do.

The palace guards at the gate ushered her inside with a sense of urgency, an attendant rushing off to inform her brother that she'd been found.

Her heart rose in her throat. Of course he'd be frantic, if word had been sent from Alara that she'd gone missing. She hadn't spared a thought as to how he would be affected by this.

When she finally laid eyes on her brother, Varrian was more disheveled than she'd ever seen him. His dark brown hair looked as though he'd run his hands through it repeatedly, making it progressively worse each time. There were dark circles beneath his eyes and his skin looked pale.

"Annie," he exclaimed, taking a step toward her. She thought for a moment he might comment on *her* appearance. She hadn't had time to freshen up before meeting him. But he said nothing. "I received word from Alara that you'd gone missing and now here you are. What are you doing here? *How* did you get here? What on earth happened?"

She sighed. *What, indeed.* She hadn't thought of an excuse he likely would believe and decided instead to tell the truth, starting with the ride with Kain that had gone so horrifically wrong, to stowing away on Berchmoore's ship, to being *rescued* by pirates and dropped off in Daera once more.

Varrian stared at her. "Which of the bastards hit you?"

Unconsciously, Annie reached up to touch her cheek. The bruise must have faded a bit by now, likely turning a nice shade of yellow. With everything else that had happened, she'd all but forgotten that one of Berchmoore's men had struck her.

"Funnily enough, the bruise was the privateers' fault. This privateer—Berchmoore, his name is—he ran from the pirates. And there's something else. The pirates took all his supplies and among them, they found Daeran provisions. The pirate captain claimed Berchmoore has been preying upon Daeran ships."

Her brother waved a hand dismissively. "Unlikely if he's an Alaran privateer. More likely, this man—Berchmoore, you said his name was?—far more likely he took them from the pirates who took them from us. *Or,* for all you know, the pirate could be lying about where the supplies came from. Perhaps he had them all along. You can't trust that sort."

But Annie didn't think so. Why would Ben rob a Daeran vessel of its cargo only to give it back to the people, as she'd seen him do on the beach? Unless he believed that was the only way its arrival could be guaranteed, if he took it before another pirate did.

Still, his own obvious dislike of Berchmoore could be coloring his view of the situation. Perhaps Berchmoore really had taken it from another pirate, instead of attacking Daeran ships as Ben seemed to think he was.

Suddenly, when faced with Varrian's cool rationality, she felt a fool for believing Ben, even for a moment. She didn't know him and what she did know of him was no reason to think him trustworthy.

Wasn't the fact that he could be charming when he wanted only further proof of how deceptive he could be?

And like a fool, she'd fallen for it.

"Maybe you're right," she said softly. "But there's something…strange going on in that kingdom, Varrian." She thought of Kain's odd behavior, the argument she'd overheard him having with the queen, the king's supposed memory loss, and the fact that Alara had hired *pirates* to solve the piracy epidemic.

Varrian looked at her sharply. "What do you mean 'strange'?"

In the end, though, when taken altogether, none of those things that bothered her pointed to anything specific. "I don't know…just a feeling I got."

"A feeling is no use. I need something more definite if I am to act." He sighed. "No doubt you're tired, Annabelle, after your ordeal. You'll be wanting rest and a hot bath. I'll send word to Alara that you're safe and sound and arrange for your trip back on the first available ship."

"*What?*" Annie cried. Surely she hadn't heard right. Surely he wouldn't send her back. Not after everything she had just told him. "Did you not hear what I said? I can't go back. You know what kind of person Kain really is. We have other options. We don't have to accept this marriage proposal. I can stay here in Daera, where I belong, where I can do more good, and continue working on my experiments. Please, Varrian. All I need is one breakthrough. I'm really close, I can feel it. I can do it, I know I can. Please!"

She was rambling now, she knew, the words unable to tumble out fast enough, tripping over each other in her desperate haste to make him understand.

She felt frantic, her heart in her throat threatening to choke her. He would understand. He had to. She would make him understand. She couldn't go back. She wouldn't.

Varrian flinched as though she'd physically struck him. "I wish there were another way. Truly, I do. If there were any other way, I would take it. But we don't have a choice. We already agreed to the alliance. To back out now would offend Alara greatly. We can't risk—"

"What?" Annie demanded, giving voice to the greatest threat she could think of. "Open war? Do you really think it would come to that?"

Alara would declare war over this?

"I don't know! But I don't intend to risk it. We're in no position to fight a war, much less one with Alara. We can't risk alienating the only ally we have. Like it or not—and believe me I don't—we need Alara's aid. It's the only thing keeping us all from starvation!"

"Oh, skies," Annie choked out, turning away. How had an already bad situation become so much worse?

She had viewed returning to Daera with a sense of eagerness. Hope, even. To return home, where she belonged, and everything was familiar. She'd been certain that Varrian would understand, that she would never have to see Kain again.

And now those hopes had been dashed upon the rocks, broken to pieces like a ship battered mercilessly by the power of the sea, unstoppable and implacable.

She was that ship, helpless to do anything to prevent or change the wave that fate had brought down upon her, sweeping her away.

Varrian let out a long-suffering sigh. "I'm not asking you to love Kain. I'm not even asking you to like him. But I am asking you to marry him. Most marriages are unions of convenience, nothing more. If Alara had a princess, I would offer my hand instead of yours. You know that. If there were another way, I would take it. But there is no other way."

CHAPTER 19

Your Majesty, as I'm sure you'll understand, King Varrian is quite concerned about the state of the famine. Very few Alaran supply ships have reached Daeran shores, and when they do, they have very few supplies on board."

Thalia turned to face Aquillus, the Daeran advisor sent on behalf of the king to negotiate for aid. He looked tired, his green eyes dull, as one without much hope. Clearly, something weighed heavily on his mind and Thalia suspected it was more than just the famine of late.

They were gathered in the throne room; the light filtering through the windows was gray—one of the few days in Alara that wasn't completely sunny. The sky had been overcast all day, as if an omen. The king sat on one of the thrones behind Thalia. She'd been forced to have him present for the discussion. One must keep up appearances, after all.

She summoned a token smile, meant to put the advisor at ease. "Of course I understand the king's concern, but I assure you, we're doing all we can. Unfortunately, the pirates are still a threat, but we're working to eliminate them."

Behind her, the king snorted. "I told you it was a bad idea to hire those privateers. Little good they've done."

Thalia shot him a glare. "Once the seas are safe, our supply ships can reach Daera without fear. To that end, I think we have a mutual goal."

Aquillus bowed his head. "Indeed, Your Highness."

A pounding sounded on the throne room door, reverberating around the chamber like a death knoll. "Enter," Thalia called, grateful for the interruption.

A livery-clad servant strolled in, bowing to her. "Your Majesty, one of the ravens has just arrived. We've received word from Daera. The princess has been found. She is safe at the castle with her brother and will be returning to Alara as soon as possible."

Aquillus let out a breath. "At last!"

Well, Thalia thought, *finally, some good news.* She dismissed the servant with a wave of her hand. The man bowed again and retreated, nearly colliding with Kain as the prince burst into the room.

Thalia frowned at the sight of him. He'd gone out for an early morning hunt with some of the noblemen's sons and she hadn't expected him back until the afternoon at least.

"You'll never guess what happened," Kain was babbling as he strode into the room, completely oblivious of what had just transpired. "William brought down that stag we've been trailing for weeks. You should have seen the size of it! The antlers alone—"

"*Wonderful,* dear," Thalia said, cutting across him. "We've just received excellent news. No doubt you'll be most pleased to hear that Princess Annabelle has been found safe and sound in Daera. I fully expect her return within the week."

Kain's face was a blank mask that somehow failed to convey pleasure. "Oh," he said flatly. "Good."

"I'll have to see to the wedding preparations, of course. I think sufficient time has passed to allow Her Highness to settle in."

"Yes…" Kain said. "Only, I'm not entirely sure she's suitable. I mean, she ran off and was kidnapped by pirates. Hardly appropriate behavior."

"*You* were with her," Thalia pointed out.

He shrugged. "She was lost in the confusion."

"She likely feared for her life after you started a riot."

"A riot!" Kain cried indignantly.

"Yes. Starting a melee in the marketplace, pelting some poor peddler with his own produce. Honestly." Thalia shook her head in disgust. "Hardly proper deportment for a member of the royal family!"

"It was the peddler's fault," Kain protested. "You know how the common rabble are. He was probably hoping the crown would compensate him for produce that was too rotten to be sold anyway."

"Be that as it may," Thalia hissed, no longer certain she was grateful for the interruption to the negotiations. She was glad of any excuse or reason to put Aquillus off, but Kain's attitude nearly made her change her mind.

This wasn't the first time he'd done this. It was almost as though he did it purposely to get on her nerves.

"You might want to consider showing a bit more decorum when the princess returns. She's going to be your future wife, after all."

"I didn't ask for a wife!" Kain exploded.

"As prince, it is your duty—"

"I didn't ask to be prince!"

"Well you've certainly asked for everything else since! It's time for you to grow up and start acting more responsible. You're going to rule this kingdom one day. Act like it!"

Kain glanced over her shoulder, looking to his father as though for support. When none was forthcoming, he let out a huff and turned on his heel, stomping back out the way he'd come.

Thalia let him go.

She sighed, turning back to Aquillus. "My apologies. He's at a very trying age. Do you have children?"

"No, Your Majesty."

Consider yourself lucky.

She was under no illusion as to what her son was: a spoiled, self-centered brat. But none of that would matter if he'd only shown a glimmer of the same power that flowed through her veins.

Thalia was relieved when the meeting concluded and she could retire to the privacy of her own chambers. She had much to think about.

If the pirates had dropped Annabelle off in Daera, why not Calida and Lorelei as well? But for the moment, her sister was the least of Thalia's worries. Mordred's report that a sky witch had been on board that pirate ship alarmed her far more.

Thalia hadn't believed there to be any sky witches left living. They'd all been killed, systematically hunted down and eliminated, starting with the ones at the monastery the day it was destroyed. It was nothing but a ruin now, deep within the Witch Wood, said to be haunted by the spirits of the witches murdered there.

But it was possible that one might have survived—or been born since. And if they were in league with pirates, there was no telling where their loyalties might lie. *Hardly with you, after what you did.*

Of all the witches, a sky witch posed the biggest threat to her, one who could perhaps match her power and use it against her. They had to be killed, whoever they were.

The risk was simply too great.

* * *

Darkness had fallen by the time the *Phoenix* docked at Amberleigh's port. The buildings were aglow with warm light, lanterns lit around the dock. Ben had purposely waited until dark before entering the pirate haven. It had always been a safe place for a pirate, or at least as safe as could be expected, but being so close to Alara made him wary. It wouldn't surprise him if they tried to pin the princess's disappearance entirely on him.

Going ashore, he skipped the taverns and gaming houses, walking along the white sand, heading straight to Rosa's.

She looked surprised to see him. "Ben! What are you doing here? Haven't you heard?"

"Heard what?"

She ushered him inside her office quickly, casting a look out into the corridor as though afraid he'd been followed. It was no secret that he made a habit of visiting her; perhaps that contributed to whatever was worrying her.

Horus hopped off his shoulder to perch on the windowsill, keeping an eye out through the gauzy curtains.

Rosa shut the door and doused some of the lanterns until only a few candles remained burning. The lighting turned dim and ominous. Strange shadows were cast, giving her a grave countenance.

"Berchmoore is here," she said softly, although they were the only ones present. "Or at least, he was when I went into town earlier. Word is there's a price on your head. The Alaran navy is out looking for you."

"How much?"

"What?"

"How much are they asking for my head?"

"Five hundred ducats."

"Five hundred! I'd have expected no less than a thousand!" He put a hand to his heart, mockingly offended. "I'm wounded."

Rosa made a sound between her teeth. "Skies damn it, Ben, this is no laughing matter. Can't you take something seriously for once? What have you done to raise the ire of the Alaran royal navy? Were the crown jewels on board one of the ships you looted?"

He sighed, running a gloved finger along the wooden surface of the table. He couldn't feel its grain against his skin, one of the many things he disliked about wearing gloves. "More like the crown, in a manner of speaking. Or a member of."

"So that explains it." She sank down into one of her plush chairs, blonde ringlets bouncing. "I'd heard rumors that a pirate had kidnapped the princess. I didn't know it was you. What were you thinking?"

Ben held up a hand. "First of all, I didn't kidnap her. I rescued her from Berchmoore, who probably kidnapped her himself, although he claims otherwise. Secondly, what was I supposed to do? Leave her there with him?"

"Well he conveniently left that part out of his story. But you should weigh anchor and get out of here. If he sees your ship—"

"Aye. I'll see to it as soon as I get back."

"You should lay low for a while," she said, standing once more and taking a step closer to him. "At least until the uproar dies down."

"I can't," Ben shook his head. With Calida and Lorelei back in Daera, there was no reason not to continue their supply drops. "I have Daera to think of."

"And who will think of Daera if something happens to you?" Rosa gave him a pitying look. "How long do you think you can keep this up?"

Ben felt his jaw clench. "As long as I have to. As long as it takes."

"With the two kingdoms uniting, there won't be a need anymore. Alara has promised to aid Daera. And an entire country can do a lot more than one man." Her tone was gentle, but the words still stung. She'd wounded his pride.

He snorted. "You believe that? You know what I've seen. You know their 'aid' is a lie."

"Still," Rosa insisted. "You have to realize that with more and more pirates turning privateer, the days of piracy are numbered."

"Funny. Berchmoore said the same thing to me the other day. 'Times are changing' or something to that effect."

"He's right. What are you going to do when those times do come?"

Ben shrugged. He'd never really given the matter much thought, but it was common knowledge that pirates didn't typically live long lives. And so he'd never thought that far ahead.

"Maybe I'll go to the east. Explore different lands. Get a proper job and work for one of the merchant companies."

Rosa didn't look convinced. "You? A merchantman?"

"The sea is my place," he said firmly. It was the one thing he was certain of. "And I'll be damned if I leave it behind."

CHAPTER 20

Ben knew something was wrong the moment the docks came into view. He could see men swarming the deck of the *Phoenix*, the air filled with the sharp reports of gunfire, fire visible as charges were ignited. Shouts and cries of pain rang out. Something splashed as it fell into the water—a body being dumped over the side.

He stopped short, heart thudding in his chest, hardly believing what he was seeing. Despite an anchor watch, the *Phoenix* had still been boarded. And he could see the silhouettes of more men on the dock, attempting to climb over the railing.

Ben had little doubt as to who the men were or who had sent them. Rosa had warned him about Berchmoore. It seemed even the cover of darkness hadn't been enough to conceal his ship's identity. Ben cursed under his breath. He should have taken her around and dropped anchor in one of the coves, but he'd stupidly assumed they'd be safe here.

And now his ship was being swarmed with privateers, out for his head.

Well, he'd have to put a stop to that. He thrust out both hands, commanding the water to push against the ship's hull. No doubt the anchor was still dropped and the sails had been furled while in port, making the ship doubly harder to move than it normally would have been.

Under ideal circumstances, the sails would have been unfurled, the canvas properly set, and at least some wind already aiding him in the task of moving the vessel. Ben had never attempted something like this, but he felt a moment's satisfaction as the *Phoenix* began to pull back from the dock, cutting off the would-be boarders.

The effort left him shaking, cold sweat breaking out over his skin as though he'd suddenly taken ill. Horus tightened his grip on Ben's shoulder as he bent double, gasping, heartbeat thrumming in his ears.

"*Careful,*" the hawk warned. "*Don't overexert yourself.*"

The bird's voice sounded muffled and far away.

"A bit late for that," Ben panted, straightening.

His arms were still trembling, but he had solved the immediate problem. No more of Berchmoore's men could board his ship and the ones that had already done so could be easily picked off by the men he'd appointed on anchor watch.

Or so he hoped.

But now he faced the problem of him being trapped on shore, separated from the *Phoenix* along with any other crew members who had gone ashore—which had been the majority, including both Terrance and Sharpe.

If Sharpe had stayed on board, I bet she'd have spotted the boarders and raised the alarm before they even had a chance, he thought bitterly, but there was nothing for it now.

He needed to get word to the rest of the crew to get back to the ship and stay out of sight while doing so. The boarders who had been cut off from the *Phoenix* were now standing guard along the docks, a few of them splitting off from the main group to head further into town.

"*They're looking for you,*" Horus hissed. "*They didn't see you on deck, so they must assume you're still on shore.*"

Which I am. "Horus," Ben whispered, ducking behind the corner of one of the shorefront buildings. Here, at least, he was covered in shadow and not easily seen. "I need you to round up any of the crew who went ashore. I'll stay out of sight until we can make our move." *Whatever that might be.*

"*Aye, sir,*" the hawk replied, launching himself into the air.

All he would need to do was fly over Amberleigh, shrieking an alarm call, and the crew would make for the docks, knowing what it meant.

Provided they weren't too far into their cups already, or otherwise occupied.

Ben cursed again, angry at his own foolishness. Why had he thought this would be easy or that he'd be safe here? He thought back to his argument with Calida over the overt use of his power and how assured he'd been that no harm would ever befall him because of those very abilities.

That might yet be true, but first they needed to get out of here and the rest of his crew, skilled as they might be, had no such power to rely on to get them out of a scrape. They relied on him and he'd led them into a trap.

Footsteps crunched on sand, alerting him to the approach of one of the privateers. Ben peered around the corner and then darted back hastily. He had no choice but to move or remain there and be discovered.

Fortunately, he'd been to Amberleigh many times throughout the past twelve years and knew the place like the back of his hand. He slipped away from the building he'd been hiding by and dashed into one of the side streets.

Amberleigh was lively as always, filled with the sounds of music and laughter, but all Ben could hear was the blood rushing in his ears. He couldn't remember the last time he'd felt so vulnerable, so exposed. It was the complete opposite of the role he'd grown accustomed to—being the one everyone else feared or respected. The eagle among the rabbits.

Now he felt like the rabbit, alone and frightened, waiting for the eagle to swoop down upon him and sink its talons in. He kept glancing anxiously over his shoulder, in each direction, expecting to see one of Berchmoore's men or hear a cry as someone spotted him. But there was nothing.

Ben forced himself to take a deep breath. He'd faced dangerous situations before, far more daunting than this. He hadn't become captain for nothing. He still had his cutlass with him and a pistol. He could still put up a fight, even separated from his mighty *Phoenix*.

He took the pistol from his belt, holding it ready in one hand. A gunshot would draw unwanted attention, but he didn't want to risk light glinting off a blade and giving away his position.

"*Ben*," a voice hissed from behind.

He whirled, raising the pistol, recognizing the voice as his brain raced to catch up with the rest of him. He let out a short breath, lowering the gun. "Sharpe. Terrance."

And there they were, his faithful quartermaster and sharpshooter, joining him in the darkness. "We 'eard 'Orus and 'eaded for the docks," Terrance explained. "But Sharpe spotted the guards waiting for us."

"Who are they?" Sharpe asked. "Some of Berchmoore's?"

Ben nodded, briefly explaining what he'd seen of the boarders on deck, but leaving out the part about moving the ship back.

"'Ow are we gonna get back on board?" Terrance asked.

They couldn't afford to wait around for every single crew member that had gone ashore. It was too much to hope for that each one had heard Horus's call and heeded it. Ben loathed the idea of leaving any men behind, but they had to go.

"We can't afford to wait around. The longer we stay, the more likely that we'll be discovered." Ben turned and began leading the way back toward the docks. "We'll have to swim for it."

Terrance looked rather appalled by the idea. "But I can't swim."

"Of course you can't," Sharpe muttered.

"I know," Ben replied. He'd known that Terrance was deathly afraid of drowning since they'd been cabin boys. "But you're not going to drown. Trust me. Sharpe and I won't let that happen."

Ben trusted his ability to control the water enough to keep Terrance afloat until they could be hauled aboard the *Phoenix*, but after how tired the earlier use of his power had left him, he wasn't as confident as he would have liked.

Not that he could tell Terrance any of that.

Terrance looked marginally less terrified than he had, but they had no other choice. "Trust me," Ben repeated.

The dock would have provided a more direct route out to the ship, but it was impossible with the privateers still standing watch. Luckily, the beach offered a straight route to the water, allowing them to walk in with as little splashing as possible.

The three of them waded out until the water was too deep to stand in any longer. Most seamen were, surprisingly, poor swimmers, considering their choice of profession. The threat of being washed overboard in a storm was quite high, yet most didn't know how to swim at all.

Ben was a passable swimmer, better than most perhaps because of the type of witch he was, but layers of sodden clothing made things difficult. Perhaps he should have been less vain in his choice of attire, but he hadn't planned on going for an unforeseen swim.

Terrance thrashed around at first, making it all the harder to keep his head above the surface, but he finally settled down, realizing that he wasn't in any danger, and they made it the rest of the way to the ship without incident.

Sharpe treaded water, her stray strands of hair hanging limp around her face, as she shouted up at the ship. "Oi! Throw us a line!"

At first, Ben was afraid no one had heard, but a moment later, a line was thrown over the side, slapping down between them in the water.

"You first, Terrance," Ben instructed.

Constantly manipulating the water to keep him afloat was draining his energy and his waterlogged red coat was weighing him down. It was all he could do to keep his own chin from going under.

Terrance grabbed ahold of the rope and slowly made his way up, bracing his feet against the hull as he climbed and disappeared over the railing.

Two ropes were thrown this time and Ben grasped his gratefully. He was thoroughly exhausted and sopping wet by the time he was hauled up, thankful for the feel of solid wood beneath his boots.

He looked down at his signature coat, feeling a flicker of irritation. Saltwater wreaked havoc on clothing. He supposed he could always give it a little help in drying out in the privacy of his cabin, but not yet. There was work to be done first.

The skirmish on board had ended, but the aftermath remained. Blood stained the deck and would have to be scrubbed clean. The bodies of the boarders had been tossed overboard and only those of any crewmen who were lost remained. They would need to be sewn into their own hammocks and committed to the sea.

"Orders, sir?" one of the sailors inquired.

Ben glanced back at Amberleigh, only a short distance behind. If they left now, they would be leaving men behind, of that he was certain. But they couldn't afford to stay.

If any of the privateers had returned to Berchmoore to warn him that the *Phoenix* had pulled away from the dock, he might very well be readying his own ship to come after them and they needed to be well away by then.

"We'll aweigh," he replied, somewhat breathlessly. "Make ready all canvas. We're getting the hell out of here."

But the respite was short-lived. Within the hour, Berchmoore's ship had pulled out of Amberleigh's harbor and could be seen in the distance, steadily trailing them.

The other ship's lanterns were lit, making no attempt at stealth, confident that their quarry would not escape this time.

Ordinarily, Ben would have thought little of it. The *Phoenix* could outrun the other ship easily enough, with his assistance. But he'd exhausted himself pushing the *Phoenix* out of the harbor earlier and then trying to keep Terrance from drowning while swimming out to the ship.

He wasn't confident that the *Phoenix* could outrun the approaching vessel, at least not for long. It would require pushing his strength to the absolute limit.

Vainly, he ordered the wind to push against the sails, giving the *Phoenix* a little nudge, but it didn't last long and he nearly collapsed to the deck from the effort.

Much as he hated it, it was smarter to save his strength for any engagement that might come. He would need it.

If only there was a storm nearby that I could push into Berchmoore or that we could disappear into.

But though the night was overcast, the clouds were ordinary enough. And attempting to summon a storm would take more energy than simply outrunning the privateer.

Ben stood at the helm, glancing back toward the other ship, Horus perched on his shoulder. "What should we do?" he murmured, the words meant only for the hawk's hearing.

"He'll never stop hunting you," Horus replied softly, even though there was no need. None of the others could hear his speech. But the tone of his voice suitably fit the grave

situation. *"You may evade him, but he'll keep chasing you. He's out for blood."*

"And not likely to let us go," Ben finished. He sighed. It was a foregone conclusion, and one they were prepared for, but not ideal.

Still, they could give it a go and attempt to outrun the approaching vessel without any magical assistance.

Hours slipped by, each crew member tensely maintaining their position, as the sky began to lighten with dawn's approach. The *Black Dagger* drew ever nearer. Outrunning the privateer would be impossible.

Ben turned, Horus taking to the air, as he shouted the commands to bring the ship about. They were going to have to turn and face Berchmoore with gun ports open, guns bristling—all forty of them. "Make clear and ready for an engagement!"

Preparing a ship for engagement was a complicated task. Each member of the crew had a role to play and everyone needed to know precisely what it was, where they were expected to be, and what they were required to do.

Sharpe made her way up into the ratlines along with some of her fellow musketeers, although some would remain on deck. Just under half the crew would be manning muskets, tasked with clearing the enemy deck of men and picking off any who attempted to reach the helm or fire guns. Even with the big guns at their disposal, muskets were just as important, if not more so. A skilled crew could get off anywhere from fifty to one hundred shots per minute, sending a hail of lead down upon Berchmoore's men.

Ben felt dread trying to claw up his throat. Broadsides were devastating and not often used by pirates hoping to take a prize, due to the terrible damage it would do to the vessel. And a prize that sank to the depths was of no use at all.

But the approaching vessel was not some helpless merchantman. In a rare reversal of role, the *Phoenix* found herself the prey.

She boasted thirty-six sixteen-pound guns—sixteen on the upper deck and sixteen on the lower gun deck, with two bow chasers in the front and two stern chasers in the great cabin. There were four swivel guns, brought up from below and mounted at the rails.

Hammocks needed to be stored, shutters secured at any windows. Gun crews checked and arranged their equipment. Large tubs of water were placed on deck in case of fire. Fighting sail was set, allowing the ship to be managed by only a handful of men, while also improving visibility.

Ben stood on the quarterdeck, Terrance at the helm. Everyone had assumed their positions and the only thing left to do was wait until they were within range.

Waiting was the hardest part, Ben had found. Those tense moments, filled with dread, knowing that something was coming, but unable to see its outcome. Even if victory was won, there was no telling how many might be lost—or what state his beloved *Phoenix* would be in.

The massive behemoth came about, her movements excruciatingly slow without Ben to aid her, until she faced the way she'd come.

Through Horus's linked vision, Ben could see the repairs to Berchmoore's stern had been hasty and incomplete, no doubt hindered by the privateer's desire to get after the *Phoenix*.

"Are we in range?" Ben shouted up at Sharpe. It was still much too far for the great guns, but perhaps the muskets could be brought to bear.

Sharpe fired off an experimental shot, the report echoing loudly in the relative silence. "Negative, Captain!"

Ben stared forward as the two ships neared each other, nervous despite his faith in his ship's firepower. The only thing they could hope for was that they weren't boarded. If there was anything bloodier than a broadside engagement, it was hand-to-hand combat in close quarter spaces.

Horus returned to Ben's shoulder and then, all too soon, it began. As soon as they were within range, the musketeers on each ship started exchanging fire. One of the men in the rigging was hit and he fell to the deck below with a sickening, bone-crunching thud.

The *Dagger* had already rolled out her own guns. The orders of when to fire were up to the gunner or whoever commanded each of the gun crews. Ben could do nothing but watch helplessly as the two ships drew abreast of each other.

Not a second was wasted. The air was filled with the roar of the guns as both ships fired a broadside at each other. The *Phoenix* shuddered from the impact of the guns recoiling, the deck pitching beneath their feet. Ben kept his balance only with practice, his ears ringing. The ship shook beneath another impact as the shot from Berchmoore's ship struck home.

Dimly, over the fading roar still echoing in his ears, Ben heard the crashing of wood. Somewhere, glass shattered. Splinters flew into the air, pieces of wood tossed as though they weighed nothing, and Ben raised an arm to shield his face, feeling sharp pricks of pain as some of the shards pierced his skin.

Smoke choked the air, heavy with the tang of gunpowder, but he felt a moment's satisfaction at seeing the damage inflicted on the *Dagger*. The railing had been shattered and jagged holes now riddled the hull—unfortunately above the waterline.

A musket ball whizzed past Ben's ear and he flinched, feeling his hair stir in its wake. A second broadside volley went off, smashing into the stern. A flying piece of debris struck him on the side of the head and he went down, feeling the deck pitching beneath him.

Dazed, ears still ringing, Ben glanced up, squinting through the smoke to see Berchmoore's ship beginning to retreat. The second broadside had punctured several holes near the waterline and when the *Dagger* shifted just right, water poured in. She'd soon be listing badly; the more water that rushed in, the easier it was for more to enter the hold.

She was sinking, albeit slowly. The carpenter would be hard-pressed to repair holes of that size in time. They could man the pumps all they wanted, but it was a losing battle.

Ben allowed himself a grim smile and got to his feet, wincing. He turned and any satisfaction he may have felt vanished. He had seen the aftermath of such skirmishes before, but it never failed to become any less gruesome or horrifying to behold.

Shot from cannons hurling through the air could easily take off limbs or decapitate a man completely. A quick death, but an ugly one. Ben felt bile rise in the back of his throat and forced the feeling down. It had been a long time since he'd last been sick at the rail—not that there was much of a rail left to be sick over.

He inhaled deeply, surveying the scene before him, breathing in the smell of blood and gunpowder. Things were likely little better on the gun deck. Somewhere a man cried out in pain. The ship's surgeon would see to those who were injured and do what little he could for them.

"Captain!" He looked up to see Sharpe hurrying toward him. She appeared unharmed aside from a gash on her arm where something—likely a musket ball—had torn through her sleeve to the skin beneath. "You're injured."

Ben reached up to touch his temple and his gloved fingers came away slick with blood. He wiped it off impatiently on his trousers. "I'm fine, Sharpe. Glancing blow. Doc can see to it later. How many did we lose?"

"Ten at least, sir. Maybe more."

He nodded curtly, still feeling a bit dazed, and set off to survey the damage. The sun had fully risen, illuminating the carnage in unflinching clarity. One of the cabin walls had been hit, much to his annoyance, and one of the windows broken. Some of the rigging had been damaged, but the sails seemed unharmed—thank the skies—having been furled prior to the engagement.

The starboard side had borne much of the brunt of the attack, being the side that had faced the *Dagger*. There were several holes in the hull that would need to be repaired the next time they were in port, but nothing near the waterline. The *Phoenix* had had the advantage of the weather gauge.

But the most alarming revelation was that the rudder had been damaged in the skirmish. The *Phoenix* was a sitting duck.

Fortunately, there'd been no fires. The crew set about making a running repair of the wounded ship as best they could. To Ben's displeasure, Berchmoore's ship still drifted nearby, at a discreet distance, as though refusing to give up even as she slowly sank. He worried they might decide to try again, despite the ship's fatal injuries, and his suspicions soon proved to be correct.

As soon as the *Dagger* realized the *Phoenix* wasn't going anywhere and guessing as to why, the other ship crept closer in preparation to board. The *Phoenix*'s gun ports were still open, but there was no one to man the guns. Everyone was busy assisting the injured or seeing to repairs.

"Prepare to be boarded!" Ben shouted as the first grappling hooks were tossed over. Cursing, he ripped his cutlass free from his belt.

With their own ship sinking, Berchmoore's men must have been desperate to think they would take the *Phoenix* by force and claim her as their own. Ben didn't intend to make it easy for them.

The first wave of boarders were easily repelled by gunfire, but pistols held only a single shot. There was no time to reload with the second wave right behind them and the sound of clashing steel rang out.

The air was a cacophony of sound. Horus shrieked, diving down to rake the boarders with his talons. The deck was pure chaos, covered in writhing, struggling figures. The wooden boards were already stained scarlet in places and Ben had to take care not to slip on any of it. He gripped his cutlass tightly with gloved fingers, raising the blade as one of Berchmoore's men recognized him and came charging.

The two swords met with a clang, the impact rattling Ben's arms. They paused, staying locked together for a few moments as each exerted force against the other. Ben grit his teeth, pulling back, preparing himself for the next attack.

Horus swooped down on the man's left, screeching. In the instant the man was distracted, Ben slammed the pommel of his sword onto his head, watching as he crumpled to the deck—unconscious or dead there was no way of knowing.

A musket ball whizzed past, missing by a mile, and he whirled to see two more of Berchmoore's men. One held the musket that had fired and the other appeared to have grabbed the gun in an attempt to intervene, perhaps explaining the poor aim.

"You idiot!" the second man shouted. "You're not supposed to kill 'im!"

Aye, Ben thought grimly. *Berchmoore will want that honor for himself.*

"Sail, ho!" a voice bellowed—Sharpe's of course. She had the best eyes of any human aboard and had returned to her usual place up in the lines, firing down at the boarders.

Ben didn't have to reply with the usual, "Where away?" He looked up and saw the sighted vessel instantly.

Fear sank its claws into him, sweat breaking out on his skin, breath hitching in his chest. The ship was close enough to identify and there was no mistaking it. She was an Alaran warship, larger than the *Phoenix*, probably with a crew of some five hundred men on board.

If the *Phoenix* were to challenge a ship of that size, they would be blown to pieces, even more than they already were. Ben would never have attempted such a thing even with his ship in perfect condition. But with the rudder disabled, the decision had been taken out of their hands.

He closed his eyes. All at once, Berchmoore continuing to trail them made a horrible kind of sense. He'd known his ally was not far behind, waiting to intercept them. Or at least it had worked out that way. He could do nothing but watch as the Alaran warship pulled up on the *Phoenix*'s other side and gangplanks were dropped.

They might have been able to successfully fend off Berchmoore and his men, but now they were severely outgunned and unable to run. If they attempted to fire on the warship, she could simply respond in kind and send them all to a watery grave.

Ben looked around desperately, hoping to locate Berchmoore. Perhaps if he could overpower the privateer, he could use him to barter for their safety or escape—if the Alaran ship cared at all for him. But in all the chaos, he saw no sign of the other captain and he had little time to search. Men were streaming off the Alaran warship, choking the already crowded deck.

He was soon engaged by a large, broad-shouldered man, freshly off the Alaran ship, if his naval uniform was any indication. He was much stronger than Ben and it was all he could do to keep the man's blade away from him. He was starting to fear he might not be able to disarm the man or hold out much longer, when he was saved by a shot from somewhere. The man sank to the deck like a stone, his sword clattering to the ground.

Blinking in surprise, Ben turned to the next opponent, only to have the butt of a musket slam into his stomach. He gasped, doubling over, the point of his cutlass dipping toward the ground. He would have cried out in pain if he'd had any air left in his lungs to do so. He drew in a ragged breath through clenched teeth and glanced up to find a pistol pointed at his face.

"Drop it," the sailor ordered, nodding to the sword.

With a grimace, Ben tossed his sword to the deck below. All around him, he could see the fight going equally poorly for the rest of his crew. Terrance had been overwhelmed at the helm, Sharpe had been forced down from her vantage point above.

As quickly as it had begun, it was over, the air suddenly quiet after the din of battle.

"Well, well, well," a familiar voice crowed and Ben shut his eyes as Berchmoore strode up to him, looking for all the world like the cat that got the cream. "I told you one day that your luck would run out, Knight. You just didn't listen."

"Now you show yourself," Ben muttered. "If you're gonna kill me, then kill me. But don't stand here talking my ear off."

"Sadly, I'm not being paid to kill you," Berchmoore replied, looking truly upset by the fact.

"Is this the captain?" a second man asked, joining Berchmoore.

Ben didn't recognize him, but assumed he must have been the commander of the Alaran warship. He had an air of authority about him. His dark brown hair was meticulously styled and his green eyes were hard.

But it was the man who accompanied the newcomer that held Ben's attention. Though he had only seen him briefly in the dark, during a storm, there was no mistaking Mordred. The witch-hunter was even more unappealing in the daylight. Ben cast a quick glance at Sharpe. Her eyes were wide with fear, yet burned with a hate so intense, it was a wonder Mordred didn't burst into flames on the spot.

"This is 'im, sir," Berchmoore confirmed.

"Good," the green-eyed man said, stepping forward. "There are one or two questions I believe you can help us with, pirate. Berchmoore here says you were the one who took the princess from him. Where is she?"

"She's not here," Ben replied, lifting his chin defiantly. If they hoped to intimidate him, they'd be sorely disappointed. "I dropped her off safely in her own kingdom."

"Did you now? Well, that was good of you. What of your other passengers?"

Ben raised his eyebrows in mock confusion. "And what passengers would those be?"

"You assisted two women in escaping," Mordred spoke up. His black, soulless eyes were far more chilling than the other man's. "I saw them leave on your ship. Where are they?"

"If they're still 'ere," Berchmoore added, "we'll find them."

"Sorry to disappoint you gentlemen, but this is a pirate ship," Ben pointed out. "Not a ferry. We don't take on passengers."

The man with the green eyes opened his mouth to say something, but Mordred cut him off. "No mind. If they are still on board, they will be discovered. And if not, it's likely they were returned to Daera, along with Her Highness." He turned to his companion. "I will continue my search for them there when our business here is concluded, Rodek."

Ben felt a flicker of fear for Calida and Lorelei. Mordred had correctly guessed that he had returned them to Daera and he would soon be hunting for them once more. He felt an overwhelming urge to warn them, but he couldn't possibly send Horus without these men noticing.

He cursed inwardly; he'd tried to tell his aunt that it was foolish to return to Daera, but she hadn't listened. She'd insisted it was safe now that Mordred had moved on, but he would return and they had no way of knowing.

"Very well," the other man—Rodek—conceded. "Now, Captain, we come to the matter of the witch on board. Who are they? One of the crew or a passenger you likewise dropped off somewhere?"

Ben scoffed, trying to mask his mounting fear. Clearly, they weren't referring to either Calida or Lorelei. Mordred knew both of the women were witches.

How had they found out there was another witch on board? He thought of the wave he'd summoned to crush Mordred's rats and Calida's warning and inwardly cringed.

"Don't be daft," he snapped. His mouth felt so dry, it was difficult to speak. "There is no witch on board. If there was, I'd know of it."

"He's not going to tell you," Mordred hissed.

"Maybe 'e can be persuaded," Berchmoore growled, cocking back a fist. Before Ben could move, Berchmoore's fist had slammed into his stomach, driving the air painfully from his lungs.

He doubled over from the force of the blow. He gasped in pain as a second fist connected with his cheek, catching him off-guard and knocking him to the deck.

Squinting up, Ben could see Sharpe desperately trying to shake free of the men who had ahold of her, spitting with rage, still trying to defend her captain to the bitter end. He subtly shook his head at her and made no effort to get to his feet. It was far better to let your opponents think you were weak and defeated than to actually be so.

Blood was gushing from his nose and Ben used the jabot hanging around his neck to try and staunch it, propping himself up with one arm. For a moment, he feared his nose was broken—not that it would be the first time.

"What do you think you're doing?" Rodek was demanding of Berchmoore. "The queen said she wanted him alive."

Ben's ears perked up at that. The queen wanted him alive? Whatever for?

"I know what she said," the privateer retorted. "But she didn't say anything about 'im 'aving to be pretty."

Rodek huffed. "Well, pirate?"

"I told you," Ben replied. "There is no witch."

"You could try putting fuses 'twixt 'is fingers," Berchmoore suggested helpfully.

"That won't be necessary," Mordred said coldly. He'd turned and was surveying each captured crew member in turn. "I know who the witch is." He came to a halt in front of Sharpe.

"Her?" Rodek asked incredulously.

"Aye," Berchmoore nodded enthusiastically. "It must be 'er, all right. She always was a strange one, that Sharpe. Able to 'it a man from eight 'undred feet or more, even in a storm. Unnatural, like."

"Ah, yes, I remember," Mordred said. His tone was soft, gentle almost, and it made Ben's skin crawl. "Indris, all those years ago. With skin like that, how could I forget? You need only look at her to realize she's a witch."

Sharpe struggled against her captors again, desperately trying to break free and flee from the witch-hunter. Her eyes were terrified, the rage Ben had seen earlier leeching away.

"She's the witch, is she?" Rodek murmured. "Fine. We'll take her. Now that we have what we need, you can kill the others."

The two men that had ahold of Sharpe's arms began to pull her away, dragging her toward the Alaran warship. Crying out in frustration, she fought fiercely, but they were too strong for her. Her wide eyes met Ben's, silently pleading for him not to let them take her.

Ben would have bet any amount of money that Sharpe was not actually a witch, but she had kept secrets from him before. Whether she was a witch or not wasn't really the issue.

They were taking her, going to punish her, in his place. She had suffered at Mordred's hands before and fought hard for her freedom. She likely had never expected to encounter him again, much less find herself once more at his mercy.

Ben bowed his head briefly, closing his eyes as he wrestled with the hardest decision he'd ever had to make. And yet, in the end, the choice was straightforward.

He couldn't let them take Sharpe or kill the rest of his crew. He had no idea what they would do to her, if they would simply kill her outright or torture her first. She deserved neither.

He was responsible for his crew and their wellbeing. If he could prevent their deaths and save Sharpe from Mordred, he had no right to do anything less.

Briefly, he considered lying, claiming that there had been another passenger and that he'd dropped them off at some obscure location. He could even stall further by offering to take them to the exact place. But sooner or later, they would know it was a lie and come after him and Sharpe all the more aggressively, putting all his crew in even more danger.

It wasn't fair to any of them. Least of all her.

"Stop!" he cried, rising to his feet. Blessedly, his nose had stopped bleeding, but he scarcely noticed, his heart was beating so hard. "She's not a witch."

Mordred, who had begun to follow after the men dragging Sharpe away, stopped and turned. Sharpe was watching Ben. Her clothing was rumpled from her struggle and her braid had started to come undone.

"She's not the witch," Ben repeated softly, now that all eyes were on him. He reached up and tugged off his right glove, holding up the exposed back of his hand for all to see. "I am. I'm the one you want."

Murmuring broke out among the crew. Some were astonished, hardly daring to believe it. But Sharpe didn't look the least bit surprised. Strangely, she looked like she might cry.

Ben could do nothing but stand there, feeling naked and exposed now that his secret was out. He'd done the one thing Calida had told him to never do—take off his gloves, or the one that mattered anyway.

"Y—you?" Berchmoore sputtered, gaping at him and unpleasantly revealing the poor state of his teeth. "Well! At least that explains 'ow the *Phoenix* was able to move so quickly. It was you doing it all along!"

Mordred had a grim look of satisfaction on his face, but Rodek stared at Ben as though he'd sprouted a second head.

"Well," the witch-hunter said, striding forward. "Thank you for being honest. Now that he's told us who the witch is, and it happens to be him, there's no reason to keep him alive. Two birds, one stone." He drew a dagger out of his belt, a long, curved, wicked thing and Ben paled at the sight of it. "You can leave the unpleasant task to me."

"*No,*" Rodek snapped. "This one we keep alive. The *queen* will want to see him."

For a long breathless moment, Ben thought that the witch-hunter would refuse to listen.

Then, reluctantly, Mordred put the dagger away, looking none too pleased at being overruled. "Fine."

Rodek gestured to one of his men. "Fetch some irons."

The man departed to do as he was told. Ben slipped his glove back on. There was no need for it now, but he felt better having both of them on. It made him feel almost normal again, back in control of the situation, as though he hadn't just announced his most damning secret to the entire world.

"Rodek," Berchmoore spoke up. "I 'ate to mention it now, but my ship was badly damaged in the skirmish. I'm afraid I'll need a new one—"

"The crown will see that you're provided with one," Rodek said shortly.

"Yes, of course," Berchmoore said quickly. "But I was wondering if I might 'ave this one."

Ben stared at him in a mixture of outrage and astonishment. *The audacity!* "You can't take the *Phoenix!*" he snarled. "She's mine! She belongs to me."

"Can't see as you'll 'ave much use for 'er," Berchmoore replied, "when you're swinging from the gallows. Or perhaps a pyre would be more appropriate."

"If that's what you want, Berchmoore," Rodek said quietly. "I have no objection."

"You bastard!" Ben growled. "You can't do this!"

He lunged forward, intending to wring Berchmoore's neck with his own two hands, but he was grabbed roughly, his arms pinioned painfully behind his back.

"We'll never follow you!" Sharpe snapped at the privateer. "Some of us are still loyal, even if you aren't."

"Then you'll 'ave to swim 'ome," Berchmoore replied, without a shred of remorse.

The man had returned with the shackles and Rodek jerked his head toward the Alaran warship. "Secure him below."

The man stepped forward but Berchmoore held up a hand. "There's just one last thing." He grinned wickedly at Ben. "I'll be taking that coat. It should 'ave been mine, after all. Just like the *Phoenix.*"

Ben glanced around, but no one was going to come to his aid.

It took every ounce of willpower and self-control Ben possessed to keep his face an impassive mask as he slowly shrugged off his signature scarlet coat and tossed it across to

Berchmoore. The privateer caught it with undisguised glee and pulled it on, discarding his previous blue one.

"Ah," he sighed. "At last. I've been waiting for that for a long time."

Rodek nodded once more to the man who held the shackles. Ben felt his arms grabbed again but this time he didn't offer up any resistance, his hands held out in front of him. A moment later, the metal clicked securely around his wrists.

He was marched past Berchmoore, toward the waiting Alaran warship, careful to keep his eyes trained on the deck.

"Make sure you cover his head," Mordred said ominously as they passed. "A sky witch can't use his powers if he can't see the sky. We all have our weaknesses…"

Ben hardly noticed as he was marched below and secured in the Alaran ship's brig. He couldn't see the sky locked down in the hold, but they placed a hood over his head anyway.

All he could think of was that Berchmoore had the *Phoenix*.

And his crew could either join him or drown.

CHAPTER 21

The captain saw the ship first and Annie rushed to the rail, fearing the worst. Despite the two escort ships that Varrian had once again sent to accompany her on her return journey to Alara, she was more fearful than ever that pirates might try something. But her fears were assuaged at once upon seeing the sight laid out before her.

There was indeed a ship out there, but it was sinking. In fact, half of it had already slipped beneath the water. There was no saving it now.

"Shall we see if there are any survivors?" the captain inquired.

He may have been the commander of the ship, but she was still royalty and her word was law. If she wished to continue straight on to Alara, and leave any potential survivors stranded, they would do so.

"Yes, of course," Annie said, more tersely than she'd intended, but she felt slightly insulted that the captain would even consider her doing anything less.

But as they turned and crept closer to the doomed vessel, she began to wish she'd made a different choice. Even half-submerged, she couldn't fail to recognize the sinking ship as Berchmoore's *Dagger*. She'd spent enough time sequestered on it. Annie wondered briefly what sort of ill fortune the ship had encountered. It was in bad shape, riddled with holes and blasted to pieces. It looked like a toy ship that a toddler had thrown to the ground.

Well, if Berchmoore himself is among any survivors, I'll tell the captain to let him sink.

She looked down as she heard a faint cry for help, eyes scanning the water until she made out a drenched figure desperately clutching a piece of shattered wood, likely from the sinking ship. Annie let out a gasp of surprise.

There was no mistaking the woman in the water, with her dark skin with its light patches. She was the woman from Ben's crew and now Annie could see others floating in the water, trying to hold on. What were they doing here? There was no sign of the *Phoenix*.

"Throw them a line!" Annie cried.

The crew hurried to rescue the stranded sailors and bring them on board. It seemed to take an eternity. Annie hurried over to them as they were hauled on deck, dripping wet.

"Your Highness," the woman exclaimed, as though Annie were the last person she expected to encounter—and that was probably true.

Annie nodded to her. "I'm sorry, I don't know your name."

"Sharpe," the woman answered, turning to her companion. "And this is Terrance."

"Right." Annie hadn't bothered to learn any of the names of the pirate crew during her brief stay on board and she regretted that now. She'd learned the name of only one and she didn't see him. "What are you all doing out here? Where's Ben?"

Sharpe was trembling, likely from exhaustion rather than cold, since the water was quite warm this close to Alara. "We were attacked," she gasped. "First by Berchmoore, then by an Alaran warship. Our rudder was disabled so we couldn't run. We managed to sink Berchmoore's ship, but he took the

Phoenix. He told us we could either sail under him or swim our way home." She turned to look at the sailors gathered behind her. "We're the ones who refused. What's left of us, anyway."

Annie felt her stomach clench. If Berchmoore took the *Phoenix*, that didn't bode well. "And Ben?"

It was Terrance who replied. "The Cap'n was taken by the Alaran warship. They've taken 'im back to Alara, no doubt to stand trial."

None of them said as much, but Annie knew Ben was as good as dead if that were true. She found herself surprisingly saddened by the thought. The Daeran people would be expecting him to return, but he never would. Who would look out for them now?

"I'm sorry," she said simply, knowing how inadequate it was.

"Your Highness?" It was the captain, coming up behind her. "Shall we drop off the survivors in Alara?"

Annie looked at Sharpe and Terrance and saw the look of alarm in their eyes. They were pirates. To take them to Alara would be handing them a death sentence. And Annie had seen the way they'd helped her people. They'd helped *her*, come to think of it.

She hadn't had them fished out of the water only to condemn them to a different sort of death.

"No," she said firmly. "Take them back to Daera on one of the escort vessels at once."

"But Your Highness," the captain protested. "The king ordered the escorts to stay by your side at all times."

"This close to Alaran waters, Captain, I think one escort will be sufficient protection," Annie replied coolly.

He sighed. "Very well, Your Highness. It shall be done."

"Thank you, Captain." Annie turned back to Terrance and Sharpe. "I can't get your ship or your captain back for you, but I can see you safely back to Daera."

Sharpe cocked her head as though studying her. "You know, you're not so bad, princess."

Annie summoned a small smile. "I'm beginning to think you're not so bad either. It's the least I can do after seeing the way you helped my people." Her smile faded. "What will you do now?"

Sharpe turned to Terrance as though looking for guidance. "Find Calida, I guess. Tell her what happened."

"I'm sorry," Annie said again, noting the bleak look in their eyes. "I wish you good luck."

"Luck," Terrance murmured. "We're going to need a lot of that."

* * *

The remainder of the voyage passed by uneventfully. What little remained of the *Phoenix*'s crew had been sent back to Daera on one of the escort ships, just as Annie had ordered, leaving her with only one other for protection. The sun was out in full force, bathing everything in Alara with its glow. She was met at the docks to be escorted to the castle once more, though with less fanfare than before.

Queen Thalia and Kain were waiting in the throne room to welcome her back and to her surprise, the king was present as well. She had seen little of him during her time in Alara—not even at dinner.

Annie could not bring herself to look at the prince. The king seemed to be off in his own little world, eyes glazed as usual, hardly paying her any mind, and it was all she could do to meet the gaze of the queen.

"We're so pleased you arrived safely, Your Highness," Thalia remarked, breaking the silence. As she drifted closer, Annie once again smelled her unusual perfume.

"Thank you, Your Majesty," Annie replied. She thought her voice sounded rather flat, but the queen seemed not to notice.

"I'd sent out many patrols and even naval fleets to search for you," the queen added. "But to no avail. We were all quite worried and you can imagine our relief when your brother wrote to us."

Annie felt her face flush. "I'm sorry, Your Majesty. I didn't mean to cause you any inconvenience."

Thalia waved a hand. "Now, now, that's all in the past. The important thing is that you've returned to us, safe and sound. I shudder to think how those pirates must have treated you. It must have been a very frightening experience."

Annie briefly considered contradicting her and claiming it actually wasn't all that bad, considering how it could have played out, but decided against it. Thalia likely wouldn't believe her and what would be the point? Clearly, they'd heard something about what had happened, probably courtesy of Berchmoore. Let them believe what they wanted.

"Yes," she said simply. "It was quite dreadful."

"Well, fear not, Your Highness. You're quite safe here."

"Thank you, Your Majesty." Annie felt herself flush again. She wasn't afraid of anything in the palace!

She was relieved when a servant approached, saving her from any more unwanted platitudes. He bowed to the queen and spoke in a low voice. "Pardon the interruption, Your Majesty. Rodek's ship has returned."

Thalia brightened. "Ah, excellent." The servant scurried away and the queen turned to Annie apologetically. "Excuse me, Your Highness. I must go see if Rodek's efforts were successful."

Annie had no idea what she was talking about, but she curtsied and watched as the queen departed the throne room, disappearing from view as the double doors shut.

She'd crossed over to one of the windows behind the thrones. The king had sunk down onto one of the thrones as though his knees pained him.

She peered out, eyes searching the harbor beyond. She wondered if Ben were on any of the ships or if he'd already arrived and been executed. If not, perhaps it wasn't too late for her to try and do something. *Like what?* There was nothing she could do now.

To her annoyance, the prince walked up to join her at the window, and she did her best to studiously ignore him.

"I'm glad they didn't harm you," he said. "The pirates, I mean. That was quite lucky."

She realized that what he'd said did not mean the same thing as *I'm glad you're back*. She didn't really care if he was glad to have her back or not. She wasn't glad to be back in *his* company, but she couldn't very well say that to his face, no matter how tempting.

"Yes, that was lucky, Your Highness," she said dryly. No matter what he had said, or might say, she would not call him by his name again.

"Pirates," he said with feeling. "Filthy dogs, the lot of them. Ought to be put down."

Annoyance flared within her as her thoughts returned to Ben, how he'd rescued her from Berchmoore, how he'd helped her people, and been captured by the very kingdom she now stood in. It was possible he was already dead or well on his way.

Despite everything he'd done, she'd given him nothing but her contempt. And now she would never get the chance to put that right.

"Actually," she said coldly, hoping to shock Kain, "I was rescued by pirates."

The look on his face almost made it worth it. "Rescued?" he exclaimed. "They kidnapped you!"

"No. They rescued me from that horrid privateer, Berchmoore, and took me safely back to my own kingdom."

The prince snorted. "They probably wanted to ransom you for themselves, only they got cold feet and backed out at the last moment, deciding it was safer to drop you off in Daera than risk their own necks."

"You know nothing of them," she retorted.

"And you do?" he shot back. "Have you met every pirate?"

"And you have, I suppose!" she challenged.

"No, but I have enough sense to know they're not heroes and you shouldn't make them out to be," he said, then sighed, continuing in a lower tone. "You really shouldn't have run away that day, Annie. Then they wouldn't have kidnapped you."

"I wouldn't have run away," Annie said indignantly, "if *you* hadn't created a disturbance in the street."

"In all actuality," the prince replied haughtily, "the peasant is the one to blame. He's lucky I didn't have him publicly flogged."

"Skies, you're insufferable." Annie rolled her eyes. "It was your inappropriate behavior that compounded the problem."

"*My* inappropriate behavior! I hardly call climbing into a crate and stowing away on a ship full of men appropriate behavior."

Annie glared at him, her face aflame, but could summon no witty retort to prove him wrong.

He kind of had a point this time.

* * *

Thalia met Rodek and Mordred in one of the reception rooms, ordering everyone out, including the two guards who had been standing by the far door.

"Where's that privateer, Berchmoore?" she asked. There was no sign of him.

"His ship was damaged in the engagement, Your Majesty," Rodek answered. "I gave him permission to take the pirates' ship, but it was also damaged. He'll have to limp it into port to make repairs."

"I see," Thalia said impatiently. "Were you successful?"

"Yes. We found the witch and we've brought him in. It was the pirate captain himself. I think you'll be most interested to see him."

Thalia stared at her advisor for a moment, trying to discern what he meant. There must be something special about this witch indeed, if they'd brought him here to her instead of simply killing him on the spot.

She turned to Mordred. "Did you find my sister?"

"She was no longer on board," he replied. "But since the pirate dropped the princess off in Daera, I have good reason to suspect he did the same for Calida and Lorelei. I will return there as soon as the business with the sky witch is finished."

Thalia nodded. The sky witch was the greater threat anyway. "Very well. About this witch—are you sure he's the one? Did you find a mark?"

"He confessed to being a witch," Rodek replied, "but whether he's the sky witch, we don't know, without a demonstration of his powers. The mark is on the back of his right hand—he showed it to us himself—and I suggest you take a look at it."

"Bring him in," Thalia ordered. "I'd like to see it."

"Yes, my queen." Rodek walked over to the door and pulled it open.

A third guard ushered the captured pirate inside and Rodek shut the door behind them. The guard halted in front of the queen, keeping a firm grip on the pirate's arm. Thalia could not see his face, concealed as it was beneath a black hood, but her eyes roamed over what she could see of him briefly.

He wasn't tall, only about average height, wearing a frilly white shirt, black trousers, black boots, and a pair of black gloves. His wrists were manacled together.

Without saying a word, Thalia motioned to Rodek, who stepped forward, tugging off the right glove. Instantly, the pirate clasped his hands together, the left concealing the right, and Rodek had to forcibly thrust his hands apart, holding up the right for her to see.

She sucked in an involuntary breath, blood running cold as she saw and recognized the witch-mark on the back of his hand. Black spots danced at the edges of her vision and she sank down onto one of the velvet chairs. She blinked, trying to regain her composure.

Resisting the urge to yank the hood off and gaze upon the face of the captured man, she gestured for them to escort the prisoner out. The chains connecting the shackles clinked as the guard removed the witch-pirate from the room.

"Your Majesty?" Rodek inquired, when the door had been closed once more.

"You were right," she breathed, "to bring him here."

Her mind was awhirl. Suddenly, everything made sense, the pieces falling into place. And yet, nothing made sense.

How could this have happened? How could she not have *known*?

"What should we do with him?"

She thought quickly. What would the pirate think? He must assume he was here to be executed for his crimes. After all, he was guilty not only of piracy but also witchcraft as well. It would be best to allow him to think that for the time being.

"Take him to a cell. As you said, we don't yet know if he is the sky witch. If he thinks he is here to face execution, he will likely try to use his powers to escape and then we will know for certain. Mordred, I would like your assistance with that, when the time comes. But first, I'd like to speak with the pirate alone."

"Are you sure that's wise?" Rodek asked. "He might try to use his powers against you and escape then."

"I can handle him if he does. But I think it far more likely he'll wait until he's alone, so he won't be interrupted."

"*If* he is a sky witch," Mordred drawled.

But Thalia had seen the mark and knew what the witch-hunter did not.

* * *

Ben had no idea where he was. The hood had not been removed since it had been placed over his head, forcing him to rely on his other senses, though they were of little use in helping him identify his surroundings.

He seemed to be marched from one place to another. Without his vision, he had to rely on the guards leading him so as not to trip. Their footsteps echoed on the hard floor, possibly stone of some kind.

They can't be taking me to the gallows, surely. There hasn't even been a trial yet. But perhaps that didn't matter in Alara. After all, they weren't known for being the most merciful of kingdoms.

They came to a sudden halt and without warning, the hood was pulled off and Ben gasped, squinting in the sudden light. He stood before a large set of double doors.

"In you go," said one of the guards, pulling open one of the doors just enough to let him pass, and giving him a shove inside.

The shackles had been kept in place. The room was empty of people, aside from two guards stationed on either side of a far door, and Ben started forward slowly, taking in its splendor.

The ceiling high above was domed and made purely out of glass, giving a view of the sky. The sun streaming through was blinding after spending so much time in darkness. There were also slim windows straight ahead of him, behind two ornate thrones atop a raised platform.

The thrones looked as though they were made from solid gold, inlaid with colored pieces of glass.

Why would they bring me here?

"At last," a feminine voice exclaimed suddenly, making him start and spin around. "The famed captain of the *Phoenix!*"

He hadn't heard the woman enter and for a moment, it seemed as though she'd simply materialized from thin air, though Ben knew that was impossible. Her voice was deep and had a natural sultry quality to it, echoing strangely throughout the vast chamber.

She wore a deep red dress of the finest silk that shimmered in the sunlight like a brand of fire. For a split second, he thought of Calida, though he didn't know why. This woman's hair was red also, but a darker, less vibrant shade, and her eyes were dark blue, not gray. From the circlet at her brow, he guessed she must be queen Thalia and his mouth suddenly felt dry as he realized whose presence he found himself in.

Should he bow or get down on his knees and beg for mercy? His pride would allow for neither. If he was going to die—and it was inevitable that he was—he would do it without a trace of fear, no matter how afraid he might actually be.

"I'm not her captain anymore, I'm afraid," he replied, then hastily added, "Your Majesty." He wasn't going to grovel but neither would he be disrespectful.

She smiled and drew closer. He watched her warily.

"What's your name?" she said softly.

"Benjamin," he replied. "Benjamin Knight."

"Is that your father's name?"

Ben realized he didn't know. Calida had never spoken of his parents' names, only what had happened to them. He'd just assumed that Benjamin was the name his mother had chosen for him before she'd died and that Knight had been his father's last name.

"I don't know," he confessed, feeling that the truth was best. "It's the only name I've ever known."

"But surely you must know your father's name," the queen suggested.

"He's dead. So is my mother. They both died when I was young. I never knew them."

"Who were they? What did they do?"

Ben looked at her, wondering why she seemed so interested in his personal history. Perhaps it was a trap or a test of some kind. He only hoped that he was passing, if that were the case.

"My father was a sailor and he died as one. My mother was a common prostitute." He shrugged. "That's how they met."

Queen Thalia's eyebrows rose and he caught a glint of something in her eyes—amusement? "Who had the raising of you, then?"

"My aunt."

"Is she still living?"

"Yes." *Last I heard, anyway.*

She let out a tinkling little laugh. "Don't tell me you don't know her name, either?"

"Calida."

"How old are you now, Benjamin?"

"Twenty."

"Rather young to be the captain of your own ship."

It wasn't, really. Most pirates were quite young, but he also knew that Calida had been right when she'd suggested that the reason he'd risen so quickly through the ranks, and the reason Captain Lussard had chosen him as his successor, had been because of his being a witch.

But there was no point going into any of that with the queen. Instead, he asked the question that had been nagging at him. "Why am I here, Your Majesty? Am I a prisoner?" He thought he knew the answer, but he wanted to hear it for himself.

She smiled again. "You can make yourself one, if you choose."

Her answer only made him more confused than he had been before.

She gave him a pitying look. "Though, you are a witch, as I understand."

There was no point in denying it, not when he'd already admitted it to the rest of the world. "I am."

"You are aware, I think, of Alara's policy regarding witchcraft, as well as piracy."

He nodded. Again, there was no point in denying it. It wouldn't change the truth.

"This should come as no surprise, then." She nodded, signaling to someone behind him. He glanced over his shoulder to see the two guards approaching. They took ahold of his arms and began to take him away. "Farewell, Benjamin."

With the hood gone, Ben could clearly see where he was being taken, as they led him through numerous corridors. None of it was familiar, and there was no reason that it should have been. It felt more like a giant labyrinth, meant to confuse and bewilder, than a palace. But the ground gradually sloped downward and Ben could guess where he was headed.

His fears were confirmed as they passed through a thick wooden door. The air was musty and damp down here, the stone floor and walls dripping with moisture. There wasn't much light; what little there was streamed through the windows that were set just above ground, at the top of the ceiling, and from torches set along intervals.

The guards stopped before one of the cells, pulled open the door with a screech of iron hinges and pushed him inside, blessedly removing the shackles from his wrists. Ben rubbed the raw skin gingerly as the door was shut and locked, watching the guards as they trooped away.

The floor of his cell was sparsely covered with dingy straw. An uncomfortable-looking wooden bench hung on one wall, suspended by chains. Somewhere, a rat scurried in the dark and Ben shuddered, remembering the wave of rats Mordred had sent after them.

He silently cursed Berchmoore for putting him in this position, recalling what Sharpe had said to him all those years ago, and yet not that long ago at all, after he'd banished Berchmoore from the *Phoenix*.

She had approached him, saying, "You could have killed him—and all the others—for mutiny. Why didn't you?"

Ben had sighed, walking toward his cabin. "I don't know. He's a good sailor, but he lets pride blind him. I guess I hoped that Berchmoore might make something of himself somewhere else, given the chance, because he certainly wasn't going to as long as he stayed here."

"Or come back to bite you in the arse, more like," she countered. It was just like Sharpe to cut straight to the heart of the issue. "We haven't heard the last of him."

"I didn't think Captain Lussard would have done it," Ben said, feeling the need to defend himself.

Captain Lussard hadn't killed those whose attempted mutiny resulted in Sharpe becoming a member of the crew. Ben knew that, in hindsight, Sharpe suspected Berchmoore might have been the instigator behind that incident as well, planting the idea in the others' minds.

Certainly, he had coveted Lussard's position for some time. Being patient had yielded him nothing. Rather than finding himself named Lussard's successor, Berchmoore had been passed over, the position falling to Ben.

Of course, aside from his skill as a sailor, Lussard had known that Ben was a witch and those skills would only help him further be the leader they needed him to be. But Ben also wondered if Lussard had suspected Berchmoore himself.

Whether he'd been involved in the last mutiny attempt or not, after being passed over, Berchmoore no longer made any attempt at hiding his feelings.

He'd played on the feelings of some of the other men, their jealousies and insecurities, and simple greed. But his mutiny had ended much the same as the first.

"You're not Captain Lussard," Sharpe pointed out.

"No," Ben said, more sharply than he'd intended. "I'm not." He hadn't meant to snap at her, but he tried so hard to be like his former captain and mentor and yet was all too aware of his shortcomings in that regard.

Sharpe had followed him inside his cabin. "Look, I'm not saying that I disagree with you. I'm just worried that the men will see it as weakness. There are rules for a reason, Ben— Captain. The code says that Berchmoore and his accomplices should have been killed for mutinying."

I'm just worried that the men will see it as weakness. The words rang in Ben's ears, along with those yet unspoken. *And you don't need to give any more of them a reason to mutiny, to think you're soft.*

"I know what the code says, Sharpe," Ben muttered. "But what's done is done."

What's done is done. That had been two years ago.

If only he had listened to her when he had the chance. And now it was too late. *Sharpe…* She was probably dead now, choosing a watery grave as preferable to serving under Berchmoore. Loyal to the end, but little good her loyalty to him had done her.

And little good your sacrifice did either, a mocking voice hissed in his mind.

If he'd only listened to her, she would still be alive and none of them would be in this mess. He should have listened to Calida, come to that, when she'd warned him about the blatant use of his power. It had been that very power that he'd believed would keep him out of danger.

How wrong he'd been.

But maybe it could help him now.

Slowly turning in the center of his cell, Ben studied his current surroundings. What did he have to work with?

He'd had time to rest on the way to Alara and the dungeon was quite damp, close to the water table. If he could somehow use that, perhaps build up enough pressure, he might be able to fracture the foundation, collapse a wall and escape.

Where he would go after that, he didn't know, but one thing at a time. First, he had to get out and he'd be damned if he surrendered to his fate without a fight.

Ben took a deep breath, casting an anxious glance around, but he couldn't see any guards. Remembering what Mordred had said about a sky witch needing to see the sky in order to draw on his power, Ben looked up at the thin window near the ceiling. He could just make out a strip of blue, but it was enough.

Odd, knowing that he was a witch, that they would choose to put him here, where he could use his power. A trap, possibly? Even so, Ben had no choice but to risk it. To wait here only ended one way.

Drawing his focus into one singular goal, Ben concentrated on the water in the ground beneath him and commanded it to rise to the surface. He was met with strong resistance; the stone prevented the water from rising, but he urged it onward, straining against the solid rock. His only opponent was the earth, defying him.

A large crack ruptured the ground beneath his feet and he staggered back as it crept up the wall. The water rushed forward like a geyser and Ben shaped it into a powerful wave, the same way he had against the rats, slamming it into the wall. A jubilant thrill rushed through him as the stone gave way beneath the weight and force of the water.

Sunlight streamed through the opening he had made and Ben stepped out onto sand. He needed to hurry; someone must have heard that and they'd soon come investigating and find him gone.

But he'd only taken a few steps when queen Thalia herself emerged from the bushes that stretched on either side of him, standing directly in his path. "I must say, I knew you were a sky witch, Benjamin, but even I'm impressed."

He exhaled heavily. He didn't dare to hope she was alone—especially since she seemed to have anticipated this—but she appeared to be. "I don't want to hurt you. Let me pass."

He'd never used his abilities to harm anyone before, and he wasn't quite sure how to go about it, but he would if she forced his hand. He was too close to tasting freedom not to try and he certainly wasn't going to hang around to keep his appointment with the gallows.

She laughed, not looking the least bit intimidated by his threat. "I doubt you could hurt me, Benjamin, but you're welcome to try."

Clearly, she had no intention of getting out of his way. He sighed. Maybe he could summon a stiff wind to knock her off her feet and make a run for it?

The wind he summoned wasn't as strong as he'd have liked; breaking out of the dungeon had proved more taxing than he'd bargained for.

The queen merely staggered in the breeze. She waved a hand and the wind stopped for a split second, before whipping up again and Ben gasped as sand flew into his eyes, stinging and momentarily blinding him.

But that wasn't what startled him the most. *The queen is a witch!* And more than that—she was a sky witch herself. The queen of Alara, the kingdom notorious for witch hunts, was a witch!

"You'll have to try harder than that, Benjamin."

He stared at her, suddenly uncertain what to do next. Likely anything he tried, she could counter. But surrender wasn't an option. He tried to emulate what she had done, and throw sand up into her eyes, but she merely calmed the wind almost as soon as he'd summoned it. There was no water nearby to use aside from that which was underground.

He tried summoning a strong enough wind to throw her off her feet, but she turned it back on him, knocking him down. Ben gasped as he hit the ground.

It was impossible to defeat her using magic; everything he did, she turned against him. The only thing he could hope to do would be to overpower her physically.

Gritting his teeth, Ben scrambled to his feet and rushed at her, but he didn't get very far. He staggered, gasping, suddenly feeling like he was choking. He couldn't draw breath or breathe at all. He doubled over, clutching at his chest, panic shooting through him. He could feel the blood rushing in his ears, his heart thudding, and still he couldn't get any air in.

Ben looked up to see that Thalia had one hand thrust toward him, fingers curled into a fist. *She's drawing the air out of my lungs!* he realized, sinking to his knees, feeling his strength leeching away.

He had never considered using his abilities in such a way, but if a sky witch could control air, it was possible.

His vision was turning black at the edges. He slumped to the ground, feeling the smooth white sand beneath his cheek. His last coherent thought before the darkness crashed down was that he needn't have been so worried about the gallows.

This was how he would die.

* * *

Thalia lowered her hand abruptly. Benjamin had stopped struggling and now lay still. His muscles had gone limp in that final moment as he succumbed and she studied him, surprised by how peaceful his features looked, almost as

239

though he were merely asleep. But she knew better. He looked less like the powerful, confident pirate captain and more like the child he was.

A faint breeze stirred a few strands of his golden hair as Mordred stepped out from the bushes, regarding the motionless body. He nudged Benjamin with a boot, but there was no response.

Thalia had only asked Mordred to be present, out of sight, in case Benjamin proved to be more powerful than she anticipated and she needed the witch-hunter's assistance in subduing him.

He hadn't been needed, of course, although Benjamin *had* been more powerful than Thalia had hoped.

"You're playing a dangerous game," Mordred warned.

Thalia grinned. "But it's my game to play."

CHAPTER 22

Ben came to slowly, unsure where he was or how he'd come to be there. At first, it almost felt like he was floating, weightless, disconnected from his body, and then it all came rushing back. The queen confronting him outside the dungeon and overpowering him. His eyes flew open.

He was in a large room, the lighting dim, coming from a few lit candles positioned around the room. A large tapestry hung on the far wall. A dresser stood along the other, with a mirror and there was a wardrobe as well. A chair was seated in front of the dresser and there were a few more chairs spread throughout the room. There was a sofa and a canopied bed that he was currently lying on. A room divider stood not far from the bed, though what, if anything, lay behind it, Ben couldn't tell.

Wincing, he eased himself up into a sitting position. There was no one else in the room. He stood, walking over to the room divider and finding an ivory bathtub behind it, already filled with water, though it had probably long since gone cold. He ignored it for now and moved over to the tapestry, pushing it aside, half-expecting to find a window concealed beneath, but he was met with solid wall.

Of course, he thought, letting the fabric slide back into place. Why would they allow him to have a room with windows, which only gave him access to his powers? Powers he'd used in an attempt to escape, proving he wasn't to be trusted, and this was his punishment.

Though most perplexing were his surroundings themselves. Why hadn't he simply been killed, as he'd believed to be happening before he'd lost consciousness? At the very least, why hadn't he been returned to a more secure cell, one without a window?

Ben doubted that this was the grandest room the palace had to offer—he would expect those to have windows—but it was a marked improvement over a dingy cell and he wasn't about to complain about that. But it did puzzle him.

He sank back down onto the corner of the bed, mind burning with questions and mulling over what had happened.

The queen was a witch, and a sky witch at that. She had to be, to be able to manipulate the wind as she had done. But that made no sense. Alara was the kingdom famous for its witch-hunts. It had become so severe that innocent people were hunted down if they happened to have an unfortunate mark, even if it was only a birthmark or a scar. In most cases, it wasn't a witch-mark, but they were still convicted of witchcraft and burned at the stake nonetheless.

It was a terrible fate and apparently quite gruesome to watch as the accused were slowly, agonizingly burned alive. Ben thought, given the choice, he'd much rather be hanged as a pirate than burned as a witch. Both were unpleasant ends, but he could only hope his neck snapped and it would be quick, rather than slowly being consumed by flames.

One of those two options was what he had believed awaited him upon his arrival in Alara, yet here he was, still very much alive.

The witch-hunts had gone on for years, as long as he had been alive. He didn't remember a time without them. They still happened even now, though less frequently since there were fewer witches to hunt, convict and burn. But they'd *always* been sanctioned by the crown.

And here was queen Thalia, a witch herself. An image of Mordred suddenly came to mind. A witch, but one that willingly hunted down and killed his own kind. Was the queen the same or was there another explanation? What would make a witch kill their own? Mordred probably did it to save his own skin, working on the orders of someone else, but what reason did Thalia have?

A knock sounded at the door and Ben looked up, startled. He hadn't even thought to try the door. He'd merely assumed it would be locked. When he didn't answer, the door swung open to reveal a servant, judging by the man's livery.

"The queen requests your presence," the courier announced. "You're to come with me."

Ben sighed but offered up no resistance as he got to his feet and followed the servant. He noticed there were two guards stationed outside his door as they passed, one on either side. *So I am still a prisoner.*

He expected to be taken back to the impressive throne room where he had met the queen earlier. Had it been yesterday or merely a few hours ago? He realized he didn't know how long he'd been unconscious. Through the windows they passed, he saw the sun was lower in the sky than it previously had been, but that meant nothing if it was an entirely different day.

The servant did not take him back to the throne room, but to a large conservatory, filled with many colorful, exotic plants that would not survive Daera's cooler climate. The air was heady with their scent, nearly making Ben choke. He didn't recognize any of the flowers, having spent most of his life at sea rather than on land.

The ceiling was composed of a glass dome, the same way the throne room had been, and the presence of so many windows throughout the palace suddenly made sense. It was more than an aesthetic choice; with the sky visible, the queen could call upon her powers with ease, even indoors.

Queen Thalia still wore the same red dress so he assumed it must still be the same day. She turned as they arrived, smiling, and dismissed the servant so that the two of them were alone. At least Ben assumed they were. He couldn't see any guards standing nearby, though he supposed it was always possible they might have been hidden among the foliage.

But after their previous encounter, he doubted the queen felt that she was in any danger in his presence.

She considered him briefly, waiting until the servant's footsteps had receded, and then said, "You're quite the talented witch, Benjamin, though untrained."

He glanced at her, uneasy. "Thank you, Your Majesty."

"I could teach you how to use your powers even more effectively, in ways you've never guessed at."

I bet you could, Ben thought, thinking of the way she'd nearly crushed his lungs. His chest still ached from the experience and he resisted the urge to massage the sore muscles. "It's a generous offer," he allowed, knowing she was waiting for a response from him. "But why are you making it?"

"It's not often one gets to meet such a talented sky witch," she said simply.

"You were waiting for me outside the dungeon. You knew I would try to escape."

"It was a test, Benjamin, nothing more. And you passed it with flying colors. If I wanted you dead, you would be."

Ben believed her and it was not a nice feeling. He frowned. "With all due respect, Your Majesty, why am I here?"

"You belong here," Thalia answered. "It's where you were born."

Ben couldn't conceal his surprise. "I was born in Daera," he corrected. "I told you so earlier."

"You were *raised* in Daera. Most people don't remember the exact place they are born, only where they grow up."

Ben considered what she said. He supposed it was possible that he could have been born in Alara and Calida had fled to Daera with him when the witch-hunts began. That must be what the queen meant. But how could she know such a thing?

He was on the point of asking just that when she surprised him yet again by saying, "I'd like very much for you to join me at dinner this evening."

He gaped at her. What on earth did she want him at dinner for? He met her gaze briefly and saw there was something hungry in the depths of her eyes, eager even, and he suddenly had the feeling that Thalia knew more about him than she was letting on.

"An attendant will be sent to fetch you when it's time," she added, as though this were a completely normal request to make. "Until then." She nodded to him and waved a hand to the servant standing off in the distance to escort him back to his room.

One didn't refuse a direct request from a queen, Ben supposed as he was led away.

Not that he'd ever been given the chance.

* * *

"It's good to have you back, miss, safe and sound," Maddie murmured as she fussed over Annie.

The princess had retreated back into her own quarters after her encounter with Kain and being informed that the queen had wanted the throne room empty for her own use. The maid was busy arranging her hair, still damp from the bath. Annie sat in front of the dressing room mirror, staring at her reflection, wearing nothing but a velvet robe. She had bathed upon returning to the palace in Daera, but spending another week aboard a ship on the return voyage to Alara had made her desperately yearn for another one.

"Imagine!" the maid exclaimed, seemingly unbothered by Annie's silence. "Being kidnapped by pirates. That must have been very frightening!"

"So everyone keeps saying," Annie muttered as Maddie began piling her curls atop her head in the beginning of some elaborate up-do, pinning them in place.

"You must be so brave, Your Highness."

"Well...I didn't have to stay there very long."

"Oh, yes. You said you were rescued by other pirates. What were they like?" Maddie seemed not to understand the distinction between pirates and privateers. Or perhaps she knew what everyone else failed to acknowledge.

Annie hesitated, blinking at her reflection. "They were...nice enough, as far as pirates go." The last thing she wanted was to think about Ben's fate and what had happened to the others.

"Think of it. You got to meet the captain!" Maddie sighed wistfully. "Was he handsome?"

Annie felt a sudden twist in the hollow of her stomach. She fingered the hem of her robe, as though that simple action would distract her. "Yes," she said simply. "In a roguish sort of way."

Maddie made a show of fanning herself. Annie thought the girl had missed her true calling, being a maid. She ought to have gone into the theater. "You don't know how lucky you are, miss."

Annie didn't feel particularly lucky. She was back in Alara, the last place she wished to be. The people of Daera were still starving, she was no closer to finding a solution to help them other than this beastly marriage arrangement, and the man who had been helping them, in his own way, was dead.

"Now..." the maid went over to one of the wardrobes, thrusting the doors open wide to reveal the gowns hanging within. "We need to find you something nice to wear to dinner tonight, my lady."

Annie turned. "Is a dignitary dining with us tonight? Or one of the lords?" *Please, not one of the lords.* She had worn plenty of plainer dresses to dinner before, reserving the more formal evening gowns for when a guest was expected.

"I don't know who the guest is, miss, I'm sorry," Maddie replied. "Just that there is to be one." She reached into the wardrobe, pulling out a deep violet gown. "How about this one?"

It was high-necked and backless, looping around her neck, the full skirts reaching all the way to the floor, embroidered with silver thread. There were no sleeves.

"Fine," Annie answered. "It's fine, Maddie."

She barely glanced at it; the thought of seeing Kain again at dinner and being forced to exchange inane trivialities with him set her teeth on edge. It almost made her want to feign an illness and not attend dinner at all.

But she couldn't be ill all the time. Sooner or later, it would have to be faced.

Duty came before desire.

* * *

Ben glanced up at the carriage clock on the mantel. The hearth remained unlit, leaving the room without its main source of light, but the Alaran air was too warm for a fire.

That was another thing he would have to grow used to—consulting a clock for the time rather than relying on the ship's bell.

The clock read five. Ben didn't know what time dinner was, but he knew he couldn't wait around forever. He'd already bathed earlier, thinking it probably prudent given the circumstances. It was a luxury not often afforded on board a ship.

Ceasing his pacing, he crossed over to the wardrobe in the corner, pulling the doors open and blowing out his cheeks as he surveyed the contents within. The fabric all looked far nicer than anything he'd worn.

What I wouldn't give just to have my coat back, he thought as he skimmed through the clothes. The thought of Berchmoore standing at the helm of *his* ship, wearing *his* coat, sparked a fierce anger inside him and he silently vowed that one day he would make the privateer pay dearly for that slight.

And then, just as quickly, the anger faded and he sighed, realizing the impossibility of that task. Berchmoore was long gone if he knew what was good for him. Ben's crew was divided, the loyal ones dead and drowned and the rest turned traitor, though he could hardly blame them.

He paused and pulled out a deep blue frock coat, trimmed in gold. He liked red much better, but he supposed it would do. *The queen knows I'm a pirate, so she can't expect too much of me, can she?*

He slipped it on, over a plain white shirt, gray waistcoat, and black trousers, keeping his black boots with their gold buckles. He didn't know if the queen would have anything to say about them, but he had to retain something of his identity.

Glancing in the mirror, Ben didn't think he looked much like his usual self. He certainly didn't feel it. The clothing was far too formal, stiff, stodgy, uncomfortable and unfamiliar. The starched collar of his shirt in particular threatened to choke him. He ran a gloved hand through his hair, trying to smooth it down. He huffed at the end result, thinking if anything, he'd only managed to make it worse.

Now there was nothing to do but wait.

At precisely six, an attendant arrived, just as promised, to escort him to dinner. The guards posted at the door did not follow, but there were guards stationed all along the corridors, as though to discourage him from trying anything. Where could he really escape to? He didn't know where these halls led and even if he did, getting out of the palace would be nearly impossible.

His escort at last stopped before a door and Ben took a deep breath, bracing himself for what promised to be a trying evening.

* * *

The door was thrown open with a flourish and Annie looked up to see who it was they were expecting. Her eyes widened, though she managed not to gape through sheer force of will. Whoever she had been anticipating, the man standing before her was not it.

For a moment, she feared she was seeing a ghost, so certain had she been that he was dead. But there Ben was, standing before her. There was a cut, right before the bump in the bridge of his nose, and dark purple bruising beneath his eyes. Those eyes scanned the room quickly, taking in its details and occupants.

The dining hall was a long, narrow room. The main table dominated the center of the room, equally long and narrow, used only for banquets or other official occasions. With only a handful of them present, they would be seated at the smaller table on the other end of the hall. There were two massive white hearths at either end of the room and the heads of each table rested beneath them.

Above each hearth was the head of a massive stag, fur a russet color, antlers sprawling toward the ceiling. Unlike most of the other rooms, the ceiling here had a solid roof, not made of glass. The long walls had windows set into them, their panes made of colored glass that could not be seen through.

Ben's gaze landed on one of the panes depicting a sailing ship, its white canvas taut with an imaginary wind. He tore his gaze away and turned his attention to the others in the room.

Kain was seated adjacent from Annie, Aquillus on her right and Rodek on Kain's right. Thalia sat at the head of the table. The seat on the other end remained empty, as usual.

Thalia rose to her feet, taking in Annie's reaction. "Ah, yes. I believe the two of you know each other." She indicated the empty seat on Annie's left. "Please, join us, Benjamin."

Ben swallowed, trying to mask his nerves, but Annie saw it. He made his way across the stone floor to the chair Thalia had indicated and sank down into it.

He glanced sidelong at Annie. "Glad to see you made it back safely, Princess," he murmured.

She nodded politely to him, whispering, "Captain."

Desperately, she wanted to ask him what on earth he was doing here at the palace, much less attending dinner with them, but she could hardly do so with everyone else present.

She forced herself to hold her tongue and bide her time. Questions would have to wait.

"Now then," said the queen, resuming her seat. "Since we're all here, we can begin."

"Hold on," Kain interrupted with a scowl. Annie groaned inwardly. She should have known it was too much to hope that he'd simply remain silent. "Who's this?"

Clearly, he was referring to Ben, who was glancing uncomfortably around the room, from one person to the next, probably wondering if he should answer the question at all and if so, what he should say.

But Thalia saved him. "We have Benjamin to thank for the princess's safe return."

Kain's scowl deepened and he glared accusingly at Annie. "You claimed that you were rescued by pirates." She could tell he was making the connection in his mind, drawing the conclusion as to who, or rather what, Ben must be. "I don't see why a pirate should be allowed at our dinner table."

Annie flushed, embarrassed to be in any way associated with the prince. She wondered what Ben made of the slight, but she didn't dare look at him.

She felt him lean in close and caught a hint of sandalwood as he whispered in her ear, breath brushing against her skin, "Your charming fiancé, I presume?"

Fortunately, the food arrived at that moment, a line of servants entering through a discreet wooden door at the far end of the hall, each bearing a silver platter.

There was a roast, already carved, fresh loaves of bread from the ovens, a large tureen of soup beside an assortment of cheeses and sausages. There was fruit everywhere Annie looked. Bowls of diced fruit, some iced, and even chicken, served with thinly sliced nuts and some kind of apricot. A cake was placed at the other end of the table, topped with ripe strawberries.

It was far more food than their group could possibly eat and Ben took it all in with wide eyes. Was he wondering how many people in Daera this could feed, as Annie was?

Kain seemed to notice Ben's hesitation. He smirked and picked up a piece of his silverware, holding it up and waggling it so that it caught the light. "This is a fork, pirate," he said, then set it down and picked up his knife. "And this is a knife."

Beneath the table, Annie clenched her hands into fists. "I don't think you need to tell a pirate what a *knife* is, Kain."

Out of the corner of her eye, she saw a small smile appear on Ben's face.

Kain's own face had turned white as a sheet and then flushed an unappealing shade of red. "Wasn't sure. I mean, what with him being a pirate and all. We know how to use silverware because we're not heathens."

"I wouldn't be so sure about that," Annie muttered.

Ben ignored Kain, finally settling on what appeared to be some sort of small guinea fowl marinated in a vibrant, dark reddish-brown sauce. Annie had tried a bite of it on an earlier occasion. It was quite rich and slightly spicy, sending her tastebuds quivering.

Kain's face screwed up in distaste. "I pity you, Annabelle. Being trapped on a boat, surrounded by a bunch of dirty, unwashed sailors who never saw the need to acquaint themselves with a bar of soap."

"Yes, well, it's a pity your tour in our navy didn't last longer, Kain," Thalia remarked dryly. "It might have done you good."

"You know I can't stand boats, mother," the prince grumbled. "I get seasick, to say nothing of the smell."

"Well it's not for everyone," Ben said. "Some people just don't have the constitution for it." He took a sip of wine, glancing at the prince over the rim of the glass.

Rodek snorted in amusement. Kain shot him a filthy look before turning the same gaze on Ben.

"What are you saying? That I'm deficient somehow? I *do* have the constitution for it. Mother, must we sit here, listening to this tramp insult us? At our own table, no less."

"You were the one who brought up your seasickness," queen Thalia replied. "Though, I'm glad that you insist you have the constitution for it. I think you should try again."

"I will not," Kain retorted.

"You'll do as you're told!" Thalia snapped, her dark blue eyes suddenly blazing with anger.

Kain slammed a fist down on the table, making the plates rattle, Annie jump, and Ben pause with a fork halfway to his mouth, a small potato speared on the end.

"I'll ask father!" the prince cried. "He won't make me go."

Ben's eyes flicked to the empty seat at the head of the table, but he kept quiet.

"Kain, you know better than to trouble your father with such trivial matters."

"You're just trying to send me away! To get rid of me. You're ashamed of me, is that it? I've always been a disappointment to you, haven't I? And this is your neat little solution. Out of sight, out of mind!"

"It's settled, Kain, now calm down. You're behaving like a child."

"It certainly is settled, because I'm not going anywhere!" the prince shouted, leaping out of his seat and storming from the room. Over his shoulder, he added, "You can't get rid of me that easily!"

The sound of the slamming door echoed throughout the hall. Thalia sighed. "I apologize for his outburst and less than courteous behavior, especially toward you, Benjamin. I'm afraid his manners leave much to be desired."

Ben said nothing, but his eyes slowly drifted over to meet Annie's, his brown eyebrows raised. She shrugged helplessly.

Aquillus cleared his throat. "I was going to inquire how go the wedding preparations, but perhaps such discussions should wait until the prince is present?"

Thalia waved a hand. "There's no need. The princess has only just returned, after a somewhat trying ordeal. I think it best not to rush things."

Annie let out a silent breath of relief. Anything that delayed her marriage to Kain, she would gladly take, but at the same time, she knew it was only prolonging the inevitable. Perhaps it would be better to get it over with as soon as possible.

And she knew the only reason Aquillus was anxious to speed things along was that the alliance would not be official until the wedding took place. He was as desperate for aid for the Daeran people as she was.

Conversation stalled after that, those that remained preferring to dine in silence. When at last dinner came to an end, the queen rose, bidding them all a good night and the guards that had been positioned on either side of the door came forward to accompany them back to their respective rooms.

Annie, of course, was always accompanied wherever she went, it seemed, especially following her stowaway incident. But the guards' presence also made her wonder what Ben's role here was.

Was he a prisoner? She had been startled to see him and no explanation had been given for his being there, other than they had him to thank for seeing her safely to Daera and thus, back to Alara.

But there had to be more to it. Terrance had definitely made it sound like Ben had been taken prisoner.

The two of them walked together, behind the guards in front. Annie slowed her pace, falling back slightly from their escorts. Catching on, Ben did the same.

"What are you doing here?" Annie hissed, taking advantage of their temporary privacy, the question she had kept bottled up at last springing forth.

"I don't know myself," Ben whispered back. "I don't know why I'm being treated like a guest and not a prisoner, or why I'm even still alive for that matter. Not that I'm complaining."

"I thought you were dead," Annie murmured, trying to keep her voice steady. It would not do to betray any hint of emotion. Not to him. "Sharpe and Terrance told me what happened."

"You've seen them?" He turned to her, a trace of urgency in his voice.

Annie nodded. "On the way here. My crew pulled them and the others out of the water. Those that were left, anyway," she added, recalling the sharpshooter's words and repressing a shiver. "They told me about Berchmoore taking the *Phoenix* and you being captured. I sent them back to Daera on one of my escort ships. I didn't know what else to do."

His blue eyes softened, looking at her with such gratitude, it was almost tender. "Thank you."

She looked away quickly. "I never got the chance to thank you for what you did for the people of Daera." She didn't say what they must both be thinking—that it was highly unlikely for that to continue. Not with him here and the *Phoenix* gone.

"No need to thank me." They walked a few paces in silence and then he spoke again. "I noticed the king wasn't present at dinner."

"He rarely is. He's not well. Supposedly, anyway."

Ben gave her a funny look, but before he got the chance to say anything more, the guards slowed up ahead as they reached Annie's door.

She stopped in front of it. "Well, this is me. Goodnight, Captain."

"Goodnight, Princess."

She stepped inside, shutting the door behind her and leaning against it, listening as the footsteps on the other side of the door moved along.

She stiffened as another, solitary set of footsteps approached, the knock following a few moments later.

"Yes?" she hissed, her heart ratcheting out of all proportion. Who could be knocking on her door at this time of night?

"It's Aquillus, Your Highness."

Letting out a breath of relief, Annie turned and opened the door, revealing the advisor standing there, light shining on his silver hair.

"Apologies for disturbing you, Highness, but do you have a moment?"

"Of course. Come in." She stepped back, allowing him into her sitting room.

"I will only take a moment of your time." The velvety material of his coat whispered as he stepped inside, shutting the door behind him.

Florence should have been present in order for their meeting to be proper, but Annie wasn't about to fetch her.

"I didn't think it appropriate to say anything at dinner, but I wondered, when you spoke to your brother, did he say anything about the reports I've sent him?"

Annie frowned. "No." And she hadn't thought to ask.

Aquillus clasped his hands. "I thought as much."

"Why? Is it important?"

He shook his head. "No, I've…just been keeping him informed of discussions with the queen regarding the aid shipments."

"And how go the negotiations?"

"Slow, as to be expected. I don't think queen Thalia is in too much of a hurry. And why should she be, until the wedding has taken place?"

Annie fought back a scowl. *Ah, yes, the wedding…*

"I expected to hear from your brother," Aquillus added. "Word of the conditions in Daera, or an acknowledgement that he'd received my letters, if nothing else."

"But you haven't heard anything?"

"No."

"That doesn't sound like Varrian."

"I am in agreement with you, Highness. But the queen assures me that the letters have been sent. Perhaps they've been delayed. So much is uncertain in life. So much can go wrong…"

"Perhaps," Annie said, though she wasn't convinced.

Aquillus smiled. "No matter. I'll keep trying, never fear. I merely wondered if your brother mentioned anything."

"No, sorry."

"I expect he was so surprised—and relieved—to have you back safely that every other matter was of no importance."

"I expect you're right."

"Well, goodnight, Your Highness. Sorry to have troubled you."

"Not at all," Annie assured him. "It was no trouble."

But he *had* troubled her, she thought as he left, shutting the door behind him with a soft click and once more leaving her alone with her thoughts.

She massaged her temples, feeling overwhelmed with all that had happened. Ben was in fact not dead, but alive and here at the palace. The negotiations were proceeding frustratingly slow while her people starved. And if Aquillus's letters never arrived, Varrian had no earthly idea what was even happening.

What she needed was a long rest, to set aside her troubles for a while and come back at them from another angle when she was ready.

But her mind was too awash with questions to even consider sleep at the moment. Without bothering to change out of her evening gown, she pulled the door open again and set off down the hallway, her back straight, her stride purposeful.

If she was going to be stuck here, she might as well try to make some more progress with her experiments. That was at least something she could do, to make herself feel like she was contributing something rather than standing around, waiting, going mad.

Perhaps if she could figure this out, there would be no need for the wedding. She shuddered at the thought.

Her workshop was exactly as she'd left it, pale moonlight streaming through the windows. Her plants had been neglected while she'd been away and Annie quickly took stock of their conditions. She trimmed and pruned, removing dead or dying leaves or shoots, watering and repotting where needed, her hands falling back into the familiar routine.

Some of the tension she'd been carrying with her fell away as she worked, the movements comforting in their way. The smell and feel of soil, to focus her attentions on something outside of herself. She still had far to go if she were to succeed, but so long as she were here, at least she was working toward that elusive goal. She wasn't going to wake up one day and find the problem had magically solved itself.

When there was nothing more to be done, Annie turned her attention to the other plants in the conservatory. It was time to see what Alaran plants she had to work with.

The conservatory stood at the very top of one of the palace spires, the circular room completely surrounded by windows, the ceiling another glass dome. She glanced down at the lights of the towns spread out below, impossibly far away. They were another world entirely, not quite real.

Moonlight illuminating her way, Annie navigated around the room, identifying what plants she could, considering them and taking mental notes for later.

The air was cloying with their competing scents, the room choked with plants, nearly sprawling on top of each other. She almost tripped over the vines of one, snaking out across the floor. Others were coiled tightly in on themselves. Some were unfurled and bold, others hid, concealed beneath the leaves. There were flowers and blooms, thorns and berries. Some leaves were jagged and prickly, others waxy, and still more Annie knew better than to touch. She reached out, running her fingers over a velvety leaf.

She had nearly made a full turn around the room when she stopped short. *Thalia!* Annie whirled around, expecting to see the queen behind her, silhouetted in the doorway, and prepared to explain what she was doing there, although she wasn't doing anything wrong.

But there was no one there.

Annie took a deep breath, trying to still her racing heart, and inhaled a lungful of Thalia's perfume. The scent was what made her think of the queen, her mind immediately leaping to the most logical conclusion—if she smelled the perfume, the queen must be here.

But there was no queen, only her perfume. Annie took a few more steps, the pungent aroma growing stronger, until she came to the source.

Concealed beneath the fronds of a fern sprouted a cluster of berries, the leaves large and petal-like, with red veins running through them. The berries themselves were small, each cluster hardly bigger than the tip of Annie's finger. But there was no mistaking their distinctive coloring: black where the fruit met the stem, slowly brightening into a vivid blood red.

It was the leaves that gave off the perfume. Annie now knew that she had never smelled it before, but she had read about it, the description of the aroma so accurate that she'd felt as though she knew the smell at once.

Certainly, she knew the plant. It had a variety of colorful names, devil's blood and silk snare among the more common. The first was due to the color of juice within the berries. The second referred to the silky feel of the leaves and how addicting the plant could be.

But she knew it best by another name entirely: *bellavexis*.

It had been commonly used as a sedative in the past, quite a powerful one. It kept patients docile and compliant, but, as it was later discovered, was very addictive. For that reason, among others, prolonged use was discouraged.

It was also an effective treatment for anxiety, but its very effectiveness came as the result of another unfortunate side effect. The plant dulled both emotion and memory, sometimes erasing the latter completely, and much of the person's personality along with it.

Annie sucked in a shaky breath. Silk snare was a dangerous plant even when one knew what they were doing. What it was doing here in the conservatory, Annie didn't know. Nor why queen Thalia smelled so strongly of it.

The smell was strong but not unpleasant. It was possible that Thalia simply liked the perfume and kept a plant growing here for that very reason.

But Annie wasn't sure. The earlier misgivings she'd expressed to Varrian about something being wrong in Alara came creeping back. The easing of tension she'd felt working in her laboratory had vanished.

She let the ferns fall, hiding the silk snare once more. Turning, she fled the conservatory for the safety of her room.

CHAPTER 23

Sharpe suppressed a sigh as she stepped off the escort ship and onto the pier in Daera, not far from where they had once dropped off supplies. Rain fell softly from the sky, a chill wind whipping off the sea. Her surroundings reflected her bleak mood, suiting her just fine.

She turned to face Terrance. Horus perched on his shoulder, his feathers damp and bedraggled. During the crossing, she had spoken at length to Terrance about what they should do upon arriving in Daera.

He'd been all for trying to find some way to help Ben, but as Sharpe had pointed out, he was beyond helping now. As quartermaster, Terrance ascended to the rank of captain in Ben's absence. He was their leader now and she looked to him as one.

They were a small group—or smaller than she would have liked. Sharpe was so used to having a crew of over one hundred and fifty men working alongside her and now there were only a handful, the rest having thrown their lot in with Berchmoore or else drowned. Those that survived had done so only by desperately clinging to any handhold they could find.

"What do we do now?" she murmured, leaning close to Terrance.

"We need to find Calida and tell 'er what happened," he answered. "She needs to know, even if there's nothing to be done. 'Orus can show us the way."

Sharpe looked at the bird. "All right," she conceded. "Should we find a pub somewhere and wait for the rain to pass before we head out?"

Terrance shook his head. "This is Daera. We could be waiting for a while." He turned to the hawk perched on his shoulder. "Lead on, 'Orus."

Sharpe's eyes followed the bird as he took off, their motley crew setting after him, trudging their way through the mud. She had never ventured into Daera before and had to admit that she had never wanted to. The ravaged kingdom was a depressing sight.

Everywhere one looked there seemed to be houses with roofs missing or collapsed, windows boarded up or broken out. The villages weren't so bad—at least they still held a trace of life—but the individual houses further on, that once must have been farms, were lifeless husks.

Some of them had caved in entirely, obviously abandoned, and others had crumbled when the earth fell away beneath them. Sharpe wondered if the people who had once lived there had moved on voluntarily, seeking a better life elsewhere, or whether they were all dead, victims of the famine.

She shuddered, eager to move on. She believed in ghosts and wouldn't have been surprised to find them lingering here.

Thankfully, they didn't come across any villages filled with the dead, the way some rumors claimed.

Calida's cottage was located deep in the forest, nestled among the trees and nearly completely overgrown with ivy. Sharpe doubted they would have been able to find it at all if not for Horus's guidance and part of her understood why Calida must have felt safe from Mordred here.

Mordred. Sharpe suppressed another shiver at the mere thought. She'd have to warn Calida and Lorelei. The witch-hunter would be on his way back, if he hadn't already arrived.

She realized, as they walked up to the door, that Calida might not even be home. If so, they didn't know when to expect her back and could be in for a long wait. But she glimpsed movement from within as she rapped on the door and a moment later, Calida stood there, peering at them in bewilderment.

"What are you doing here?" Her gray eyes went to the hawk, but he made no sound.

"Something's 'appened," Terrance said simply. "May we come in?"

Calida regarded him, her lips thinning, dread entering her gaze. But she stood aside to let them pass without a word.

Their group may have been small, but in the tiny house, there seemed suddenly to be no room.

Still, despite the small size, Sharpe had to admit it was a cozy sort of space. The furniture was worn, but comfortable. Blankets and spare shawls draped over the backs. Candles were lit around the room and somewhere, unseen, she could smell incense burning.

A warm fire crackled in the hearth and Horus flew over to perch on the arm of a chair beside it. Sharpe found herself drawn to it, for its warmth as much as the comfort it provided.

In this, at least, luck was with them. Lorelei was already there, seated in one of the chairs. She rose to her feet as they entered. "Calida? What's going on?"

Calida shut the door when the last of them had entered and re-latched it, leaning against its frame for a moment as though in need of support.

She took a deep breath and turned to face the room. "It's Ben, isn't it?"

"'Ow did you know?" Terrance asked.

"Because I knew he'd be here himself, otherwise."

Sharpe let Terrance tell the story—adding in a few details herself that he'd left out, but that she felt were pertinent—from Berchmoore taking their ship, to Ben being taken by the Alaran vessel and the rest of them left to drown if the princess hadn't come along.

Calida remained standing throughout the tale, but she sank down onto the worn sofa, near where Horus was perched, as the story came to its end. Sharpe had never seen anyone look more defeated than Ben's aunt did in that moment.

She felt compelled to say something, anything, to fill the silence. The room had fallen deathly quiet except for the crackling of the fire and the occasional shifting of a log. "I'm sorry. We thought you should know."

Calida raised her head. "We have to help him."

"'Elp 'im?" Terrance said, mirroring Sharpe's own surprise. "But 'e was taken to Alara. 'E'll be dead by now."

"No. He won't." Calida rose to her feet again. "Trust me. It's in the queen's best interest to keep him alive."

"But why would she do that?" Sharpe demanded. "How can you be so sure?"

In spite of herself, she felt a surge of hope that perhaps Ben might not be dead after all. The idea was ludicrous—and getting her hopes up even more so—but Calida seemed absolutely certain.

"Because," Calida replied, a flash of rage sparking briefly in her eyes, gone so fast Sharpe wasn't sure she'd seen it. "Queen Thalia is my sister."

Sharpe sat there, stunned, trying to make sense of the information.

"You?" Terrance exclaimed. "The queen of Alara is *your* sister?"

He didn't add what some of them were likely also thinking: *Then why are you living here in this skies forsaken kingdom?*

"There's no time to explain." Calida's tone brooked no argument. "Ben is our priority now."

"What about Mordred?" Sharpe asked. "He's still out there, looking for you. He's on his way, if he hasn't arrived already."

"Hang Mordred!" Calida snapped. "We have to do something to help Ben. This is exactly what I—" She glanced at Lorelei, "—what *we* never wanted to happen. This is why we did what we did in the first place."

"But don't you see?" Lorelei spoke up. "That's probably the safest place of all for him to be. Thalia must realize who he is."

When Calida next spoke, the tone of her voice sent gooseflesh crawling over Sharpe's skin.

"That's what I'm afraid of."

* * *

Days passed by with no word from the queen. She hadn't offered up any more interesting bits about Ben's past or made good on her offer to train him. He remained sequestered in the same room without windows, with the requirement of attending dinner every evening.

He was no closer to finding out why exactly he was there and he was getting tired of waiting. If the queen wouldn't be forthcoming, he would seek the answers out for himself. He had tested the door to his room and found it unlocked. All he needed was the perfect opportunity and a little help.

Ben wasn't sure where to start, but inspiration sought him out one afternoon. He'd been taking a nap in his room, bored by the isolation, when he was awoken by the sound of voices just outside the door, one of them raised and angry.

He blinked, unsure whether he had dreamed it or not, and climbed out of bed, stealing over the floor on bare feet and pressing his ear to the door.

"I insist you let me in!" a male voice demanded. It was the raised voice and the owner did not sound the least bit pleased, but it was unfamiliar and Ben couldn't place it.

"Sorry, sir," a second male voice replied. "No one is to enter."

"On whose orders?"

"The queen's, sir."

"This is ridiculous!" the first voice cried. "I am the king!"

Ben drew back from the door in surprise. The mysterious, aloof king of Alara, who was supposed to be ill, according to what Annie had told him.

Although, when he'd asked her why the king had been absent from dinner and she replied that he was ill, she hadn't seemed convinced. He'd wanted to ask her what she meant, but hadn't gotten the chance.

"Apologies, Your Majesty. But no one is allowed inside."

"I know there is someone staying in that room and I want to know who."

Wrapping his fingers around the door handle, Ben slowly eased it open and peered through the thin crack. He could just make out the figure of the king and his first thought was how little Kain resembled him. The king had blond hair, tending toward gray, and his blue eyes were several shades too light to match the prince's.

"There you are, Your Majesty!" a new voice boomed, making Ben duck back slightly. He didn't have to see the newcomer to know who the voice belonged to. He'd heard it back on the *Phoenix*, the day he'd been captured. "You mustn't go wandering off like that. We've been looking for you."

"Ah, Rodek," said the king, sounding slightly mollified. "Just the man I want to see. Tell these guards to let me pass. I want to know who our guest is." He gestured to the door.

Ben thought it odd that the king, of all people, was telling someone else to give orders that he could not.

"Now, Your Majesty," Rodek soothed. "There's nothing to see behind that door. Come along, now. You're not feeling well. You need to take your medicine. Take him to his quarters."

The two guards moved forward to usher the king away. "Let go of me!" he demanded, struggling slightly, but he was no match for the two younger men. "I wish to speak to whoever is in that room!"

"Oh, sire, there's no one in there."

Ben watched until they had vanished from view before carefully closing the door once more. Why were they trying to keep his presence a secret from the king? Why had Rodek lied about no one being in the room?

Suddenly, he wondered if the guards posted at the door were less to keep him in and more to keep the king out. But why?

Perhaps if he could find out the answer to that, he could learn the reason he'd been brought to the palace in the first place. But for that, he'd need someone to help him, someone who knew the castle a lot better than he did, and someone he could trust.

He approached Annie after dinner one evening. She was once again dressed fabulously, this time in a green gown that matched her eyes, the silk rippling around her like waves. Her hair was pinned up, leaving her slender neck and shoulders bare, and secured in place with gold hairpins that matched her earrings. A few strands of hair remained loose, framing her face charmingly.

Once again, they were accompanied by guards on the way back to their rooms, as well as Annie's personal chaperone, a withered older woman.

Ben leaned close to Annie, his voice barely a whisper so as not to be overheard. "I need a favor."

She glanced at him and the two of them dropped back slightly, slowing their pace. To his surprise, she linked her arm with his, as though they were enjoying a pleasing stroll together. He wasn't sure it was entirely appropriate, with her engaged to another man, but he wasn't going to complain.

"What is it?" she asked.

"I need answers," he confessed. "I'm no closer to learning why I'm here and I want to take a look around and see if I can find anything. I heard the king outside my room earlier. He knew I was in there and he wanted to see me, but Rodek wouldn't let him in." He shook his head. "Something is…off about all of this. But I need your help."

"My help?"

"You know your way around this place much better than I do."

She looked up at him. "You want me to help you snoop." The tone of her voice made the notion sound scandalous, but from the smirk on her face, he could tell she was jesting.

"Yes. Will you help me?"

For a moment, he expected her to say no. She owed him nothing and he was a pirate, after all—that breed she so despised.

Or rather, he had been a pirate. With no ship or crew, he wasn't sure what that made him now.

Annie had turned quite pale and he was on the point of asking her what was wrong when she replied, somewhat breathlessly, "Yes, I'll help you." She turned to face forward again. "You're not the only one who wants answers."

Ben suppressed the urge to ask her what she meant by that. He'd gotten what he wanted and there would be time enough for questions later, when they could speak more privately.

He glanced over his shoulder. "We'll need to find a way to ditch your chaperone. She follows you everywhere."

Annie rolled her eyes, her color returning. "Don't remind me. They seem to think my virtue is in danger of being compromised."

He couldn't help but tease her. "Or maybe they're worried you'll be kidnapped by pirates."

She turned a becoming shade of red. "Don't worry about Florence. I'll figure something out. But we'll need to wait until everyone is asleep."

"Fine. Do you have a clock in your room?"

She nodded.

"All right. At exactly one, tonight, then. Where should I meet you?"

"Outside my door. But how are you going to get away?"

He smiled grimly. "Don't worry about me. My door isn't locked. I somehow get the feeling that the queen isn't too concerned about me escaping."

* * *

"Thank you so much for agreeing to this, Maddie," Annie said, grateful that Florence was in the other room. When in the presence of her maids, Annie was in little danger. She was already in her nightgown, as part of the deception, and the maid was busy taking the pins out of her hair for the night.

Maddie was thrilled that Annie had chosen to include her in the ruse. Too thrilled, perhaps, all things considered.

The maid stifled a laugh. "I can't believe you're sneaking out, miss. You're not going to see the prince, are you? Not dressed like that, I wouldn't imagine!"

She referred to the fact that Annie would be borrowing one of Maddie's plain muslin dresses, disguising herself as a maid so that if anyone saw her, they'd think nothing of it and probably ignore her altogether. Servants could be essentially invisible when they chose.

Annie had to agree that sneaking out dressed as a maid for an assignation with the prince hardly seemed logical, though for all she knew, Kain could have a thing for servant girls.

"No," she admitted, seeing no harm in it, since Maddie was already in her confidence. "I'm not."

"Someone else? How exciting! Who is it, then?"

Maddie believed she was sneaking out to meet a man romantically, and Annie saw no reason to disabuse her of the notion, since it was the most logical explanation.

"You know that pirate captain you were asking me about? It's him."

"Skies!" the maid exclaimed. "Well, don't worry about a thing, miss. My lips are sealed."

"I know. I can always rely on you."

"Well, I'd best let you get to bed, miss." Maddie winked at her. "Goodnight, my lady."

"Goodnight."

Annie waited until the maid had departed for her own quarters and then the waiting began. She didn't want to climb into bed and risk accidentally falling asleep and missing her meeting.

The hours wore on and it became increasingly difficult to stay awake, but at last the clock read half past twelve.

She stood, listening, but the bowels of the palace remained quiet. She went over to the wardrobe, where Maddie had stashed an extra pair of clothing earlier. The maid had a fuller figure than she did and the dress fit a bit awkwardly, but the point wasn't to be fashionable but invisible.

Annie inexpertly pinned her hair back up, snatching a few of the gold hairpins. They were the only ones she could find, but they'd be hidden beneath her cap, where they wouldn't be seen. She jammed the cap over her head and surveyed her handiwork in the mirror. Strands of hair stuck out from under the cap, but she supposed it suited the look of a maid who had snuck out for an assignation.

If we get caught, she thought suddenly, wondering how they would explain themselves. Then, just as quickly, *We won't get caught.*

Taking a deep breath, she opened the door and peered out. The hallway was clear and she stepped out quickly, shutting the door behind her. It wouldn't do for anyone to come upon her leaving that way, not when maids had their own entrance.

Annie reached up, fiddling with her cap as she waited for Ben to arrive. What would she do if he never showed up?

"*Annie*," a voice hissed from behind.

She jumped, a yelp starting to spring from her lips even as she turned around. A hand clamped gently over her mouth, filling her nose with the scent of leather, cutting short her cry.

"Relax," Ben whispered. "It's me."

She grabbed his wrist and shoved his hand away, embarrassed by her reaction and angry at herself for it. "I know that. You scared me is all." She hadn't even heard him creep up behind her.

"I wasn't sure it was you at first, dressed like that." He took in her appearance, eyes glittering with amusement.

For his part, he was dressed the same as he'd been at dinner, although he'd shed the outer frock coat and now wore a white silk shirt. The collar was undone and Annie tried not to stare at it.

"I told you I'd find some way of getting out. This way, if anyone sees us, they'll think you snuck out to see one of the maids."

His eyebrows rose but he refrained from comment.

"So where do we start?" she asked, eager to be off.

"The king. Why would Rodek lie to him? He—the king—didn't look ill when I saw him earlier. Isn't there supposed to be something wrong with him?"

"I think there is," she said, not wanting to explain the suspicion that had taken root in her mind ever since that night in the conservatory, as insidious as the plant that had put it there.

At first, she'd thought the king was a drunkard and that illness was just the excuse the rest of them gave to cover it up. But if she was right, the alternative was so much worse.

"Do you know where his quarters are?"

Annie nodded. "Yes. They're right across from the queen's. Follow me." She had taken to roaming the castle in moments when she was bored, though somehow, her steps always seemed to lead her back to the conservatory and what it implied.

She turned and began leading him down the darkened corridors, their footsteps nearly silent on the stone floor. There were no torches set into wall sconces to light their way; the moonlight streaming through the windows and glass domes was more than sufficient.

"I hesitate to ask," she said suddenly. "But…those bruises…" The bruising she had noticed the first night at dinner had begun to fade and turn yellow, much as her own bruise had done.

"Berchmoore," he answered, bitterness clear in his voice.

"There seems to be little love between the two of you."

"No."

"What happened?"

She heard him sigh. "He was a member of the crew once, under Captain Lussard—the captain before me. Lussard recognized my talent for sailing and saw that I rose through the ranks quickly, all the way to quartermaster. Berchmoore didn't take too kindly to being passed over for the position. He'd served under Lussard for a long time and felt that the rank should have been his. And then when Lussard named me his successor as captain, it was just a step too far for Berchmoore. He gathered together some others who were disgruntled for one reason or another and attempted a mutiny."

Annie looked at him in alarm and he went on quickly, "They failed, obviously, but instead of killing them as the pirate code demands, I let them go. But I told them they should, under no circumstance, expect to be accepted back. Berchmoore's nurtured a grudge over it ever since. He still wanted to be captain of the *Phoenix* and I guess now he's got his wish."

"I'm sorry," Annie murmured.

He shrugged. "It's not your doing."

"But it is, though, isn't it?"

"What do you mean?"

"Guards," she hissed suddenly.

There was nowhere to go in the corridor, no columns or tapestries to hide behind. Ben pushed her suddenly against the wall, leaning close to her, one arm propped against the wall, blocking her face from view of the guards. To them, it would appear as though they were merely a man and a maid having a conversation—or stealing an intimate moment.

Annie drew in a sharp breath at Ben's close proximity, inhaling his sandalwood scent. Her heart thrummed in her chest; he wasn't touching her, but there were mere inches separating them and it would only take the slightest movement to close the distance.

But Ben didn't notice her reaction. His eyes were on the guards, watching subtly until they'd moved on. He stepped back, giving her some space, and she let out a breath.

"What did you mean?" he asked again. "That what happened was somehow your fault?"

"Well…if I had never run off and stowed away on Berchmoore's ship, you never would have rescued me and taken me to Daera. And no one would have thought you'd kidnapped me and then gone after you."

"Maybe not," he conceded. "But Berchmoore's had it in for me even before you came along. We'd have clashed sooner or later."

"But you could have handled him," Annie said morosely. "Couldn't you? It was the Alaran warship that sealed it and that never would have happened if it weren't for me."

"Annie, you don't know that," Ben said firmly.

Her chest tightened. He'd called her by her name. Not *princess*. Annie.

"Berchmoore's new ship was a lot more powerful than I gave him credit for. If anything, what happened is my fault, for being cocky and thinking I could handle whatever came at me."

Annie drew herself up, happy to drop the subject. "Well, the coast is clear. Come on; it's not much further now."

They reached the hallway containing the doors to both of the royal chambers without further incident. They were at the corner of a corridor, peering around, when Annie said, "All right, stop here." She pointed, indicating the two doors ahead. "That's the queen's chambers, adjacent to the king's."

Ben was about to say something when Annie suddenly hissed a warning and dragged him behind one of the pillars, having seen who was approaching. Neither of them could risk being seen by him.

As they watched, a familiar figure drew near the queen's chambers and entered, disappearing inside.

"Was that Rodek?" Ben murmured, his breath warm on her ear. "What's he doing, going into the queen's chambers at this time of night?"

Annie gave him a wry look. They both knew the only likely explanation.

Ben gave a low whistle. "Well, that explains a lot."

"All right, listen," Annie spoke quickly. "Guards patrol this hallway in front of the two chambers, walking past every few minutes. If we want to get inside and find the king, we need to move fast before they come back."

Ben cast a swift glance around, in either direction, peering through the dark. "Let's go."

They stole out into the hallway, halting in front of the king's door. Ben reached out, grasping the handle and turning. It didn't budge.

"It's locked."

"Guess we should have expected that," Annie remarked.

Rodek had entered the queen's quarters without any trouble, but perhaps he'd had a key.

"I could open it, maybe, if I had something to pick the lock with."

Annie frowned, peering at the lock. She gasped, reaching up beneath her cap to pull out one of her hairpins, causing a lock of hair to come tumbling down her face. "Will this work?"

Ben blinked, considered. One end of the pin was very sharp and thin. "It might at that," he said, taking it and turning back to the keyhole. "You're certainly full of surprises, princess." He stuck the sharp end of the hairpin inside and began fiddling with it. "Keep an eye out, will you?"

Annie's heart beat faster with each second that ticked by. They were in the hallway, out in the open, she standing and Ben kneeling by the door. There was nowhere to hide and by being so exposed, they risked certain discovery.

Annie gripped the skirt of her—no, Maddie's—dress with clenched fingers. They'd wasted too much time. The guards would be coming back at any moment.

She shuddered to think what the queen, and Kain, would have to say if she were discovered with Ben, who was trying to break into the king's rooms, while she stood by, dressed as a servant.

What if Kain refused to marry her and the wedding was called off, the alliance with it? She could be risking everything!

Suddenly, she realized what a stupid idea this had been. How had she ever allowed Ben to talk her into this?

"Hurry, Ben!" she hissed.

"I'm trying!" he muttered. "I've never picked a lock with a hairpin before…"

Annie kept casting anxious glances in either direction, expecting to hear a shout and see guards hurrying in their direction. *Oh, skies…*

There was a sudden click. "I've got it!" Ben exclaimed softly, just as the first hint of footsteps could be heard, rounding the corner, straight for them.

For a moment, the two of them stared at each other, frozen in fear. Then Ben stood, pushing the door open and stepping inside. Annie followed in a flurry of skirts, heart in her throat. He closed the door behind them and they stood there, breathless, hearts hammering. The footsteps kept coming, reaching where they'd been only moments before, and then passing by.

There was no cry of outrage, no guards seizing her.

Annie looked at Ben, pushing hair out of her face. He flashed her a roguish grin and she found herself smiling back. It was all she could do to repress the irrational urge to laugh.

What the hell was she doing, roaming about the palace halls at night, picking locks and ducking into forbidden quarters with a pirate?

Then, as if realizing where they were and what they'd done, they turned to face the rest of the room.

And there, seated on a chair in front of a crackling fire, was the king.

CHAPTER 24

For a long moment, neither of them moved. The king sat facing the fire; he hadn't turned or gotten to his feet when they'd entered, shutting the door softly behind them. Ben still had ahold of the door handle and he forced his fingers to let go, releasing it. His other hand gripped Annie's golden hairpin, and he slipped it into his pocket, his hands damp with sweat within his gloves.

"Who is it?" the king demanded, craning his head to see around the back of the chair. "Who's there?"

They stood in a spacious, well-appointed sitting room, the walls papered scarlet with gold motifs.

Annie glanced at Ben and then stepped forward cautiously. "I'm sorry for disturbing you, sir."

"Princess Annabelle? Skies above, I nearly didn't recognize you, dressed like that!"

"Yes, it's me, sir." Annie stepped around to the side of the chair where he could see her better. "And I brought someone with me, that I think you wanted to meet."

The king rose from his chair. Annie motioned for Ben to come closer. He hesitated for a second, then crossed the room, grateful for her lead, coming to stand beside her. He blinked, taking in the man before him. It was much easier to make out his features at such close proximity.

He had blue eyes, very much like Ben's own, only slightly less vibrant, dulled perhaps with age. They were nearly the same height. The firelight illuminated the wrinkled and weathered face of the man who had tried to gain entry into his room.

"Ah, yes," the king murmured. "The mysterious guest in the west wing, kept locked up and under guard. I know how that feels."

Ben didn't bother to correct him, licking his lips nervously. "You wanted to speak to me, sir?"

The king nodded, scratching absently at his beard. "Yes…I wondered what reason Thalia would have for bringing a stranger here."

"Do you know why I'm here?" Ben asked eagerly.

But to his disappointment, the king shook his head. "I'm just as in the dark as you are, I'm afraid. Thalia doesn't see the need to consult me in such matters. She thinks I'm nothing but an old fool and maybe I have been…" His eyes, which had grown foggy for a moment, sharpened suddenly as they focused on Ben. "Who are you?"

"Benjamin Knight, sir. Former captain of the *Phoenix*."

The admission hurt.

"Hmm," the king murmured. "Doesn't sound familiar. How long have I been in here? I lose track of time…" He trailed off, turning to stare into the fire.

Annie reached out to place a hand on Ben's arm. "Maybe we should go," she whispered.

Ben felt a sharp pang of disappointment. He didn't want to leave just yet. They'd only just arrived and they'd learned nothing. The king had no answers to give them. The man was more lucid than Ben had expected, given what he'd heard, but there was something clearly wrong with him.

He should have expected nothing less. He'd been a fool to get his hopes up.

He opened his mouth to agree, preparing to admit defeat, but a knock at the door interrupted him, making both of them freeze. Annie's hand gripped his arm painfully tight. She looked up at him, her expression frightened at the prospect of being discovered.

"Who is it?" the king called.

A male voice spoke from the other side of the door, "It's time for your medicine, Your Majesty."

The king waved an angry arm at the door, but of course, the other man could not see it. "Oh, go away," he growled.

"The queen insists, my lord. How else will you get better?"

"I have visitors!" the king protested. Annie flinched.

The servant was not to be put off. "You must keep up your strength, sire."

"Oh, very well," the king consented, but he still didn't sound overly thrilled. "Come in, then."

In less time than it took to fully think about what they were doing, Ben grabbed Annie's hand and pulled her over toward the window. The sitting room had nowhere else to hide and the bedroom was on the other side of the room, too far to reach in time. That left only the tall window, with curtains so long, they pooled onto the floor. Ben flung them back and he and Annie quickly stepped behind them, drawing them closed again as the door swung open.

They stood there, breathless, pressed against the window, side by side, the curtains shielding them from view. Ben peered out between the small gap that separated the two curtains. He felt Annie press close as she did the same, her hair brushing against his cheek.

A liveried attendant entered, carrying what appeared to be a glass of red wine. He set the glass down on a side table next to the chair and looked around. Ben held his breath, but the servant's gaze slid right over their hiding spot as it passed around the room.

"Where are your guests?" he asked.

The king glanced around, too, as if in befuddlement. He hadn't seen them dart behind the drapes. "Oh, they were just here a moment ago…"

The servant gave him an indulgent smile. "Well, I'm sure they'll come back once you drink this."

The king grumbled something under his breath, but he tipped the wine glass back and took a sip of the contents. The servant waited expectantly.

The king lowered the glass, glowering at him. "What are you waiting for?"

"I was instructed to wait until you'd finished all of your medicine, sire."

"I'll finish the rest of it later. Now go away. I'm tired and I wish to be left alone."

The servant hesitated, but apparently the king still carried some authority, for he bowed a moment later and departed, closing the door behind him.

"They're always giving him some sort of medicine," Annie whispered. Ben could barely hear her, her voice was so quiet. And her hair smelled distractingly of jasmine. "But I don't know why."

No sooner had the servant left than the king set the glass back down on the table with a sigh. Ben waited a few more moments before he dared push back the curtains and retreat from their hiding spot.

Annie strode forward with purpose and snatched up the wine glass, sniffing it, the color draining from her face.

"What is it?" Ben asked.

"*Bellavexis.*"

He frowned. "What?"

She made a face. "Devil's blood. Silk snare."

"Oh." Ben recognized the plant by its common names. "*Oh.*"

"Oh, yes," Annie agreed, turning to the king. "I don't think you should drink this anymore, Your Majesty." And then, to emphasize her point, she tossed the glass's contents into the fire, the liquid sizzling as it met the flames.

Ben lowered his voice to a hiss. "Why the hell would they give him silk snare?"

"I don't know," she whispered. "But I had a feeling... I found some of it in the conservatory the other night. Where it came from or why it's there, I don't know, but something is not right..."

Ben glanced at the king. The man had paid them no heed since they'd stepped back into view.

Annie returned the glass to the table, empty with only a few dark drops left in the bottom, appearing for all the world as though the king had ingested the whole thing.

"We should go," she said softly. "We've spent too much time here as it is. Someone will notice we're missing."

Ben sighed, not at all satisfied, but he realized she was fearful of discovery. It wasn't fair of him to ask her to do this. If it had just been him, he'd have stayed and risked it, but it wasn't just him. He had to consider that.

"You're right. Let's go."

Annie opened the door a crack, peeking out cautiously. "It's clear. Hurry."

They darted out into the hallway, Annie leading back the way they'd come.

"Did you find what you were looking for?" she asked after they'd gone some distance.

"No," he admitted. "But thank you for assisting me."

"Think nothing of it."

They parted ways at her room and Ben made his way back to his own quarters, trying not to feel too disappointed. As he reached the door, he glanced over his shoulder, feeling eyes on him—and not that of the guards.

A lithe orange fox crouched behind one of the pillars, eyes glinting as it watched him. Ben had never seen the creature before, but there was something intelligent in its gaze that made him uncomfortable. Something unnatural and yet familiar.

He gladly shut the door on the beast.

The summons from the queen the next morning did not come as a surprise. *We must have been seen,* Ben thought, hoping Annie wouldn't be punished for her part in this. He'd have to tell Thalia that sneaking into the king's quarters had been his idea and any punishment ought to be his alone.

To his surprise, he was taken once more to the conservatory, leaves and branches brushing against his shoulders as he made his way to the center, the glass dome high above his head. The sunlight streaming through the multitude of windows landed hot on his skin, already conjuring a thin layer of sweat.

The conservatory brought back memories of last night, what Annie had said about silk snare in the king's drink, and what it meant. He swallowed as he approached, unable to shake the feeling that he was a man walking to his own execution.

Had he finally worn out his welcome at the palace? Was this subterfuge the last straw? Had the queen tired of him? Would she order his death?

Ben had expected to have met his end by now. A reprieve was not the same thing as a pardon and that was what his time at the palace had been—a reprieve. There was only one way this ended.

A white wrought-iron table and two chairs had been set up in the middle of the room, a tea service laid out on the table, along with toast, eggs, sausages, jars of preserves, and fresh oranges. The china looked so delicate, he thought it might shatter at the slightest touch.

Thalia was dressed in a deep blue gown this morning, high-necked, with strings of beads around her shoulders. She was already seated in one of the chairs and gestured for him to take the other.

He did so, warily regarding the fox that wound itself around her legs. "Your familiar?"

She smiled. "Most people think Jade is nothing more than a pet. But yes, she is my familiar."

So that's who ratted us out.

The queen waved a hand at the food spread out before them. "Help yourself." She held out a bottle. "Would you like some brandy in your tea? You may need it."

Skies, he really was dead. Ben nodded, bracing himself for the conversation to come. He was just tentatively reaching for a piece of toast when she spoke again, "Regarding last night—"

"It was my idea," he said quickly. "I only wanted answers. I still don't know why I'm here."

Thalia smothered her piece of toast with some of the orange preserves. "I suppose it's time I told you the truth."

"I'd like that, Your Majesty." *I think.*

"Though," she added warningly, "I imagine it will be difficult to hear." She sat back in her chair, regarding him. "What did your aunt tell you about your parents, again? That they were commoners?"

He nodded. "And dead."

"Well, that's not true, because your parents are very much still alive. I can see my sister didn't tell you everything."

The brandy-laced tea went down the wrong way and Ben coughed, fighting to keep his composure as his chest started to burn.

His voice came out hoarse and strained. "*What?*"

"Calida is my sister," Thalia replied, completely composed. "And you are my son."

Ben stared at her. The rows of plants on either side of the room seemed to stretch in front of him and he shot a suspicious glance at the tea.

He might have thought she was mocking him if she didn't look so damn serious. He shook his head, but it took a few moments for him to find his voice again. "No. That's not true. My parents were common and they died."

"That's what Calida told you and it's hardly surprising, given the fact that she *stole* you from me."

Ben shook his head again, but the lightheaded feeling wouldn't go away. "No. This is not real. This is not possible."

"I can see you're going to be difficult to convince, which is unsurprising given the circumstances. Skepticism is a good quality to have, Benjamin." She stood, pushing her chair back and turned around so that her back was to him. "But I imagine this ought to look familiar."

She gathered her hair and pulled it over her shoulder, leaving her back exposed. The dress she wore was backless, stopping at the base of her spine. And there, at the small of her back, exposed now that her long hair was no longer in the way, was a witch-mark.

Identical to his own.

Thalia let her fiery hair tumble back down and faced him again, resuming her seat.

Ben found himself utterly speechless, his mouth opening and closing ineffectually like a fish out of water, unable to deny the proof he'd seen with his own eyes. Her mark was identical in every way to the one on the back of his right hand and there was no denying what it meant.

"But how?" he finally managed to choke out. "Why would Calida do such a thing?"

"Because she's jealous."

"Of what?"

"Of me. She wanted Niklaus—the king—for herself. She wanted to be queen, to better herself." The queen sighed. "But to understand that, I have to explain the way Alara used to treat witches. It used to be that whenever a witch was a child, they were sent to a monastery to be trained how to use their powers. When they graduated, they would go out into the kingdom to be laborers in the fields, or keep the weather calm on board ships, whatever job best suited their particular gifts. Calida and I were sent to the monastery, but Calida wasn't satisfied with the future that awaited her. She didn't want to be just another servant of the kingdom.

"When king Niklaus—or prince, as he was then—came to visit the monastery with his father, to look at the newest batch of graduates, he saw me." Thalia smiled at the memory. "It was my looks that interested him in the beginning, but he came back and as we got to know each other, we fell in love."

"But I thought a prince had to marry a princess," Ben interrupted.

Thalia shook her head. "Maybe elsewhere, but in Alara, the monarch can marry whomever they wish. But Niklaus wasn't king yet and the old king didn't approve of me. So we had to wait. Calida was jealous that Niklaus had chosen me instead of her." She sighed. "It was…trying, our having to wait. Niklaus wanted his father's approval, but he refused to give it, and that led to a lot of tension between the two of us. We fought, more than either of us would have liked, and Calida was there to comfort me. She would always tell me how reasonable I was being and how unfair Niklaus was.

"It was only later that I realized that she was visiting us separately, saying the same things to Niklaus. She would tell him that I was the unreasonable one and that I didn't understand him the way she did, trying to turn us against each other." The queen's eyes narrowed in anger, her lip curling. "My own sister. The one who should have been there for me when I needed her most, betraying me behind my back."

"So what did you do?"

"When I found out what she was doing, I convinced Niklaus to have her sent away," Thalia said ruefully. "There was nothing else I could do. I couldn't sit by and let her destroy our relationship and everything we had fought so hard to build. I thought that was the last of it, until I sent Rodek and Mordred out to hunt down the pirate who had supposedly kidnapped the princess. Rodek recognized your mark when he saw it and knew I needed to see it, too, so he brought you here to the palace. As soon as I saw it, I knew what must have happened."

"What did happen?" Ben had drained his tea while listening to the story and he poured himself some more, grateful for her suggestion of adding something stronger to it.

"All these years, I believed Kain was my son, while Calida was probably laughing wherever she'd holed herself up, knowing that she had taken my true son and I none the wiser. She had to have help, stealing you away. I believe it had to be Lorelei, the midwife, who helped her, seeing how she fled the castle shortly after. You were a newborn; I barely had the chance to look at you and then Lorelei was bustling you away, claiming it was her duty to look after you, and that I needed to rest. All I can think of is that she must have taken you out onto one of the balconies, some place open, and put you in something that Calida's hawk could carry away. A basket, perhaps. It would be easy enough.

"Horus carried you away in that basket, delivering you safely to Calida, who was still staying in Alara at that time. She couldn't have been far away. She put a replacement in your stead and sent the basket back."

"Kain?"

"Exactly. But she knew I'd seen your mark, so she placed a false one on Kain's right hand, just like yours, so I suspected nothing."

"But…our eyes," Ben protested, desperately latching onto anything that would disprove this wild tale. "Kain has dark blue eyes like you. Mine are lighter."

Thalia shrugged. "With newborn babies, one looks much like another, I'm afraid. Yes, your eyes are lighter. Just like your father's."

He had seen those very eyes just last night. He stared at Thalia, his gaze greedily searching her features for the similarities between them.

There were few. He resembled his father in almost every way. But there was no denying the bump in the bridge of her nose, exactly identical to his own. Such a bump could only be the result of a broken nose or genetics. And while Ben had broken his nose more than once, he'd had the bump for as long as he could remember, even as a child. Before he'd gone to sea.

Absently, he reached up, running a gloved finger over the bridge of his own nose.

Thalia added softly, "No doubt Calida believed you should have been her and Niklaus's child instead of mine."

The queen's words had a ring of truth to them. Ben's mind raced. Nearly everything Calida had ever told him had been a lie. She had stolen him from his true parents and let him believe they were dead. But she'd also stolen from him the life he should have had. He should have grown up here, in the palace, with the best of everything at his fingertips, never fearing he might miss a meal or having to look over his shoulder for danger.

Suddenly, he knew what Thalia had meant when she'd told him he belonged at the palace and that he'd been born there. He'd thought she meant Alara in general, but it was so much more than that.

He could have known what it was like to have a family, instead of just being raised by an aunt.

But then, I never would have gone to sea and become a pirate. He'd meant what he'd said to Rosa about the sea being his place and him not wanting to give it up. He loved it, but that still didn't excuse what Calida had done. And there was simply no denying the truth of the witch-mark.

I'm *the prince,* Ben realized, as the full weight of that revelation settled upon him. A royal. The future ruler of a kingdom. And Kain, the one everyone believed to be the real prince—including Thalia until recently—was an imposter.

What would Annie think if she knew? Annie…who was engaged to the prince of Alara, who wasn't who she thought he was. *That would make her engaged to me!*

The ground beneath his feet suddenly felt unstable and Ben was glad he was already sitting down.

"It's a lot to take in, I know. That's why I waited to tell you. I wasn't sure how to go about it—or that you'd even believe me."

Ben shook his head, trying to clear it. "If that was how Alara used to be, with the monastery and all that, how did we get to where we are now? With the witch-hunts?"

"Ah," Thalia sighed. "I'm sorry to disappoint you further, but Calida wasn't the woman you thought she was. As I said, Niklaus and I couldn't marry until the old king died. Calida must have thought she could speed that process along, while also taking my place. She used her knowledge of plants to poison the king. She thought she could frame me for it, but the truth came out." Thalia shook her head. "Regicide is a terrible crime and all witches paid the price for her treachery. Niklaus loved me and so I, at least, was safe. But the others…"

She summoned a smile for him. "Don't worry. You're safe here. Nothing's going to happen to you."

He looked up at her and for the first time, thought of her as being more than the queen. She was his *mother.* He had no idea what it was like to have a mother. Calida had been the closest thing, but she had been his aunt. And she could be…distant at times. There had been something about her, about their relationship, that made Ben believe that having a mother must feel different.

He had been happy, not knowing the truth that had just been revealed to him. But he'd only lived with his aunt until he was eight, when she'd sent him off to sea.

And yet, here they were, the two of them, despite all of Calida's efforts to keep them apart.

Thalia stood and made her way to his side of the table, touching his cheek with one hand. He looked up at her, into the eyes of his mother.

"I can't get back the time Calida took from us. The time we should have had together. But you're here now and I can promise you, nothing will take you away from me again."

CHAPTER 25

The *Phoenix* dropped anchor off Daera's coast, unable to put into port, on a morning that dawned chilly and damp. Clouds obscured the sky, threatening rain, but so far it had yet to break free. One of the longboats was being prepared to take Mordred ashore. He'd been forced to find passage back to the northern kingdom somehow and he saw using one of Alara's own privateers as the perfect opportunity.

Mordred paced the deck as he waited, impatient to begin his search for Calida. It had taken longer to arrive than he would have liked. He'd have left sooner if he hadn't had to stay to placate the queen. It was precious time lost. There was no telling where Calida may have gone during that time.

He turned to Berchmoore, who was leaning against the rail, which had been newly repaired. "Good luck with your 'unting!" the privateer called. He began to turn as though to head to his cabin,

"Wait," Mordred ordered. The privateer tensed, halting in his tracks. "I need you to stay here, anchored, until I return."

"What?" Berchmoore exclaimed. "That wasn't part of the deal."

"You'll be compensated for your trouble, of course. I need you to wait here so that I can return to Alara once I've concluded my business here."

"You can 'ire another ship."

"I can also sink that new tub of yours, if I see fit," Mordred snapped, his patience wearing thin. "And seeing as how you're captain, you might just go down with it."

"We're losing a lot of potential loot, sitting 'ere waiting for you," Berchmoore groused.

"You'll lose a lot more if you cross me," Mordred promised. "I'll make it worth your while. Besides, this shouldn't take long," he added, with more confidence than he felt.

"Fine," the privateer consented reluctantly. "You know where to find us."

* * *

It had been decided that Sharpe would remain with Calida and Lorelei while Terrance and the rest of the crew went into the villages by the coast to keep an eye out for Mordred, since the witch-hunter would be certain to recognize her.

Horus sat upon Terrance's shoulder, the bird's keen eyes scanning the streets around them. Calida had come to the conclusion that they didn't have time to sit around and wait for Mordred to find them, so they would come to him. As soon as the witch-hunter was spotted in Daera, Horus would fly back to Calida and give her Mordred's location.

Calida would handle the rest, making sure she was seen and then luring Mordred away.

Horus made a soft sound and Terrance looked up, sucking in a sharp breath. There, anchored off the coast not far from their former rendezvous site, was the *Phoenix*. She looked beautiful, even in the gray lighting, her red sails furled as she bobbed gently in the water. The holes that had been blown in her side were patched and her brown hull gleamed. There wasn't a shred of damage on her.

Terrance crept closer, remaining on the outskirts of town. A longboat was put ashore and he recognized Mordred among those present. They deposited him on the beach and he stalked away, leaving them there, as though waiting for him.

"All right, 'Orus," Terrance whispered. "Go find Calida. I'll tail 'im."

The hawk nipped the top of his ear affectionately, as if to remind him to be careful, and then he was gone.

* * *

Calida opened her door to let Horus in when the hawk came back to the cabin.

He landed on the back of a chair. *"Mordred is here,"* he reported. *"In the town of Steelrest. Berchmoore is anchored off the coast, waiting for him."*

Fetching her cloak and leaving Sharpe safely behind in her cottage, she set out. Little over half an hour later, Calida found herself walking the streets of the village.

Lorelei hadn't liked Calida's plan, when she told her that this was their chance.

"Chance to do what?" Lorelei had demanded.

"To put an end to him."

"Calida, you can't be serious. How do you intend to take on Mordred, knowing what he's capable of?"

"We'll set a trap for him," she replied. "Lure him out."

"How?"

Calida had pursed her lips. "You aren't going to like it. I'm the one he wants the most, so I'll go into the village and lure him away, into the forest. There, I can utilize my power fully."

"You seem to be forgetting that he can also utilize his powers fully there, too. He's an earth witch, just like us. Let me go with you. Lead him to where I'm lying in wait, and then we can both attack him. Surely even Mordred cannot take on two witches at once."

Calida didn't want her friend to risk herself, but knew the wisdom of her words and that there would be no dissuading her. "I don't like you taking that risk."

"It's a risk I'm willing to take. It's time we end this. In that, we agree."

Steelrest was a large town, its proximity to the harbor making it a center for trade and business—or it would have, if times hadn't been so hard. The rain had held off for the day and the streets were flourishing with activity, the townspeople taking advantage of what passed for good weather in Daera these days.

People bustled about, coming and going, frequenting certain establishments and going about their daily tasks. Sailors were always coming ashore here and plenty of the businesses catered to the tools of their trade.

Some had set up makeshift stalls, hawking what paltry wares they could. Others, dressed in filthy, tattered rags crouched in doorways or alleys, reaching out with skeletal, claw-like hands, desperate for charity that was not forthcoming.

Calida tried to ignore the clothing of those she passed, patched and mended well beyond the point they should have, because they couldn't afford new garments.

She wasn't sure if she could even find Mordred in the throng, but she was confident that he would find her if nothing else. She scanned the crowd for a tall man dressed in black, deliberately leaving the hood of her cloak down, exposing her tell-tale red hair.

She passed a stall selling fish that smelled like they were rotting and remembered she would have to return to the market soon, not to lure Mordred out, but to buy more food, such as it was. Her pantry was beginning to look sparse.

If this all went according to plan, of course. Her pantry really was the least of her concerns.

Passing by the fish, she stopped in front of a chandler's window, pretending to study the candles within. As she did so, the space between her shoulder blades prickled uncomfortably. She turned slowly, glancing at the crowd around her, and caught a glimpse of a figure in black.

Mordred's eyes met hers. Without waiting to see if he set off in her direction, Calida whirled and strode away, as quickly as she could without drawing further attention to herself.

Following the road that led out of town, she prayed that none of the townspeople would try and stop her. They knew her and she didn't doubt they would try to intervene if they perceived she was in some sort of trouble. The last thing she needed was for one of them to get hurt.

Mordred wouldn't think twice about harming an innocent bystander. The image of Daniel's ruined house flashed into Calida's mind, along with the knowledge of his wife and children buried within.

Fear threatened to climb up her throat and it was all she could do to keep her pace leisurely and natural, knowing that Mordred was behind her. Her pulse thudded painfully hard, blood rushing in her ears. The other witch could be sneaking up behind her at that very moment and she wouldn't know until it was too late.

But Calida forced herself to keep walking, trusting in the fact that there was little he could do to her in public without drawing everyone's attention. Once she reached the woods, though, she had no such assurance. And she could see its edge up ahead, rapidly nearing.

Calida glanced over her shoulder. There was Mordred, still following behind, though perhaps slightly nearer than before. She met his dark gaze once more and then turned, lifting her skirts, and broke into a run.

The forest soon surrounded her. Her boots no longer clopped on the cobblestones, but thudded softly on the mossy floor, strewn with fallen leaves and pine needles. The thick foliage seemed to muffle all sound apart from her frantic pulse and harsh breathing. There were no birds that she could hear.

She was tempted to throw her cloak away, feeling it was slowing her down, billowing out behind her like a sail and catching the wind. But she didn't. She might have want of it after this was over.

A quick glance behind revealed that Mordred had pursued her, as she had expected, his own cloak spread out behind him. But he was too close. His longer stride meant that he was slowly gaining on her and he didn't have cumbersome skirts to deal with, either.

Calida gasped as she ran, spurring herself on, tree branches whipping past her face. The cold morning air seared her lungs. The ground was wet from last night's rain and she nearly lost her footing on the slippery leaves, but managed to regain her balance at the last moment and keep going. A fall now could mean death.

She let out a cry as she was suddenly jerked to a halt, her cloak digging into her neck. Brambles had sprung up behind her, digging into the woolen material and pulling her to a stop.

Her suppressed panic surged to the surface as Mordred slowed and approached. It was too soon! She hadn't reached where Lorelei had agreed to wait for her.

She'd have to confront the witch-hunter alone.

Calida turned to face her pursuer. Her boots and the hem of her dress were damp, splashed with mud. Her wild mane of red hair was even more tangled than before and she stood there, fighting to draw enough air into her lungs.

"Thought you could outrun me, did you?" Mordred asked.

She did not reply, glaring at him. This was the man who had killed Daniel and his entire family, and who had helped kidnap her nephew. She waved a hand and the brambles that had ensnared her fell away.

Mordred spread his hands. "There's no ship for you to escape on this time, Calida."

She snorted, her eyes tracking a brown and white body as it deftly flew between the trees, alighting in one. Sleek black forms dotted the tree limbs beside Horus. The hawk had gathered the crows for her.

Earth witches could communicate with animals other than just their own familiars, at least so far as to give them commands. And she'd always had a way with birds.

She reached out toward the crows with her mind, sensing their collective consciousness, and gave them an order. *Kill him.*

As one, the black birds swooped down from their perches, filling the air with their raucous calls. Mordred whirled and in an instant, they had surrounded him, pecking and scratching with their talons, beating at him with their wings. The witch-hunter cried out as he ducked, shielding his head with his arms. Thick vines began wrapping around him, creating a shield.

The vines twisted around his body like a cocoon, preventing the birds from reaching him. They were too large to slip through any gaps. As Calida watched, in the blink of an eye, thorns erupted from the vines, spearing the still-writhing crows.

Those that had escaped, she ordered to disperse. They retreated back into the trees, waiting. Calida gasped as she felt something sharp wrap tightly around her leg, yanking her to the ground. She glanced back to see a briar had twined itself around her calf. She sought to rise, but more sprouted from the ground, undulating unnaturally, lashing themselves around her limbs, holding her fast.

Mordred disintegrated the vines around him and stalked forward. "Oh, Calida. You always were rather uninspired in a fight."

Calida pulled against her bonds, feeling the thorns bite into her flesh, but the briars were too thick to break. She looked up, expecting to see a wave of rats cascading down upon her. It would be just like Mordred to pick an end so cruel, but there was just him standing there, with a dagger in one hand.

He hefted it, light glinting off the blade.

A gunshot rang out, impossibly loud, and Calida cried out, thinking for a moment that she must have been hit. But then she looked at Mordred, at the round hole that had sprouted in the middle of his forehead.

He toppled to the ground without a sound, the brambles holding Calida unraveling as his power over them ceased.

Panting, Calida scrambled to her feet, gingerly touching her wrists where the thorns had bit into them.

Sharpe stood behind her, pistol still raised, the barrel smoking. She lowered it slowly and shoved it back in her belt.

"Sharpe," Calida breathed. "How did you—"

"Thought I should follow you," the pirate said simply. "And a good thing, too. Besides, after what he did to me and my captain—" She looked down at Mordred's corpse, his eyes staring sightlessly at the sky, a mild look of surprise frozen on his features. "—he was mine to kill."

"Is it over?" a voice called. A moment later, Terrance burst out of the trees and ran up to them.

"You were supposed to stay away," Calida scolded softly. "Both of you."

Not being witches themselves, they wouldn't have stood a chance against Mordred. She barely had herself. She hadn't planned on Sharpe hiding in the shadows with a gun, but she should have.

Fortunately, neither had Mordred.

"What about 'is familiar?" Terrance asked, nudging Mordred with his boot. "Shouldn't we find and kill it, too?"

"No need." Calida shook her head. "Once a familiar has bonded with a witch, if the witch dies, so does the familiar."

"What's happened?" Lorelei cried, the moment she came into view, breathing hard from the run. "I heard a shot."

"Mordred's dead," Sharpe called. "It's over."

"Not quite," Calida corrected. "Now we focus on helping Ben."

"But 'e's in Alara," Terrance protested.

"Then we must go there."

"We don't have a ship," Sharpe pointed out.

"Then we'll find one," Calida said, a sly gleam entering her gaze. "And I think I know just the one."

"You don't mean—" Terrance's eyes widened and a grin spread across his face. "You *do* mean."

Calida bent down, removing Mordred's cloak. She regarded the young man standing in front of her. "Yes, I think you're just about the right height." She draped the cloak over Terrance's shoulders and pulled the hood up, concealing his face.

"I see what you're thinking," he remarked. "But I don't look anything like Mordred."

"And thank skies for that," Sharpe muttered.

"Berchmoore will notice right away that something's off."

"Not after nightfall," Calida replied. "He'll see only what he's expecting to see: Mordred returning with his prisoners."

Terrance shrugged. "Worth a go."

Calida knelt down beside Mordred. "Help me with his clothes."

"What about the body?"

Sharpe's lip curled. "Leave him to the rats."

CHAPTER 26

Annie parried Kain's attack, nimbly leaping backward out of range. The sharp *ting* of their rapiers meeting and the shuffling of their feet echoed around the room. It was a long room, in the shape of a rectangle, completely devoid of decoration or furniture of any kind aside from hard-backed chairs lined along the walls, beneath narrow windows. Florence, her chaperone, sat in one such chair, but they were otherwise alone, left to their fencing.

Annie gripped her blade tighter, savoring its familiar weight, the feel and shape of it. How good it felt to have a sword in her hand again, even if Kain was the one she had to spar with.

She would have preferred Ben as her partner. She didn't know if he knew how to fence, but surely a pirate had to have some skill with a blade. But when she'd gone looking for him, she'd been unable to find him. Annie had gone to his room and knocked, but there had been no answer and she was beginning to worry that they'd been seen sneaking around that night.

It was unlikely she would have been recognized, dressed as a maid, but he might have been, and she thought perhaps he'd been punished somehow.

Rain poured down outside, streaking the windows, making riding impossible and relegating them to indoor activities. And so Annie was stuck with Kain for company and poor company he was.

Annie gasped as the tip of Kain's rapier struck her in the shoulder. The jackets they wore ensured that the blade wouldn't penetrate, but it would still leave a bruise.

"You seem a bit distracted, princess," Kain taunted. "What's wrong? Still brooding over that pirate, are you?"

For the sake of galling him, she replied, "As a matter of fact, yes."

He snorted. "I can't understand why mother keeps him around. She's probably hoping to turn him into another of her privateers, I suppose, so he can pretend to hunt down the pirates, too."

Annie froze, yanking her face-guard off. "What do you mean, 'pretend'?"

"That's all they do, isn't it? Poor Annabelle. Still so slow." He lunged forward, stabbing wildly at her.

She scurried backward, frantically parrying. "Kain! I don't have my helmet on."

"Well what did you take it off for?" He didn't slow or cease his attacks. If anything, it seemed he was hellbent on landing a hit, only the tip of his sword was swiping too near her face.

"Stop!" Annie cried.

It was easy to block his attacks, so wild and unsteady they were, but it was the principle of the act that angered her. Kain knew as well as anyone that you didn't attack your opponent without the proper protection. This was supposed to be a friendly duel, after all, not a fight to the death on the battlefield.

Through the wire mesh of Kain's own helmet, Annie caught a glimpse of bloodshot eyes and suddenly understood why his attacks were so erratic. "You're drunk!" How had she not noticed before?

And what did he think he was doing?

"Well it seems to work for my father," he retorted. "And I think I know why. It's not him, it's my mother. That woman would drive any man to drink!"

Letting out a hiss of disgust, Annie beat his blade aside and lunged forward, striking him in the chest, her sword flexing.

"We're done here," she declared, marching away from him. She tossed her rapier into one of the weapon racks and didn't look back, not waiting for Florence to catch up.

She shook slightly as she walked, though whether from fear or lingering anger, she wasn't entirely sure. If she hadn't been paying attention or such a skilled fencer, Kain could have blinded her. What was he thinking, attacking her without her helmet on? Then again, if he were drunk, he likely wasn't thinking much at all. *Or about the only thing he ever seems to think about. Himself.*

What had he meant when he said all the privateers only pretended to hunt down pirates? Was he right in thinking that's why the queen had kept Ben here, that she wanted him to become a privateer, too?

It seemed far-fetched to her. But she'd have to ask him. Perhaps Thalia had said as much to him. If she could ever find him…

Annie pushed sweat-dampened hair out of her face. Hadn't Ben made a similar insinuation all those days ago, when she'd accompanied him to one of the supply drop-offs? That Alara's aid was little more than a sham?

She rounded the corner and suddenly there he was, as if conjured by her thoughts. She let out an involuntary cry as she nearly collided with him. "There you are!"

Ben looked surprised to see her, or perhaps it was her fencer's attire that caught him off-guard. His frock coat was gone and he wore only a white collared shirt, tucked into black trousers and the same boots he'd had from the beginning.

"Where have you been? I looked for you earlier." She bit her lip. "You're not in any trouble for sneaking around, are you?"

"No." He shook his head. "No."

"Good. The queen hasn't asked you to become a privateer, has she?"

Ben blinked at her. "No, what gave you that idea?"

Annie rolled her eyes. "Just something that Kain said. He thinks that's the reason Thalia's keeping you around. But he said something else to me just now, admitting that the privateers only pretend to hunt down the pirates."

He leaned against the wall. "Well, it fits with what I said about Berchmoore having Daeran supplies on board. I didn't think he'd gotten them from another pirate. More likely, he's still a pirate and is preying upon Daeran ships."

Annie tugged off her gloves. "I told that to Varrian, but he didn't believe me. Alara hired the privateers to hunt down the pirates. What's the point if it's nothing more than some elaborate charade?"

Ben shrugged, glancing around as though to make sure they weren't being overheard. Florence hadn't caught up to Annie after she'd stormed off and she didn't really care where the chaperone had gotten to.

"The only thing I can think of is that it must benefit Alara somehow to keep the pirates around. They're a convenient scapegoat, don't you think?"

"What do you mean?"

Ben rubbed at his eyes. He didn't look as though he'd slept at all since they'd seen each other last. "I mean, Alara can just blame all its problems on the pirates. How's the aid coming along?"

Annie narrowed her eyes. "You know, Aquillus mentioned something odd to me the other night. He's frustrated. He says the reports he's sending Varrian don't seem to be getting through."

"How do you mean?"

"He never hears anything back from my brother, but Thalia assures him the letters were sent."

"I wonder if they'll try to blame that on the pirates, too," Ben muttered.

"I don't see how they could," Annie pointed out.

"No, but they blame the pirates for the aid shipments not getting through."

"But that makes sense, though. Of course the pirates are targeting merchant ships and taking everything of value. That's what you do, isn't it?" She summoned a small smile to rob the words of their sting.

Ben shook his head. "The pirates are a problem, I'm not saying they aren't, but they're not *that* bad. I've targeted Alaran ships in the past, figuring the only way the aid shipments would arrive in Daera was if I saw to it myself. There were very few supplies on board, much less than I would have expected. When I asked where the rest were, they claimed they'd already been taken by other pirates."

Annie shrugged. "So?"

"It sounds plausible, but unless the pirates had a tiny sloop for a ship, they'd have taken everything. That's what pirates do. They're greedy by nature. They're not going to willingly leave something valuable behind unless they're forced to because they have no room for it. That explanation might be true on occasion, but every single time? And besides, I can tell you for a fact—there aren't that many sloops on the Atlas Sea."

"Let's say you're right," Annie said. "If pirates didn't take the rest of the supplies, what happened to them?"

"I don't think they were ever on board in the first place," Ben said grimly. "That way, if the Alaran ship arrived in Daera without encountering any pirates, they can always say they did and deliver as few supplies as possible. If they *do* encounter any rovers, they'll take what little there is and," he shrugged carelessly, "oh well, blame the pirates."

Annie stared at him. What he said made a horrible kind of sense. It was terribly clever at the expense of her starving people. "But…why would Alara do that? We have an alliance! They agreed to send aid."

What the hell am I engaged to a man like Kain for otherwise? It can't all be for nothing!

"The alliance hasn't been finalized yet, though, has it?"

"You think that's why the queen is in no hurry for the wedding to take place?"

"I don't know," Ben admitted, looking suddenly pale. "But I do think Alara likes having Daera depend on them. And as long as the famine continues and the people need food, they'll be dependent on Alara for aid."

Annie peered at him. "Are you all right?"

"As well as to be expected. Just tired, is all. I'm not used to spending so much time on land."

Annie frowned. He was stuck here, surrounded by souls he barely knew, with his ship captained by his rival and his crew scattered to the four winds.

Little wonder he was miserable.

* * *

Calida glanced down at the ropes binding her wrists together, her eyes following the single rope that trailed from her bonds to Terrance's hand, hidden beneath the folds of Mordred's cloak.

Sharpe and Lorelei were similarly 'bound', but it would take only a flick of the wrist to be free. The rest of the crew had remained on shore. If all went according to plan, they would send the longboat back for them once they had successfully taken control of the *Phoenix*.

The three of them ought to be enough to achieve that. It would happen quickly and no one on board would be expecting such a thing. Sharpe had made it sound like all they had to do was point a gun at Berchmoore and it would be over. Calida hoped she was right about that.

"Are you sure this is going to work?" Terrance hissed as they approached the longboat that had remained on the beach, waiting for the witch-hunter's return.

"Yes," Calida replied. "Providing you don't talk. And pull your hood down lower."

Terrance reached up and tugged the cloak's hood lower, casting his face into shadow. He had donned Mordred's black tunic as well. It wasn't a perfect fit, but Calida prayed the darkness would conceal that.

"You know what to do?" Sharpe whispered.

"Yes," he replied breathlessly.

"All right. Here goes."

They had reached the longboat. Terrance said nothing and the women climbed in with him following. The men that had been posted to wait for him pushed the boat out into the water and then they were rowing out toward the waiting *Phoenix*.

Terrance sat with his back to the men, facing his prisoners, shoulders hunched. Calida felt Sharpe tense beside her. The pirate's eyes were wide, her fists clenched as they drew nearer to the frigate and Calida realized this must be the first time Sharpe was afraid to approach her own ship.

Her own heart began to hammer uncomfortably and her palms felt slick with sweat. What if the plan failed? What if Berchmoore wasn't taken in by the disguise? How then would they find a way to help Ben?

But the longboat reached the larger ship without incident and was slowly hoisted up. No one called out or tried to stop them.

The lanterns lit on deck threatened to give them away, but Terrance had the hood pulled practically over his entire head and his hands were hidden within the cloak.

Calida had never met Berchmoore, but she recognized the man immediately. He wore Ben's red coat. A surge of anger lashed through her, red-hot and quick as a whip.

"Well it's about time," he remarked, striding up to them and placing his hands on his hips. "But I see you've got the women with you so I suppose this wasn't all for naught. Bad luck to 'ave a woman aboard, though." His gaze landed on Sharpe and his eyebrows shot up. "Well, well. You've brought me Knight's little 'arpy. Maybe not such bad luck, after all."

In the blink of an eye, Terrance had thrust the cloak aside, raising and cocking the pistol he held, the barrel aimed squarely at Berchmoore's forehead. His crew reacted, drawing weapons of their own. Lorelei, Calida, and Sharpe had shed their bonds, pistols drawn.

Berchmoore was sputtering, hands raised ineffectually. "Wh—what is this?"

"This," Sharpe growled, "is a mutiny. I'd expect you of all people to recognize one, Berchmoore. We're taking back our ship."

Terrance glanced around at the crew. At least half of them had served under Ben and then deserted. "I was your quartermaster," he called, using the tone of an officer giving an order to his men, brooking no argument. "With Ben gone, I am your captain now."

"Drop your weapons," Sharpe snarled.

"Call the men off," Terrance murmured to Berchmoore. "Unless you'd like a bullet in your skull."

In the breathless seconds that followed, no one moved. The air crackled with tension and Calida feared they would refuse. The crew greatly outnumbered them.

Berchmoore ran his tongue over dry lips. "Put your weapons down. Do it!"

The first sword dropped as one of the pirates loosened his hold. It slipped through his fingers, clattering to the deck, and like a herd of sheep, the others followed suit, abandoning their arms.

"Who are you?" Berchmoore demanded, his eyes on Calida. "What 'ave you done with Mordred?"

"He's dead and you'll be joining him if you don't cooperate."

Sharpe bared her teeth. "I say we kill him and throw his body to the sharks." She advanced on him, gun raised.

"Wait!" Berchmoore yelped. "Parlay! I can be of use to you."

"How?" Calida asked, ignoring Sharpe's snort.

"I—I know things. You want to know what's going on in Daera? Why nothing's getting better? Surely you've wondered why the aid shipments rarely ever get through?"

"And you know, do you?" she asked, not bothering to keep the skepticism out of her voice.

"He's lying," Sharpe hissed.

Berchmoore nodded, ignoring her. "I know. And I'll talk. But not to you. I want to speak to the king."

"The king!" Sharpe exclaimed. "What the bloody hell for? We can't go to the king. We're pirates!"

"Because," Berchmoore retorted. "'Ow do I know you won't just shoot me once I've told you what you want to know?"

Calida's eyebrows rose. Given the daggers Sharpe was glaring at Berchmoore, she thought it a fair assumption to make. At least with the king, he had a chance at clemency.

And Calida had wondered about the very things Berchmoore had spoken of. She had her suspicions, of course. She wouldn't put anything past her sister. But she had no proof and nothing could be done without it. King Varrian wouldn't believe such things without incontrovertible evidence.

Now here was one of Alara's privateers, willing to turn evidence against the crown. Berchmoore might very well be the proof they needed. And squeal he would, once they took him to the king. The only other option offered to him was about as attractive as the gun barrel Sharpe was shoving in his face.

As for the *Phoenix*'s crew being pirates…surely the king would go easy on them once he learned what they'd done for the people of this kingdom. Ben had never targeted a Daeran vessel. They were more like privateers than Berchmoore—attacking the ships of one nation for the sake of your own—or they would have been, if Daera had seen fit to give them a license.

Calida wanted nothing more, now that they had control of the ship, to set sail for Alara as soon as possible. But she'd meant what she'd said when she told Ben's crew that he was safe for the moment. She couldn't ignore the opportunity Berchmoore provided them. This could be their chance to expose Thalia and bring some much-needed relief to this decimated kingdom.

"Fine," she told Berchmoore. "We'll take you to the king."

She turned, feeling the cool night air ruffle her hair for a moment, and held up one arm. Horus came swooping down to land, wrapping his talons carefully around her arm.

"Go ahead of us to Alara. Find Ben and tell him what's happened."

The hawk eagerly unfurled his wings and sprang into the air. Calida watched him until he vanished out of sight, swallowed by the darkness.

Wherever Ben was, his familiar would find him.

CHAPTER 27

The following day dawned bright and clear, much to Kain's relief. He needed to get out of the castle. It seemed stifling inside and he couldn't bear the thought of running into either that bothersome pirate, his fiancée, or his insufferable mother.

He stepped out into one of the walled gardens, letting the sun touch his skin and the wind play in his hair. There were no glass domes here. Unlike the conservatory, this garden was completely natural.

The garden was longer than it was wide, surrounded on all sides by stone. There was a gate on either end, beneath an archway, the only entrances. Small flower beds and shrubs lined the pathways, a small pool in the very center, the fountain within bubbling quietly.

Kain paused to watch a bee investigate a nearby flower before continuing on his way.

Initially, he'd wanted nothing more than to be alone, but he spotted his father sitting on one of the stone benches in the garden. He was sitting in a slightly slouched position, his hands clasped loosely together, eyes staring off into the distance. Kain doubted he was seeing anything at all.

Despite the heat, his father wore a frock coat, though unbuttoned. It hung loosely from his frame. The silk shirt beneath was unbuttoned at the collar and it seemed to fit far better, though it protruded from the waistband of his trousers where it hadn't been tucked in all the way.

Kain moved over to the king, suddenly feeling the need for company. At the very least, his father wasn't going to insult him, make him feel less than enough, or try to get rid of him by sending him back out onto one of those horrid ships. After all, that was the only reason his mother had suggested such a thing at dinner: to get him out of the way.

Kain sat down, glancing at his father, the man he barely knew. "She banished you as well, didn't she?" The king made no reply. "That pirate is still here. I wish she'd send him away, but she won't. And do you know why? I saw them both, the day he first arrived, fighting outside the dungeon. He'd somehow managed to escape and she was going to stop him." He scoffed. "He's a sky witch, just like her."

He waited for his father to say something, but wasn't entirely surprised when he didn't. He hadn't even grunted to show he'd heard.

Kain went on doggedly, his frustration seeking a way out and boiling over. "I never had any powers. I was always a disappointment to her. And now she's found someone who does." He kicked out at a loose stone. "Oh, why am I even talking to you?"

He got up and stalked away, feeling no better than he had before his confession.

But the king had heard every word.

* * *

Thalia glanced over at her husband, clad in his dressing gown as though about to retire for the night. Soon enough she would send for his medicine and an attendant would put him to bed. But not just yet.

His chair was seated at a slight angle, as was hers, before the crackling fire. It really was too warm in Alara for such indulgences, but that afternoon had brought a chilly rain.

Niklaus had demanded a fire and she humored him. He probably felt the cold more acutely than she did and it was best to keep him happy if she wanted answers.

Which was precisely why she had chosen to spend the evening with him instead of occupying her time any way else. Jade, her fox, had informed her that Benjamin had paid the king a visit and she wanted to know what, if anything, he'd said. She didn't imagine there was much Niklaus could tell him, and at that point, Benjamin hadn't known the truth, so he couldn't possibly have asked about any of that.

Still…if Niklaus had asked him the same sort of questions she herself had done when Benjamin had first arrived, he might have mentioned Calida's name.

"I was told you had a visitor," she said mildly. "Benjamin came to see you, didn't he? What did you talk about?"

Her tone was encouraging enough, but it didn't fool him. He turned those clear blue eyes on her and she froze. "Don't think I don't know what you're doing."

A thrill of fear shot through her. What could he possibly know?

Thalia forced a laugh. "What do you mean?"

"Tire of Rodek, did you?"

Thalia stared at him. Niklaus's expression gave nothing away, but he didn't appear the least bit angry for having known about her and Rodek's involvement. And that angered her. She hadn't exactly expected to make him jealous, but for him not to care at all…

"What does Rodek have to do with any of this?" she demanded, realizing that perhaps he truly didn't know anything.

"Collecting another young man, are you? One who is gifted this time?"

"*Benjamin*? Don't be absurd!" Thalia would have found his assumptions amusing, he was so far off, if it weren't their own son he was talking about.

But how had the king found out about Benjamin's abilities? Surely the boy wouldn't have been stupid enough to admit it to him? Or perhaps he'd heard rumors of the witch they'd brought to the palace and put two and two together.

"You decided you didn't want to wait on Kain any longer," Niklaus accused. "He came to me earlier, feeling like you're casting him aside for someone else, since you think he doesn't have any powers."

"I *know* he doesn't," Thalia retorted. *Clever of Calida to ensure that Kain had a witch-mark. She knew I'd look for it and so it had to be the same.*

It explained why she had believed Kain to be a witch all those years, yet he'd shown not a shred of ability. If there was a mark, there had to be powers. Unless the mark was a fraud as well.

"You can't possibly think you're going to put Ben on the throne, simply because you're tired of waiting on Kain. He's not the prince."

Oh, if you only knew. "I'll do what I like." Thalia rose to her feet, pointing a warning finger at her husband. "And you will not oppose it."

Clearly, Niklaus was more aware and lucid than she'd believed. How long had this been going on? She had to admit it had been clever of him to trick her as he had, pretending to still be unaware and docile, and all the while he'd been listening, gathering information, drawing conclusions. Who knows what he might have heard?

And he had played his part so well, none of the rest of them had thought anything of it. He'd been essentially invisible, seemingly harmless. But he was anything but. Depending on what he heard and what he knew, he could pose a serious threat to her, especially now that Benjamin was here.

He might threaten to undo everything she had worked so hard to build, everything she'd waited so patiently for.

The only saving grace was that he didn't know that Benjamin was his son. Or was he merely pretending about that, too?

One thing Thalia now knew for certain was that Niklaus was no longer afraid of her, if he had ever been. The defiant gleam in his eyes reminded her too much of her sister and if he wasn't afraid of her, there was no guarantee that he wouldn't try to cause trouble, if only to get back at her.

She supposed she could use Benjamin to threaten him, keep him in line. Surely he would do as he was told for the sake of his own son. But that would mean telling him the truth and there was no way to know what he might wish to tell Benjamin then.

No. Thalia could no longer trust her husband to stay out of the way.

* * *

Sharpe paced her cell like a caged animal. Calida had expected her to calm down and give it up by now, but she had persisted, her eyes still blazing.

Calida, for her part, had slumped down to the bench in her meager cell, regretting her decision to bring Berchmoore to Varrian. She supposed she should have foreseen this conclusion, but she had thought…what had she thought? She had certainly hoped that the king would believe their story and take action to make it right, and not to punish them, at the very least, for bringing it to his attention.

But as far as Varrian was concerned, they were all pirates and he'd had them imprisoned until he could verify that what they'd said was true. It was reasonable, Calida supposed, but it made her antsy, knowing they were losing precious time sitting here.

"You shouldn't have listened to him," Sharpe snapped, for at least the fifth time. "You should have let me shoot him while we had the chance."

The main door to the dungeon opened at that moment, saving Calida from having to reply. Two guards marched in, dragging Berchmoore between them.

"I was brought 'ere against my will!" he cried shrilly, his voice echoing off the walls. "I'm a lawful privateer; ask Alara, they'll vouch for my credentials. I didn't steal that ship, I commandeered it after mine was destroyed in the engagement. A ship for a ship!"

The guards shoved him into one of the empty cells and shut the door with a clang.

"It's too late now to take back what you said, you idiot," Terrance muttered.

Whatever Berchmoore now claimed, he'd already confessed the truth to Varrian, as he'd promised, knowing his neck was on the line if he didn't. Calida had been right: Alaran privateers were being paid to ignore the pirates rather than hunt them down and to prey upon Daeran ships instead. It could be considered a blatant act of war. Calida felt no better for having been right and she doubted Varrian did either.

"I'm the victim 'ere!" Berchmoore shot back. "I was only doing my job. You lot are the pirates."

"Oh, put a stopper in your gob," Sharpe growled. "Coming here was your idea, remember?"

Calida listened to them bicker, leaning her head against the wall. At least she had sent Horus on ahead. Ben wouldn't be entirely alone.

* * *

"Do you think there's any truth to it?"

Varrian considered one of his advisors for a moment. He was never truly without an advisor, but he was beginning to sorely miss Aquillus, especially at a time like this. He could have used the other man's advice.

But he had neither the benefit of Aquillus's presence nor his wisdom. He'd heard nothing from the advisor since the initial few reports, informing him that they had arrived in the southern kingdom without incident and that he expected negotiations to begin soon.

He wondered how Annie was taking it, being back in the one place she least wanted to be, with people she'd been desperate to flee from.

Worry knotted itself around his stomach. She'd tried to tell him that something wasn't right in Alara. Perhaps he should have listened.

Varrian mulled over what he'd just been told. He wasn't sure he trusted anything that man, Berchmoore, said, remembering the name. Annie had said he was the man who ran from the pirates instead of doing his job and engaging them, putting his own neck above all else.

He hadn't believed her when she'd mentioned her suspicion that Berchmoore was preying upon Daeran vessels. It had been a pirate, after all, that had suggested such a thing to her in the first place.

But now Berchmoore had put his hands up to it and, more alarmingly, he claimed not to be the only Alaran privateer to do so.

Such an act would be inexcusable at any time, but during the famine, even more so. Added to the fact that very few aid ships arrived from Alara, it looked even more damning. They'd certainly seen no improvement since agreeing to the marriage and sending Annie to Alara.

The lack of communication from Aquillus troubled him. The only other missives he'd received had been from queen Thalia herself, informing him when Annie had gone missing so that he'd already been aware of the situation when his sister had arrived in Daera. And then there had been a letter informing him that she had arrived safely once more.

Since then, silence.

"Yes," he said slowly, at last giving his advisor an answer. "To some of it, at least. I've sent men to the villages along the coast, asking if this woman Calida's story is true."

She claimed to have, along with the pirates, arranged to have Alaran supplies dropped off in villages. If that were true, the townspeople would attest to it. They had no reason to lie.

An odd situation, to be sure. Varrian did not approve of piracy in any form. Up until this meeting, he'd believed the pirates to be to blame for the lack of Alaran aid getting through. But with Berchmoore's admission, that might be less accurate than he'd thought.

It would be ironic if, by stealing from Alaran ships, the pirates had brought the people of Daera more aid than their supposed ally to the south.

Alara can simply deny anything Berchmoore has said, he thought to himself. *And none of the other privateers are going to spill their guts.*

Berchmoore would be thrown to the wolves and Alara would happily wash their hands of him.

CHAPTER 28

Ben stopped outside the corridor that led to the king's chambers, pausing behind a pillar. He glanced around to make sure no one had followed or was watching him. After Thalia's familiar, of all things, had spotted him last time, he wasn't taking any chances.

The coast was clear. He was just about to step out from behind the pillar when the door to the king's chambers suddenly opened and he froze, ducking back out of sight.

But it was only Aquillus, the Daeran advisor. He didn't linger, but continued hurriedly on his way. Ben wondered briefly what business the advisor had with the king, waiting until Aquillus was well out of sight before approaching the door.

The king himself answered.

"You've come back, have you?" he asked, regarding Ben with those eyes that were so familiar—and now he knew why. "I thought you might."

He stepped aside and Ben crossed over the threshold, casting a final glance over his shoulder, to make sure that Thalia's fox hadn't followed him this time. The hall was empty.

The hearth was unlit, unlike on his previous visit, and the curtains at the window had been thrown back, allowing the bright light of day to stream in, giving everything a crisp, clear look. The king moved over to his chair, gesturing that Ben should take the other. He did so reluctantly, unsure now that he was here what exactly had made him seek his father out.

Ben studied the man with new eyes, no longer seeing the king but the man who was his father. Did the king even know? He'd given no sign upon their last visit.

"So," Niklaus said, breaking Ben out of his thoughts. "What brought you back?"

Ben took a deep breath. "I have questions that need answering," he said honestly. "Though I don't know if you'll be able to help me or not."

The conversation he'd had with Annie about the privateers still lingered in his mind. He was certain that it was true, and had been for some time, but had no real proof. He didn't feel he could approach his mother over the issue. If she had been purposely withholding aid, she wouldn't be likely to admit to it, and Ben didn't think it wise to broach the subject.

But his father might know.

"I can certainly try," the king offered.

Ben licked his lips. "What do you know about the privateers?"

Niklaus snorted. "A bad idea, I thought, when Thalia first suggested it. But she got her way, as she always does."

Ben toyed with the decision and then came to the conclusion that he had nothing to lose by admitting his suspicions. "I have reason to believe that the privateers aren't hunting down the pirates, as they were hired to do, but targeting Daeran ships."

The king's brow furrowed. "Why do you believe that?"

"I've found Daeran supplies on board some of Alara's privateers and I don't think they took them from pirates."

"It's possible," said his father slowly. "But I'm afraid I wouldn't know. The privateers are Rodek's responsibility, not mine."

"But…this is your kingdom. Surely you must know what's going on."

Niklaus shook his head. "It's Thalia's kingdom. Has been for a long time…" His eyes narrowed and he leaned forward in his chair. "Who are you, boy? I've heard you have powers that match Thalia's own. Is that why she brought you here?"

Ben looked at him in surprise, wondering how he had come by such knowledge. Perhaps the queen had told him herself.

He ducked his head slightly. "Yes, that's true. I have her powers because I'm her son." His gaze flicked back up to meet the king's. "Your son."

The king was silent for a long moment, his eyes never leaving Ben's face. At last he said, "I see it… My son. It explains so much." He blinked, gesturing helplessly with his hands. "Where have you been all this time? How is this possible?"

Ben realized his father couldn't possibly have known. His shock was too genuine to be affected. And his questions mirrored Ben's own when he'd first been told.

"I grew up in Daera," he explained. "I lived there until I was eight, then I went to sea, where I've been ever since. My aunt, Calida, had the raising of me." He didn't add that it was Thalia's belief that Calida had stolen him away.

Niklaus's eyes had a far-off look, staring past Ben as if he didn't see him at all. For a moment, Ben wondered if the king had been taking more of his supposed medicine and it was affecting him. He'd seemed remarkably lucid up to this point so perhaps he'd taken Annie's advice to heart and refused to take any more of the foul stuff.

"Calida…" he whispered, so soft Ben almost didn't hear. His eyes glistened with moisture and he shut them tightly, as though trying to blot out an unpleasant memory.

Ben looked down at his hands, assuming his father must be remembering how Calida had manipulated and tricked both he and Thalia.

But he was wrong.

"Oh, Calida," the king murmured, looking as though the weight of the world had descended upon his shoulders. "I'm sorry… How could I have forgotten?"

Ben frowned. If Calida had betrayed both the king and queen, why would Niklaus apologize to *her*? A more likely reaction would have been resentment, even if it had faded over time.

"You knew her?" he asked. According to Thalia, of course the king had known her, but his reaction didn't fit with the story Ben had been told.

If what Thalia said was true, why did he react with such sorrow instead of hate?

Niklaus looked up. "I loved her."

Ben stared at him, a chill creeping over his arms.

"I loved her…and I lost her. And now here you are. My son." He reached out, laying a hand on Ben's shoulder, his grip surprisingly firm despite his fragile appearance. "Calida's son, in a way, since she raised you. The son we should have had together."

Ben suddenly found it difficult to breathe. The room, despite its lack of a fire, felt suffocatingly hot.

All those years, he'd believed himself to be an orphan and now he found himself sitting across from his father, who had been here all this time.

The king looked as if there was something more he wanted to say. Ben felt much the same way, overwhelmed by the gravity of the situation. What did one say to a son or a father whose existence they had been unaware of until recently? How did one acknowledge and bridge the gap of all the time that had been lost?

Ben wasn't even sure it was possible.

But before either of them could find the words, someone pounded on the door.

Niklaus looked up, all thoughts of Calida and the past forgotten, alarm written across his face.

"Quickly!" he hissed, springing to his feet with more dexterity than Ben would have thought. "You must hide. She won't be pleased to know you've seen me."

"Why?" Ben asked, also rising, but his father took him by the shoulders and shoved him toward the entrance to his bedchamber.

The king's fear sparked his own, spurring him to action. If his father had reason to be afraid in his own room, in his own kingdom, Ben thought it prudent to take heed.

He caught only the barest glimpse of a lavish bedroom before he threw himself to the floor, wriggling under the bed—just as the door opened. He hadn't heard the king ask who was there or give permission for anyone to enter.

The bed was canopied, with the curtains reaching to the floor. They were partially drawn, obscuring part, but not all, of Ben's hiding place. He stayed very still, heart thudding against the floor as he tried to slow his breathing, afraid that at any moment, someone might glance over and see him.

But the bedchamber was dark and no one looked his way. Their attention was reserved for the king.

Several liveried guards had trooped into the room, followed by Rodek.

The advisor stopped before Niklaus, looking down his nose at the king, the man who should have commanded his respect. "You're to come with us, Your Majesty."

"Where?" Niklaus demanded. "Why?"

"I think you know why," Rodek said softly. "You've been asking questions, about things that don't concern you."

The king took a step back. "What is this?"

Rodek nodded to the guards, who stepped forward, taking hold of the king's arms.

He struggled, but there were too many of them, their grip too strong. "Unhand me! That's an order. I'm your king!"

Rodek ignored him, walking to the far end of the room, where Ben could not see. But he could still hear and what he heard sounded like a window latch being opened. "Take him away."

The guards began to shuffle forward, dragging the king along with them, until they, too, were out of view. Ben's muscles froze in horror as he realized what they were about to do.

But, no, surely—

Should he burst free of his hiding place and try to stop them? There was an open window right there, allowing him access to his power. To the best of his knowledge, neither Rodek nor the guards were witches. He ought to be able to subdue them, even outnumbered.

On the other hand, he'd seen his father's fear. Was this what he'd been afraid of? Had he known this was about to happen? He'd warned Ben to hide and stay hidden.

He hesitated and that hesitation cost them both.

The king's protests abruptly cut off, replaced by a chilling scream, which rapidly grew fainter until it cut off altogether.

Ben bit down on the leather of his glove, trying to stay silent and process what had just happened.

"Let's go," Rodek murmured.

Laying on his stomach beneath the bed, Ben watched their feet, listening to their receding footsteps as they left the way they'd come, the door clicking shut behind them.

Then all he could hear was the sound of his own frantic heartbeat. He dared not come out, for fear they'd come back for some reason, or that they weren't truly gone.

But he also knew better than to linger too long. Every moment that slipped by brought a greater chance of discovery.

Slowly, his heartbeat settled. He didn't know how long he remained—an hour? A few moments?

That last awful scream rang in his mind, endlessly, until he could bear it no longer, torn by the agony of not knowing what just happened, dreading that it was nothing good, wondering if there was anything he could do, or whether it was too late, and the lingering fear of revealing himself.

Whatever had happened here, he was not supposed to witness it.

He crept out from beneath the bed, wincing. One of his arms had fallen asleep and his muscles were sore from the tension running through them.

His eyes went first to the door, fearing that at any moment, it would crash open and he would be discovered, crawling out on his hands and knees.

But it remained closed. No one came.

Next, his gaze flicked to the open window, the gentle breeze flowing through it ruffling his hair.

Ben felt like a marionette as he slowly approached the window. His movements were not his own, his body an alien, foreign thing, at once obeying and defying him.

He didn't want to look.

He had to look.

Reaching the windowsill, Ben reached out, placing his palms flat upon it, and leaned over the edge. It was a dizzying height, plummeting to the ground below. The ground here was grass rather than stone, but it had done little to soften the king's fall.

Far below, made to look small by the distance, lay his father where he'd been pitched out the window, his limbs twisted at unnatural angles, his body broken.

Sucking in a sharp breath, Ben ducked back inside, but the image remained. The king had been murdered and he had witnessed it.

His father, dead, just like that. The father he had only just found.

Dazed, Ben straightened up and hurried from the room, unable to move fast enough, knowing it was unwise to linger or hesitate. The rational part of his mind that was still working knew there was nothing he could do for his father now. That window of opportunity had closed.

Oh skies, why hadn't he done something? He could have stopped them. His father was dead and he could have saved him. Instead, he'd hidden beneath the bed like a coward.

He managed to stumble back to his own room, locking the door behind him. He made it to the bin beside the desk, sinking to his knees, the bile rising in his throat.

He felt physically sick with fear and the tumult of emotions warring within him. He wanted to be sick, if only to ease the feeling, but he couldn't.

Ben knelt there on the floor, shaking, keeping the bin close just in case. He had seen skirmishes, been involved in engagements and boardings. He had seen the devastation cannons could wreak on a human body, had seen men shot, stabbed or blown to pieces. He'd thought himself numb, used to such things, but this shook him in a way he hadn't expected.

How frightened his father must have been in his last moments, as he hurtled to the earth, knowing how this would end. Knowing that no help was coming. Knowing the horrific pain that waited at the end, only moments away.

And then nothing.

Slowly, as his racing thoughts quieted, a different sort of fear took hold. Something was very wrong in this palace. The king of Alara had just been murdered in cold blood, casually tossed out the window, leaving gravity to do its work.

What the hell was going on?

He glanced at the locked door. He had no idea what was going on, the machinations at play, and that made him powerless. Possibly surrounded by enemies. Were they his enemies?

The only thing Ben was sure of was that he didn't know who he could trust.

When the knock came, it sent his heart surging as if he were back in the king's quarters and not his own.

He jerked to his feet. "Who is it?" he demanded, more sharply than he'd intended, fearing that Rodek had somehow learned that he was there and now had come for him, too.

There was no window in his room and so they'd have to come up with another, creative end for him.

"It's Annie," came the reply, her voice slightly strained. "Please let me in. Something terrible has happened."

His mind instantly went to the king, but how would Annie have found out about that already? With great trepidation, he moved to the door, sliding back the bolt and beginning to pull it open.

She pushed into the room as soon as the door began to move. Ben stepped back, startled by the sudden movement and then grew angry at himself for being so skittish. He was losing his nerve, confined in this place.

He shut the door quickly, bolting it once more. It was entirely improper for him to be in the same room—his room, no less—with Annie, alone, and have the door locked. But propriety be damned, he wasn't taking any chances.

Ben turned to her. She had her back to him, her arms crossed, and he realized she was shaking. All thoughts of his own fear vanished, wondering what could have happened to make her this way.

"Hey," he said softly. "What's wrong?"

She whirled and there were tears streaking down her face. "Aquillus has been arrested!"

"What?" Ben exclaimed. "Uh—here, you'd better sit down." He gestured to the bed and she made her way over to it under her own power, then sank down onto the edge as though her strength had left her. He joined her. "Under what charge?"

Her eyes were wide and fearful as she looked at him. "Conspiring to murder the king."

"That's ridiculous," he scoffed, mind racing once more. "Why would Aquillus do that?"

She shook her head rapidly, black curls bouncing, desperate to make him understand. "You don't understand. The king is dead. They found his body outside." There were tears in her voice and she sounded like she might break down entirely at any moment, but she somehow held it together. "It appears as though he fell out of the balcony in his room. They're saying Aquillus pushed him. He was seen leaving the king's chambers."

Ben had seen Aquillus leave himself, but the king had been alive and well when Ben had seen him shortly after. He knew it to be a lie, but Annie hadn't seen what he had.

"What was Aquillus doing there, did they say?"

"He had a scheduled appointment to speak to the king about the aid negotiations. He was to meet the king in his quarters on account of him not feeling well."

It made sense. Annie had said that Aquillus had previously expressed frustration, feeling he was getting nowhere with the queen, so he had chosen to approach the king instead.

"But why would Aquillus want to murder the king?" Ben asked, trying to determine the arguments that were being used to frame the Daeran advisor.

"He wouldn't!" Annie cried, her hands held out helplessly. "That's just it. Aquillus would never do something like this. I've known him all my life!"

"Calm down," Ben ordered, taking her hands in his own. They were so much smaller than his. "I believe you."

She swallowed, her lips pressed tightly together.

He looked at her, saw his own fear mirrored in those green eyes, and came to a decision. Here was someone he could trust, perhaps his only ally in the entire castle, now that his father was gone. She was an outsider, just as he was, caught up in something neither of them understood.

She had offered to help him find answers when no one else had. She was here on behalf of the Daeran people, the same people Ben and his crew had risked so much for. They both wanted the same thing.

He resisted the sudden impulse to reach out and brush her tears away. It would have been intrusive. But he hated seeing her like this, knowing there was very little either of them could do about it.

He looked away, biting his lower lip.

"Aquillus is being framed, Annie," Ben muttered. "That's not what happened. I know because I was there."

"You were?" she whispered, glancing at the door, as though fearful they would be overheard.

He nodded. "No one else knows. I'm only telling you because I trust you."

He blinked, caught off-guard by his own admission and how much he meant it. At some point, things had changed, from her refusing to tell him who she was and him exasperated with her, to finding an unlikely ally in this foreign kingdom.

"What really happened?"

"I saw Aquillus leave as I was arriving, but he didn't see me. I'd gone back to speak to the king—"

He didn't explain why he had wanted to see the king. Thalia had asked him to keep his true identity a secret for the time being, a completely reasonable request, he supposed, when one considered the turmoil such an announcement could cause.

Everyone believed Kain to be the prince, including Annie, and Ben didn't know how she would take the news. He didn't want to be the prince. He didn't want her to think of him that way.

"—And I was in the room when Rodek and several guards arrived. But they didn't see me. *They* threw him out the window, Annie."

"Oh, skies," she breathed.

"They killed him."

Anger twisted Annie's lovely features. "But why? Why would they murder their own king and try to frame Aquillus for it?"

"I don't know."

But Annie answered her own question. "For the same reason they would refuse to send aid to Daera. If they frame a Daeran advisor for it, it gives them the perfect excuse to break off the alliance. They could declare war if they wanted to! We have to send word to my brother!"

"But how? You said so yourself that none of Aquillus's reports were getting through. Think that was by mistake?"

"Of course not."

If Horus were there, she could write a letter and send it back with him. But the hawk wasn't there. Ben didn't know if he would ever see his familiar again. Or his crew. He missed them both dearly.

He yearned for Terrance's or Sharpe's advice about what he should do, but they were gone, back in Daera. An ocean separated them. And Berchmoore had the *Phoenix*.

Thinking of them now only reminded him of how alone he truly was. He had only one person on whom he could rely and she was sitting before him.

"We'll figure something out," he assured her. "But in the meantime, don't tell a soul what I've told you. Something is going on and I'm not sure what it is yet."

"I won't. I swear it."

He reached out suddenly, gripping her arms just below the shoulders. "I know you won't. But for skies' sake, Annie, *be careful.*"

Ben didn't know if he could bear to lose her, too.

CHAPTER 29

I want to see him," Annie said suddenly, wiping at her eyes with one hand.

"What?"

"I want to see Aquillus," she insisted. "I haven't been able to speak to him since they took him away. I thought maybe…" She looked at him with a trace of guilt. "Well, you were first brought here as a prisoner, weren't you? I thought you might remember the way to the dungeons."

Ben sighed. From the look on his face, she guessed he didn't find the idea agreeable. "It was a while ago, Annie. I wasn't exactly focused on where I was going at the time. I had other things on my mind."

She looked at the floor. "Right."

He tugged at the gold loop in his ear. "I can try," he conceded and then, seeing the hope that must have sprang into her gaze, hastily added, "Try, mind you. That doesn't mean we'll find it."

Impulsively, she reached out and grabbed his hand, feeling the leather beneath her fingers. He always seemed to wear gloves—at least she'd never seen him without them—and she didn't know why.

Perhaps they'd been horribly scarred from his time aboard ship. Or perhaps he found touch somehow repellant, the feel of skin on skin.

Either way, if only her chaperone could see her now. But she had left Florence behind, darting away to tell Ben the news as fast as her feet had been able to carry her.

"We need to hurry," she said, tugging him toward the door. "There's no telling what they'll do to him."

Ben led the way without further protest, unlatching the door and casting a nervous glance about before stepping out into the hall. Annie stuck close to him as they navigated the corridors. Though she knew her way around the castle better than he did, she didn't know the way to the dungeons.

It soon became clear that Ben was struggling to remember the way himself. They were forced to backtrack multiple times, taking one turn after another. Annie had the feeling they were getting hopelessly lost and wasting precious time. Her patience wore thin and she struggled to hold it together.

She never should have asked him to do this. It wasn't fair.

At last, the ground began sloping downward beneath their feet and Ben let out a relieved sigh. "This is it."

The air grew colder and Annie shivered, wrapping her arms around herself. They were stopped at a large wooden door, metal bars across the top, by two guards.

"Halt," one instructed. "No one is allowed entrance, by royal decree."

Ben didn't look as though he wanted to tangle with the guards, but Annie hadn't come all this way for nothing. She stepped forward, tilting her chin up, and assuming her most haughty tone, one used on recalcitrant servants and accustomed to getting her way.

"As princess of Daera, I insist you let us pass. One of my subjects has been imprisoned under dubious charges and I demand to see him."

The guards shuffled nervously, glancing at one another.

"*Now*," Ben snapped, coming to her aid. She hadn't heard him use that tone since he'd given orders aboard ship. "Unless you'd like us to inform the queen that you denied Her Highness entry."

"No," said the first guard hastily. "That won't be necessary." He pulled open the heavy door and stepped aside to let them pass. "Ten minutes."

"Thank you," Annie said stiffly and marched inside, the heels of her boots echoing against the floor.

The air on the other side of the door was even colder and she wrinkled her nose in distaste. It was damp and dark, the only lighting coming from lit torches. There were thin windows near the top of the walls, but the sun was on the wrong side of the building to stream through.

She spotted Aquillus instantly and hurried over to his cell, aware of the guards posted throughout the dungeon. She would need to take care that nothing that was said reached their ears. Ben glared at the guards warily and came over to join her.

"Aquillus!" Annie whispered, taking in her advisor's disheveled appearance. He'd been sitting on the bench, head bowed, but he rose to his feet and approached as she called to him.

His white tunic was smudged with dirt, his collar torn as though he'd put up a fight, and there was a bruise darkening his jaw.

"Your Highness!" the advisor exclaimed. "What on earth are you doing here? Are you hurt?"

"Me?" Annie said, surprised at the question. "I'm fine. Aquillus, they're saying that you murdered the king. That you were seen leaving his room and witnesses heard arguing. He was found dead shortly after, on the grounds as though he'd been pushed out the window."

"It's utter nonsense," Aquillus hissed. "I did pay the king a visit, that much is true, and hardly a secret. I made an appointment beforehand. But he was alive and well when I left him."

Annie clutched at the bars that separated them. "We have to send word to my brother. Varrian will sort this out."

Aquillus shook his head. "You know I've tried to send him messages, for all the good it did. I heard nothing; I doubt any of them were ever sent at all."

"You think they were lost deliberately?" Annie asked, even though she thought she already suspected the answer.

"I wouldn't have thought so, but then, I wouldn't have expected to be accused of regicide either. Yet here we are."

"Why would they accuse you?" She'd already gone through theories with Ben, but she wanted to hear what the advisor thought. "Or not send your reports?"

"I don't know, my lady, but don't trust anyone." Aquillus's green eyes burned into hers. "The queen least of all."

* * *

When he'd seen Annie safely out of the dungeon, Ben went immediately to find his mother. Aquillus seemed not to trust Thalia and Ben wasn't sure he did either, but he wanted to find out what she believed had happened. Perhaps he could convince her of Aquillus's innocence. He didn't know the man well enough to judge his character, but in this at least, he was guiltless.

He found her in the throne room, speaking quietly with Rodek. Upon his entrance, they each looked up and without another word, Rodek strode away, leaving the mother and son alone.

If she was irritated by the interruption, Thalia didn't show it, turning her undivided attention to her son. "Ah, Benjamin. There you are. I'm afraid I have some rather bad news."

"If you're referring to father, I've heard," he said, walking up to her, fighting to appear outwardly calm, the memories still too raw and close to the surface.

Her dark blue eyes softened. "Yes, it's terrible. To find the father you never knew you had, only to lose him so soon. I'm dreadfully sorry." For a moment, he thought she might wrap her arms around him in a motherly gesture of affection, but then she seemed to change her mind at the last moment. Not having made the formal announcement yet, no one knew the truth of their relationship and it would demand an explanation if anyone were to see.

The words threatened to stick in Ben's throat. "For better or worse, I didn't really know him that well. The Daeran advisor has been arrested for it," he added, grateful to move on.

"Yes, several witnesses claim they saw him entering and exiting the king's chambers shortly before he was found dead, and that they heard arguing within."

"What witnesses?"

"The guards."

Ah, Ben thought grimly. *Of course.* There were guards seemingly everywhere, so they would make perfect witnesses. But they could also be bribed or ordered to say they heard and saw something that in reality never took place.

And he knew they were lying, simply saying what they'd been told to, though on whose orders he wasn't as sure. If there really had been witnesses of some kind, they would have mentioned that he had gone into the king's quarters after Aquillus left.

If not for his hidden identity, he might have found himself accused of the king's murder and not Aquillus.

"It's merely a precaution," Thalia added, "until we can determine how exactly the king met his death. It could be nothing more than a tragic accident and a very unfortunate coincidence that Aquillus happened to be there. But until we know for sure, I can't have him roaming the palace halls freely. I'm sure you understand."

When put like that, it sounded so reasonable.

"But why?" Ben demanded. "Why would Aquillus put the alliance at risk by killing the king? Daera relies on us for aid. What would they gain by betraying their ally?"

Thalia shrugged. "Perhaps the Daeran delegation came here under false pretenses. Maybe they don't need our help as much as they claim. Perhaps he became frustrated with the pace of our negotiations and decided to take matters into his own hands."

Ben had seen the state of the Daeran people firsthand whenever the *Phoenix* had arrived to drop off more supplies. The townspeople along the coast weren't as poorly as those further inland, because at least they had access to the sea for food. He helped see to that. But he'd heard stories of people so thin that the skin hung off their bony frames; of entire villages starving to death and their neighbors too weak to bother burying them, so the corpses rot where they lay.

Daera most certainly did need Alara's help.

He looked at his mother, studying her features that were at once familiar and yet the face of a stranger. Did she know or suspect that the man she had been talking to before Ben's arrival was the killer? Rodek had had a hand in it, at least, and the guards had been acting on his orders. Was he acting on someone else's orders or was he making a play for the crown?

If the Alaran advisor acted alone, then Ben's mother was in danger just as much as anyone.

How much did she know? Should he tell her? What if he said nothing and she fell victim next? His earlier feeling of guilt returned with a vengeance, roiling in his stomach. He'd had the opportunity to save his father and had done nothing. He didn't want the death of his only surviving parent on his conscience as well.

And yet, she was the queen of this country and had always seemed to be in more control than her husband. His father had said as much to him—that Alara was Thalia's kingdom.

His mother did not strike him as the type of person to be easily duped or to not know what was happening in her own kingdom. No one was infallible, of course, but there were only two possibilities.

Either she didn't know or she did—and that meant she was lying. If she were willing to lie about this, the next logical, inevitable question arose.

What else had she lied about?

There was no denying the witch-mark she had shown him, but was what she claimed about Calida and her motivations true? Or had that been a lie as well, meant to deceive him and endear him to her side?

"Benjamin, are you all right?" She reached out to him. "You've gone pale."

He cleared his throat, forcing himself to pay attention. "I'm fine." To his relief, his voice sounded almost normal.

In the end, despite what she might know or suspect, Ben could say nothing. He had told Annie not to trust anyone and he'd meant it. She was the only one he could trust. Anyone else was simply too great a risk.

The doors to the throne room opened and Kain strode in, blessedly taking Thalia's attention off of Ben.

"Mother, I must speak with you," the prince announced. He wore some sort of uniform, looking quite regal and self-important.

Seizing his chance, Ben gave the queen a small bow, keeping up appearances in front of the false prince. "I can see the prince has something on his mind, so I'll take my leave, Your Majesty."

She nodded to him and he turned and walked away, grateful to get out from under her gaze.

* * *

"What was he doing here?" Kain hissed the moment Benjamin was out of earshot.

"More to the point," Thalia said, staring down at him. "What are *you* doing here, Kain?"

He was dressed in a scarlet dress uniform, with gold braid and epaulettes, black trousers and matching boots, and his usual white gloves.

For a moment, she hoped he'd reconsidered her suggestion that he take up his naval tour again. That would get him nicely out of the way, which was why she'd made the suggestion in the first place. And now with the king dead, it was more important than ever.

But as ever, he disappointed her.

"I was just wondering when I'll be crowned king," he said, adjusting his collar. "I mean, if a king dies on the battlefield, whoever is heir ascends to the throne almost immediately."

"You know it's much too soon for that," Thalia replied.

The man he believed to be his father wasn't even dead for a whole day and here he was, eager to take the man's place. She might have found his attitude repellent, but the sheer audacity, the scope of his ambition, brought out a grudging admiration in her.

He might not be her son, but perhaps she could see some part of herself in him.

"The proper period of mourning must be observed and there's to be an inquest to determine whether the Daeran advisor is guilty or not. And Daera must be notified, of course."

She did not tell him that she had no intention of seeing him crowned king. That role belonged to another and he'd find out for himself soon enough.

Though perhaps he had a point. The coronation should be held sooner rather than later. She'd send a messenger later today.

"Besides," Thalia added, beginning to walk away. "Your father did not die on the battlefield. We're not at war yet."

"What does that mean?" Kain called after her.

She paused and shrugged in that way she had. "Who knows what might come of this unpleasant business?"

And then she was gone.

* * *

Kain stared after her, feeling foolish. He should have known better than to think he'd receive a straight answer from her, much less the answer he wanted.

Maybe she thought him heartless, coming to her so soon after his own father was found murdered, all but demanding to be made king in his place. He should have thought of that, of how it would look.

But he hadn't thought of that, his actions driven by his own insecurity. The fear that his mother was trying to replace him, to cast him to the side. If he were crowned king, she wouldn't be able to get rid of him so easily.

He wanted her to approve of him, and ever since that damned witch-pirate had arrived, Kain had found himself cast aside even more than usual. Thalia had found someone new, someone more interesting and gifted than he'd ever be.

Would his mother push him aside in favor of the pirate? Would she chose a stranger over her own son? Bad enough he already suspected she'd only suggested he return to the navy as a means of getting him out of the way. Out of sight, out of mind.

She wouldn't have to look at him every day and be reminded of what a failure her son was. What an embarrassment to the crown.

He was sad about his father. The man had been distant, but there had been a time when things were different. At least the king had never seen him as something to be disappointed in, rather than viewed as a member of the family. A son.

Kain blinked in surprise, finding his cheeks were wet. He tore one of his useless gloves off and reached up, fingertips meeting tears.

He needed that crown. If he were made king, his mother wouldn't be able to ignore him. She would need him. He would be important, maybe even finally important enough for her.

He might even outrank her.

Kain took a deep breath, smoothing back his hair. He just had to be patient. Wait until the mourning period was over and then they could proceed with the appropriate ceremonies.

His time would come. He just had to wait a little longer. After all, he'd been waiting his entire life for this moment, hadn't he? Isn't that what Thalia had been preparing him for, in her own forceful way? All the lessons, all the times she had sat him down and commanded him to make water ripple or a plant to grow.

But even as he tried to reassure himself that all would be well, the fact remained that he still couldn't do any of those things his mother put such value on. He still couldn't command the waves or breathe life into the wind.

But Ben could.

CHAPTER 30

Calida allowed the guards to escort her into the Daeran throne room with no small amount of trepidation. They had been waiting for several days in the cells, anticipating word of their fate. Perhaps now it had finally arrived, though she couldn't fathom why she was the only one being summoned to the king's presence.

The outer doors opened, revealing a long, rectangular chamber. With the dim lighting streaming through the windows and only the flickering orange flames from the various torches, the room had a dark, sinister air. The deep violet coloring would doubtless have looked gorgeous in the brilliant sunlight, but without it, the effect was dark rather than regal.

Varrian looked even more grave than the last time she'd seen him, when they had confessed their reasons for coming. The lines in his face seemed too deeply etched for one of his relatively young age. Calida felt sweat break out over her palms and she wiped them on the skirt of her dress.

This couldn't bode well.

He wasted no time in explaining why he had summoned her. "I have just received word from Alara," he announced, hands clasped behind his back. "The king is dead. My top advisor, Aquillus, has been accused of his murder."

The room seemed to tilt around her and Calida's legs buckled, sending her to her knees. Niklaus, dead? No! It couldn't be. How had it happened?

She felt a scream rising, building up from within, but no sound emerged. The pressure only continued to grow, becoming painful, but there was no release.

Even as the thoughts raced through her mind, she knew what had happened. No matter what Alara claimed or what the official verdict was, she knew. This advisor had nothing to do with Niklaus's death.

Her sister had.

But why now? Calida had learned long ago that Thalia had little love for the king, so why would she wait until now to make her move?

And Ben…what must he think?

Calida felt one of the guards grab her arm roughly, hauling her to her feet. She staggered for a moment and then found her footing. She could mourn Niklaus later. Right now, cold hard logic was needed, especially if she were going to help her nephew. She had to get him out of there.

Varrian's expression was one of mild curiosity, courtesy of her display of emotion, but he didn't comment on it. "I can't believe that Aquillus is guilty," he continued. "There will be an official inquest into the king's death, of course, but if they're willing to accuse Aquillus in the first place, I can't believe they plan on pinning the murder on anyone else."

Mutely, Calida shook her head.

"Naturally, I can't sit idly by and allow my advisor to be executed for a crime he didn't commit. The idea that he is in any way guilty is ludicrous. We are on the brink of an alliance with Alara! Why would Aquillus, or anyone from Daera for that matter, put that at risk? I must go to Alara myself."

"I don't think that's wise, Your Majesty," Calida spoke up, finding her voice. "I don't think we can trust the southern kingdom, and your advisor being accused of the king's murder reeks of a plot. I do not think Alara intends to honor the alliance and I fear that if you travel there, you will be putting yourself in grave danger."

Varrian's eyebrows rose a fraction. "I had considered such things myself. I realize Daera is vulnerable right now, with the famine as bad as it is. That's why we were forced to turn to Alara in the first place. If Alara wanted to destabilize the kingdom further, disposing of me would be the next logical step. But I have no choice. I must go."

"You'll be giving them exactly what they want!" Calida protested. "You'll be playing into their hands."

"What else am I supposed to do?" Varrian exploded and Calida took a step back at his raised tone. "My sister is there! If we are in as much danger as you think we are, I cannot leave her there alone."

"Send me. With the crew of the *Phoenix*. I, too, have a family member in the southern kingdom who is in danger. I will see that both of them are safe, if I can."

She fell silent, listening to the drum of her own pulse, waiting to see what his answer would be.

His dark blue eyes were narrowed as he stalked toward her. "Who are you, that I should put such trust in you?"

Calida drew herself up. "Thalia is my sister."

He looked her up and down. "To my knowledge, Thalia has no sister."

"Yes, well, I'm sure she would prefer it that way."

"No love lost, is that it?"

"Yes. Give me the chance and I will make sure that Thalia never threatens your kingdom again."

"You said you had a family member in danger. Not Thalia, surely?"

"No. My nephew. The captain of the crew currently sitting in your cells."

Varrian opened his mouth, a look of alarm coming over his features, a thousand questions no doubt on the tip of his tongue, but Calida held up a hand, forestalling him.

"Whatever's going on in Alara, it's not what you were led to believe. I believe my sister to be responsible for the famine plaguing Daera, the alliance offered under false pretenses. Certainly, you know the truth behind the privateers."

He let out a long sigh. "So Alara is to be our enemy, rather than our salvation."

"They always were."

"And you would ask me to entrust the safety of my sole remaining family into the hands of pirates." He grimaced, but went on before she had the chance to argue. "I trust pirates very little, but at the moment, I trust Alara even less." Varrian ran a hand through his hair, leaving it tousled. "I had my men validate the story you told me, of how you and the pirates distributed supplies to some of my subjects, who also confirmed it." He gave her a small smile, full of irony. "It appears the lot of you may have done more for my people than all of Alara has thus far."

Pushing her luck, Calida decided to step forward. There were now less than three feet between the two of them. "If you entrust this to me, I will not fail."

Perhaps it was something in her voice or the look in her eyes that convinced him. Perhaps something of her hatred for her sister shone through, a force so powerful it left no room for doubt. Either way, she was grateful when he acquiesced with another sigh.

"Very well. Take the *Phoenix* and its crew. Go to Alara, get my sister—and Aquillus—out of there, if you can. Bring them home."

Calida let out another breath. "Thank you, Your Majesty."

From the tightness around his mouth, she knew he wasn't happy about this turn of events. "I will take your advice and remain here, but I will, however, send word ahead that I am coming. Perhaps, if you are right, Alara will take the bait and reveal their true intentions."

* * *

The impact of something striking Annie's window made her jolt awake, heart hammering, wondering what on earth could have made such a sound. Her window was high enough that nothing should have been able to reach it, but still the noise continued.

She sat up in bed. One of the windows hadn't had its curtains drawn. Silvery moonlight dappled the otherwise velvet darkness of night. One of the maids must have forgotten to close the drapes. She should have remembered to do it herself, but she'd had other things on her mind.

That evening, at dinner, Thalia had announced that the coronation would be held the next day. Tomorrow. Or was it today? How late was it? Through the darkness, Annie couldn't read the clock at the other end of the room.

Either way, it seemed much too soon for her. Kain had looked positively smug at the news, seated across from her at the dinner table.

It had been a miserable affair all around. She'd felt horribly awkward seated there, with the king only murdered that afternoon and the advisor of her kingdom locked in the dungeons for it.

No one spoke of what had happened, for which she was grateful, but the empty chair at the head of the table had seemed more glaring than ever, knowing that its occupant would not be there that night—or any night ever again.

Annie had picked at her food, though it smelled and looked delicious, unable to conjure much of an appetite. Ben hadn't fared much better and when Thalia made her announcement, he'd gone paler than she'd ever seen him, his tanned skin blanching.

He excused himself shortly after, claiming he felt ill, and she could well believe it.

Something slammed into the window again and Annie choked off a gasp, clenching the silk sheets in her fists. She could just make out a shadowy figure swooping and capering outside.

All at once it dawned on her what she was seeing and she threw off the covers, racing to open the window.

Horus immediately flew into the room, perching on the back of one of the chairs. The hawk's chest was heaving, his beak open slightly, wings drooping.

"Horus!" Annie exclaimed softly, casting a furtive glance at the door that separated her quarters from that of her servants. The last thing she needed was for Florence to burst into the room, demanding to know what *that filthy animal* was doing in here. "What are you doing here?"

Even as she asked the question, she realized why the bird had come to her—and a good thing, too, because there was no way Horus could tell her himself. From her previous visits, she recalled that Ben's room had no windows. Naturally, the hawk was looking for him, but couldn't find him. He had seen through her open window and decided that she might be able to take him to wherever Ben was.

"You're looking for Ben, aren't you?"

A faint nod.

"I can take you to him," Annie said, snatching up a dressing gown and throwing it over her nightgown. "Come on."

She held out one arm and Horus hopped up to perch on it, talons wrapping firmly but gently around her sleeve. She silently marveled at the bird's weight and yet how gentle he was.

Cautiously, Annie eased her bedroom door open and darted out, excitement and terror surging through her veins. She didn't know what explanation she would give if she were caught roaming the halls in the middle of the night with a raptor perched on her arm.

Now that the hawk was here, they could send a message back with him, ensuring that at least one of Aquillus's reports made it through. But she didn't think queen Thalia would be too pleased to learn of their subterfuge and so she had to be careful. No one else could know what they were doing.

She and Ben had to remain on the queen's good side. Especially Ben. He was only a pirate and expendable if he were caught undermining the plans of anyone here in the palace.

Annie still didn't know why Ben was at the castle. If the queen hadn't approached him with the intention of recruiting him for the privateers, she could think of no other reason for him to be there. Perhaps Thalia found him amusing?

Regardless, Annie was grateful that she had at least one ally in the palace. Someone who was in the thick of it just as deeply as she was, whom she could rely upon.

Funny how she had once thought him no different from other pirates, blaming him for her kingdom's ills. And now he was her ally, of all things.

She reached his bedroom door without incident. The guards that had stood watch on either side had long since been removed. Annie rapped softly and when there was no answer, pounded once with her fist.

Perhaps he was a deep sleeper or still felt poorly from dinner.

The door opened a fraction and Ben was standing there, blinking at her through bleary eyes, golden hair tousled. His feet were bare and he wore a loose white shirt and dark trousers. The first several buttons on his shirt were undone and it was half untucked. He looked tired, as if he hadn't slept at all.

Annie tensed at the sight of him, realizing how inappropriate this meeting was and how much trouble they'd be in if they were caught.

Ben's gaze sharpened instantly upon seeing Horus and he opened the door wide to admit her. "Horus! Where did you find him?"

Annie answered once she was safely inside and the door closed. "He was outside my window. I think he must have been looking for you, but since your room doesn't have any windows, he couldn't find you and came to me instead."

He turned to the hawk. "What are you doing here?"

Annie listened as the bird let out a series of low sounds, meaningless to her, but Ben seemed to understand. He glanced from the bird to her, but said nothing.

"You speak hawk?" she asked, when it seemed the conversation had ended.

Ben gave her a lopsided, wry smile, but there was little amusement in it. He sighed, running a hand through his hair and only making it stand up worse. "My aunt and crew have captured the *Phoenix* from Berchmoore. Last Horus heard, they were taking him to speak to your brother."

"Varrian?" Annie said in surprise. "Why?"

"Apparently, Berchmoore's willing to turn queen's to save his own neck. After all, he's nothing but a legal pirate and he was preying on Daeran ships. We were right."

Annie brightened. "There's the evidence we need!"

"Maybe and if we send Horus back with word of what's been going on here, it'll prove that Alara's not holding up their part of the bargain."

"I can write up what Aquillus told me," Annie said. "Just let me fetch some paper and ink from my room." She dashed breathlessly back out into the hallway, returning with the parchment, ink well, and pen.

She plopped down at Ben's dressing table and immediately began to compose a letter to her brother, explaining that none of Aquillus's reports had been sent and the suspected reason why, along with his belief that no aid had been sent. She included a bit about the king's death and

Aquillus being accused, even though she suspected Thalia had already sent official word of it to Varrian. She wanted her brother to hear it from his sister, almost pleading with him to do something.

She wrote as fast as she dared without blotting the ink. Finally, she was done, her wrist cramping. She blew softly on the ink to help it dry and sat back in the chair.

Ben had sank down onto one of the divans, Horus perched on the arm. He ran his fingers slowly over the hawk's feathers, but his blue eyes were watching her.

Annie blushed beneath the scrutiny, though she wasn't sure why. With no windows, the room was utterly dark aside from a few lit candles, their light lending an intimate feel. She was in his bedroom, in the middle of the night, in her nightgown.

She cleared her throat, desperate to steer her thoughts in a different direction. "Are you feeling any better? You left dinner early."

He broke eye contact. "A little."

"What do you think of the coronation being held so soon?"

He opened his mouth to say something and then hesitated. Annie waited patiently, not wanting to push him. Finally, he sighed. "I think it's too soon. It's hardly appropriate, is it?"

"Certainly unprecedented. I think Kain's pleased, though."

"It won't last," Ben muttered darkly. "Is that dry yet?"

She turned back to the stationary. "Oh, I think so." She rolled up the piece of paper and held it out to Horus.

"Take it directly to the king," Ben instructed. "Or, failing that, make sure it gets to Calida. She'll know what to do with it."

Horus nodded, wrapping one foot around the rolled letter. Annie took the hawk back to her room and opened the window once more for the bird to get out.

She watched as he launched himself out into the clear night, taking all her hopes with him.

* * *

Ben lay awake after Annie had left. No sooner had Horus found him than he found himself missing the hawk all over again, a connection and reminder to his not-so-distant past.

At least Terrance, Sharpe, and some of the crew were safe. And Mordred was dead. He would never threaten anyone again, not that Ben had shared that news with Annie. She didn't know the witch-hunter and there was no reason she should have.

She wasn't the witch. He was.

Ben sighed and rolled over for what felt like the thousandth time. His eyes physically ached from tiredness. The bed, which was much softer than his own, ceased to feel comfortable in that moment. He'd had trouble sleeping, to adjusting to life on land, since he arrived, missing the shifting of the *Phoenix* beneath him, the familiar creaks and groans of the wood.

Here, it was too quiet. Too still. There was nothing to keep his thoughts at bay. He didn't even have a window to look out of.

He should have told Annie that he was a witch, to give her a real explanation as to why he and Horus could communicate. Why hadn't he? He'd wanted to tell her, so why hadn't he? Come to that, he'd wanted to confide the truth of his real identity to her.

But he hadn't, fear killing the words before they'd even had a chance to take flight. Fear of how she would take the news. Fear of what she would think of him.

When had her opinion of him mattered so much? He couldn't explain it. He shouldn't have cared, but he did.

What would she think when she found out she was actually engaged to him?

She'll find out anyway, a voice whispered. *Tomorrow at the coronation.*

Ben shook the thought away. He didn't know that. He didn't know what Thalia intended for tomorrow. She hadn't discussed it with him, much to his annoyance. He should have sought her out, he supposed.

And said what? That he didn't want this, that this wasn't who he was? That he was just a pirate, not some long-lost prince? That this was a responsibility that he didn't want? That all he wanted was to return to the sea, where he belonged, with his crew and his *Phoenix.*

And that was what he wanted, more than anything. But what could Thalia do about any of that? She might be the queen, yes, but he was the prince, whether he wanted to be or not. He *was* her son. The throne of Alara rightfully was his. He'd been born to it, even though he'd had no training or tutoring, no experience or knowledge of what it meant to be a prince, a future leader of a kingdom.

What he wanted didn't matter.

But he didn't know if Thalia intended to crown him king at tomorrow's ceremony or continue the charade and name Kain king, like he wanted, instead.

Ben would have preferred that. So what if Kain was a pretender, wasn't the real prince? At least this was something he wanted.

He sighed again, waiting to see if sleep would finally claim him and take him away from all of this. If he couldn't dream, he could at least imagine he was back on his beloved *Phoenix,* surrounded by his crew and their chatter, the sturdiness of the helm beneath his hands, the canvas taught above his head, the creak of the ropes, the water parting before the frigate as she sliced powerfully through the waves, the smell of salt in the air, and the wind on his skin.

That was where he belonged.

* * *

"Wake up, my lady!" Maddie's voice broke through the thick layers of sleep. The maid thrust the rest of the curtains back, bright sunlight flooding the room.

Annie groaned, covering her face with one arm. She'd returned to bed after her late-night excursion, but still felt the effects from it. "It's so early," she complained, not knowing or caring whether that was true.

"It's the special day," Maddie replied.

Of course. The coronation. She couldn't forget even if she wanted to. "It's too soon," she muttered, more to herself than to the maid.

Maddie shrugged. "It's not up to me, miss. Perhaps Her Majesty thinks it will do the people good, to see their prince crowned. The news of the king's death must have been mighty upsetting, after all."

"I suppose," Annie grumbled, forcing herself out of bed.

A coronation meant pageantry, pomp and circumstance, a whole lot of fuss for nothing. But she, as the prince's fiancée, would be expected to attend and look her best.

She allowed Maddie to do her hair and help her into her gown, which was the scarlet color of Alara. It seemed inappropriate when she wasn't even married into the Alaran royal family yet, but she supposed they all needed to match. To display a united front.

The coronation ceremony was to be held at the palace chapel, which bore more resemblance to a cathedral. Tall marble pillars supported the vaulted ceiling. The walls were composed almost entirely of stained glass, but the dome of the cathedral was ordinary glass, allowing the sunlight to fall on the raised dais.

In addition to the two rows of seats stretching back toward the door, there were two balconies on either side of the room, on the second floor. Scarlet banners, emblazoned with Alara's proud golden griffin were draped from the ceiling. As she stared at them, Annie wondered how much such a large piece of fabric must weigh, should it come crashing down.

It was midafternoon before the ceremony proceedings got underway. Annie had hoped to see Ben beforehand, but he hadn't been in his room when she'd called.

Thalia stood in the middle of the raised platform, looking radiant in her scarlet gown, which shimmered as she moved like jewels made of blood. To her left stood Kain, dressed in the red uniform jacket with its gold epaulets, black pants and matching boots.

Annie stood off to one side, on the edge of the platform, on the same side as Kain. To her surprise, Ben was also present, on Thalia's right, dressed much the same as Kain. She couldn't fathom why he should be there, dressed in royal regalia, and in such a central position where people couldn't help but notice him for his close proximity to the queen.

But she supposed Thalia must want him there for some reason and he needed to match Kain or else the effect would be ruined.

She caught his eye and tried to smile. Ben didn't smile back. If anything, he looked more like he was facing an execution than a coronation ceremony, where the only thing that was expected of him was looking suitably stoic.

The lords and ladies of Alara, most of whom had been present the night of the ball, filed into the cathedral, taking their places alongside the raised dais in two rows. There were plenty of empty seats—not everyone being able to attend on such short notice—but to Annie it seemed as though every peer of the realm had been invited.

No doubt they had scrambled, canceling all other plans, to attend an event that was not to be missed. Coronations were few and far between. If they wondered at the speed of it all, they seemed not to show it, eager to take in the spectacle.

The air quickly grew warm with so many bodies present. The sunlight beating down through the glass dome made Annie's bare arms feel uncomfortably hot, a thin trickle of sweat running down the back of her neck. She could feel it gathering on her chest, sticking to her corset.

Thank the skies Maddie had been thoughtful enough to hand her a fan. With a flick of her wrist, Annie snapped it open and began fanning herself surreptitiously, feeling overwhelmed, standing at the front of the room, all eyes turned in her direction.

She hoped this infernal ceremony would be over soon. It was the last thing Kain needed—another reason for his ego to become even more inflated than it already was.

She glanced over at him. He made no attempt to disguise the glee on his face and Annie felt disgust roil through her at the sight. It would seem he loved taking possession of the crown more than he'd loved his father.

When at last the crowd had assembled, Thalia stepped forward. The acoustics in the building were excellent and her voice carried without forcing her to shout.

"Thank you all for coming on such short notice to this prestigious occasion. As you all are no doubt aware, such haste is not customary when it comes to crowning the heir. Niklaus's death was a tragedy, one I intend to see put right, and we mourn him, each in our own way. But nothing about this coronation ceremony has been ordinary, as you will soon see for yourselves.

"What you are about to learn will sound incredulous. At first, I hardly dared believe it myself. But I have seen the proof with my own eyes and there can be no denying the truth."

Annie frowned. What on earth was the queen talking about? Had she uncovered the king's true killers and was prepared to denounce them, here and now? She could think of no other *truth* Thalia could be referring to, given the circumstances.

"It has recently come to my attention that this young man you see before you—" She gestured at Ben. "—is the son of the late king Niklaus and I, stolen from us shortly after his birth by northern conspirators—my own sister, no less, who left a fraud in his place."

The final echoes of her words resounded throughout the room and faded, met with stunned silence. Annie couldn't make out much of their expressions from where she stood, but she could see astonishment, plain as day.

Her own lips were parted in stunned silence and Kain's mouth hung open in silent outrage, no trace of his earlier smug expression. Annie tried desperately to catch Ben's eye, but he wasn't looking at her.

Ben, the prince? Kain, a fraud? It made no sense. Ben was a pirate—

Then, without warning, the silence of the chamber was shattered as murmuring broke out, rising to a cacophony as voices rose to be heard over one another.

Thalia raised a hand for silence and to Annie's astonishment, the crowd complied, perhaps curious to see what she would say or do next.

"The king is dead and his heir must take his place." She gestured to an attendant, who stepped forward to recite the royal oath.

Annie felt strangely weightless, lightheaded, adrenaline coursing through her veins, surging faster and faster courtesy of her bounding pulse.

Ben was the prince? Thalia's son? Heir to the kingdom that seemed to bear such hidden hostility to her own. She had confided all her fears and suspicions to Ben and all the while, he was the queen's son.

Now his presence at the palace made a horrible kind of sense. Had he been playing her for a fool this whole time?

Oh, skies.

The cathedral felt warmer than ever. She flapped her fan frantically, but it brought no relief. She felt the blood rush to her feet, black spots dancing before her vision. The ceiling seemed to spin as the cathedral toppled around her, the sounds of the ceremony fading away to a dull roar.

She did not know that Kain fortunately darted forward to catch her before she crashed to the ground, lowering her gently.

And so she did not hear as the lords cried out in protest, demanding proof of Thalia's claims. She did not see Thalia reveal her own witch-mark to the gathered crowd or Ben forced to remove his glove to reveal his own, identical to hers.

* * *

"Annie!" Kain slapped her face lightly. She moaned, eyelids fluttering. Her pulse was fast but strong, her skin pale.

Satisfied that she was in no danger, Kain ripped off his own white glove, shouting, "I have one just like it!"

He wasn't about to sit idly by and let his mother—no, the queen—take this from him. His position as prince was the only thing he had. He may not have powers like her or her real son, but the title was his. She couldn't take it away from him! Not like this, not in front of everyone.

Thalia's glittering eyes turned on him, resentful that he had spoken up, commanding him to back down, but he refused. "If you are my son," she ground out, "then prove it."

She flung her arm out, wind whipping up suddenly throughout the cathedral, sending the heavy banners displaying Alara's griffin whipping wildly. Some of those assembled cried out, ducking in the force of the sudden gale.

Thalia lowered her arm and the wind ceased, the only sound the flapping of the tapestries as they slowly began to settle.

Kain felt his face heat at the humiliation. An identical mark he may have, but it carried no weight. No matter how hard he tried, he could not replicate her demonstration. Years of training, lessons, attempting to perform tasks far simpler, had all ended in failure.

He hung his head and stepped back. He wanted this so badly, it was a physical ache inside of him. But wanting wasn't enough.

"No?" Thalia taunted, turning to Ben and nodding.

He did not flinch, his face an impassive mask as he stepped forward, lifting one hand. The wind sprang back up, not quite so aggressive. This breeze was a gentle caress, unlike his mother's vicious tempest, but the fact that he commanded wind of any kind was proof enough.

It brushed against the cheeks of those assembled, stirring their hair and gently swinging the banners until it, too, faded away.

There were no more protests after that. The attendant recited the oath and Ben gave his solemn pledge to uphold it, his voice flat, eyes unblinking, staring out at nothing.

With the oath at its end, Ben rose from where he'd knelt. A crimson, furred cloak was placed around his shoulders. Thalia retrieved the crown from its place on a scarlet cushion at the rear of the platform, carrying it in both hands, the gold winking in the sunlight.

To Kain, the scene seemed to unfold at a snail's pace, everything moving with an excruciating slowness, as the queen hefted the crown and Ben bowed his head to her. She placed the heavy gold coronet atop his head and stepped back, her dark eyes glowing with pride.

She gazed at him in a way she had never graced Kain.

Ben lifted his head and stared out at his assembled subjects, the sunlight streaming through the ceiling alighting on his golden hair, making him look every inch a king.

Jealousy cinched tight around Kain's gut. And yet, even as he stared at the pirate-turned-prince, he couldn't summon up the resentment he wanted.

If the crown had been placed atop his own head, Kain would have felt triumphant, vindicated at last. On Ben's face, there was no hint of the joy Kain had anticipated. The light had gone out of his eyes, leaving only hollowness.

Thalia stepped back. "I give you your future king," she announced and applause rose up from the crowd.

Whether they approved or not, they dared not show disrespect.

* * *

When Annie came to, she was back in her room, Maddie fussing over her, fanning her face and dabbing at her cheeks with a wet cloth.

The maid let out a sigh of relief. "Oh, miss, you gave us a right fright, you did."

"What happened?" Annie asked groggily, pushing the maid's hands away and sitting up in bed.

She still wore the scarlet dress from the coronation, the skirt slightly rumpled now.

"You fainted at the coronation ceremony," Maddie replied. "Not that anyone could blame you, of course. I think the announcement came as quite a shock to everyone—"

But Annie was no longer listening. At the mention of the coronation, the memories came flooding back, tightening her chest. There was at least one person who hadn't been surprised by the announcement. Ben hadn't looked the least bit taken aback by the news.

He was the prince and he had known.

He had known—and he hadn't told her.

He had known what was about to happen. She was certain of it. How long had he known? Why hadn't he confided in her?

Kain wasn't the true prince at all. She wasn't engaged to him. That came as a relief, of sorts, but it was short-lived. No, Kain wasn't the prince and her fiancé. Ben was. She was engaged to marry him. And she felt like she didn't even know him.

He had kept this a secret from her. What else had he kept hidden? What more wasn't he telling her?

Her heart seized painfully. The only emotion stronger than her hurt at that moment was her fear. She had been sharing her suspicions about Alara, the queen, the privateers and pirates with him, confiding openly. And the entire time, he was really the queen's son. For all she knew, he could have been in league with whoever was behind this horrid plot, and she had been confessing thoughts that could be construed as treasonous.

Had anything he told her been true? Aquillus was facing down a murder charge—regicide. Was what Ben said about being in the king's room when the murder happened true? Or was he somehow behind it? Did he have a hand in setting up Aquillus?

Was *he* the one responsible? When he learned about his true identity, did he see disposing of the king as a way of obtaining more power? The throne would be a temptation for most, that kind of power a heady, intoxicating thing.

Annie shook her head, her cheeks heating with a mixture of fear and shame for thinking such things, even for a moment. She would be stung if the roles were reversed, if Ben ever thought such things about her.

She bolted for the door, not knowing where she planned on going, but knowing she wanted to be alone.

She yanked open the door and found herself face to face with Kain, standing outside her room, still in his uniform.

"I came to see if you were all right."

Surprised, she felt a sudden stab of pity for him. He'd been betrayed just as she had—she was certain he hadn't known beforehand the way Ben must have. Kain had been cast aside and humiliated in front of all those people.

What had Thalia called him—a fraud?

Suddenly she saw in Kain a potential ally. At the very least, someone to vent to, who was just as hurt as she was.

"I'm sorry," she blurted out. "I didn't know."

"No," Kain muttered.

Annie gestured helplessly with her hands. "None of this makes any sense! How could he be her son? He's been a pirate all these years!" She didn't understand what the queen had meant about her sister…did she mean Calida? Calida was Ben's aunt and that would make her Thalia's sister if Ben was the queen's son.

A muscle ticked in Kain's jaw. "I shouldn't be surprised. Not really. She was always going to pick him, even if he wasn't her real son."

"But *why?*" Annie demanded, only puzzled further by Kain's certainty.

His lip curled. "Because he's a *witch*."

CHAPTER 31

Ben strolled absentmindedly along the shoreline, letting the waves roll over his bare feet. He'd rolled his pants up to his knees, carrying his boots in one hand. Where the sand met the trees, guards stood in the shadows, keeping an eye on him. Each held the reins of a horse, or remained seated on their mount. One held the reins of Ben's horse as well.

He sighed, eyes focused on the ground, the sand beneath his feet and the warm water that rushed over them. He'd come here to escape the palace for the first time, but he could never be truly alone outside the castle walls. The guards would accompany him everywhere he went, never leaving his side. Of course, they wouldn't let the prince just wander off.

The prince…

It was late in the afternoon, the day following the queen's announcement. For Ben, the shock had yet to wear off. He'd known it was coming, of course, but hadn't wanted to believe.

The dread had faded now that the announcement had finally been made, leaving behind an emptiness. He felt more alone than when he'd first been taken to the palace. He hadn't seen Annie since the coronation ceremony, but he couldn't forget the look, of mixed incredulity and horror, on her face when the announcement had been made. It wasn't the reaction he'd hoped for, but the one he had feared.

But more than that, he realized what this meant for his life and future moving forward. Even though Terrance, Sharpe and the rest of his crew had succeeded in claiming the *Phoenix* back from Berchmoore, he couldn't escape with them back out onto the open sea and a life of freedom.

Not now.

Not if he was the prince of this kingdom, with responsibilities and duties to fulfill. He'd known that from the moment Thalia first told him the truth, but it hadn't truly settled in until now.

That life was over, the door closed.

And Thalia seemed to know it. She'd given Ben a new room, larger and more lavishly decorated than before, but the important thing was that it had windows. She trusted him enough now not to use his powers to try and escape. Or she knew that by making her public announcement, she had essentially sealed his fate. His hands were tied. He couldn't go anywhere even if he wanted to.

And, skies, did he want to.

At his core, in his soul, he was a pirate, not a prince. Sailing was all he knew how to do, but he was good at what he did. He loved it. Lived for it.

Even now, burdened by the knowledge of his new identity, the ocean called to him. He had directed his horse here, to the beach, where the ocean lapped at the shore. It called to him and he yearned to go back.

It wasn't the most glorious life, but it was his. He didn't know the first thing about running a kingdom, court etiquette, or playing politics. No doubt he'd be terrible at all three, and yet he would be expected to do all of those things, now that the king was dead and he, as the heir, was set to take his place.

He sank down onto the sand, feet just out of reach of the waves, dropping his boots beside him. He breathed in deeply, lungs filling with salty air. It was a hint of freedom, tantalizingly close, frustratingly out of reach.

Ben glanced up at the sound of approaching hoofbeats, the knot in his stomach tightening, the weight in his chest nearly crushing. Annie slowed the white horse to a halt and slowly dismounted.

Her expression was somber as she looked at him. For a moment he thought she'd come alone, but then he spotted her own entourage of guards, lingering a respectful distance away. He waited for her to speak, but she didn't come any closer.

Gone was the scarlet gown she'd worn for the coronation, replaced by a cream shirt beneath a violet corset vest, riding trousers and knee-high boots. Her black hair was unbound, long and wild.

She wrapped the reins around her knuckles. "I didn't expect to see you here," she said at last.

It wasn't a hello, but Ben would take it.

"Are you all right?" He had seen her collapse during the ceremony, but there had been nothing he could do. There was no way he could have reached her in time to catch her. That task had fallen to Kain and at least in this, he had done the right thing.

She nodded. "Fine."

He hadn't imagined or mistook the look in her eyes at the ceremony. That wary trace of fear still lingered.

"Am I really that scary?" he asked softly. She looked away for a moment. "I'm still the same person I was before."

"Are you?" she countered. "Who were you before? I'm not sure I know. I'm not sure if I ever knew."

"I've never lied to you about who I am."

She pursed her lips. "Then why didn't you tell me?"

"The queen asked me not to. And I was afraid…"

She crossed her arms, looking down. "What about being a witch? You didn't tell me that either."

Ben sighed. "Something I've been told my whole life to keep a secret? And I was afraid of what you might think of me." He felt his face grow warm. Her opinion of him carried far more weight than it should.

He hated making the admission, of admitting to such weakness, but she deserved an explanation and he had none to give her but the truth.

"And for good reason, too, it seems," he added.

"That's not fair!" Annie cried. "What am I supposed to think? This whole time I've been trusting you, confiding my suspicions about this kingdom to you and you're the prince! How do I know you didn't have something to do with this plot to frame Aquillus?"

Ben glared at her, stung by her lack of faith in him. "I told you the truth about that, remember? I put my own neck at risk telling you that. How could you think so little of me?"

She had the grace to flush, looking away.

"You saw what I did for the Daeran people," he added, tone softening. "That wasn't some elaborate trick to gain your trust. I'm still the same person I always was."

"No, you're not," she said, but she let go of the horse's reins and walked up to him. "You're a prince now."

"No," Ben corrected. "I'm a pirate."

That earned him a small smirk, Annie plopping down onto the sand beside him. "And here I thought I was going to marry a spoiled brat, only to end up with a pirate prince instead."

"If the alliance goes through," Ben muttered darkly. He frowned, not wanting to think about the proposed marriage now that he would be taking Kain's place.

But she pulled all the thoughts back. "So…are you my fiancé now?"

"It would appear that way…"

To his surprise, she laughed. "Well, don't look so disappointed."

"You're not the least bit bothered by this?"

She shrugged. "Honestly, I don't see that we can do much about it. And admittedly, I'd rather marry you than Kain."

"Thanks, princess," Ben muttered, wryly.

Annie was silent for a moment, the only sound that of the waves washing in, and then she said, "Are you really a witch? Kain said he saw you and the queen fighting the day you were brought here. That you'd used your powers to break out of the dungeon."

Ben sighed, tugging off his leather gloves. There was no reason to wear them now with his secret out. The cool breeze felt good on his skin. He tilted his right hand so that the mark was facing her, clearly visible.

"So that's why you always wore gloves," she murmured.

"I *wanted* to tell you," he said quietly. "But I never told anyone, not even my crew. Some of them probably suspected, but they didn't *know*." He'd wanted to ask if she knew the queen was a witch, but that would have required him to explain how he'd come by such information and admitting that he was a witch himself.

"I still wish you'd told me. But I suppose I understand why you didn't." She tilted her head, looking up at him. "What else are you keeping from me?" Her tone was light, teasing.

Ben couldn't resist teasing her back. "Only that I'm quite looking forward to our wedding night."

Annie gasped in mock outrage, shoving against his shoulder, making him laugh. "Skies, you certainly know just what to say to a girl. How romantic."

"I can be very romantic when I want to be."

"Uh-huh." She shook her head, a slight smile on her lips. "How do I know you wouldn't just bewitch me with one of your spells?"

"How do you know I'm not doing it right now?" Ben countered, his voice a low purr, leaning closer to her.

He could smell the jasmine in her hair, see the rapid rise and fall of her chest.

"If you are, it's not working," Annie whispered. She didn't pull away.

"Are you sure?"

Her lips parted in a nervous exhale, Ben's gaze tracing the movement. "Maybe."

He had the sudden urge to kiss her, right then and there, but he wasn't sure if she felt the same and he wasn't going to ask her, for fear of looking even more a fool.

Besides, it wouldn't be the right time or place, with an audience of guards behind them.

He pulled back, breaking the brief moment. "We'll fix this," he murmured. "With Aquillus. Together."

Annie sighed. Did she sound disappointed or was that just his imagination? "I'm afraid," she admitted. "I don't know what's going on, but it worries me."

"I won't let anyone hurt you," Ben promised, looking intently into her eyes.

The words had sprung to his lips before he even realized what he was saying, but he was startled by how much he meant them, how desperately he wanted to protect her from all of this, whatever it was.

He hoped he hadn't just made a promise he couldn't keep.

CHAPTER 32

Sharpe hated being below deck. The air was cramped and smelled of the damp, though she knew it only got worse the further down one went. She wasn't meant to be down here—it was so unlike her usual haunt up in the lines. How could she be expected to keep an eye out for other ships or mount a defense from down here?

Of course, for the time being, she wasn't supposed to. The *Phoenix* sailed out in front of the two Daeran ships, giving the appearance of an escort, on Varrian's orders. The king himself had remained behind in Daera, as Calida advised, but he'd sent word ahead to Alara that he was coming. For all the southern kingdom knew, he was on board one of the other two ships.

What Alara would do with that knowledge remained to be seen. Calida was of the opinion that her sister intended to weaken and eventually take over the northern kingdom, and what better way to go about it than assassinating the Daeran king at sea, leaving the pirates to no doubt take the fall for it.

Sharpe fully expected Alara to mount some form of assault; she didn't trust the southern kingdom at all. Without Varrian, the Daeran people had only the princess to look to—and she was safely ensconced in Alara, set to marry their prince. Alara would have control of both kingdoms once the marriage went through—all hinging on whether a suspected assassination attempt succeeded.

Sharpe smirked to herself.

She almost hoped the Alaran navy did attack, if only so she could go out into the fresh air and have something to do. It was unspeakably boring, being relegated below decks for days on end. Like the rest of the crew, she was used to always bustling about.

But she knew it was foolish to wish such a thing. Boredom was preferable to a massacre.

Depending on how many ships Alara chose to send, the two Daeran vessels and the *Phoenix* might not be enough to mount a defense. They might all end up on the bottom of the sea and then what?

Sharpe fingered the musket in her hands, running her fingers over the many carvings she had adorned it with over the years. At least she had it back. It had been left behind on the *Phoenix* when Berchmoore had taken the ship and she had despaired of ever seeing it again. Yet here they were, with control of the ship, and Berchmoore nothing more than a figurehead.

Calida and Lorelei had been sent below as well. They couldn't risk anyone who might be on board the Alaran ships recognizing them and blowing the entire charade. If this were to work, they needed to believe that the *Phoenix* was still their loyal privateer.

Sharpe glanced over at the other two women. Calida's expression was difficult to read, but Lorelei appeared anxious, as she had ever since they'd set sail.

The *Phoenix* had seen battle before, but without their captain, Sharpe wasn't as sure of her prowess as she had once been. The ship no longer moved with the same speed or grace without Ben to magically manipulate it—and that's what he'd been doing all these years. Sharpe knew it as soon as he'd taken off his glove and revealed that he was a witch—to save her.

She hadn't really been surprised; she'd suspected a long time ago but Ben had never chosen to reveal his secret to her. It was his to keep, just as the truth about her past had been hers to keep or reveal as she chose.

But she did feel guilty now and not a little bit impatient. What were they doing wasting time out here when her captain needed help? She owed him for what he'd done, giving himself up so that Mordred wouldn't take her instead.

She shuddered to think of it now. She hadn't felt such raw terror in years as she had in that moment, fearing that Mordred was about to take her again, that she was powerless to stop him, and not knowing what he might do to her.

Sharpe had felt that way, years ago, as a child on Indris. And once she'd learned to shoot, she'd determined never to feel that way again. She gripped the musket tighter. No, she refused to be afraid as long as she had a gun in her hands.

In that moment, though, she hadn't had a gun or any other weapon. She still remembered the look Ben had given her, his wide blue eyes meeting her terrified gaze. He had understood.

A cry went up from above, putting an end to her reminiscing and Sharpe stiffened. A sail had been spotted—more than one by the sound of it.

She got to her feet, ducking beneath the low ceiling. "Stay here," she instructed Calida and Lorelei. "I'll check it out."

Witches they might be, but the two women were useless in a fight out on the open water. Earth witches were restricted to being on land for the use of their powers and it would not help them here.

Sharpe headed for the stairs leading to one of the hatches, wishing that Ben were there. His powers would have been far more useful. And then she chided herself. *If he were here, we wouldn't be in this mess.*

She poked her head above deck, hailing the first passing sailor. "What is it?"

"Two Alaran warships," came the terse reply.

"Our welcoming party," Sharpe muttered as she looked around.

It could have been exactly that, nothing more than escorts sent to meet them and see them safely to the Alaran harbor. But she knew such was not the case when the first shot rang out—and not from one of their own.

A cry went up. "All hands!"

That's your cue. Sharpe heaved herself up onto the deck, clutching her musket and made for the ratlines, along with the other musketeers.

She paused halfway up the lines, taking in the two enemy ships before her. Their white sails billowed, gun ports already open, guns bristling menacingly. They were both ships of the line, bigger than the *Phoenix*.

Fortunately, the gun ports of both Daeran ships were already open, guns prepped in case of an engagement. It was three to two, but they were right to be nervous.

Sharpe looked away and continued upward until she reached one of the crow's nests. She could feel the *Phoenix* moving beneath her, turning toward one of the Alaran ships in preparation for the engagement. From her vantage point, she could make out the enemy crew, scurrying about on deck. Her musket had already been loaded and she brought it to her shoulder, sighting down the barrel.

Maximum firing range for a musket was five hundred yards. It had taken her a while to transition from aiming and firing on land to adapting to the rolling, pitching motion of a ship. But she had done it.

She took a deep breath, taking aim at the man at the wheel, and pulled the trigger. She was rewarded with the sight of her quarry crumpling to the deck. In less time than it took to tell, Sharpe had torn open a cartridge, primed the gun, emptied the powder down the barrel, thrust the ball and cartridge into the barrel and then slammed the butt of the musket on the floor of the crow's nest, allowing the weight of the ball to rest against the powder.

She then cocked, aimed, and fired again.

She continued to individually pick off men one by one, but she remained aware of the rest of the skirmish taking place around her. The *Phoenix* had engaged the larger of the two ships, along with one of the Daeran vessels. The roar of the guns and thick, choking smoke filled the air, partially obscuring her vision, but she was high enough to avoid the worst of it.

The ship rocked beneath her with each volley and she had to compensate for the movement, taking her shots while the guns were being reloaded. Splintered wood and sailors alike were sent hurtling through the air with each shot, the acrid smell of gunpowder filling the air. It was nearly impossible to miss from this distance.

With both ships bombarding it at once, the Alaran vessel was unable to board.

No doubt it had been caught off-guard when the *Phoenix*, a ship believed to be its ally, turned on it. Slowly, she could see that the Alaran ship was sinking. The sailors on board began to panic as their impending fate dawned on them. They were too far out to swim to shore and no one on board the Daeran ships were going to take pity on them.

With its target incapacitated, the *Phoenix* turned to the remaining Alaran ship, only to find that it had already been taken care of—but not before taking one of the Daeran vessels down with it.

Sharpe breathed a sigh of relief. It hadn't been pretty, but it could have gone a lot worse. Given what they suspected about Alara's motivations, every man on board had known the risk.

It was over as quickly as it had begun, the roar of the guns falling silent. Slowly, still trembling from adrenaline, she made her way safely down. The *Phoenix* had sustained damage of her own, but it was nothing compared to what had been suffered in her previous battle against Berchmoore and Rodek. The remaining Daeran ship looked the worse for wear, but she judged her still sea worthy.

Those on board must have felt the same, for the ship slowly came about, turning back toward Daera, its role fulfilled. The *Phoenix* would be able to make port in Alara, under her privateer guise, but it would be unwise for the Daeran ship to remain with them.

Sharpe's boots landed softly as she hopped down onto the deck, moving toward Terrance and Berchmoore at the helm. "All right, Berchmoore. We've done our bit. Now it's your turn."

Proceeding with the next part of Varrian's plan, it was up to Berchmoore to report to the palace and tell Alara what they most wanted to hear—that the Daeran king had been killed in the ensuing skirmish.

* * *

The silence of the palace cathedral was absolute. The slightest shuffle or movement sent sound echoing into its furthest reaches. *Skies help anyone who sneezes in here,* Ben thought wryly.

Gone were the massive crowds that had attended the coronation, leaving the building hollow and empty. The red banners still hung far above his head, motionless. The sky above was overcast, muted light filtering through the glass dome.

At any other time, such silence would strike Ben as oppressive, so used was he to the constant sound of the sea. Privacy was nearly nonexistent on a ship, silence even more so. But he had sought solitude, knowing he would be unlikely to come by much of it in the future.

Before him, the stone casket of the king, his father, was laid out for mourners to come and pay their respects a final time before it would be committed to the vaults and catacombs beneath the chapel. The king's likeness graced the top of the coffin, captured in stone, a sword held between his hands, a crown atop his head. He looked somehow younger set in stone, free of the guilt or whatever it was that had plagued him in life.

Regret was probably a more accurate term. Ben was certain that was what he had seen in the king's gaze and heard in his voice the last time they had spoken, when he had mentioned Calida. Why his father should ask someone like Calida for forgiveness, given what she had supposedly done, still bothered Ben. And now he would never have answers.

He sighed, gazing at the casket before him, wishing he'd gotten the chance to get to know his father. He felt only a deep-seated disappointment and a longing for what might have been, but no grief, sharp and piercing. It made him feel guilty. This was his father, after all. He should have felt sorrow at least.

The creak of the chapel door opening made him turn from where he sat in one of the pews. Someone had tried to open the door quietly, but had failed, the sound reverberating throughout the chamber. Kain stood in the entrance, looking like he'd been caught at something. He began to back out.

"You don't have to leave," Ben said.

Kain hadn't been the friendliest person during the time they'd known each other—far from it—but Ben couldn't help but feel sorry for the former prince, having his title stripped away and reduced to a laughingstock in front of all the peers of the realm. Ben couldn't blame him if he was more than a little angry.

"And stay here with you?" Kain countered. "I'd rather not."

"Look, I didn't ask for any of this," Ben said quietly. "I'd much rather have you be the prince, go back to my ship, and leave all of this behind, believe me."

Kain paused in the doorway, looking thoughtful, and Ben expected him to turn and leave. But he stepped inside, walking down the aisle toward him. "I'd help you do that if I could," he said, then added quickly, "For my own gain, you understand."

Ben half-smiled at that. "Of course. But I don't think it's possible anymore. Once, maybe, but not now."

"No." Kain kicked out halfheartedly at the end of one of the pews. "Heavy is the crown…" He sighed and sank down onto the pew, maintaining a distance between him and Ben.

"It was heavy," Ben admitted, thinking back to the coronation, the moment Thalia placed the crown atop his head.

They were silent for a few moments in their respect for the casket laid out before them. *We have that in common, if nothing else.*

Ben nodded to it. "Were you…close?"

Kain had known the king far longer than Ben had. His whole life, growing up as a fraud in the castle, believing the man to be his father. *We both grew up as frauds. Pretending to be someone other than who we really were, and each unaware of it.*

Kain let out a bitter laugh, somewhere between a snort and a soft chuckle. "I don't think I was ever really close with either of my parents. Or rather, your parents."

Ben rubbed at the back of his neck. "I was always led to believe my parents were dead."

"And now one of them is." Kain crossed his arms. "I would say that it was a shame it was him and not the queen, but I suppose that's a terrible thing to say."

Ben glanced at him, one eyebrow raised.

"I never liked her," Kain muttered. "She was always so demanding. I was always trying my best to please or impress her and it was never enough. Nothing I *ever* did was good enough. And now I know why."

Ben licked his lips nervously, half fearing that at any moment, Kain would become angry and storm off. "What does she want? You've lived here all your life. You must have some idea what's going on."

Kain shrugged. "I don't know anything. I was never deemed important enough to know."

Ben gestured to the coffin. "Do you believe the Daeran advisor killed him?"

The former prince gave him a look. "Do you?"

Ben smiled ruefully, wanting to admit what he knew to be the truth, or at least to reply that no, he didn't believe it. But he was too afraid, remembering how he'd asked Annie not to tell a soul, out of fear.

He and Kain might be united in their mutual circumstances, but that didn't make the former prince trustworthy.

"She never liked him," Kain added. "The king."

"I spoke to him," Ben admitted. That much, at least, was safe since Thalia already knew he'd spoken to the king once. "He seemed…perfectly normal, for the most part. Why was he always given medicine to take if there was nothing wrong with him?"

"I wondered about that. Sometimes I thought he was just a drunk and that my—the queen—was too ashamed of him to say so, so she invented some story about how he was ill to explain his absences during hangovers or whatever. But other times… Well, if I didn't know any better, I'd say it almost seemed like she was drugging him to keep him out of the way."

"Why?"

Kain shrugged again. "The only thing I could think of was that he must know something he wasn't supposed to, something she didn't want anyone else to know."

Like the truth about him, Thalia, and Calida?

"Other than that, I don't know." Kain got to his feet, a wry smile quirking his lips. "Part of me is glad that I don't have to worry about trying to please her anymore. It's hard to envy you your new position, having lived it all my life." He shook his head. "I don't know what she has planned for you."

CHAPTER 33

Horus must have spotted the *Phoenix*'s telltale red sails, for he found them before the Alaran coastline was even in sight. The hawk clutched a rolled piece of parchment in his talons, which he offered to Calida. She listened to the hawk at length and then told the others.

The note was from Annie, the princess, addressed to her brother, but they had already left Daera far behind, along with the king, so Horus had delivered the letter to Calida, the only other person best placed to know what to do with the information.

"The Daeran advisor, Aquillus, has been attempting to send reports back to the northern kingdom," Calida said, rolling the parchment once more. "But none have arrived. Little wonder, I should think."

Other than that, the letter seemed to add nothing new and even if it had, there was nothing they could do but stick to the plan.

When the *Phoenix* docked at the Alaran harbor, Berchmoore set off to report to the queen alone. Sharpe disliked letting him go free, out of her sight, but she supposed they'd just have to trust him. It was unlikely and would also be unwise for him to betray them and the plan at this point. He was far too involved and Sharpe didn't think the queen the most merciful of people. If she were to learn that Berchmoore had played a role in the deception, however unwillingly, it would go poorly for him.

They would just have to trust him, but after what he'd done in the past, Sharpe found she was unable to.

* * *

Annie didn't know what to expect when queen Thalia summoned her to the throne room. The room was empty, save for the two of them and a handful of guards. Annie swallowed her apprehension as she approached the queen, viewing her through a far more wary lens than ever.

Was this about the wedding? Did Thalia want to hold the ceremony soon, now that Ben had been crowned the true prince? Or was it about Aquillus, still languishing in his cell? Had the results of the inquest been returned, finding him guilty?

"Your Highness," the queen nodded to her.

"You wanted to see me?"

"Yes." Thalia clasped her hands before her. "I'm afraid I have some rather bad news."

Annie's throat tightened, convinced that she had been right about Aquillus. She braced herself, preparing to be told that Aquillus had been found guilty and sentenced to death.

"Naturally, you know I sent word to your brother after this tragic incident with king Niklaus and the Daeran advisor." Thalia paused and Annie nodded. She continued, "I received word that Varrian intended to travel here to Alara himself. However, I was just informed that his ship was set upon by pirates before he could arrive. I'm afraid there were no survivors."

Annie's breath caught in her chest, a pressure lodged in place. "You mean…Varrian's dead?"

"Yes, child." Thalia laid a hand on her arm. "I understand this is hard for you, especially given recent events. I'm afraid the wedding will have to take place sometime soon, seeing as how you are now Daera's ruler. The two kingdoms must be united. But don't worry about that now—you'll be given time to mourn, of course."

Annie scarcely heard her. All she could think about was that her brother was dead. Her brother, the one she was relying on to fix this mess. To prove Aquillus was innocent and demand that Thalia let him go. To demand that Alara honor its agreement and actually send aid for once and for the privateers to do what they were supposedly hired for in the first place—hunt down the pirates.

The pirates who had sent her brother to a watery grave.

Varrian had risked crossing the sea to be here in person and paid the price for it.

She swallowed. "If you'll excuse me, Your Majesty?"

"Of course."

Somehow, Annie managed to bob a curtsy and then fled from the room as fast as walking would take her. At least the tears waited until she was in the privacy of her own room before they spilled out across her cheeks. Annie sank to her knees by the bed, fingers clenching the sheet that hung over the side, trying to smother the sobs that threatened to break free.

She had never been close to Varrian. The twelve year age gap between them had made it hard to relate to one another. But he had always tried to look out for her in his own way.

As soon as she'd heard that Aquillus had been accused of murdering king Niklaus, she'd known that her older brother wouldn't stand for it. That he'd be on his way here to set things right.

And now he was gone, leaving her the unprepared ruler of a decimated kingdom, set to marry into the Alaran royal family.

Exactly where Thalia wants me.

She was more alone than ever, caught in a web that was more tangled and vast than she could have imagined.

A knock sounded softly on the door. Annie tried to snap at whoever it was to go away, but her voice wouldn't work. The door eased open and she cursed herself silently for not having thought to lock it. But then she saw it was Ben and she sought to rise and rush to him, but couldn't seem to find the strength.

It didn't matter. As though he could sense her need, he shut the door and crossed the room, kneeling beside her and enveloping her in his arms. "I heard. I'm so sorry."

There were so many things Annie wanted to say to him, but could do nothing but sob into his shoulder, the velvet material of his outer coat growing damp with her tears. She was embarrassed and ashamed that anyone should see her like this, especially him.

She wanted to apologize for causing such a scene. Not one usually given to tears, she chalked it up to the amount of stress she'd been under ever since she'd arrived.

Her experiments, all but abandoned now, had failed to produce results. Her engagement and impending marriage to Kain, whom she had viewed as brutish. Finding herself aboard Berchmoore's ship and then Ben's. The truth behind Ben's real identity and what that meant for the both of them. And now this.

It was all too much.

Pull yourself together!

They needed to figure out what to do, now that they would receive no help from her brother. Annie took a deep breath, pulling away, even though it pained her to do so. She wanted nothing more than to let him keep holding her, enveloped in his strong, lean arms and sandalwood scent, his body warm against hers.

Instead, she pushed her hair back from her face, swiping impatiently at damp eyes.

"I don't want to give you false hope," Ben murmured. "But we don't know that what we were told is true, blaming what happened on the pirates the way they are. We all know the truth about that."

Annie scolded herself for not having thought of that, instead assuming the worst possible scenario and letting it overwhelm her. "You're right. I don't know if I even dare hope, but…" Anger suddenly set in, the heat of it crawling across her skin. "I mean, really! It's exactly what she wants."

"What do you mean?"

"Thalia! She told me that I'll have time to mourn, of course, but the wedding is still going to take place. It wouldn't surprise me if she wants to hurry things along now that my brother is dead. I'm the ruler of Daera now and if I marry you—"

"Thalia will have control over both kingdoms."

"Exactly. She's still the queen. She's still in charge. I wonder if this isn't what she wanted all along and that's why the marriage was proposed."

"Maybe." Ben shrugged. "It's possible she's only waited this long because once she found out that I was her son, she had to postpone things. She wasn't going to let you marry Kain once she found out the truth."

"No," Annie said bitterly, then a terrible thought struck her, her momentary hope leaching away. "Just because pirates may not be to blame, that doesn't mean that Varrian still lives."

"We don't know," Ben agreed. "But Berchmoore was the one to deliver the news to Thalia. Last we heard, my crew had succeeded in taking the *Phoenix* back from him. Something about this whole story doesn't add up."

Annie wanted to believe him, to latch onto any shred of optimism she could, but she knew it would only lead to more disappointment. Thalia wasn't the sort of woman to leave anything to chance and if she had arranged this for whatever reason, she would be thorough.

Whether by the hand of pirates, or the queen's own, Varrian was dead.

*　*　*

Calida went ashore shortly after Berchmoore. It would have been more convenient to travel in the same longboat, but they couldn't risk being seen together, even though she doubted anyone in Alara would recognize her after twenty years.

She traveled alone, the muscles in her arms and back straining as she worked the oars, Horus perched on the prow. It was arduous work, but she was strong, and more than that, determined, knowing that each stroke brought her one step closer to Ben.

If everything went according to plan, she would not be the only one rowing when she returned to the *Phoenix*, anchored a respectful distance offshore. She would have her nephew to help her.

Pulling the boat up onto the sand and securing it, Calida paused to rest from her exertions, eyeing the castle just visible in the distance. Somewhere in there, both her nephew and her sister waited. She wanted nothing more than to storm that castle, confront her sister and end this madness once and for all.

But she would get just one chance to confront Thalia, if she were lucky. One chance was enough.

Calida nodded to Horus. "You know what to do."

With a dip of his head, the hawk took to the air, soaring toward the distant palace. Whatever happened, however this day played out, Calida was certain of only one thing—she would see Ben safely back aboard his ship and away from this place with all haste. Whether she would get to be a part of that plan, she was less certain.

She had left Sharpe and Terrance behind, even though they could have been useful. They were not witches and had no part in this bitter rivalry that had destroyed an untold number of lives. If Calida had any say, it would not destroy them as well.

Lorelei, on the other hand, had been harder to convince. Unlike the others, she knew well what Thalia had done and what was at stake. She'd wanted to accompany Calida, to see an end to it, for what Thalia had done to her and Daniel as much as Calida.

In the end, she had remained behind as well, admonishing Calida to be careful, but accepting that this was her fight. Thalia was her sister and had cost her more than any of the others. Her hatred for her sister ran so deep that she'd been willing to have her banished to another kingdom, sent from the only home she'd ever known.

And while Calida was not so vain as to think Thalia had created the famine as a means of flushing her out, the same could not be said of the witch-hunts.

Horus had long since vanished from sight. Calida blinked, unsure how long she had stood on the beach, lost in the past, a stiff wind darting through her hair and catching at her skirts.

It had been worth it, to take one last long look at the kingdom that had been her home. She might not ever lay eyes upon it again. It was certainly a beautiful place, the water clear as crystal, a lovely shade of blue-green, the sun streaming down from a sky filled with large clouds.

Snatching one of the ship's lanterns out of the bottom of the boat, she turned and began walking. She had a little ways to go on foot, but she knew these paths well, having utilized them often enough after a night of sneaking out of the monastery.

There was no monastery there now—not anymore—and she wasn't entirely sure what sort of sight would greet her when she arrived, but it seemed only fitting somehow that this should end where it all began.

Certainly, she would be undisturbed there, until Ben could find his way to her.

* * *

Now that Ben's room had windows of his own, Horus came directly to him rather than Annie. He'd developed a habit of leaving the windows thrown wide open. Some of them were tall doors, made mostly of glass, that opened out onto balconies. When he was alone, Ben liked to go out onto the balconies, or at least have the windows open, letting in the strong breeze and the fresh air, bringing a hint of salt from the sea.

Other than Annie, he sought out little company, slowly growing more comfortable with solitude. It was in one such moment, when he was in his room alone, that Horus found him.

It was late, night already having fallen. There'd been no further word on Annie's brother's fate, and she had been absent from dinner that evening. Ben couldn't blame her. Such meals were quickly growing tiresome—and far too uncomfortable.

He hated sitting at the same table as Rodek and Kain, though the latter was far less acerbic toward Ben than he had been. It was all Ben could do to sit down to a civil dinner with his father's killer. The king's absence seemed more overt than ever, as did Aquillus's. If there had been any further word on the advisor's fate, he wasn't aware of it.

And then there was his mother. Ben still didn't know how far to trust her, what she did or didn't know. Her expression was inscrutable and if she were bothered by the palpable tension around the table, she didn't show it.

But Ben wasn't merely imagining it. He could tell Kain felt it, too, but no one dared say anything.

He had rarely been so relieved to retreat back to his own quarters. He inquired after Annie along the way, to see if she were hungry, offering to fetch something from the kitchens for her. But she had declined.

He couldn't blame her for feeling the way she did. Ben thought that if he stayed here much longer, confined within these walls, he might just go mad. If he wasn't already.

Really, he should have just gone to bed, given how poorly he'd slept since he arrived here. The longer he put it off, the more he risked being unable to fall asleep when he did eventually go to bed. The last thing he needed was to spend another sleepless night. Whatever was going on in this palace, he needed his wits about him.

But even knowing that, he stayed by the balcony, staring off into the distance, at the towns below, and the warm lights he could see, each one representing someone he didn't know, who, for whatever reason, had also put off retiring for the night, giving them something in common.

He felt he could have stayed there forever, enjoying the rare moment of peace. Not everything was right with the world—in fact very little, if anything, was—but in that moment, it felt like it could be. And then Horus swooped down through his window on nearly silent wings.

Ben was surprised to see the hawk back so soon, but Horus quickly explained. The *Phoenix* was here, anchored off the coast of Alara, and Calida was waiting for him at the edge of the Witch Wood.

"The Witch Wood?" Ben repeated. In all the time he'd spent in the southern kingdom, the name meant nothing to him

"I'm to take you there now," the hawk replied. *"Can you meet me outside the palace?"*

Ben had never tried to sneak out of the palace. The only time he'd left the castle, he'd been accompanied by guards. But he glanced down at the witch-mark on the back of his right hand, bare now. He'd ceased wearing gloves since the coronation ceremony and it was still an odd sensation to be able to feel the texture of things when he touched them.

He was a pirate. A prince. A witch. He could manage this.

The palace was dark and quiet, the corridors mostly deserted, but Ben still took some of the lesser paths he knew of, thinking he would have a greater chance of going unseen.

It took him far longer than he would have liked, having to double back on a couple occasions and even getting lost for a few moments, finding himself in passages that were unfamiliar. But he valued subtlety over speed.

He could hardly leave via one of the main entrances, which were guarded, so he ducked out of the servants' entrance. There were no servants about to notice him. Their days began quite early and they were all no doubt asleep.

Ben debated taking a horse from the stables, but decided against risking it. Horus was waiting for him, circling above lazily and Ben set off on foot after him, quickly regretting his decision not to take a horse.

The hawk quickly led him out of town and into the forest, the lights and sounds of civilization fading into the distance, silence swallowing them. It was difficult navigating the uneven terrain in the dark and Ben swore as he nearly lost his footing more than once.

It was a pity conjuring light wasn't part of being a sky witch.

His feet hurt by the time they reached their destination. What little of the forest he could see looked the same to him and he wondered how much further they had to go when his surroundings began to suddenly change, a sense of wrongness coming over him.

Thick fog melded with the trees, floating between the trunks. Ben suppressed his sudden unease, continuing after Horus. There was something inherently *wrong* about these woods. A subtle background noise had risen up, enveloping him in its near constant hum. A ghostly murmur sounded to his left and he jumped, feeling goosebumps erupt over his skin. He stood still, listening to the uncanny sound.

It was almost as though he could hear voices, but the moment he tried to focus on any single one, it faded away, dissolving into nonsense, words he couldn't make out, the thread lost.

Calida stood ahead of him, a lantern in one hand, and Ben moved toward the light with relief.

"What is this place?" he demanded.

The trees had iron nails driven into them and through the fog, he could see ruins. Stone walls, some collapsed, others yet intact. There was no breeze at all.

"The Witch Wood," Calida replied. "It's rumored to be haunted by the souls of the witches who were killed here, and those murdered in the witch-hunts. If you believe witches have souls, that is."

"What about those ruins?" Ben nodded to them, wishing he had a weapon of some kind. Though what good it would have done against ghosts, he didn't know.

"Where the Erlohn monastery stood. It was once where all Alaran witches were trained."

"I know about the monastery," Ben said. "Thalia told me."

"Oh, yes? What else did she tell you? Did she tell you that she's the one responsible for the monastery becoming the Witch Wood?"

He looked at the ground. "She said you were jealous of her and the king and that you stole me as a baby." He looked up. "Is that true?"

Calida sighed, her expression hard to make out in the lantern light. "Yes, that much is true."

"Why did you do it? Thalia said it was because you believed I should have been your child and not hers. Is that true as well?"

"If I'm honest with myself, I was jealous. Bitter, too. You should have been mine and not hers. And you would have been, if she hadn't taken Niklaus from me."

Ben shook his head. "She accused you of doing that to her."

"Of course she'd say that. That's what she always did, spinning the truth backward, just enough that it had a ring of authenticity to it and you believed her."

"Then what really happened?" Ben challenged. "You dragged me all the way out here to this skies-forsaken place. Now I want the truth."

"I met Niklaus when he and his father toured the monastery. I loved him and I still do, even with him gone. I have no doubt Thalia had a hand in that. She never loved him, she was only jealous because he'd shown interest in me and not her. She always was ambitious. She wanted to be queen so that she could make something more of herself. She wasn't happy with just being ordinary, believing herself destined for something more, something greater.

"But Niklaus had chosen me, so she needed to devise a way to separate us. We argued a lot, he and I. His father didn't approve of me and it created tension between us, since we couldn't marry until the old king was dead. Niklaus wanted his father's approval, but he refused to give it. And after every argument, wouldn't you know, there was Thalia. My faithful sister, come to comfort me, telling me that he was being unreasonable and that I was the fair one. Little did I know, she was visiting him as well, saying that I was being childish, selfish, that I didn't understand him the way she did."

Ben felt his skin crawl. It was eerily similar to the tale Thalia had told him, the very same only with the roles reversed.

"I admit that I wasn't as good of a companion to Niklaus as I should have been," Calida confessed, bitterness evident in her voice. "That is true, but it doesn't excuse what she did! She turned him against me. And had me banished from the castle. From the kingdom. So when I heard that the two of them had a child, a son, I was consumed with jealousy. I vowed that if I could not have the man I loved, then my sister could not have her true son, either."

"So you stole me and put Kain in my place." Ben could not keep the accusation out of his tone, frustration boiling over. "My entire life has been a lie! His as well."

"What would you have rather had me do?" Calida challenged, her anger rising in response to his own. "I wasn't going to leave you there, with all your powers, and grow up with her as a mother. How do you think you would have turned out? You'd have been like Kain, only worse, because you *had* inherited her powers. Thalia would have corrupted you, made you into a tyrant like her."

"You don't know that," Ben protested, but his voice lacked conviction. He exhaled slowly. "How did you do it? How did you steal me from her?"

"It would have been impossible without Lorelei. She was a midwife in the castle. She placed you in a basket on the balcony for Horus to steal and bring to me. After which, she fled to Daera with me. At the monastery, Thalia was always looking for others whose gifts might prove useful to her once she was in a position of power. That's why she chose Lorelei and Mordred.

"I don't know what she told you about the witch-hunts, but they were a way to eliminate competition. Thalia realized the only people to truly pose a threat to her were other witches and so she devised a way to eliminate them."

"She said you poisoned the old king and that all witches paid the price."

"The old king wasn't poisoned and certainly not by me. But his death was hastened along, yes. Thalia was responsible for that, but I could never prove it. No one could. But all witches did pay the price. Niklaus was half driven out of his mind with grief. He became convinced—whether through Thalia's influence, I don't know—that witches were dangerous. That they posed a threat that could bring down the throne. I'd like to believe he later came to realize what a mistake it had been, to paint all witches with the same brush, but by then it was too late. The damage was done.

"And of course, Thalia did nothing to discourage him. If nothing else, it was a convenient way to hunt me down once I was banished and ensure I could no longer cause her any more trouble. She didn't believe what she'd done would sit well with me, or that I'd let it go, and she was right."

Ben gaped at his aunt. "You're telling me that the witch-hunts were partially put in place as a means of getting rid of you?"

"That's how ruthless my sister is," Calida said firmly. "I think you know now why you cannot remain here. You may be her real son, but don't think for a moment that she won't turn on you. Blood means nothing to her."

"I can't just leave."

"You must. You have no idea the things she's capable of."

"How do I know I can trust you?" Ben demanded. "Either of you? How do I know which of you is telling me the truth?" He was suddenly angry at Calida for what she'd done, tired of all the lies, and unsure of who to believe. "You lied to me. You told me my parents were dead!"

"Thalia is dead to me, as far as I'm concerned. And Niklaus was as good as, under her control."

"That's no excuse!"

"I did it to protect you!" Calida snapped. "I couldn't risk Thalia finding out the truth about who Kain was."

"And who is he, really?"

"An orphan. The child of some commoners who were either dead, couldn't afford to keep him, or simply didn't want him. What difference does it make? I found him on the streets. He wouldn't have lived on his own and if he had survived, the only life he would ever know would be one of deprivation, begging for food, not knowing where his next meal would come from or if there would be one at all. By doing what I did, I gave him a better life, but he's no witch's son, which is why I had to put a fake mark on his hand, the same as yours. Thalia may not have paid much attention to your appearance when you were born, but you can be sure she noticed your mark. It was all she looked for, all she cared about, because it meant you were a witch, just like her."

Ben shook his head. "You've interfered in both of our lives. This isn't fair to either of us, me or Kain. Neither of us asked to be caught up in your petty feud."

"And I didn't ask to be betrayed by my own sister," Calida retorted. "But here we are. Perhaps I should have told you the truth, but I truly did believe it was for the best if I didn't."

"Just like not telling me that I was a witch? Was that for the best, too?"

Calida ignored the barb. "You've had some dealing with my sister by now. You know what she's like, what kind of woman she is. Knowing that, given the taste of the royal life you've had and the life you had aboard the *Phoenix*, which would you have rather had growing up?"

Ben knew the answer, but he refused to admit it to her. What she had done was still wrong and he didn't want to tell her that she was right, about anything.

"You're going to have to decide who to believe, Ben," Calida said softly. "Because we can't both be telling you the truth."

He sighed, crossing his arms. "Tell me this. Is Annie's brother alive? Or was Berchmoore telling the truth when he reported him killed?"

"Oh, he's very much still alive, safe back in Daera."

Ben let out a breath of relief, thinking of how pleased Annie would be at the news.

"But the assassination attempt on him was all too real," Calida added, explaining about the attack on the Daeran ships and how Alara had believed Varrian to be on board one of them. "I think that speaks volumes about my sister's true intentions. She wants to weaken Daera. That's why she created the famine in the first place."

"What?"

"She's a sky witch, Ben," Calida said, with a kind of patience that was infuriating, as if what she had just said hadn't further shaken the already crumbling foundation Ben felt he stood on. "Like you. She can manipulate the weather, create storms. She's the one who makes it always rain in Daera so that the crops don't get enough sun and rot in their fields. I'm certain of it."

Ben stared at her, unable to conjure a single argument or seemingly rational thought. It made a terrible kind of sense. He didn't know why he hadn't thought of it before.

Daera's situation went beyond a streak of bad luck or a mere pattern of bad weather. There was design, intent, behind this. Sky witches could indeed control and manipulate the weather. Hadn't he done it often enough aboard the *Phoenix*?

Other than himself, Thalia was the only other sky witch he knew.

There were simply too many things pointing in the same direction. Taken separately, one might not have thought anything of it, but when viewed together…

Calida must have seen something in his expression, his anger and doubt draining away, leaving behind an emptiness.

She reached out toward him, offering one hand. "Come with me, Ben. The *Phoenix* is waiting just offshore."

The *Phoenix*. His crew. The sea. Freedom.

His heart ached with a longing so fierce it physically hurt.

But he shook his head. "Annie's still at the palace. If what you say is true, I can't leave her behind. I won't."

Calida lowered her hand, studying him. "You care for her, don't you?"

Ben blinked at her, the words sinking in. He did care. He was surprised by the admission, by how much he *did* care. And yet, at the same time, it didn't surprise him at all.

Somewhere along the line, things had changed.

He had changed.

"I suppose I do," he said quietly.

"Go then," Calida relented. "Quickly."

CHAPTER 34

The trip back to the castle took longer than Ben would have liked, but at least it passed without incident. He'd been unspeakably relieved to leave the Witch Wood behind, his thoughts churning. Should he believe what Thalia told him, or Calida, the woman who had raised him for eight years?

The woman who had stolen him away from the life he should have led, by her own admission. But he didn't have to think too hard to know that the royal life was not one he would have chosen for himself. Perhaps if it was all he'd ever known, his answer would have been different.

He belonged to a different life. One of freedom and danger, yes, but was the palace any safer? He was beginning to have his doubts.

He wanted nothing more than to flee down to the shore, to see his beloved *Phoenix* again and sail away, back to where he belonged. But he couldn't do that without Annie. Even unsure where the truth lay among all the lies he'd been told, he was sure that leaving Alara was a wise thing to do.

At least until they understood what was really going on. And if Calida was telling the truth about his mother causing the famine…

It was almost too horrible to contemplate, and yet, Alara didn't seem too keen on actually helping its northern neighbor. All signs pointed to the contrary. Perhaps that would explain why.

As if conjured by his thoughts, he rounded the corner and nearly collided with his mother. Ben had been careful to use the servants' entrance again and had encountered no one in the halls. It was even later now, his walk back having taken far too long, but the sky was still velvety dark, no sign of dawn on the horizon.

"Benjamin." She smiled at him. "A bit late, isn't it?"

He forced himself to look at her without flinching, unsure what, if anything she knew or merely suspected. Was this woman, his mother, responsible for the deaths of hundreds—thousands—of Daeran people? Was she capable of something so ruthless?

"I couldn't sleep," he answered, then added, "Mother."

Her dark blue eyes studied him for a moment more and then she nodded. "Very well. Perhaps you'll have better luck now."

"Perhaps." He ducked his head and went on his way, happy to have escaped unscathed.

Rather than going directly to his room, he stopped before Annie's, knocking softly, hoping to avoid the attention of her chaperone.

A moment later, she poked her head out and beckoned him in silently. She was still dressed, in a silk blouse and trousers, making him think she hadn't retired for the night either. Her feet were bare, though, rendering her a few inches shorter without the added height of a heel.

"I've just been to see my aunt," Ben explained, casting a quick look around to be sure they were alone. "She's here, in Alara, with the rest of my crew and the *Phoenix*. Your brother's alive, Annie. It was all just a ruse."

She visibly wilted with relief. But as he further explained what had happened, and the dark implications of Alara attacking a ship they believed Varrian to be on, her frown only deepened.

She let out a long breath. "It's a direct violation of the alliance. An act of war."

"I don't think there is an alliance anymore," Ben said grimly. *If there ever was.*

Annie walked over to her balcony. The doors were closed, but she opened them and strode out onto the stone platform, overlooking the towns below and the sea beyond, moonlight shimmering off its surface.

Ben joined her. He could almost imagine he could hear the sound of the waves rolling in, but it was too far away. Too far away to see the *Phoenix* from here, but he looked anyway.

How should he tell her that he was going to leave and he wanted her to come with him? Would she even want to?

What if she refused? What would he do then? Give in to his heart's desire and go back to the *Phoenix* or give in to his other desire?

Ben leaned his arms on the railing, studying her profile. The way the moonlight illuminated her features, lending them a softness that sunlight lacked, made his pulse quicken. Standing so close to her in the middle of the night didn't help matters any. His eyes roamed over the way her thick black curls fell over her shoulders, her nose that was slightly upturned, lingering on her lips.

"What else did your aunt say?" she asked, turning toward him.

Ben quickly turned away, feeling himself flush, hoping she hadn't noticed the way he'd been looking at her.

Turning his thoughts back to Calida quickly brought reality crashing down.

"She said some rather interesting things," he replied, "about my mother. She accused Thalia of being responsible for the famine plaguing Daera." It hurt to admit that. *My own mother…the cause of so much suffering.*

Annie blinked. "How is that possible?"

"She's a sky witch." Ben spread his hands, the moonlight playing over the bare mark. "Like me. She can control the weather if she's powerful enough. And I think she is." He remembered the day he had fought her outside the dungeons, the raw strength behind her attacks.

Annie digested the news in silence. It didn't matter how much aid Alara sent if their queen was continuing the bad weather that afflicted Daera, day after day without end.

"I'm sorry," Ben whispered, the sheer horror—and shame—threatening to undo him. How could he be the son of someone so cruel?

"For what?" Annie said, facing him. "You're not her."

"I feel like I should do something, though. How can I sit back, knowing this, and not do anything to stop her?"

Calida wanted him to run, to leave all of this behind, and the idea was so tempting, he was ashamed by the cowardice of it.

He was the prince of Alara, but he'd also grown up in Daera. Didn't he have a responsibility, to both kingdoms, to try and set this right?

It was a responsibility he'd never wanted, but it was real. It was his. And he couldn't deny that.

Annie shook her head. "Don't. Don't challenge her, Ben."

He knew she was right, but that didn't make it any easier. He might have been the prince, but he was little more than a stranger here, unfamiliar with all of this. What difference could one man make?

He closed his eyes and let out another sigh. Then he opened them again and looked at her. "What would I do without you, Annie? My voice of reason."

"I'm sure you'd manage somehow." But he thought she was blushing in the silvery light.

She seemed so different to him now than she had when he'd first taken her off Berchmoore's ship. He smiled at the memory, thinking of how she'd refused to tell him who she was.

She noticed the look. "What?"

Ben sobered slightly. "My aunt wants me to leave with her. Right now. Tonight. I said I wasn't leaving without you."

She looked at him with wide green eyes.

He forged ahead. "You know, when I first met you, I thought you were insufferable."

"And now?" she asked, a little breathlessly.

"I think," Ben said, leaning a bit closer to her, "I want to kiss you."

There was no doubt about it, she was definitely turning red now.

She took a deep breath, but she didn't pull away. "I think I'd like that."

Before he could lose his nerve, Ben closed the distance between them, pressing his lips against hers, softly at first and then with more urgency. Annie reciprocated, her lips parting beneath his. His hands trailed down to her hips, pulling her against him, wanting more. He wanted to touch her, to feel every inch of her against him.

He threaded his fingers through her silky hair, breathing in her jasmine scent. His touch grazed her skin, relishing the feel of it against his own, without gloves to get in the way.

He felt her thin fingers playing through his own hair. He broke away, trailing his lips along her jaw, down to the soft skin of her throat. He could feel her pulse, fast and strong, and he felt a thrill go through him as she let out a small sound of pleasure, her breath hot on his cheek.

Ben would have happily seen how much further it would have gone, but time was a precious currency slipping away each moment they delayed. With a frustrated growl—and no small amount of restraint—he pulled back, both of them breathing hard, his skin awash with heat.

Annie laughed suddenly. "What would Florence think?"

Ben chuckled as he pictured the chaperone's horrified face. It would be a sight worth paying for.

"Perhaps we can scandalize her later. Right now, we need to go. I don't want to leave without you." He leaned his forehead against hers, arms still around her waist. "I don't want to have any more adventures if you're not a part of it, right there beside me. Whatever happens, I want to face it with you, Annie. Will you come with me?"

"Of course."

He smiled, relief coursing through him. "Princess," he murmured, leaning forward to kiss her again, knowing they should have already left.

He was nothing if not weak. She made him weak. *But if this is what weakness feels like, then I never want to be strong.*

It was a much slower kiss, more akin to smoldering coals than the raging inferno that had nearly consumed them both mere moments ago. Ben was content to take his time, but they didn't have time to spare.

Annie pulled back suddenly, as if something had just occurred to her. "Aquillus! And what about Maddie and Florence? Much as I hate having a chaperone, we can't leave them behind."

"There's no time."

"Aquillus, then," she said stubbornly. "I won't leave him to answer for a crime he didn't commit."

"All right. We'll take him with us," Ben assured her, glancing over his shoulder at the room behind. "Do you have everything else you need?"

"Nothing I can't leave behind. You?"

He shook his head. He'd brought only the clothes on his back when he'd arrived and he'd be content to take nothing more with him when he left.

He took her hand and began leading her toward the door. "Come on."

* * *

Aquillus looked up at the sound of the dungeon door opening. Thalia stepped through, gesturing with a flick of her fingers for the guards to leave them.

The advisor sat on the edge of his cot. "Come to tell me it's over, have you? That I have a dawn appointment with the gallows? Or do you intend to burn me as a witch?"

"Not quite." She looked down at him. He must truly have given up all hope to take such brazen a tone. "I've come to inform you that king Varrian has been killed in an engagement with pirates."

"What?" he exclaimed, his expression turning stricken. "It can't be! You're lying."

Thalia thought it amusing how he had seemed unconcerned when it came to his own fate, but he was devastated over the death of his king. "I'm afraid not. The wedding between Princess Annabelle and my son will go forward, of course. The kingdoms will be joined. But I can't rule both Daera and Alara at the same time. I'll need a steward in Daera, someone I can trust." She looked at him pointedly.

Aquillus narrowed his green eyes at her. "Why offer such a thing to me?"

She shrugged, gesturing at the cell around them. "Seems a better prospect than what you've currently got going for you."

He scoffed. "I would be nothing more than your puppet."

"Oh, don't be like that. Most men would leap at the chance you've been offered and you'd do well to consider it."

Thalia crossed her arms behind her back, fingering the handle of the dagger she'd hidden there. She found it a comforting presence, whether she intended to use it or not.

"I'm not going to be your pawn."

Footsteps shuffled in the passage outside. Thalia frowned, preparing to snap at the intruding guard that she had specifically stated she wished to be alone.

But it wasn't a guard. Rodek stood in the hall outside the rows of cells, a rolled piece of parchment clutched in one hand.

"A message for you," he said, pitching his voice low. "It was delivered by your sister's hawk."

Thalia froze, staring at him as if she hadn't heard him right. Quick as a viper, she snatched the missive from her advisor. There was a single sentence, quickly read, her eyes greedily devouring it.

Meet me at the monastery.

Leave it to Calida to refer to the Witch Wood as the monastery it once was, rather than the ruin she'd made of it. She crumpled the letter in her fist.

Calida was here, in Alara. Thalia had no idea what had become of Mordred. Berchmoore had had no answer to give her when she'd pressed the privateer earlier, but if her sister was here, it seemed she had either slipped the witch-hunter's grasp or put an end to his hunting days for good.

Either way, it didn't matter. In twenty years, never had Thalia come so close to having Calida in her grasp. It was an opportunity not to be missed. Calida would be waiting for her, but Thalia was confident she could handle her. She'd always been stronger, even then.

Aquillus had noticed her reaction, taking in the crumpled letter, still clenched in her fist. "Bad news?"

"No," Thalia murmured. "Quite the opposite. Though the same can't be said for you."

He barely had a chance to move as she whipped the dagger free of its hiding place and buried it, to the hilt, in his side, slipping between the ribs. The Daeran advisor let out a choking gasp.

Thalia pulled the blade free and straightened, wiping it on the hem of her skirt. Aquillus slumped against the wall, one hand pressed to the wound, but without prompt medical attention, he wouldn't last long. And none would be forthcoming.

She turned to Rodek. "I think it's time I paid my sister a visit."

He nodded. "I'll go with you."

It was on the tip of her tongue to refuse his offer, to say that there was no need. But there was no harm in letting him tag along like the faithful dog he was. Calida was hers to finish, but it never hurt to have someone watching your back.

"As you wish."

CHAPTER 35

The dungeon was deserted when they arrived, which Annie found odd, but she wasn't going to waste valuable time questioning good luck. Without the guards present, there was no one to steal or demand the key from, but she pushed the issue aside. They would figure something out. If nothing else, perhaps Ben could pick the lock again.

Boots scuffing on the stone floor, she hurried over to where Aquillus's cell had been, only to stop short, letting out a gasp.

The Daeran advisor was slumped against the wall, his skin ashen, eyes closed. His tunic was stained a deep scarlet, the coppery tang of blood thick in the air. It was everywhere, his clothes, his hands, puddled on the floor beneath him.

Annie turned away, gagging at the sight, the smell of it. Ben, likely more accustomed to such things, stepped up to the cell door.

"He's dead," he murmured, confirming her thoughts. No one could lose that much blood and live.

Skies, there was so much of it. A little blood went a long way, but even so…

"We're too late," she whispered.

She took a step closer, wondering who had done this and why. Surely Aquillus had posed little threat, locked away in a cell. But then, Alara thought that Varrian was dead. Perhaps there was to be no trial. Annie knew that Aquillus was innocent, even if she didn't know what had been the intended result of all of this.

Maybe this had been the plan all along, to quietly remove Aquillus and whatever obstacle he represented.

"There's nothing we can do for him now," Ben said quietly. "We need to go."

Annie straightened, her emotions compressing into one hard lump. She could untangle it later. She clenched her hands into fists, her anger such that it burned cold rather than hot.

It frightened her, how calm she felt given the force of her anger. It made her feel dangerous, capable of anything.

"Not yet," she replied. "There's something I need to get first."

Ben followed behind her as she hurried to the room where she had sparred with Kain. Along the way, she passed the corridor that would lead her to her work room and she felt a pang of loss at the idea of leaving it all behind.

Only now she knew how futile it had all been. If a sky witch were responsible for the famine, it didn't matter how hardy the plants she crossbred were. The magic would find a way to kill them.

When she thought of all the time she'd wasted, all the soaring hopes and crushing blows she'd endured along the way, Annie wanted to scream. It had all been for nothing.

The real solution was, in theory, much easier.

To stop the famine, all they had to do was get rid of the sky witch behind it.

Easier said than done. Thalia must have been quite a powerful witch to create and maintain the famine.

She glanced at Ben as they ran through the empty corridors, footsteps ringing out. But no one came, drawn to the noise. Their attention must have been required elsewhere.

Annie wondered if Ben realized what needed to happen. This only ended one way. Either they succeeded, or the famine would continue.

Thalia had to be stopped. Hopefully, that task would fall to her sister, but if not, Annie wondered if Ben had it in him to do what needed to be done. He wasn't close to Thalia, and whether he felt any warmth toward her, Annie couldn't say, but she was still his mother.

She darted into the room, striding over to where the racks of rapiers stood, snatching one. The blade glinted in the low light. Through the window, she could see the faintest hint of dawn staining the sky.

The cold steel in her hand instantly made her feel better. She might not have any magic of her own, but neither was she helpless.

She turned to Ben. "After what they did to Aquillus, I'm not going anywhere unarmed. Do you want to take one?" She gestured to the racks.

There were plenty and they were real enough, sharpened and deadly. It might not have been the kind of sword he was used to, but they were better than nothing.

He shook his head, flashing her the back of his hand, witch-mark on full display. "I'll be all right."

It was hard to argue with that. "Then let's go."

* * *

The darkness of the wood enveloped Thalia as she entered, moving at a careful walk, not knowing where her sister was hiding. She could feel Rodek's presence behind her, his steps quiet but heavy on the forest floor. His hand was at the sword at his side, ready to rip the blade free at a

405

moment's notice, though it would be little use against a witch with full access to her power.

Mist swirled around her skirt as it always seemed to here. Though the sky was lightening beyond, no trace of sunlight pierced through the thick tree branches. Malaise settled over her, a feeling of dread that threatened to distract her.

The ghostly murmurs continued to whisper in her ear. She could feel the iron nails studded into the trees, dampening her power, and stayed as far from them as she could. But if they weakened her power, so too would Calida be similarly affected.

The first of the ruins came into view and there was Calida, dressed in a dowdy gray-blue dress. She looked like the commoner she was compared to Thalia's regal scarlet gown.

"Hello, sister."

It was the first time they had seen each other in twenty years. Faint lines had appeared around Calida's eyes and mouth—as had happened to Thalia herself. Her hair was wild and curled, a vibrant orange, while Thalia's own was a deeper red and straight.

And yet for all that, Calida had always been the more beautiful of the two. Even now, though no one could call Thalia anything but attractive, she was still overshadowed by her older sister.

Calida stared evenly back at her. "You're no sister to me."

Thalia ignored the jab. "What a battlefield you've chosen," she retorted, nodding to the ruins behind her.

"I thought you'd appreciate the irony," Calida remarked, taking a step forward. "I knew you'd come, though you might have left your loyal dog behind."

A hiss of metal rang out as Rodek began to slide his sword free, but Thalia flung out one arm, stopping him. This was her fight, this feud that had simmered for so long, now at last boiling over.

The air suddenly smelled like rain. Thunder rumbled overhead and, if possible, it seemed to grow even darker in the Witch Wood. Thalia could see enough of the sky through the trees to call upon her power. But they were also on land and Calida could make the most of her own.

Her sister turned and ran toward the ruins, still remarkably intact with stone stairs leading up into the various towers and wings that had once made up the monastery.

"Running again?" Thalia taunted. Leaving Rodek behind to watch her back and see to it that they were not disturbed, she charged after Calida.

Calida turned as she reached the top of the wall. Thalia was still navigating the stairs. Her sister mentally yanked on one of the dead trees and sent it toppling toward the stone stairs.

Thalia's eyes widened at the sight of the tree falling toward her and she flung up one hand, hurling it aside with a concentrated blast of wind. It collapsed harmlessly onto the ground with a crash. The wind redoubled all around, tearing at Calida's hair and clothes, threatening to push her off the wall.

Calida let out a growl of frustration, a sound that Thalia savored. She had access to both wind and water, giving her an advantage. Calida was left with only control over the earth, since there were no animals in the haunted wood to come to her aid.

Calling on her power, she hefted loose chunks of rock from the ruins, hurling them toward Thalia, who merely summoned the wind to divert them or send them flying back toward her sister. With each stone that slammed into the damaged wall, the rock cracked and crumpled, weakening just a little more.

Calida slammed her foot down on the wall beneath her, a crack spreading out toward Thalia, the ruins trembling from the impact. Thalia cried out, losing her footing, falling to her hands and knees. Before Calida could take advantage of her opportunity, a bolt of lightning arced down, striking the ground at her feet.

She was thrown from the force of the blast. A faint smell of burning hung in the air. While she lay dazed, Thalia got to her feet.

Calida reached out to the tree roots concealed beneath the ground, calling them up. The roots broke free, snaking up the sides of the wall and lashing around Thalia's legs, dragging her to the ground once more.

The queen let out a scream of rage as the roots began to drag her toward the edge of the wall, her fingers reaching out desperately for a handhold and finding none. The sharp rock sliced through the skin of her fingers as she scrabbled for a hold.

Calida sought to rise, watching as her sister was tugged toward her doom, when she suddenly gasped and sank down, clutching at her chest as Thalia crushed the air out of her lungs.

As she weakened, so did her hold on the tree roots. Thalia shook free from their grip, scrambling up, staring down at her sister in triumph.

* * *

Ben saw the storm gather over the Witch Wood before they'd even arrived, dark clouds swirling and writhing in their wrath, lightning flashing ominously within. He urged the horse on faster, Annie's arms wrapping tighter around him.

Throwing caution to the wind, they had taken one of the horses from the stables, no time to make the trip on foot. He could feel the animal's muscles straining beneath him, pushed to its limit.

The horse skid to a halt at the edge of the woods, rearing in fright and nearly throwing them both. Annie cried out. The animal snorted, tossing its head, refusing to take another step.

Ben swung his leg over the saddle and dismounted, helping Annie down. Together, though he dreaded setting foot in the place again, they ran into the Witch Wood.

Almost at once, he spotted his mother and aunt up on the wall. For a moment, he thought perhaps Calida was about to win, only for his mother to pull the same trick she had on him that first day in Alara. She was crushing Calida's lungs.

His own lungs were burning from his sprint, desperate to reach the two women before it was too late. He started forward, only to come up short, his path blocked by Rodek.

The advisor drew his sword. Ben hesitated. Could he use his magic against another human, the way his mother did?

Annie darted forward, rapier raised. She looked so small compared to Rodek's muscular frame. But she was quick. Rodek blocked her sword with his own and she deftly parried.

"Go!" she cried.

The last thing Ben wanted was to leave her there. He'd never forgive himself if something happened to her. He'd made her a promise. But if he didn't, Calida would die.

Trusting that Annie could look after herself, Ben dashed forward with a muttered curse, his eyes locked on the two women on the wall.

He raced up the stone steps two at a time, nearly tripping in his haste. Calida had sunk to the ground, her struggling feeble. Ben reached the top of the stairs, where it met the flat stretch of wall, just as his mother drew a dagger from her belt. Without stopping to think, he threw himself between the two sisters.

"Stop!" he cried.

A flicker of surprise appeared in Thalia's dark blue eyes for a moment and then was gone. She lowered the dagger at once and Ben heard Calida choke behind him as she gasped in air. He let out a sigh of relief.

"Get out of the way, Benjamin," Thalia said softly. "This doesn't concern you."

"I can't let you do this."

"You should go back to the palace. I understand if this isn't something you wish to see, but this traitor must be dealt with." She looked past him to where her sister still lay. "Or have you forgotten what she stole from both of us?"

Ben shook his head. "You were right. She did steal me from you. But now I understand why. She didn't want me growing up with a monster for a mother."

Thalia raised her hands in a placating gesture, her tone calm and reasonable, a stark contrast to his own, as if to emphasize how unreasonable he was being. "I don't know what sort of lies she's told you—"

"You're the liar," Ben spat. "I've known that ever since you killed my father."

The queen frowned. "What?"

"It wasn't Aquillus. It was Rodek. I knew that from the start, because I was in the room at the time, hidden. The story about Aquillus was all a lie to frame him."

"Rodek?" Her expression took on a mask of horror. "I had no idea. After this is over, I will see this put right."

"Drop the act, mother. There's nothing Rodek does that you don't know about. That's why you brought him here."

Thalia was unflappable. "And why would I do that? Why would I have my advisor murder my husband?"

"Why do any of it?" Ben challenged. "Why lie about the privateers? Why claim they were hired to hunt down pirates when they're nothing more than glorified pirates themselves? Why the elaborate charade of the marriage proposal and alliance with Daera? Why send out Alaran ships in an attempt to assassinate the Daeran king? Why lie about sending aid shipments when you've caused the famine all along? Everything you've done, every move you've made was to weaken Daera, to make them ripe for the taking." He stared at her. "Tell me it isn't true."

Ben knew that even if Thalia denied it, he couldn't believe her. But he had seen the suffering of Daera's people and desperately didn't want the woman who was his mother to be capable of something so cruel.

Thalia drew herself up, defiant. "Your aunt always did think too small. Don't tell me you're the same. I had to work with what options I had available to me. Kain exhibited no powers—and now we all know why. I couldn't hope to take Daera by force. I had to try something else. But now…" Her eyes gleamed. "Now that you're here, Benjamin, together we can conquer the northern kingdom and take it for our own."

"How could you do it?" Ben cried, disgusted that she thought he would ever help her do such a thing. "How could you let innocent people starve?"

She looked at him with such pride, even now, and for all the wrong reasons. She wasn't proud of him. She was only proud of the reflection of herself, of her power, she saw in him.

"How could I do it?" Thalia exclaimed, voice at last growing shrill. "We were meant for more, you and I. Something greater. I didn't want to be just another common laborer, sent off to help wherever my particular gifts were deemed of most benefit to the kingdom. Alara may be known for witch-hunts now, but this kingdom wasn't kind to witches even before I became queen, Benjamin. We were just tools to be used, no better than slaves. I wanted more than that. I was meant for more than that!"

"Alara may have been cruel to you, but now you're no different. Your actions led to your fellow witches being persecuted. People are dying in Daera, looking to you for aid. You're in the position now to help them, to do something good, to make a better world than the one you knew. And yet you do nothing!"

Thalia scoffed. "People like us would have nothing if we didn't take it. No one helped me get to where I am now. Why should I help those who did nothing to help me? But what do you know of the world? You're just a boy, playing at things you don't understand."

"I know more than you think I do," Ben retorted, knowing that he was about to cross a line, but the moment to pick a side had come. His mother's ambition had gotten out of control and had to be stopped. "I gave food to some of those people. Supplies I stole from Alaran ships and probably some of your privateers. Ships with Daeran supplies on board and there's only one explanation as to why that might be."

He curled his lip, making no secret of his disgust for her and what she had done. "Your precious privateers have done nothing to curb the pirate scourge. I was one; I know how much of a problem the pirates are—and they are a problem. But not nearly as much of one as you make them out to be. They're just a convenient scapegoat for you! If anything goes wrong, blame the pirates. When you attempt to assassinate the king of the country you're supposed to be allied with, you can blame it on the pirates! But the pirates didn't kill Varrian any more than your own soldiers did. He still lives, safe, back in Daera."

The color drained from her face, though from anger or because of how much he knew, Ben wasn't sure.

He felt a moment's satisfaction, glaring at her, daring her to contradict him. "I'm not as blind as you think I am."

"Well," she said softly. "Perhaps I should remedy that."

In the blink of an eye, Thalia hefted the dagger in her hand. Gripping it, her knuckles white, she lunged toward him. Ben's eyes widened as he realized what she meant to do and he drew back.

He wasn't quick enough.

He felt the sharp bite of the blade as it slashed across the right side of his face, digging into his eye. He cried out, recoiling from her, hands flying up to shield his face. Calida called his name.

Ben stood there, shaking, waiting for another attack to come. When it didn't, he lowered his left hand, keeping his right pressed over his eye, and peered up at his mother.

Thalia stood before him, clenching the dagger, blade stained crimson with his blood. Ben could feel the warm liquid running down his face, his hand.

She closed the distance between them and he flinched, anticipating another assault. With her free hand, she grabbed him roughly by the chin, forcing him to look at her. His hand fell away, laying bare his ravaged eye, but she didn't so much as flinch at the sight. Her face was a mask of fury and betrayal, eyes blazing, teeth bared.

"You'd do well to remember your place," she hissed. "I'd think long and hard about whose side you're on." She raised the dagger, resting the tip against his cheek, just below the corner of his good eye. "Or I'll take your other one."

Ben was trembling in her grasp and hated himself for it. Dimly, in some corner of his mind that wasn't frozen in fear, he knew he could shove her away. Summon the wind to throw her backward.

But he didn't dare.

She had taken a knife to his flesh and would do it again.

Satisfied by his apparent meekness, Thalia pushed him to the side, turning back to Calida.

With a shriek, Horus dove out of the air, his talons raking the queen's face. Thalia screamed, losing her grip on the dagger. She swatted blindly at the hawk, stumbling back in a desperate attempt to get away.

Her heels connected with the edge of the wall and she toppled backward. For a breathless moment, her arms flailed madly as she sought to regain her balance.

And then she tumbled over the edge, disappearing from view.

There was a brief, bloodcurdling shriek, then silence.

The howling wind cut out, making Ben's ears pop from the sudden drop in pressure. Calida heaved herself to her feet and made her way to the edge, peering over, before coming to join him.

"The queen?" he gasped, hand once more clamped over his eye.

Calida shook her head. "Dead." She looked at him. "Let me see." Gently, she grabbed his wrist, pulling his hand back from his wounded eye. She said nothing. She didn't have to.

"Bad, is it?"

"We need to get you back to the palace. Come on."

"Annie!" he suddenly cried, remembering. He turned, desperately searching for her, his head spinning at the movement. "Where is she?"

Calida reached out toward him. "Easy. She's right here."

Relief washed over him at the sight of Annie, nimbly running up the stone steps. But the relief vanished the moment she looked up and laid eyes on him.

* * *

Rodek had held her up longer than she would have liked. He was strong, he was fast, and Annie had to grudgingly admit that when it came to swords, he knew what he was about.

But so did she.

She had a few close calls and she knew, lurking in the back of her mind as they traded blows, parried and feinted, each trying to draw the other out, that the longer the fight went on, her chances of succeeding dwindled. Already she was tiring, while he showed no sign of weakening.

The longer she delayed, however, the stronger his anger grew. Perhaps he was insulted that a little slip of a princess could prove such a challenge. Perhaps he was just a naturally impatient man.

Whatever the case, his blows became wilder, less controlled. Annie told herself she only had to hold out a little longer until, in his carelessness, he made a mistake. As soon as she saw an opening, she would take it. No hesitation.

She yelped as the tip of his short sword sliced clean through her sleeve and into the skin beneath. His green eyes lit with triumph. He not only scented blood, he had drawn it.

Annie clenched her teeth against the pain. It was only a flesh wound, but it gave her the opening she needed. Eager to finish her off, Rodek fell for one of her feints, leaving himself vulnerable. He hadn't hesitated and neither did she.

She plunged her rapier into his chest.

She watched as he fell and then raced up the stairs. That fight, too, seemed to have ended. Calida and Ben still stood on the wall, but there was no sign of Thalia. She smiled as she crested the top of the stairs, the smile freezing and then falling from her lips as Ben turned toward her.

In spite of herself, she let out a gasp at the sight, a hand flying to her mouth.

Her horrified expression was the last thing Ben saw.

CHAPTER 36

Somehow, between the two of them, Annie and Calida managed to get Ben back to the horse, who had blessedly remained at the entrance to the Witch Wood. The sun had fully risen free of the horizon by the time they reached the palace. With both Thalia and Rodek gone, there was no one to protest as they ushered Ben inside, Calida demanding that the prince be taken to the infirmary at once.

Using her skills as a healer, she personally tended to Ben's wound, doing what little could be done for it. Annie sat nearby, one of Ben's hands gripped in her own. Throughout it all, he had yet to regain consciousness, either from the shock or blood loss, Annie wasn't sure.

Seeing the damage Thalia's knife had done made her stomach clench. Absently, she ran her thumb over the witch-mark on the back of Ben's hand. Without thinking, she'd expected his hands to be rough, but they were surprisingly smooth, protected all those years by gloves.

At last, Calida stepped back, having done all she could.

"Will he be all right?" Annie asked.

"Oh, he'll live," the witch answered. "But I fear the eye is beyond saving."

Annie gripped Ben's hand tighter. He would have a horrible scar, forever marked by what his mother had done to him. She didn't care. She only hoped he wouldn't let it bother him either.

But the loss of an eye would be a harder challenge to overcome.

He stirred slightly, the one eyelid Annie could see flickering, the other covered by a bandage. But he didn't speak and his one good eye remained closed.

She spoke to him anyway, mostly inane things, unsure if he could even hear her. She reassured him that everything was all right, that Thalia was gone and Rodek taken care of. Reaching out, she brushed a stray strand of hair off his brow, her fingertips stroking against his skin.

"We should go," Calida said softly. "Or rather, you should."

"I'm not leaving him alone," Annie insisted, preparing to fight Calida on this. Not after what had happened.

"I'll stay here with him. But I promised your brother I would bring you home."

Her brother. Annie still felt a sense of relief that she didn't know if she dared believe. Varrian was alive and he was waiting for her back in Daera.

"But the danger's passed now," she argued.

"That was the deal." Calida's tone was gentle but firm, brooking no argument. "I'll see that he's looked after. He'll still be here waiting for you when you return. Or perhaps he'll come to you."

Annie sighed, knowing when she was beaten. She pressed a kiss to the back of Ben's knuckles and stood. "I'll collect my things."

She had the time now that they weren't planning a desperate flight in the middle of the night. She had time now, too, to take Maddie and Florence with her, feeling a stab of guilt. She'd been willing to leave them behind. But things hadn't gone according to plan and there was no reason they couldn't accompany her now.

As briefly as she could, without telling them anything they didn't have to know, she explained that she was returning to Daera for the time being, on the orders of her brother. Maddie was more accepting than Florence, but there was little the chaperone could do. If she insisted on staying, Annie really would leave her behind.

She didn't encounter Kain again, which might have been just as well.

Despite Calida's protestations, Annie made her own way down to the dock, with only the two servants for company. They didn't know how far the plot against Daera went, which of the guards they could trust. She trusted only a handful of people and she was leaving two of them behind.

The longboat was exactly where Calida had told her it would be. Annie piled her belongings into the bottom of it and, with help from the other two women, managed to push the boat out into the water.

Together, they managed to row, awkwardly at first and then falling into a rhythm. The *Phoenix* still waited offshore, her scarlet sails a welcome sight. Annie's arms burned with exertion by the time she reached the ship, calling out to announce her presence.

"Isn't that the pirate ship?" Maddie asked, recognizing the *Phoenix* from when she had stalked them on their first trip to Alara.

Florence frowned, shooting Annie a look.

"Varrian sent them," Annie panted. "It's a long story. Please, just trust me."

The frigate had grown larger as they approached and she marveled at its size, knowing that it was only Ben's abilities that had made it successful as a pirate vessel. Otherwise it would have been far too slow.

Sharpe's head poked over the railing and Annie let out a sigh as the longboat was laboriously brought back on board.

"What happened?" the sharpshooter asked as soon as Annie was safely standing on deck. "We were expecting Calida and Ben."

"It's just me, I'm afraid," Annie said, hating to disappoint them. But she explained what had happened. Ben would be staying in Alara with Calida, at least for now.

Sharpe frowned. "We'll come back, then. In the meantime, we struck a deal with the Daeran king, and if it's all the same to you, princess, I'll not be accused of kidnapping you again."

Annie smiled in spite of herself. Terrance began shouting orders, setting trim and weighing anchor. Over her shoulder, Annie glanced back at the palace, made to look small by the distance, and wondered if she'd ever see it again.

* * *

Without Ben's influence, the *Phoenix* traveled much more slowly, crossing the Atlas Sea in the time it usually took a ship of that size. The wind stayed constant and favorable, at least, and Annie found she was only mildly seasick.

She stayed in Ben's cabin again, the misgivings she'd had the last time she was here gone. She slept poorly, not used to the movement and noise of the ship, wishing he were there with her.

It seemed the longest week of her life, even though she knew time passed the same, and she was relieved when the Daeran shore came into sight.

Terrance and Sharpe accompanied her, Maddie, and Florence to the palace, she supposed as a way of proving they'd upheld their end of the bargain. At Sharpe's insistence, Berchmoore also went with them.

The privateer had returned to the *Phoenix*, as ordered, after delivering his false news to queen Thalia. He had provided valuable evidence against Alara and done as they ordered. Now, it was up to Varrian to determine his fate.

A guard ran to inform Varrian of their arrival and they waited in the throne room for him to appear. Annie turned as the far doors opened and Varrian rushed forward, wrapping his arms around her and pulling her close.

It was a rare display of vulnerability that Annie could scarcely remember seeing before, without the slightest regard that there were witnesses present. Annie let him fuss over her, as if unsure if she were real or not.

He released her, stepping back, his attention turning to the pirates behind her. "You really did it. I can't tell you how many times I regretted my decision after you'd left. I expected Calida would be here."

"So did we," Sharpe replied.

Once more, Annie explained what had happened. This time, she left out none of the details she'd kept from her servants, including that Thalia had been behind the famine. That elicited a gasp from behind her, though she wasn't sure from whom.

Varrian frowned, his scowl deepening the more she told.

"Well," he said when she'd finished. "If that's true, with Thalia gone, the weather should begin to ease. It will take time to undo the damage—some of it, I'm not sure we can ever repair. But I think we can rely upon Ben to send us aid."

When he's ready. With Thalia gone and the king already dead, Ben would now become the sole monarch of Alara, with all of the responsibility that came with running a kingdom resting fully on his shoulders.

And she wasn't there to offer her support.

"It seems to me that there's just one more matter yet to be resolved," Varrian said, returning Annie's thoughts to the present. His eyes were fixed on Berchmoore.

Whether he would have pardoned the privateer or ordered him executed for his crimes, Annie would never know. She reached out, laying a hand on her brother's arm, and stepping up to the privateer.

Whatever else he might have done, he had helped them, even if his motivations had been less than noble. He had played a small role, but without him, they might not have succeeded.

There had been enough death.

Annie had to look up to meet the man's gaze, but she did so without flinching. No longer was she the helpless girl locked inside his cabin. Now he was in her domain.

"You have two hours to get a head start before I send the Daeran royal navy after you," she murmured.

"Two 'ours?" Berchmoore sputtered. "That's 'ardly fair! At least give me four!"

"Two. Not a second more."

He held out his hands, palms upward. "I don't even 'ave a ship! 'Ow am I supposed to leave?"

"Then I suggest taking yourself down to the docks and joining the first crew that will take you. Either way, get out of my sight, Berchmoore. I never want to see your face or hear your name again. Am I understood?"

His face was red, flustered, and it looked like he wanted to argue. But he bit his lip and nodded, perhaps realizing how lucky he was to be offered even that.

A chance at life was still life.

* * *

Ben stood at one of the many glass windows in the palace, overlooking the sea in the distance, mulling over all that had happened. He knew the *Phoenix* was gone from the harbor, even though he couldn't see it from here.

Gone, along with his crew and Annie.

Calida had explained to him what had been decided, and even though he understood why, that didn't make it any easier to bear.

He'd returned to consciousness slowly, the immediate aftermath of the fight hazy. He had come to in bed, his right eye bandaged and hurting considerably. Ben recalled Annie speaking to him, her tone more than the words themselves, her touch gentle.

His eye was still covered by a bandage and would be until it healed sufficiently. Neither Calida or any of the palace healers had been able to save his eye. It was blind, just as Thalia had intended. There would be a nasty scar when the wound had healed. He had worried, shallowly, what Annie would think of him now. Would she think him disfigured?

She'd been gone by the time he'd fully regained consciousness, so he still didn't know what her reaction would be. The look on her face when she first crested the stairs up to the wall kept replaying in his mind. He didn't want that to be the way she looked at him from now on.

Ben was still shaken by Thalia's behavior toward him in those final moments, her true nature revealed. She had taken a knife to her own child. He reached up to gingerly touch the bandage over his eye, thinking that if she was willing to harm her own son, there truly was no limit to what cruelty she might inflict on others.

He couldn't help but be disappointed. Knowing, or at least suspecting, what she was didn't make reality any easier to swallow. She had still been his mother and now she was dead, her reign of terror ended. A reign that never should have been hers to begin with. He found himself wishing for what might have been, but not what *would* have been.

Calida had done him a favor when she'd stolen him away. Ben shuddered to think of the person he may have become if he had grown up with Thalia as a mother.

Calida… He'd asked her what she intended to do now that both her sister and her lover—once—were gone. Would she stay in Alara, the place that had been her home, or return to Daera?

She had shaken her head. "Niklaus is dead. Daera is my home now. I'm needed there."

For now, though, she was still here, waiting, perhaps, as he was for the *Phoenix* to return.

He'd been unsurprised by her answer, but a bit disappointed. She, too, would leave him here. How could he, as Alara's sole monarch, leave now?

"I'm sorry," he had murmured. "About the king." She had loved him once, and probably still did.

Her gray eyes were sorrowful. "Yes. I'm surprised it didn't happen sooner. She never loved him."

"If…If he had lived, would you have stayed?" It was a painful question, probing into what could have been, but Ben had to know.

She'd given him a small smile. "No. Too much time had passed. We'd likely both changed too much. I, at least, am not the person I once was."

Ben suspected that even having forgiven each other, neither would have been able to forget what had happened. Thalia had changed the course of both of their lives and forever altered a kingdom.

I'm not ready. I can't do this.

He had wanted Annie to stay most of all. Ben hadn't realized just how much he'd come to rely on her, sharing his confidences with her, until she was gone. He didn't doubt she would want to return, but he was less sure that her brother would allow such a thing. Ben could always go to her, but he didn't know if he would be welcomed in Daera after what his mother had done.

With Thalia gone, the weather in Daera should slowly begin to return to normal. After a decade of rain and dark skies, perhaps the sun would shine once more and the famine could begin to come to an end.

Already, Ben had given the order to send aid shipments to the northern kingdom and this time, he was confident they would arrive.

All hired privateers would now either have to turn pirate or actively hunt down the pirates that remained. It was an odd feeling for Ben, almost as though he were betraying his former fellow sea rovers, but he didn't have a choice. A kingdom couldn't allow pirates to prey on their merchant ships and now both Daeran and Alaran vessels were off-limits.

The witch-hunts had also been officially ended, just the start of the proposed changes Ben intended to make. He didn't know much about how to be king—leading a pirate crew was one thing, but an entire kingdom?—but he intended to at least try to be a good one.

The people deserved that much.

Ben looked down to where Horus perched upon the windowsill and absently stroked the hawk's feathers, savoring the feel of the bird's plumage beneath his fingers. Horus had saved his life in the Witch Wood and probably Calida's as well.

"Penny for your thoughts."

He turned from the window, broken out of his reverie, to see Kain standing just behind him, dark blue eyes also fixed on the view beyond the glass.

"I doubt they're worth that much," Ben muttered.

Kain nodded toward the window. "You should go to her." Ben didn't have to ask who he meant.

Kain was another sort of dilemma Ben would be forced to deal with. No longer prince, but with nowhere else to go. Ben saw no reason why Kain should be banished if he didn't want to leave. There was no life waiting for him beyond the palace walls, no family to speak of.

"I can't leave," Ben replied. "Unless…" He'd given the matter a lot of thought, having little else to do while he recovered. "I have an offer for you."

Kain raised one eyebrow. "I'm listening."

Ben took a deep breath. "A stewardship."

The other man's eyes widened. "You would make me steward? Trust me to rule in your place."

Ben nodded. "As needed."

"But why? Why would you offer me this?" Kain's face flushed and he looked away, as though ashamed. "After what I did? I hated you, at first, and I was certainly less than kind— to you and Annie both."

"I wasn't here very long and I only got a small taste of what it would have been like to have Thalia for a mother. In your place, I can't say I would have behaved any better. In fact, I probably would have been worse. So even if it wasn't right, I can't say I blame you. And pragmatically speaking, you know a lot more about all of this than I do. You're born and bred to it, with years of experience that I don't have. I believe, working together, we can make this kingdom a better place. The people deserve to have better rulers, after what our mother did."

Kain didn't miss Ben's choice of words. *Our mother.* He swallowed. "It sounds like you're offering more than just a stewardship."

Ben held out one hand. "I've never had a brother before, but I think I'd like to give it a try."

Kain reached out, clasping Ben's proffered hand. "So would I." He stepped back. "That's all I wanted, really. A family. To feel like I belonged, that I was accepted just as I was, instead of never being good enough."

"I'm lucky that I have that. We're not related, but we're family all the same. My crew. My ship. That's where I belong." Ben gestured at the walls. "This is your world, not mine. I can't leave or abandon my responsibilities entirely, but...there is more than one way to serve."

EPILOGUE

Annie tipped her head back, savoring the feel of the wind brushing through her hair, the warm sunlight on her face. She had been uncertain if the feeling would ever return to Daera. She had grown accustomed to the sun during her time spent in Alara, but before making the trip there, she had forgotten how pleasant the sensation was.

She opened her eyes, surveying the scene before her. The wilted foliage was beginning to spring back to life, once more a vibrant green. The roads were no longer overrun with mud, but a soft dirt or sand. This was what Daera was meant to be.

She smiled to herself, nudging her horse into a canter. It had been three months since queen Thalia had been killed in the Witch Wood. Daera still had a long way to go, but it was beginning to make progress, so Annie could only assume that they had been right. Thalia had been responsible for the constant terrible weather that had created the famine.

To her right, she glanced out across open fields and the group of farmers who had gathered to till the land and begin planting. Calida stood among them, giving directions and aiding their efforts, as she'd been taught at the Erlohn monastery. Her red hair was unmistakable and Annie waved as she passed.

Calida had returned from Alara, but Ben hadn't been with her, much to Annie's disappointment.

After her own trip back, Annie had been exhausted and wanted nothing more than to sleep. Instead, she and Varrian had stayed up late into the night, after the pirates had gone, talking about all that had happened.

Varrian had been less than pleased by how things had played out and how much danger Annie had been in. She wasn't sure how he would feel about keeping the alliance with Alara. What she had felt for Kain had certainly been less than love, but she was sure of her feelings for Ben. And while it was much too soon to consider marriage at the moment, it wasn't out of the question for the future.

Eventually, she wore Varrian down, her brother coming around to seeing things her way. Grudgingly, he agreed to give the southern kingdom another chance. After all, if Thalia were the one behind the famine, there was no one else to blame or hold responsible now that she was gone.

Her faults, though many, were hers alone.

Annie entered the village of Steelrest on her way to the harbor, passing market stalls. The smell of roasting meat filled the air, the fruit and vegetables on display large and bright, courtesy of Alara until Daera found her footing. The way it should have been.

Annie waved to the people she passed, happy to see that they were no longer skin and bones, their cheeks no longer hollow. She was delayed in reaching the beach by the sheer number of livestock that clogged the roadways, but instead of being annoyed, she felt relieved. The animals that had once been a rare sight were now anything but.

A dog barked somewhere in the distance and a cat sat on the porch of one of the houses, licking a paw.

Annie maneuvered her mount around the crowd, impatient to reach the sea. At the sound of a shriek, she looked up, shading her eyes from the sun, to see a familiar hawk circling overhead. Her heart leapt in anticipation—and also worry.

It had been three months. Would he be as happy to see her as she was to see him? At least he would finally get to see the results of his aid efforts for himself instead of simply reading about them in her letters.

She raced down to the shore, scanning the open water for the familiar red sails.

* * *

The *Phoenix* made good time, slicing through the water like an arrow, picking up speed as Daera came into view, as if she could sense Ben's eagerness without him even having to nudge her.

He stood at the helm, dressed in his favorite red coat once more, rescued by Sharpe from Berchmoore. She'd made it a point of telling her captain upon his return that the privateer had been banished by Annie and no one had seen or heard any trace of him since.

Ben looked—and felt—like a pirate again, as though nothing had happened, with one small but significant difference. There was no trace of his black leather gloves.

He ran his hand across the wheel, feeling the grooves in the wood, witch-mark bared for all to see. No longer did he have to hide what he was.

From above, in the lines, Sharpe called out something and Ben turned to see for himself. There, along the same stretch of beach that once served as their rendezvous point, stood a lone horse and rider.

Ben smiled to himself and urged the *Phoenix* on faster.

* * *

Of course, the *Phoenix* was too large to anchor directly at the dock and so Annie waited patiently on the beach for the longboat to reach her. Even from a distance, she could recognize him, in that telltale red coat, Terrance and Sharpe with him.

Her stomach fluttering nervously, she swung down from her horse as the boat reached the shore. For a long moment, the crew was busy with the boat, pulling it up onto the sand.

And then, with that duty done and nothing more that needed seen to, Ben turned to her.

She supposed he looked a bit tired, but the responsibility of ruling a kingdom would do that to a person. A brown leather eyepatch concealed his right eye, effectively hiding the scar there. He looked at her, his remaining eye still the same, clear blue.

"What do you think?" he asked, gesturing to it.

Annie smiled. "I think it suits you." Then, dropping her horse's reins, she stepped forward into his arms. "I missed you."

"I'd miss me, too," he murmured, then laughed as she stepped back, swatting him on the arm. "I'm here now."

"There's so much I want to show you."

Ben wrapped one arm around her waist as he took in the sunlit shoreline before him. "It's beautiful."

She caught a flicker of some emotion in his one good eye, and wondered if he were thinking back on what it had cost to achieve this and finding that it had all been worth it.

He smiled down at her. "It's just as I remember."

Thank you for reading!

When I was twelve, I decided that my dream was to become a published author. I have since achieved that dream, but an author is nothing without their readers. So thank you, reader, for giving this book a chance.

If you enjoyed this book, it would mean the world to me if you would consider leaving a review on Amazon. Reviews are essential for authors. They help our books get seen, they help our book get promoted, and they can be the difference between whether or not another reader decides to take a chance on a book.

While it may sound cheesy, you are literally helping make my dream come true. So thank you again for your support and happy reading!

ABOUT THE AUTHOR

Rachel Terry grew up in a small town where nothing much ever happened, dreaming of grand adventures and far-away places, which she found between the pages of books. When not writing, she can be found reading, making YouTube videos, gaming with friends, or indulging in her love of history. She currently resides in the Midwest with her family and a cat named Crinkles.

Visit her online at: rachel-terry.com

YouTube: RachelTerryAuthor

Instagram: rterrywriter

Facebook: rachelterryauthor

LIGHTBRINGER

LIGHTBRINGER
The Guardians Duology Book 1

When an old wrong leads to war, one girl finds herself in the middle of it all.